W9-CUQ-003

Oberheide

DANGEROUS DISCOVERY

Eavin stiffened as Nicholas brought his mouth down on hers. But when he did no more than give her lips gentle kisses, she relaxed and allowed her hands to slide tentatively around the breadth of his back. His kiss deepened, and she could feel the tip of his tongue along the line of her lips. Something inside her stirred, something she had always denied and fought against, fearing the excitement it aroused. But for one night she would try to understand what it was that brought men and women together. She would never have to wonder again. . . .

Moonlight and Memories

Moonlight
and
Memories

BY

PATRICIA RICE

A TOPAZ BOOK

TOPAZ
Published by the Penguin Group
Penguin Books USA Inc., 375 Hudson Street,
New York, New York 10014, U.S.A.
Penguin Books Ltd, 27 Wrights Lane,
London W8 5TZ, England
Penguin Books Australia Ltd, Ringwood,
Victoria, Australia
Penguin Books Canada Ltd, 10 Alcorn Avenue,
Toronto, Ontario, Canada M4V 3B2
Penguin Books (N.Z.) Ltd, 182-190 Wairau Road,
Auckland 10, New Zealand

Penguin Books Ltd, Registered Offices:
Harmondsworth, Middlesex, England

First published by Topaz, an imprint of Dutton Signet,
a division of Penguin Books USA Inc.

First Printing, October, 1993
10 9 8 7 6 5 4 3 2 1

 Topaz is a trademark of New American Library,
a division of Penguin Books USA Inc.

Printed in the United States of America

To Hilary, a friend
disguised as an editor

1

August, 1813

The candles in the intricately designed silver candelabra
burned low and occasionally guttered in puddles of wax,
sending the ghostly shadows on the wall into shimmering
patterns. The silence in the room was almost as suffocat-
ing as the heat. No one cried or screamed or even cursed
as the three women worked frantically over the still figure
on the bed.

The reason for their silence stood ominously in the far
corner, out of their way, but his presence was felt even
when it wasn't seen. Anger and anguish emanated equally
from his restless pacing, the clenching and unclenching of
his fists signaling a need for violence or a release from
helpless frustration. No one was inclined to inquire.

As the limp woman in the bed finally woke with a
scream, the man in the corner dropped his glass and
rushed to her side, lifting her in his arms and murmuring
reassuring words. The candlelight caught on golden
strands of his hair but shadowed his face in bleak lines.
When he turned to speak to the women at the end of the
bed, his eyes held a strange amber glow.

"Do whatever you must to save her. The child is no
concern of mine."

Born and raised a God-fearing Catholic, Eavin
O'Flannery Dupré hastily crossed herself before wringing
out a cold cloth and coming to rinse the sweat from the
laboring woman's brow. A shiver of apprehension or pre-
monition momentarily swept through her as she touched
the moist, pale face of the woman on the bed and felt the
fevered emotions of the man at her side. But she did not
have the gift of Sight, and so could not predict the outcome of that night, other than to know that the woman

was dying. Praying silently, the whispered words a frantic plea falling from moving lips, she performed the ritual absolution, even if a priest had not been called. The man beside the bed was responsible for that lack, too, as he was responsible for the child now stripping his wife of her soul and for the heresy that would condemn that child to death if he could.

In the black of mourning, she was no more noticeable than the silhouettes of heavy furniture in the background. The man beside the bed didn't know she existed. That was the way it should be, but Eavin had great difficulty maintaining her tongue as the frail woman on the bed twisted in the agony of childbirth. Men were the root of all evil, she sometimes believed. This night came a little closer to proving it.

"He's almost here! One more push, Francine, one more push, *ma chère,*" the small woman working with the black midwife pleaded.

The man at the bedside threw her a look of loathing and continued to hold his wife as if she would escape should he let go. Ignoring him, the old midwife gently pushed Francine's extended abdomen, forcing what she was too weak to do herself. The laboring woman gave a brief scream and a shudder, jerked upward, then fell back, lifeless, into her husband's arms.

The sudden, engulfing silence broke a moment later with the shrill cry of a babe.

Wrapping the child in dry clothes some time afterward and handing her to the wet nurse, who had been acquired well before the birth, Eavin worriedly listened to the pacing of heavy boots in the study below. Nicholas Saint-Just's reaction to the death of his wife was not that of a sane man.

His grief at the death of his beloved wife was understandable. His refusal to even look at the child she had borne was not.

Eavin watched wistfully as the babe was held to the breast of the black wet nurse. Only a few short months ago, she had been dreaming of holding a child of her own to her breast. She would never have given the task to another woman as Francine had planned.

Tearing her gaze away from the object of her envy,

Eavin tried to concentrate on the actions of the man below. When he was certain his wife could not be brought back from the dead, Saint-Just had howled a curse and stormed from the room. These last hours of darkness had been spent sending messengers far and wide. Apparently they were returning with his replies, for he was yelling orders at his lackeys, donning boots instead of his house shoes, and calling for his horse. The ominous clatter of the rapier that usually hung over the mantel did not bode well for the coming dawn.

Eavin shivered and strode to the window overlooking the spacious front lawn. She would never grow used to the eerie webs of moss bearding the oak trees. In what was left of the moon's light, they seemed a product of the devil, and the appellation she had heard applied to the man below came back with prophetic timing. Old Nick. Friends and enemies alike called him Old Nick.

It wasn't because he was old, although the stories they told of him were so numerous he would have to be ancient to have accomplished them all. But she came from a race that reveled in stories, and she knew there was only a kernel of truth to the best of them. Saint-Just's past was not what concerned her, but his future was, for now hers was inextricably entwined with his.

They brought the horse, and she watched as he effortlessly gained the saddle with a leap that did not seem quite human. In the brief blur of motion before he reared the horse and sent it galloping down the drive, she noted the gleaming sword at his side, and felt pincers of fear closing around her heart.

His reputation for dueling was infamous. Should he die, she would be homeless. Again.

Eavin remembered only too well her arrival in New Orleans as a destitute stranger. The March wind had been warm, but it had whipped relentlessly at her thin petticoats and bulky bonnet as she stood on the wharf, unnerved by the foreign patois of the natives swarming around her. Even then the bales of cotton and boxes of other goods had begun to crowd the banks, waiting for ships that never made it through the British blockade. Eavin had felt dwarfed and helpless in this frightening jungle where she knew no one and no one knew her.

Her back had ached for the past week, and she placed

a hand to it as she stretched and tried to see around the
bales for some sign that someone had come for her. Her letter had gone out only a short while before she had sailed.
It was quite possible that it had not yet arrived, and she
would be left stranded to make her own way. The thought
terrified her beyond the bounds of reason, for she was all
too aware of the furtive looks she drew from the burly riv-
ermen around her.

Another ripple of pain passed through her middle, and
Eavin closed her eyes briefly and prayed for the life
within her. Dominic had left her with nothing but this
babe; she would not lose it, too. She had been mad to
come this far to a place and strangers she didn't know,
but she had been desperate enough to be mad. Dominic
had never provided a home for her. She had still been living in the boardinghouse with her mother when word
came of his death. And the only home she had ever
known had quickly become a nightmare after that.

Trying not to think of that parting, Eavin scanned the
wharf once again, finding the crowd suddenly dissipated
as the ship's passengers and contents went their separate
ways. She was alone and homeless and down to her last
penny. What would she do now?

A man walking toward the wharf began to move purposefully in her direction, and Eavin glanced over her
shoulder to see whom he must be meeting. When she saw
no one, she turned to watch him with something akin to
fear. He was tall and strode with an athletic strength that
warned his elegant clothes were little more than a disguise. But it wasn't his physical attributes that frightened
her as much as his expression. There was none. His eyes
looked at her with a curious blankness, and his words,
when they came, were curt and without welcome or any
other emotion.

"Mrs. Dupré?" At her nod, he signaled a black servant
scurrying behind him to pick up her few meager bags. "I
am Nicholas Saint-Just, Dominic's brother-in-law.
Francine sent me. You will be staying with us."

That was almost the full extent of their conversation
for the entire journey back to the plantation. Perhaps being forced to welcome a woman little more than an Irish
servant into the family had been beneath his dignity. Perhaps his mind had been elsewhere. Perhaps she had been

a mere annoyance to his plans for the day. Eavin had not learned any more in the months since that time. With Nicholas Saint-Just, any and all of those things could have been his thoughts. He was an enigma, one she would not want to cross.

And now Francine was gone, and there was no one else but him in this house that had been her home for half a year. The thought of being thrown back out into that strange world alone again terrified Eavin out of her mind.

Her gaze drifted back to the window, now empty of any human presence, and she whispered a prayer for the safety of a man who didn't know she existed.

Dawn was just breaking as Nicholas galloped with his winded stallion into the clearing made by the overgrowth of spreading oaks. The spot was time-hallowed by duelers preserving their honor. The oaks were much older than the new civilization encroaching on their preserve, but these past fifty years had seen more blood shed here than in centuries of primeval existence. Nicholas focused only on the hated figure in the clearing as he leapt from his horse to join the small crowd of men mingling beneath the branches.

"This is insane, Nicholas, you can't go through with this." The slender young man catching Saint-Just's cloak hurried to keep up with his long paces. "You will only cause more talk. They'll call the child a bastard. For love of Francine, Nick, don't do this!"

"She's dead, Jeremy. For her sake I left him alone. Now he's going to pay." The dawn's light did nothing to illuminate the stark features of the man advancing on the group beneath the majestic trees. Uncombed, Saint-Just's wild mane of hair fell across his brow and down to his uncollared shirt. Sometime during the evening he had donned the waistcoat and frock coat of a gentleman; there the resemblance ended. His eyes glittered like a feral beast's, and his muscular stride was that of a panther as he advanced upon his enemy.

Or victim. The man waiting, rapier in hand, was no match in size for Saint-Just. Half a head shorter and several stone lighter, he watched his opponent's approach with more contempt than fear. When he was within hear-

ing distance, he spoke to his companions in a voice meant
to be heard.

"The hero of the Barbary coast approaches, *mis amigos*.
Do you think he means to blow us up, too? Or did he bring
his pirate friends to—how you say?—keelhaul us? Surely
he cannot mean to use the puny weapon at his side?"

"You chose rapiers, Raphael. I will be more than happy
to meet you with any weapon you prefer. Any way you
wish to do it, I mean to remove the one you use on de-
fenseless women." Nicholas gave his opponent's tight
trousers a look of disdain and tossed his rapier to an at-
tendant to inspect.

An inward hiss of breath was his only reply as Raphael,
too, threw his rapier to be examined. Their seconds exchanged formalities, but both knew what the rules would
be. Although illegal, duels were not uncommon, but duels
to the death had only recently been adopted by this Creole
society, a bad habit learned from the Americans. The code
of honor specified such an outcome not be mentioned, but
it would be very difficult to disguise the death of either of
these prominently known men.

Within the first few minutes after the rapiers met, it became apparent that the match was more equal than expected. Saint-Just was accustomed to the weapons of his
size—rifles, pistols, swords, and knives—weapons that he
could use well with his greater strength. The rapier required greater finesse, and the dapper Raphael wielded his
slender grace well.

But as the minutes rushed closer to an hour, and the sun
rose over the horizon, throwing the clearing into long shadows from the massive oaks, the observers of this battle realized that the man with the cognomen of Old Nick earned
his name well. He merely played with his opponent, prick-
ing him occasionally to feed his anger, then letting him ex-
haust his strength before he moved in for the kill.

Raphael's seconds began to mutter angrily, but there
was little they could do. First blood counted for nothing in
this argument, and all concerned understood why. When
Raphael finally found an opening in Saint-Just's defense,
they prayed anxiously, but the larger man was quicker than
they imagined, and the blade merely cut through his clothing and scraped along his side before he lunged, piercing
his opponent's shoulder.

Cries from the onlookers did nothing to persuade the two combatants from their goals. Their brows beaded with perspiration, their breath coming a little faster, they circled, looking for further openings to close in for the kill. Raphael's fashionably cut hair fell about the immaculate folds of his cravat. The ruffles at his throat and wrists hung in tatters, ingeniously sliced to pieces by the man meaning to kill him. And now blood began to seep through the rent in his elegant cranberry coat, although it was not as noticeable as that staining Saint-Just's side.

Weary, Raphael stumbled over a tree root but recovered himself before Nicholas could do more than slice his sword arm. It was easy to see that he was on the defensive now, wearing down slowly, and for the first time fear began to flicker behind his opaque eyes as Nicholas pressed onward seemingly tirelessly.

"Nick, call it off! Can't you see he's done for? It's slaughter, damn you!"

Amber eyes gleamed golden briefly as Saint-Just's rapier caught Raphael's riposte and held it. "Shall we call an end, dear friend?" he asked with deceptive calm.

In reply, Raphael spat at his feet and spun his rapier with a lightning-like move that nearly rendered his challenger's sword hand helpless.

The match ended swiftly after that. Tired of the game, no longer fed by anger but hollow with despair, Nicholas allowed his enemy to close in, then in a flurry of movement no one could possibly describe later, dodged, swung around, and lunged, bringing Raphael to his knees with a deadly wound through his middle.

As a doctor rushed onto the field, Nicholas wiped his blade on the grass and stalked away, leaving his seconds to carry out the necessary duties. Jeremy ran after him, demanding that he wait for his wound to be tended, but the pain in his side was easier to bear than the hurt buried where no one could see it, and Nicholas kept on walking.

It scarcely seemed important whether he lived or died any longer. Gaining his saddle with a wince of pain as torn muscles pulled with the effort, Nicholas rode off without a backward glance to the scene of chaos behind him.

Let them hang him. The reason he had stayed alive all these years was dead, killed by another man's child. What purpose was there in living now?

2

"The wound in his side is not serious. He will recover, more's the pity."

Eavin glanced at Francine's mother with surprise. The small woman had seemed mild and meek since her arrival a week ago. Not a cross word had ever left her tongue. This remark about the man who had so obviously loved her daughter did not seem natural.

Seeing her daughter-in-law's look, Madame Dupré sighed and dried her hands on the towel Eavin held out for her. They had left Nicholas sleeping in his chamber. Safely in Madame Dupré's room, they could speak unheard by the servants. "He is more animal than man," she tried to explain. "Francine adored him, but she feared him, too. And rightly so. Nicholas has no control over his temper. When he is enraged, he strikes like any animal would do. Not that I can say I blame him in the circumstances, but no gentle woman could live like that for long."

Thinking of how Francine had lived in silks and lace and more comfort than Eavin had ever known in her life, she could not quite grasp this concept, and she protested. "I never saw him lift a hand to her. He treated her like the finest porcelain. They seemed to love each other very much." That was perhaps pushing it a little far, but Eavin's romantic nature occasionally colored her usual skepticism. In the few months that she had been here, Francine had never left her chambers. But Nicholas had visited her with regularity and they seemed much attached. She had seen nothing to bring on the old lady's displeasure.

"Perhaps they did, in their own ways." Madame Dupré collapsed in the nearest chair and held her fingers across her eyes. "They were friends as children. Francine may

have been his only friend. Nicholas was a strange one
even then. When his father died and left the family bankrupt, he went off to sea and promised to return for her,
and she believed him for many years."

She looked up to find the young woman who had married her only son still standing there, waiting for explanation. Isabel Dupré tried to hold a sigh of exasperation.
She could not imagine what her genteel and well-bred
young son had seen in this common Irish beauty, other
than the usual thing that men looked for. Surely he could
have had that without marriage. But it was too late for
that old quarrel, just as it was too late for this one. Both
her children had disappointed her, and now they were
dead. She wished the child her son's wife had carried
could have lived to carry on his name, but Eavin—such
a plebeian name!—hadn't even succeeded in doing that
correctly. But her daughter's child still lived, and arrangements had to be made.

"None of that matters now. The child must be baptized.
I think she should be named after Francine. Nicholas will
have to be made to see to her support now that Raphael
is dead. Not that Raphael would have had any way of
supporting her. So much has been lost since the Americans came. There is scarce room for the poor babe in my
rooms, but she is all I have left. I suppose I will have to
find some way."

The tentacles of fear returned when Madame Dupré offered no invitation for her daughter-in-law with these
words. Eavin hastily urged her to lie down and rest, not
daring to sort out this odd conversation until she was
alone in her own room.

When she finally left Madame Dupré sleeping and
found the comfort of her small chamber, Eavin lay across
the bed, mind racing despite the weariness of her body. It
was becoming increasingly obvious that the child sleeping a few doors away did not belong to the man who
owned this house, the man who had given her a home
when she had traipsed across half a continent, pregnant
and homeless and newly widowed. Dominic had told her
to come here, to his sister and safety from the insanity of
the war raging on the East Coast. Francine had been the
one to invite Eavin to stay.

And now Francine was gone. As was Dominic. And it

appeared even Francine's child did not belong here. Despairing for the poor child as well as herself, Eavin turned over and buried her face against the pillow. What would become of them all?

Exhausted, she fell asleep, but even in her sleep there was no rest. The distinguished man standing by her mother's side when she had waved Eavin off on her journey haunted her nightmares. The pressure on her breast where he squeezed it, the heat of his arousal as he pressed her against the bedroom wall, made her toss feverishly as those hated words rang through her mind.

Eavin's subconscious slowly dragged her away from that memory and into another one. This time the man smelled not of cologne but of whiskey. The realization that she had fallen asleep before locking her door came to her just as clearly as the night it had happened, just as she felt his heavy weight cover her. She screamed, but he muffled the sound with his slobbering mouth. As his hands groped beneath her nightdress, her terror threatened to overpower her as much as his greater strength, and some small part of her brain disconnected and coolly reacted with violence.

It had only been a knee to the groin that time. The intruder had heaved the best of a bottle of whiskey from his stomach to the floor. But after that Eavin had begun carrying a gun that Michael had bought for her.

She jerked awake with the remembrance of her hand reaching for that gun. Swearing, she sat up and noted the lateness of the hour from the position of the sun through her window, and she cursed again. Bemoaning her fate solved nothing. If she was going to stay here instead of being forced out into the world, she needed a plan.

When Nicholas woke some hours later, it was to find the black-clad figure of his sister-in-law grimly waiting for him, a glass of sherry near one hand and fresh bandages at the other. He winced as he reached for the glass, and she sat down beside him and held it so he could sip.

"What in hell is the brat screaming about?" The noise pounded through his brain with the remains of the brandy he had imbibed the night before.

"She is most likely hungry. Annie will see to her shortly. She will need a name, you realize."

The woman he had scarcely noticed these last months

spoke curtly, with only a vague hint of the lilting accent of her ancestors. Still, in this place the sound struck his ear oddly.

"Give it any name you like." Removing the glass from her hand, Nicholas gulped the remainder of the sherry. When she did not move, he regarded her through narrowed eyes. Until now he had barely exchanged three words with this woman. She was a mousy little thing who stayed out of his way, but because she gave Francine someone to talk to, he had made no objection to her staying. Shortly, he would be forced to acknowledge the awkward situation of her presence.

"The child is a girl, not an it. Francine wanted her very much. Perhaps you could call her Francine in remembrance."

Instead of going away, the irritating woman began probing the bloody bandage at his side. Nicholas closed his eyes and let her probe. Dominic had always been naive when it came to a pretty face, and this Irish female had more than a pretty face. Unfortunately, she had none of the manners of her betters.

It was a pity she couldn't resemble Francine more. A soft voice and delicate charm would go a long way toward ending this pain eating at his innards. With his eyes closed, Nicholas could almost see his wife's frail, blond beauty, hear her enchanting southern voice with the exotic hints of her parents' French and Spanish accents. Dominic must have gone out of his way to find a woman so opposite to his sister in looks and breeding.

Grimacing as the bandage came off, Nicholas opened his eyes again. The witch wore black as usual, but it went well with her white complexion and black hair. Heavy black brows and thick lashes should have looked coarse, but instead they accented damnably green Irish eyes and rose-stained cheeks. She never met his eyes, but he could feel the contempt with which she treated his wound.

"Call the creature anything you like, just keep her out of my sight. And hearing." The screams in the other room were escalating.

"Francine for her mother and Jeannette for St. Joan." Eavin cleansed the angry slash with a solution left by the doctor. "And Madame Dupré means to take her to New

Orleans, so you needn't worry about hearing her for long."

"Over my dead body!" Abruptly shoving Eavin aside, Nicholas threw his legs over the edge of the bed, only to discover he wasn't dressed. Holding the sheet to his waist, he shouted, "Bring the old biddy in here! And get the hell out while I find some clothes."

Not certain how well her plan had worked, Eavin scampered to do as told. It would be much more pleasurable to stay and tell the arrogant creature what she thought of him, but she knew better than to beard a lion in his den. And Nicholas Saint-Just was no less than a ferocious lion as he rose from his bed and began yelling for servants. Eavin just hoped she hadn't unleashed an uncontrollable beast.

Later she would have reason to remember the broad expanse of bandaged chest and powerful shoulders rising from that bed, but for now she thought only of the home she didn't have and would make if he would let her. It was obvious that Nicholas Saint-Just was a man alone, and men were incapable of making homes. She wanted to keep the job she had slowly created for herself these last months in the neglected mansion. And she wanted to keep the child.

Oh, how she wanted to keep the child. Sending one of the maids to find her mother-in-law, Eavin ran to the comfort of the nursery in time to see Annie take the child to her breast again. She ached to hold that tiny body, but the black nurse had just lost a child, too, and she cuddled the white infant as tenderly as anyone could wish. It didn't seem fair that she couldn't have one of her own, but Eavin wasn't one to bewail the fates and do nothing. If her choices were to stay here and fight for the child or return to Baltimore and the disorder of that boarding-house, she would choose to fight.

Comforted now that she had seen the babe quieted, Eavin returned to the hall to hear Nicholas shouting at Madame Dupré. He would tear open his stitches if he continued in that manner, but she wasn't one to interfere in what a person did to himself. He was lucky he was still alive if he had truly fought a duel this day. She wouldn't think about what had happened to the other man. She didn't know these people or their histories, and she really didn't want to know them. She just wanted to be left alone to make a place for herself.

Eavin returned to Nicholas's room in time to find her mother-in-law weeping quietly into her lace-edged handkerchief. Madame Dupré and Francine were much alike with their elegant grace and soft, swishing silks. Eavin knew very little about the kind of genteel life they lived, but she did know a distraught woman when she saw one. Entering the chamber, she put her arm around Francine's mother and lifted a questioning glance to the man still trying to shove his shirt into his trousers.

"The brat stays here. Call her Francine or Josephette or Napoleon Bonaparte for all I care, but she stays here. I'll not send her to that pit of vipers in the city. Calm down, woman, I don't mean to eat her for breakfast!" He roared this last as Madame Dupré increased her wails.

"Come, you must calm down. We can discuss this reasonably a little later. Monzure San-Juze needs his rest."

"Bloody damn hell, just call me Nicholas, or Mister Saint-Just! I'm a bloody American like everybody else now. There's no point in fracturing two languages." He stalked toward his wardrobe, ignoring Eavin's pained expression at her placating attempt to use his French name correctly.

"Sure, and we'll poison his milk should he come down to eat," Eavin murmured in a mocking brogue as she led Isabel out. The threat shocked the woman into staring at her, which had the immediate effect of halting her weeping. If the man behind them heard, he gave no indication, and the door slammed between them as they departed.

Eavin's irate expression settled into the calm mold required of any good servant. She might be out of her depth with these high-strung aristocrats, but she had enough experience dealing with people to know how to smooth over any situation. Life in a boardinghouse full of powerful and temperamental men had that effect.

"We must call for the priest and have little Francine baptized before he can change his mind." That served to distract Isabel Dupré, although frankly, Eavin fully intended to call the child Jeannette. Two Francines, even when one was dead, was more than one household needed.

Pacified that this one request would be carried out, Isabel hurried to put her plan in motion. Eavin stuck her tongue out at Nicholas's closed door and turned toward the steps and the kitchens outside. She'd not had any sleep, but that brief nap in twenty-four hours, but it was obvious that no one was going to sleep while the lion stalked the floors.

It was odd that she had never noticed Saint-Just's true nature while Francine was alive. True, the servants had whispered behind his back and even Francine had occasionally expressed uncertainty about his temper, but Eavin had always thought of Nicholas as the polite gentleman who bowed to her whenever she went in and out of the room. Perhaps he had been on his best behavior while his wife was ill and now felt the need to vent everything he had kept pent up. She could certainly understand that feeling.

She was quite certain Nicholas didn't realize who had taken charge of his kitchen and his servants and returned order out of chaos, but Eavin fully intended to remind him if the need arose. Confined to her bed, Francine had been less than useless in overseeing the help, and they had taken full advantage of the opportunity. They would do so again if Eavin left. It wasn't a large lever, but it might hold open the door until she could find another.

It would be an uphill battle all the way. Reluctant servants, a filthy-tempered man, and a country so strange that it might as well be another planet did not make the task of staying easier. But when Eavin considered what she had left behind, she set her jaw determinedly. Here was where she was going to stay.

That night, after the child was baptized and arrangements were made for the funeral and Nicholas had disappeared somewhere on his own, Eavin lay in bed wondering if she had made the right decision.

She could die out here and no one would know the difference, or even care. At least back in Baltimore she had her mother and, occasionally, her brother. Before his death, when Dominic had mentioned coming here, he had assured her that his sister and mother would welcome her with open arms, but of course, she had been pregnant then. It had seemed wisest to join his family while she carried his heir, particularly with the British sending their navy up and down the coast to terrorize seaports. But now she no longer carried a child, and it seemed the British were just as likely to take New Orleans as the East Coast.

But she had been told the Saint-Just plantation was far enough up river not to be bothered by the war and close enough to the city not to be a target of Indians. It wasn't the external dangers that worried Eavin as much as the internal ones. She had no claim on Saint-Just's hospitality any longer. It was obvious her mother-in-law had no intention of taking her in. Somehow she had to make a niche here or be forced to leave, whatever choice she would prefer. How did one go about carving a niche in emptiness?

Remembering the helpless infant sleeping in the next room, Eavin knew there had to be a way; she just had to find it. If God had seen fit to deprive her of children of her own, He must have sent her here to take care of Francine's child. The will of God would win out over the temper of a Nicholas Saint-Just.

3

Madame Dupré left after the funeral without protest. Eavin wondered mildly what Nicholas had used to buy her off, but that was of no concern to her. That he had not made any mention of Eavin leaving with her was satisfaction enough for the moment.

But it couldn't go on forever. Not knowing her place in things was almost as bad as being told she was unwelcome. Not that Nicholas ever noticed that she was there long enough to express his displeasure at her existence. When he was in the house, he haunted the main rooms, where Eavin didn't dare stray. If he ever slept, it was long after she had retired to her own bed. She made certain that meals were available at regular times of the day, but for all she knew, he never ate them. She took to eating hers in the nursery when Annie went to the kitchens to eat.

It was those times when she was alone with Jeannette that Eavin enjoyed the most. The child was a pure delight, staring unblinkingly at everything around her, crying only when something hurt, sleeping soundly after every meal. Her tiny fingers curled trustingly around Eavin's when she held her, and her head turned eagerly at the sound of her voice. Eavin's heart was well and truly lost before a week was out.

The fact that Jeannette's hair was black and not the blond of her parents only endeared her more to Eavin. It made her that much more like herself, like the child she had lost. It was a dangerous attachment, but she couldn't help herself. Her miscarriage had only been a few months ago, and the loss was still achingly real. Jeannette filled the gap that had loomed empty for so long.

If Eavin had thought about it, she would have known that she didn't miss Dominic as much as she missed the babe she had never known. But she didn't think about it. Dominic was a part of her life of which she was not particularly proud. It was better to remember her late husband with fondness and let it rest there.

But Eavin couldn't let the stalking tiger of Nicholas Saint-Just rest. She was growing too attached to Jeannette to find herself out on her ear one day. She had to confront him, one way or another, and make her position clear.

Hearing him roam the downstairs salon one night before she prepared for bed, she straightened the high neck of her mourning gown, checked the ribbons holding the black cotton beneath her breasts, and verified in the mirror that her face was unsmudged. She wrinkled up the small nose that she considered too pert for her face, bit her lips to add color, pinched her cheeks, and strode determinedly to the staircase. That her knees were quaking before she reached the bottom did not deter her in the least.

The door was open, so there seemed no reason to knock. The salon was a public room, after all, and it was only her uneasiness at her position that kept Eavin from using it. While Francine had been alive, she had been family. With Francine gone, she had no connection in this household other than as unpaid servant. Servants seldom frequented the family salon.

Nicholas was pouring liquor from a decanter when she entered. As usual, his coat and waistcoat were unbuttoned, and his cravat hung, untied, around his neck. It was as if the clothes required by civilization were too restraining, and he pawed them off as he paced the confines of the cage that was this house. Eavin shrugged away that fantasy as she approached. She was nervous enough without conjuring up wild animals.

"If you have a minute . . ." she hesitated over the proper title and settled on, "sir, I would like to speak with you."

Nicholas lifted a tawny eyebrow and merely gestured for her to take a seat while he completed filling his glass. The lamplight flickered golden over his hair as he regarded the color of the liquid impassively and waited for her to seat herself.

"I suppose you want money to return to wherever it is you came from." He spoke idly, throwing open a humidor and selecting a cigar. He gestured as if asking permission, but snipped off the tip before Eavin could give it.

Startled by this tack, she wasn't immediately prepared to reply, but she recovered as quickly as she could. "Actually . . . sir . . ."

"Nicholas. Just call me Nicholas. Or Nick. Or monster. Whatever comes easiest." He took a seat and drew on the cigar as he eyed her impatiently.

"Nicholas." Reasserting herself, Eavin began again. It wasn't easy. He was every inch the noble French aristocrat, and there were more inches than she cared to consider. She wasn't a particularly small woman, but she felt almost diminutive in his company. "I would like to stay and look after Jeannette. I realize she really doesn't need a nanny yet, but she will, and in the meantime I could help look after the household. I have been doing so for some months now, and you have seemed satisfied with my efforts."

Nicholas sipped his brandy. His side ached, but that helped distract from the aching hollowness that had taken root in his guts. He really wasn't paying much attention to the woman sitting across from him, not any more attention than he would pay the chair she sat on. Francine had bought that frivolous piece of furniture. Francine had wanted her brother's common Irish widow to stay. One was the same as the other.

"The damned house could molder back into the swamp from whence it came for all I care, but you're welcome to try to keep it afloat if you wish. The brat will need a woman of some sort to raise her, I suppose, and you're her aunt. Wherever you came from must be hell indeed if you want to stay here."

Hell wasn't an adequate description. Rising, Eavin nodded agreement. "I come from Baltimore, sir, but I prefer the quiet of the country. If you would excuse me . . ."

Bored and momentarily amused by her presumption, Nicholas gestured with his cigar. "Sit down. The brat isn't crying yet. You're as entitled to use this room as I am. If we're to rattle around in this house together, it will be a lot simpler if you don't scamper into hiding every time I walk through."

Trying to appear relaxed, Eavin returned to her seat. "I

am unaccustomed to sitting idle. I should have my mending, at least."

"You will need light for that. Call for Hattie and have her bring what you need. It's time you learned our indolent life if you mean to take up residence here."

The sarcasm tinging Nicholas's voice seemed out of place. He was raised to this kind of life. He pursued it with the same languid grace as all the other inhabitants of this tropical country. Why did he mock what he was? Eavin didn't reply but took the bell he handed her and shook it hesitantly. She was too accustomed to being the one on the other end of the call to accept its demands casually.

And Nicholas seemed to know that. He watched with amusement as the black slave appeared and took her request. Eavin knew she was supposed to order and not ask, but she had two good legs of her own and could have brought the requested mending and lamp without summoning someone to do it for her. The only reason she and the servants had managed some rapport these last months was because she made no unnecessary demands. They knew their jobs and did them when told. Fetching and carrying for someone not their mistress didn't fit into any job category that they knew.

"They'll give you grief if you're not firmer with them," Nicholas admonished as the slave hurried to carry out her request.

"If I were paid nothing for my services, I would be resentful, too." Flustered by this unanticipated converse with a man she scarcely knew, Eavin let slip what she thought rather than what she was supposed to say. She waited in horror for the explosion sure to follow.

"You just offered your services for nothing," he reminded her calmly, drawing on his cigar. "Am I going to have to listen to your complaints in recompense? If so, I'll have to rethink this arrangement."

"I am not complaining." Eavin accepted the basket of mending with a word of thanks that brought another mocking smile to the face of the man across from her. "I am merely stating a fact. If you would prefer I say nothing, then allow me to return to my room. I find it unnerving to sit in silence while someone criticizes my behavior."

"I'm certain 'unnerving' isn't the word, but I stand corrected. I get what I pay for, and if I pay nothing, then I should expect nothing. Perhaps I ought to offer you an allowance."

"That would be most generous of you, but I did not come in here to beg. Room and board is adequate recompense, although I might find it awkward in the future to come to you should I require certain necessities. Dominic left me nothing but his back pay, and I used that to come here."

"Dominic was a young fool to marry when he had nothing to his name." Sipping his drink, Nicholas leaned back in his chair and, indolently throwing one leg over the arm, stared into the cold fireplace.

"He was going off to war with every expectation that he might never return. Wouldn't you prefer to know some of the joys of life before going to death?" Eavin hadn't fooled herself into believing Dominic's passionate promises. Although he had been her own age, he had lived a protected life and was vastly immature compared to her. He had wanted a woman, one who would always be there when he came into port, and she wouldn't give into him without marriage. It had been as simple as that.

Of course, Dominic had told her embroidered lies about his loving family and grand home, and because she had known he was a gentleman far above her station, she had believed him. So they had both got what they bargained for, little or nothing.

"I would prefer to go off to war without leaving a woman and possibly children in poverty, grieving over my death. Dominic was a selfish ass, but it's a little late to tell him that now. If he'd had the money to buy you, you both would have been better off, but I suppose he should be congratulated for doing the honorable thing. One must always give credit for honor."

The tone of his voice indicated the opposite belief, but Eavin was in no position to argue either view. Honor was for those who could afford it. The rest of the world did well to stay alive as best as they could.

"I doubt that any woman could be bought for a price high enough to support herself and a child for the rest of their lives. Marriage might be a gamble, but the odds are better than what you suggest."

Nicholas laughed softly and actually turned to look at her. "You have a fascinating mind, Mrs. Dupré. Not one woman of my acquaintance would have stated her worth in such a manner. You should give the brat some interesting ideals."

Not wanting to debate that topic, Eavin remained silent, and Nicholas seemed willing to accept this end to their conversation. Calling for his news sheet and an additional lamp, he settled down to read while Eavin took up her mending.

The days turned into weeks in this odd manner. The few callers who arrived after the funeral were turned away either by Nicholas's absence or his refusal to see them, until they eventually stopped calling. Eavin occasionally felt a tweak of loneliness having no one to converse with but the black servants and occasionally Nicholas for a few minutes in the evening, but she was satisfied with her choice. Her duties here were not strenuous, and the pleasure of holding Jeannette and watching her grow far outweighed the onus of loneliness, and certainly outweighed her only alternative.

Eavin saw no further examples of Nicholas's formidable temper. She gradually became aware that he had other interests outside the plantation that drew him away from home frequently. He often went into New Orleans, where she suspected he kept an office and perhaps another house, as so many of the plantation families did. What knowledge she had of family life in the new state of Louisiana came from the house servants, but they knew little more beyond this house than she did.

She wanted to know more. If she was going to make her home here, she needed to know how people lived. But Louisiana was such a new state, with such a confused history, that there was very little to be found in Nicholas's library on the topic. Perhaps there was more of interest in the volumes labeled in French, but Eavin knew nothing of that language. Frustrated by her limitations, she began saving the American news sheets Nicholas left scattered about and reading them avidly when she was alone.

Surprisingly, the newspapers that Nicholas brought home approached the topic of war from a different angle than the ones at home. Whereas the sheets she remembered were incensed at the huge debt acquired by purchasing Louisiana Territory and wanted to give the whole of it back to the Spanish or French, these sheets swore they would be better off if the South declared independence of the elitist North and their high-handed manners. They loyally backed the president and supported the war and wanted to extend enlistments and form an army and build a navy to fight off the condescending aristocrats who would dare to stop American ships and limit their access to foreign ports.

Eavin found it difficult to believe that the aristocratic society that Nicholas lived in would condemn any form of elitism. These papers seemed to appeal more to someone like herself, someone who had little but craved the opportunity to make more. But the fact that most of this area was French-oriented and England had been at war with France since time immemorial might have some reflection on their views. Still, the France of Napoleon Bonaparte was not the France of aristocrats. It was exceedingly confusing, and she wished she had someone to discuss it with.

Throwing down the paper, Eavin went to check on Jeannette. At three months, the child was sleeping through the night, but she still felt the need to go in and touch her, feel her breathing, stroke the warm, moist hair of her head to be certain all was well. Having satisfied herself that the infant was sleeping soundly, Eavin still felt too restless to return to bed.

Nicholas hadn't appeared in the salon, and she assumed he had gone into New Orleans again. It would be nice if he left some word as to where he could be found or even if he meant to eat his meal here or elsewhere, but this was his house and she had no authority to ask him to change his ways. She made certain that there was something prepared fresh for him every day. Beyond that, Eavin could do nothing.

But she knew the bread that he hadn't eaten was still in the pantry, along with some strawberry jam, and probably the little cakes that had been prepared for dessert. Any and all of these sounded good at the moment, better than retiring to her lonely bed to stare at the ceiling until sleep came. Daringly, Eavin turned her feet toward the back stairs and the food cupboard.

She wished for some way of preparing tea. The awkward system of placing the kitchen out back, where the slaves could contend with the heat and the house's inhabitants could stay cool, was a constant source of irritation. How difficult would it be to move the kitchen into the storerooms under the lower gallery? A fire down there couldn't generate that much heat upstairs. Eavin had never seen the floods that the servants promised would come, but surely water in the kitchen couldn't be worse than the mud in the yard.

Her mother had always said that Eavin was never content with the way things were, and perhaps she was right. Why be content when just the simplest of changes could make things better? But she had no power to make changes and never had. She had hoped that might be different with marriage, but that hope was long since lost. She must learn acceptance.

Finding her way down the narrow back stairs with just a candle, Eavin gave a scream of fright when the light suddenly sent a large shadow dancing across the wall in front of her. A moment later, she recognized Nicholas, and she caught her breath as her hand instinctively flew to the unfastened neckline of her nightshift, and she edged backward up a stair. The familiar fear came back full force as it had not this past year or more, and she found herself quaking before the man with whom she must share this house.

Eavin could smell the liquor on Nicholas as he came to a halt a step or two below her. He still seemed to tower over her, but he didn't appear to be drunk as he looked at her through amused and weary eyes.

"Midnight raids on the pantry, Mrs. Dupré?"

He always said that as if the name were an unspoken jest, but Eavin had learned to ignore his sardonic humor. Retreating another step or two until his masculine proximity no longer terrified her, she recovered her wits and wished she hadn't, for then she remembered the only people who used these stairs were the servants. The slave quarters were directly out the door at the bottom. There could only be one possible reason for Nicholas Saint-Just to be visiting the slave quarters. She hadn't been widowed so long that she had forgotten a man's habits, and the smell and look of him confirmed her suspicions.

Disgust and dismay filled her, and Eavin blurted out

the first thing that came to mind. "Sure, and that is why that Jezebel is after shirking her chores and laughing about it! I've naught to say to the likes of you, sir." Lifting the hem of her nightshift, Eavin retreated hurriedly to the safety of her room, more shaken by the encounter than she would ever admit.

Below, Nicholas laughed, the sound echoing up the stairwell and through the hall after her.

"Sweet dreams, Irish," she thought she heard him call from the landing below, but Eavin buried her head in the pillows and refused to acknowledge it.

Imagining the golden Nicholas making love to that snotty black slave irked her beyond the bounds of all reason. She wanted to smack them both. And now that she recognized Saint-Just as a man just like any other, a deep apprehension began to fill the hollow in her middle.

4

Eavin hastily rose from her chair when Nicholas entered the salon the next evening. She dreaded the thought of being in the same room with him, but the scowl on his face at her movement brooked no disobedience.

"Sit," he commanded, pointing at her chair. "I'll not be judged and condemned by a damned piece of Irish skirt."

Rage rapidly replaced embarrassment and fear as Eavin did as told. She'd been forced to control her temper long ago, but letting it simmer for any length of time wasn't healthy, either. Clipping off the first words coming to mind, she opted for a more objective reply. "I don't remember judging your morals, sir, only the results."

Nicholas gave a sharp bark of laughter as he reached for his news sheet instead of the decanter. "A philosopher. How quaint. Then by your terms it would be preferable if I would fornicate somewhere outside the household."

Color flooded her cheeks, and Eavin dutifully bent over her mending and counted to ten. She'd heard men use worse words. Helping run a boardinghouse for men had taught her a great deal more than her religious background would approve of, a fact which had never bothered her mother. But somehow when this man said such a thing, the meaning seemed much more personal. Perhaps it was the fact that they were the only two people in the room, and his male dominance permeated the atmosphere. It took a moment before she could recover her tongue.

"The church teaches fornication outside of marriage is a sin." She had never discussed such a topic with a man, knew it was highly improper, but she had never learned to hold her tongue when given the opportunity to use it.

Nicholas chuckled and glanced over his newspaper.

Even in the dim light of the lamps he could see the color staining her cheeks, but he knew defiance when he heard it. In those blasted black gowns, with her hair pulled tightly to the back of her head, she gave the appearance of every self-righteous old woman he'd ever known. But he was beginning to suspect that there was more behind that respectable facade than was readily apparent. He couldn't judge by the drunken glimpse he'd had of her the night before, but the memory of her irate Irish brogue placed her in a little different category than prudish widow.

"The church teaches us to go forth and multiply," he answered wickedly.

Eavin treated him to a scathing glance. "That's disgusting."

Fully entertained now, Nicholas allowed his paper to fall to his lap. "What happens between a man and woman is not disgusting. It's perfectly natural. God created us, after all."

They were definitely treading dangerous waters. Men and women weren't supposed to discuss such topics together, and Eavin was beginning to have some understanding of why. Heat warmed her cheeks under his close regard, and she wished she had never given in to her temper. "This discussion can have no proper ending, sir. I'll thank you to discontinue it."

Nicholas grinned. Even her ears were red. He'd not thought a little Irish molly could be so prudish. One would almost think she was one of those cold fishes that called themselves ladies and pretended babies grew under cabbage leaves. But she was from one of the peasant classes, which reveled in their physical natures, and she had been married. She knew precisely what he was talking about and where it could lead.

Relenting, he picked up his paper. "They say the Indians are on the warpath again. The governor's called for volunteers."

This was at least a safer topic, if no less worrisome. "Are there still Indians around here? Dominic told me they were all gone."

"Generally speaking, the Indians have more sense than the French. They know better than to fight over a piece of worthless swamp. The rebellious ones are farther north of here. But when they go on a rampage . . ." He shrugged carelessly and looked up. "Do you know how to use a rifle, Mrs. Dupré?"

He was needling her. She could see it in his eyes. He had the most damnable laughing eyes when he wasn't raging or sulking or ignoring her. Eavin thought she might prefer to be ignored. Before she could give a suitable reply, the front door knocker thumped loudly, and she nearly jumped from her seat in startlement.

Nicholas did laugh then. "Indians aren't going to knock, Irish. You can rest easy."

Despite his sensible words, Eavin could still feel the tension in him as he waited for a servant to answer the door and announce the caller. From the number of footsteps approaching, the visitor or visitors had refused to be left waiting. Eavin glanced anxiously at Saint-Just to see if she should depart, but he wasn't paying attention to her, as usual.

"There he is, damn you! Arrest him, *señor*. No more excuses."

Eavin's eyes grew large as the two men pushed in behind the maid, filling the parlor with the scents of the night wind, horses, and leather. The man who had spoken was only slightly larger than she, with a thin mustache and graying hair and the tight, intricately embroidered clothes of a Spanish dandy. The man with him had the look of a soldier, but he wore a leather vest and an ill-fitting sack coat instead of a uniform. After so many years of living on the thin edge of it, Eavin could smell the law a mile away.

Nicholas didn't bother to rise but regarded his guests disdainfully. "So nice of you to stop by, gentlemen. What can I do for you?"

"Hang! I will see you hanged, Saint-Just."

The Spanish pronunciation of the French name was almost as intriguing as Eavin's attempt at it. She lifted her eyebrows delicately, ignoring the Spaniard but keeping a wary eye on the lawman. He had the grace to look embarrassed.

"There's any number of people I would like to see hanged, Reyes, but I generally don't break into their homes and demand it without reason," Nicholas replied calmly.

The night was too warm to demand a fire, and the room was lit only by the two oil lamps beside their respective chairs. The shadows of the newcomers danced along the far wall, over the elegant French wallpaper, the gilded mirror, and the delicate, inlaid escritoire that had been Francine's. A cold chill shivered down Eavin's spine, as if her sister-in-law's ghost had entered the room with the onset of danger. The air seemed redolent of Francine's jasmine perfume, but the men were oddly oblivious to her presence. Eavin turned to watch Nicholas, but the amber glow in his eyes warned of his dangerous mood, and she remained silent.

"Without reason! You killed my son! Murderer! You will hang. I will see you hang." The Spaniard ranted, shaking his riding crop and ignoring all else but his own rage.

Nicholas lifted a world-weary eyebrow to the lawman. "You will explain what he raves about, Brown?" An impatient French accent tinted his words.

"Someone has told him about the duel. I'm afraid I'll have to take you in, Saint-Just. Governor Claiborne outlawed dueling, and when a man dies . . ."

Nicholas waved a dismissing hand. "This is ridiculous. His son disappears and he blames it on me. Raphael was in debt up to his ears. I would think it more likely he has run to escape prison as he has done in the past, or perhaps this time someone he owed took exception to his inability to pay."

"They say you killed him the night your wife died, Saint-Just. I can't dismiss an eyewitness report."

Eavin felt Francine's ghost breathing down her neck, urging her to speak. She glanced nervously to Nicholas, but he seemed dangerously calm, his eyes glittering with something she had no desire to interpret. She turned back to the lawman, who seemed as nervous as she. The Saint-Just reputation was not for nothing, then. She coughed lightly, causing the man named Brown to turn to her.

"I do not mean to intrude, sirs." She spoke quietly, keeping her eyes on her hands folded over the mending. "But Mr. Saint-Just was with his wife that night. I was there. He never left her side. He was terribly distraught. Even . . ." She hesitated, more for effect than because she didn't know what she meant to say next. "Even afterward, we could hear him in his grief. You may ask Madame Dupré or any of the servants. This house is not so large that such anguish cannot be heard. Your informant is dreadfully misinformed."

Brown breathed a visible sigh of relief. "Thank you . . ." Suddenly realizing he didn't know her name, he turned to Nicholas for an introduction.

Blithely speaking over the Spaniard's sputtering objections, Nicholas rose and made a perfunctory bow in Eavin's direction. "Mrs. Dupré, my sister-in-law. She came to us after Francine's brother died, and has graciously agreed to stay to help me raise the child. Mrs. Dupré, may I introduce Clyde Brown? He attempts to keep some semblance of law around here."

"My pleasure, sir." Eavin attempted the gracious nod of her head that she had seen Francine use.

"The pleasure is mine, Mrs. Dupré." Unaccustomed to the graceful gallantry of the aristocracy, Brown merely turned his hat in his hands while giving her a warm smile. "Not that I think this will ever come to that, but would you be prepared to testify to what you just said in court?"

Eavin felt the flutter of fear in her stomach, the same flutter she had felt every time the law had come knocking on her door looking for her brother, but she had learned how to smile and pretend assurance. The time to worry hadn't come yet. "I hope it isn't a French court, sir. I don't speak French."

Reyes was babbling incoherently now, shaking his fist and the riding crop, and Brown merely had time to acknowledge her statement before he grabbed the older man's elbow and began to lead him out.

"I'm sorry for the intrusion, Saint-Just. Just doing my duty."

Nicholas followed them to the door. "Of course, *monsieur,* I understand perfectly."

Eavin had the feeling that the purring French accent from Nicholas was a good deal more dangerous than his usual curt American tones. She shuddered briefly, then remembering Francine's ghost, sought her presence again. Whatever had been there was gone, and she wasn't certain whether or not to sigh with relief.

Nicholas returned to the room and poured himself a brandy. When he turned to face her, the glitter in his eyes

was more mocking than dangerous. "Your morals intrigue
me, Mrs. Dupré. You disapprove of making love, but
have no qualms about lying or, evidently, murder. Would
you care to explain yourself?"

Finding her hands shaking, Eavin set aside the shirt she
had been mending. It took what remained of her courage
to face him, and she did so only once she had risen from
her chair and was prepared to flee. "I didn't lie. I merely
withheld the full extent of the truth. And if murder has
been done, that is on your conscience; I know nothing of
it. I merely did what was necessary to protect Jeannette.
Should they arrest you, she would have nothing. You, at
least, are better than nothing."

A dark smile turned Nicholas's lips at this acknowledgment. "At least I will have no trouble knowing where I
stand in your eyes, Irish. You will keep me informed
when you decide I am no longer worth even that much?"

"I think you will know, sir. May I be excused now? I
find this day has become most tiring."

She did, indeed, look suddenly very tired. Nicholas instantly regretted his facetiousness. She knew nothing of
him, yet she had done him a favor that he suspected even
his best friend would not have done. Even if her reasons
were purely selfish, they had saved him from a very unpleasant night or two. Standing there in that shapeless
black gown, she looked young and alone. He could afford
to be generous.

"How can I show my gratitude? Were it not for your
quick thinking, I might have had the misfortune to spend
the next few nights in an extremely unpleasant jail. You
deserve some reward. Perhaps a new gown or two?"

Remembering Francine's ghostly presence, Eavin
glared at him. "You might show your gratitude by giving
your daughter a little attention. A child needs a father,
and as far as she is concerned, you are hers."

Nicholas struggled with the emotion raging through
him at her words. The chit wasn't so slow as not to have
guessed that he was not Jeannette's father. His fingers
clenched around the brandy glass until he felt it crack, but
there was no denying her request. For whatever reason,
he had allowed Francine's child to remain here. She
would bear his name. He had thought that would be
enough, but the Irish widow was making it plain that she

would not consider it so. He despised interfering women, but her interference had saved him a great deal of unpleasantness.

Sensing some of his struggle, Eavin waited patiently. She owed Francine this much. Dominic's sister had taken her in unquestioningly, welcomed her with the open arms that Madame Dupré and the rest of society would deny her. Because of Francine, Eavin had a roof over her head and food in her stomach and her pride relatively intact. Francine's daughter would lack for nothing as long as Eavin was in a position to look after her.

"She is too young yet to know that I exist," was all the response she received from Nicholas.

With a look of derision Eavin lifted her skirts and prepared to leave. "A child is never too young for love. But then, perhaps you were never a child. Good night." She walked out before she could see the bleak expression on Nicholas's face.

He had only one really strong childhood memory. He had been very young, so it must have been in Santa Domingue. He could remember the blistering sunshine above and the parade of colorful dancers in the street below the balcony where he had hidden. They had seemed so full of joy and life as they danced and swung about in their brilliant costumes, the drums beating an exciting rhythm around them. They wore masks and feathers, and many of them had bare feet. He had wanted badly to join them, but before he could figure out the best method of escape, he had been dragged back into the cool shade of the salon and the door had closed behind him.

Nicholas couldn't remember what lesson it was he had been avoiding that day, but the beating he had received had taught him not to shirk another. And he hadn't. He'd gone on to excel in everything he did. It was some consolation to know that he had the ability to conquer every lesson set before him. But sometimes the childish desire to join the dancers came back.

Disgruntled, Nicholas slammed his glass on the table and strode out.

5

Eavin tried not to show her surprise when Nicholas walked into the nursery the next morning. He was dressed casually in tight riding pants that clung indecently to strong thighs, and an open-necked linen shirt that revealed too much of the sun-browned column of his throat. His overwhelming masculinity in this tiny room scented with baby lotion and milk made her more aware of the man than ever before, a knowledge that did not sit easily with her, given her past experiences with men. It took an effort to remain where she was.

Unaware of Eavin's uneasiness, Nicholas gave the infant rocking on her hands and knees on the floor a dark look of skepticism. "Should she be out of bed like that?"

Eavin wished she had one of the cool short-sleeved muslins she had seen in Francine's wardrobe. The long-sleeved gown she wore now was suddenly stifling, even though it was October and the weather should be turning cool. Ignoring her discomfort, she bent to pick up Jeannette.

"How is she going to learn what the world is like if she is not allowed out in it?" Eavin asked more calmly than she felt, handing the child to her father.

Nicholas looked stunned at suddenly finding his hands filled with a small, chubby body. The babe gurgled and blew a bubble, gazing through innocent dark eyes at the stranger who held her.

"Hold her against your shoulder. Let her get to know you," Eavin instructed, hiding her amusement. Saint-Just suddenly seemed far less intimidating in the morning light with an infant dangling from his hands.

Gingerly, Nicholas adjusted the child to his shoulder, holding her tightly as if fearing she might break or get away. A small palm patted his lean face, and he grimaced, but when he discovered she would not dive from his arms, he took the window seat and stretched his long legs out before him. With curiosity he probed tiny fingers and feet in the same way in which Jeannette explored him.

"She doesn't see many strangers. Some children are afraid of anything different. She seems to adapt quite well." Complacently, Eavin took up the embroidery in her lap.

"Francine never knew a stranger. She welcomed everyone." Nicholas felt the wrenching pain of the memory and tried to ignore it. He had been a young boy when his family had first arrived in New Orleans. He had known no one, and the circumstances under which they had arrived made the world seem an unfriendly place. But he could still remember the golden little girl stopping her duenna in the street so she could say hello. Francine had loved everybody. Unfortunately.

As if following his train of thought, Eavin replied, "There are good and bad points to that trait. We will need to teach her caution."

That he would do of a certainty. Filling with an incomprehensible urge to protect this helpless creature he had been given, Nicholas caught Jeannette in his hands and raised her to meet his eyes. The small face looked startled and a trifle wary, and he grinned. "You will learn, *enfant*. That wicked witch in black over there will teach you to keep a sharp tongue, and I shall teach you to keep a sharp knife. It's never too soon to learn."

Eavin raised her eyebrows at this, but she offered no protest. The fact that Nicholas had lowered his evil pride to come in here and acknowledge the child was sufficient to raise him a step higher in her eyes. She was well aware that some men would never have had the maturity or assurance to accept another man's child as his own. Perhaps Nicholas Saint-Just had just grown a notch this day.

"It will be good for her to become accustomed to a man's voice. She hears nothing but women as it is."

"Perhaps that is the way it should be. We could send her to the nuns when she is older, and she would never know about the male of the species." Nicholas sent Eavin a mocking look that demanded reply.

"That is a little like learning about sunshine and closing your eyes when the nighttime comes and pretending

it doesn't exist. Ignorance can be as dangerous as knowledge. More so, perhaps."

"You are a hardhearted female, Irish. Dominic is scarce
gone a year, and already you have forgotten how to weep
for him. Should you not be protesting the benefits of men
and married life rather than comparing us to nighttime?"

Eavin had never truly wept for Dominic, and this devil
seemed to know that. She had cried the night they wed,
but never again. It had almost been a relief to know that
her husband wouldn't be coming back. Only after she had
lost the child had she felt any regret.

But she wouldn't give Saint-Just the satisfaction of
knowing he'd gotten under her skin. "I am not inclined to
be sentimental. I've not had that luxury. I've learned a
few things in this life, and one of them is that knowledge
is power. Ignorance might be bliss for a while, but it inevitably leads to pain and destruction. With knowledge, it
is possible to make constructive choices."

Nicholas watched her consideringly as she spoke. He
had never made any inquiries as to her background. He
didn't even know her age. The harsh morning light revealed only a complexion as soft and touchable as
Jeannette's, and wide eyes that reflected pain and humor
and intelligence when she raised them to him. She might
even be attractive in her rather blatant peasant way, if she
ever loosed the tight confines of her hair and wore something besides sackcloth. She was so entirely different
from the malleable women of his world that he could not
help but be fascinated.

"You do not sound as if you have had an easy life.
Where did Dominic meet you?" Nicholas had not meant
to linger, but the child reclining in his lap was restful, and
his curiosity about the woman who cared for her was only
natural.

Eavin didn't think Dominic had imparted that knowledge to his family. She threw Nicholas a shrewd look
from behind politely lowered eyelashes. "My family
owns a boardinghouse. Dominic had rooms there."

A working-class family, as he had suspected. Even the
democratic Americans didn't have Irish aristocracy.
Dominic had married far below him, when he should
have been looking for wealth. No one had ever claimed
that Francine's family had a lick of sense; here was living

proof of it. Still, Nicholas could understand the boy's fascination with the exotic. He had fallen for it himself in the past.

"I suppose that is where you learned to run a large household so capably. I am fortunate. There is always food available when I want it. When I first came here, I was forced to rummage about." Nicholas grimaced as a warm, wet spot began to form on his trousers, and he held the offender from him. "She's wet," he informed her politely.

"She's a little young to know better." Eavin efficiently took the infant to a dressing table and began to strip her. "There is no need for you to linger if you have business to carry on. I only meant for you to realize that the child has needs, too."

"She needs to be kept in the barn with the animals until she learns manners," he grumbled, rising and holding the wet stain from his leg.

As the child set up a protest at being changed, Nicholas came to stand over her warily. "You will see that she has what she needs while I am gone. I will begin giving you an allowance to cover your expenses and hers. I will leave it in my bottom desk drawer. The key will be in the center drawer." He touched an inquiring finger to the infant's and watched tiny fingers wrap around it as he finished giving orders. "I will be gone three days. I should be home by six of the third day and would like to eat at seven. I would also like your company at dinner, so do not go hiding yourself away in here when I arrive. This is a damned empty house, and if I'm to spend any time here, I wish to have a little companionship."

He removed his finger and strode out before Eavin could recover from her shock and reply.

She had plenty of time to think of things she could have said over the next few days. She could have asked him what earthly good was an allowance when she couldn't go anywhere to spend it. She could have told him she had hired on as a child's nanny and not his. She could have spat in his face and kicked his shins, but she doubted that he'd notice that any more than the other protests. Nicholas Saint-Just was accustomed to giving orders and having them obeyed. Eavin didn't think it had

ever occurred to him that the recipients of these orders
might have thoughts of their own.

Clyde Brown arrived on the morning of the third day of
Nicholas's absence. A storm had briefly relieved the heat
and humidity, and Eavin had brought Jeannette onto the
gallery in an old cradle she and Annie had unearthed
from the attic. She watched as the lawman slowly
stomped up the stairs to the living quarters. He was wearing an odd felt broad-brimmed hat, but if he had any
weapons, they were on the horse standing below. When
he caught sight of her, he hesitated, then came down the
gallery to where she waited rather than knocking at the
door.

"Good morning, ma'am. Is Mr. Saint-Just at home?"

She rather liked the lawman's open easiness. He used
flat American accents to pronounce Nicholas's name and
didn't posture or pose as he awaited her reply. He even
took his hat off respectfully, and she smiled at that.

"I don't expect him until this evening, Mr. Brown. I
would hate to think you've ridden out all this way for
nothing. Would you care to have a seat and some lemonade? I believe some has just been made fresh."

He didn't seem in the least displeased at this offer, and
while Eavin sent a maid scurrying for the refreshments,
he bent over the cradle and rattled one of Jeannette's toys,
to her intense enjoyment.

When Eavin was seated again, he asked, "This Saint-
Just's little one? She's a mite dark, ain't she?"

Eavin's suspicious nature instantly returned, but she replied calmly, "Her name is Jeannette. I understand both
the Dupré and Saint-Just families are French. I believe
dark hair is more prevalent than light. Was there some
message I could forward to Mr. Saint-Just when he returns?"

Brown took a seat on the cane-webbed chair a servant
brought and accepted the lemonade thirstily. Eavin
merely took a sip of her refreshment and set it aside. The
sheriff was beginning to make her uneasy again. She
didn't know what would happen to her and Jeannette if
Nicholas were put in jail, and she didn't want to know.
The sum of money in the desk drawer seemed immense
to her, but she wasn't certain of the value of things in this
odd country. The paper bills had been in French, and

some of the coins were Spanish. She wasn't even certain what they were worth. There might be enough to get them into New Orleans and to Madame Dupré if she could figure out how to do it, but beyond that she couldn't venture a guess. And she very much wanted to stay here.

Clyde Brown regarded her speculatively. "Don't know that I should, ma'am. I don't want to disturb you. Saint-Just can take care of himself. I just thought he ought to know Reyes is bent on making trouble."

"That much is obvious," Eavin replied drily. "Do you think his son has run away as Nicholas suggests?" She knew she had made an error as soon as she let slip the familiar name, but she had taken to thinking of Saint-Just by the name Francine had used and not by his proper title. She lifted the lemonade glass to her lips and pretended innocence.

Brown didn't so much as arch an eyebrow as he finished off his drink and rose. "Well, it's unusual not to find a body if a man's dead. These French place a mighty store by honor. To my way of thinking, if Saint-Just killed Raphael, he'd have sent the body back with flags and ribbons. But then, I've only been here a year or two, and there's a lot I don't know about these people. I thank you for the lemonade, Mrs. Dupré. It's not often I get a chance to talk with a pretty lady in the line of duty."

Forgetting her gracious lady pose, Eavin rose and followed him toward the stairway. "I thank you for the compliment, Mr. Brown, but I am more concerned about Mr. Saint-Just. Do you think this Señor Reyes will cause him harm?"

"Now, I knew I shouldn't have said anything." He turned and took her hand, patting it like a child's. "Saint-Just is capable of taking care of himself. I hear he's fought with the Barbary pirates, blowed them clean out of the water. Anyone who's sailed the sea has to have a lot of backbone. And he came out here and turned this place around single-handed, beat off the alligators and Indians to get that cotton in when everyone said he was moon-touched, and he's never looked back. I don't think one old man is going to hurt him none."

Perhaps not, but there were many ways of causing hurt. Eavin watched with a thoughtful frown as the lawman rode away. She'd heard the pirate story often enough to

begin to believe it. Nicholas Saint-Just upon occasion
might play the part of languid French aristocrat, but she
wasn't blind enough to believe the pose. She could see
him sailing ships and climbing masts. She could also see
him with gun in hand, decimating alligators and Indians
and men who dishonored his wife. He had that kind of
temper.

Turning back to Jeannette, Eavin wondered what the
story was behind Francine's capitulation to a man not her
husband, but she would probably never know the truth of
that. The Francine she had known had been quiet and
withdrawn, but she had heard enough from Dominic and
his mother to know that wasn't the true Francine. She
didn't think Nicholas would have married a ghost, either,
and that's all the woman in the bed had been.

As Eavin returned Jeannette to the shadows of the
house, she felt it close around her like a prison wall. She
wanted to retreat hurriedly to the sunshine, but she recognized her foolishness. It was just a house like any other
in these parts. She had seen enough upon arriving to
know that. It wasn't even a very large house based on the
standards of her home. The brick and timber walls downstairs merely held storage and work areas. The family
mostly lived on this second story. The salons and dining
area and master suite were here. Upstairs were the
smaller rooms Eavin and Jeannette and guests used. Without the ground-floor storage area, her mother's boardinghouse had been bigger.

But Eavin felt its gloom as she climbed the stairs to the
nursery. Perhaps it was the heavy oaks with their trailing
moss and spreading shade that caused this oppressive
feeling. Perhaps it was the knowledge of the powerful
river less than a mile away, with its ability to spread and
kill that caused this tension emanating from the walls.
Whatever it was, Eavin would be glad when Nicholas returned to dispel her fanciful notions.

The knowledge that she was looking forward to his
return surprised her. Unable to lie down and rest in the
afternoon as was the local custom, Eavin found herself
searching the library in the study when Jeannette went
in for her nap. She had scarcely given Francine's husband a
thought before, other than to wonder about the stories
about him. But now she was wishing for his early return.

The loneliness must really be worse than she had imagined. Perhaps she ought to sit and write her mother a letter. That should relieve any homesickness quickly.

There was paper in Saint-Just's desk. Sitting down in his chair, Eavin rummaged through the drawers in search of writing utensils. Since Nicholas had given her his key and access to the drawers, she didn't think there could be anything of value in here and had little compunction about putting it to use. Still, she jumped as if guilty when a voice spoke.

"What you doin' in Marster Nick's desk?"

Eavin looked up to find the African woman Nicholas had taken for a mistress standing in the doorway. He cared little what his servants wore, and he had obviously paid for her services with the piece of vibrant red silk Jess wore wrapped around her now. It not only accented the darkness of her skin, but the voluptuousness of her body, and Eavin found herself staring out of curiosity. She had long wondered what the fascination was between men and women, why one woman appealed to a man when another didn't. She didn't know why Dominic had wanted her physically, or why she hadn't returned his feelings. She had heard that ladies weren't supposed to have the same feelings as men; at the same time, she had seen with her own eyes how some women were attracted to men, and the feeling seemed mutual. It was very confusing, but obviously not to this slave, who knew less than nothing about anything else at all.

"I'm going to write a letter," Eavin responded casually. It wasn't what she wanted to say, but she felt uncomfortable telling servants to get out and mind their own business. She kept thinking of them as people capable of feelings, like herself.

"You ain't got no business in Marster Nick's things. You get yo'sef out o' here." Jess raised her hands defiantly to her broad hips.

That gesture brought Eavin's attention and thoughts to even more personal things as she imagined those swaying hips being held in Nicholas's hands. She might blame the heat for her straying thoughts, but the heat was nominal this day. She looked away and began to sharpen the pen. "Why don't you just go and make yourself happy in his bed until he comes home? Surprise him. He'll be here in a few hours."

The woman's eyes grew wide and her mouth opened as if she had more to say, but abruptly she turned and stalked out.

Eavin gave a sigh of relief and stared at the paper, pen posed above it. How did she go about telling her mother that she was suffering not only from hallucinations, but from a desire to know more about a strange man's bed?

6

"If he's holed up in Grand Terre with your pirates, Lafitte, I'll blow the place to hell and back. Don't lie to me."

The black-haired gentleman with the devilish eyes stroked his mustache and watched his dinner partner with some amusement as the lion-haired gentleman paced the room. Lafitte was on close terms with many of the businessmen of New Orleans, but this was the only one who dared speak to him in such a manner. And undoubtedly the only one from whom he would allow such language.

"You and who else, Saint-Just? Don't threaten me unless you mean it. Since you have started playing nursemaid to women and children, you have sold your best ships to me. The schooners you have left may evade the blockade with some success, but they do not make good privateers. You will need cannon to reach me."

Nicholas grew dangerously still as he swung around to face the man no one sensible would ever call friend. He met the other man's eyes coldly. "And you do not think I can summon cannon? Claiborne wants you out of there, *mon ami.* I will not be very popular with the merchants of New Orleans, but I will see you pounded into the swamps if you do not turn Reyes over to me."

Lafitte had not built his empire by pushing men too far, but only as far as they would go. Smiling, he crossed a booted foot over his knee and reached for his cup. "He is gone. My men do not think highly of the Spanish. Did you know he was wearing padding under his shirt? Your blow would have killed him were it not for that."

Nicholas closed his eyes and sent curses to the heavens. Then flinging himself to the nearest chair, he reached for a goblet. "I suspected as much, but I was too wretched to care. Where has he gone?"

Lafitte shrugged, but the dangerous narrowing of Saint-Just's eyes caused him to reconsider. "The ladies nursed him to health. One of them was Mexican. My men thought she would be an attractive addition to their beds, but she had other ideas. Reyes stole some silver and a boat and the girl and left during some festivities. I would suspect that they are making their way to Texas, perhaps on to Mexico."

"If you are telling the truth, then his father is more fiendish than I have given him credit for." Nicholas swallowed heavily of the wine.

"I have heard the rumors, too." Lafitte watched him sympathetically. "They do not like you much here to believe such assinity. To believe you would kill your wife and her child is the work of fools."

"My father was accused of worse in his time, and most of it was no doubt true. Why should they not think the same of me? It's of no moment." Nicholas shrugged his large shoulders.

Lafitte snorted. "That is why you marry the lovely lady? Because you do not care what people say? Bahh, you are as big a fool as they."

Nicholas thought of Francine's lovely laughter in the days when she had been happy, remembered her look of unadulterated relief when he had made his offer, remembered the brief moments when he had held her in his arms as the tears shook her slender frame, and he shook his head. Perhaps he had been a fool for taking her in as he had, but that fool's life had been the most pleasant he had ever known.

"Honor makes a gentleman, not a fool, Lafitte. Honor may be all I have left, but I will abide by it." Nicholas rose to his feet and waited for the other man to realize the conversation had ended.

A clever man, Lafitte understood what his companion had left unsaid. Scowling, he rose and shook Saint-Just's hand. They both had led lives unknown to the idle, wealthy gentlemen of New Orleans. They both walked the city's streets in the same guise as those idle fops. But only one of them had clung to his notion of honor and deserved the title of gentleman their wealth bestowed upon them. Lafitte watched as Saint-Just strode out and wondered if it was too late to change his path.

* * *

"What in hell? Get out of here, you slut!" The furious shouts echoed through the lower rooms and up the stairs.

Eavin halted on the way down, her hand resting on the banister as a woman's whining voice replied. It took a moment before she realized what was happening, and then a slow grin began to form on her lips.

"I don't care what you thought! Get your filthy black ass out of my bed and back where it belongs! Out! Now!"

A thud followed by running footsteps indicated a forcible removal and irate retreat. Eavin debated returning upstairs, but the black maid arrived in the hallway before she could escape, and giving Eavin a scathing glance, Jess scampered away from the sound of approaching boots. There wasn't time to squelch her laughter at the insolent woman's ignominious flight before Nicholas arrived in her footsteps.

Seeing the laughter in Eavin's eyes, Nicholas's fury rose to new heights. "Who in hell gave her permission to be in here?"

"Sure, and you didn't like the surprise? A bother it is, but it kept the spalpeen out of my way. Dinner will be at seven, as you requested." Twitching her skirts, Eavin made a more dignified retreat beneath Nicholas's black scowl.

Sometimes her temerity terrified her, but Eavin gathered the shattered remains of her courage when it came time to go below for dinner. She had spent three days stewing over Nicholas's orders to accompany him at the table. She shouldn't have vented her anger by using Jess. But the deed was done and she must face up to it.

Nicholas was waiting for her as she came down the stairs, probably intending to come up and drag her down had she been a minute late. He had actually donned a cravat and brushed his hair back neatly, although he hadn't bothered to fasten any of the buttons on his coat or waistcoat. A scowl still darkened his brow as Eavin descended, but he held out his arm for her and led her into the dining room without a word of comment.

He seated her on his right and poured a glass of wine for each of them as a maid carried out the first course. Eavin eyed the array of forks and spoons with trepidation and wisely followed Nicholas's assured choices of silver-ware as the meal progressed.

"You have made your point," he finally admitted in a tone of disgruntlement as he drained his glass. "The baggage will stay in the kitchen, and I will stay out of it. Do you have any further surprises waiting for me?"

"Not of my making. The sheriff was here to see you. You might wish to speak with him sometime." Eavin answered with relief that he had held his temper, but she kept her eyes on her plate, not letting them stray to his arrogant elegance. Nicholas emanated a fierce tension that made it difficult to concentrate, much less eat.

"Brown?" He stifled a curse. "I dare say he was more interested in seeing you than me. He's never bothered to come out here before. I find it amusing that you don't even need to leave the house to find suitors."

That forced Eavin to look up. Nicholas was leaning indolently back in his chair, one elbow propped over the curved wood as he drank his dinner and watched her. Amusement glittered somewhere behind his dangerous eyes, and she tightened her lips in anger.

"I am glad you have found something to amuse you. I had supposed there to be a dire dearth of amusements in these parts."

"Sarcasm does not become a lady. There are many amusements to be had here. I was thinking it time to attend them again, although most of the frivolity has returned to New Orleans by now. I think, under the circumstances, that you should be returned to society at the same time that I am. The Howells are having a small soiree Friday night. You will be ready at half-past seven."

The fork clattered out of her hand, and Eavin retrieved it without looking at him. "I will not be one of your amusements," she said when she had gathered her wits.

"No, you will be my protective armor. I cannot think of any more formidable shield against eager young things than a matronly widow on my arm. But you cannot attend in that ghastly black. Have you nothing in gray or lavender or something less depressing to the eye?"

He was baiting her. Surely, he must be baiting her as her brother often had. Eavin raised her head to meet his gaze in defiance. "I dyed all that I owned when Dominic died. Black is all I have. And I don't mean to keep you entertained if you are bored with society. My place is here with Jeannette."

Nicholas's voice was smooth and confident as he returned to his meal. "Your place is where I tell you, Irish. This is my household, and I expect all members of it to respect my orders. Find something in one of Francine's wardrobes that will be suitable."

Men really knew absolutely nothing about anything. Glancing down at herself, Eavin tried to imagine forcing her sturdy figure into the tiny bodices and long skirts of her tall, slender sister-in-law, and without thinking, she giggled at the image produced. If she did not spill out of the one, she would trip over the other.

"You would get what you deserve should I obey that particular order." With more calm than she felt, Eavin reached for her wineglass.

Nicholas lifted a languid eyebrow. "Indeed?" His knowing gaze dropped to the shapeless bodice of her gown. Unable to ask the question that immediately came to mind, he substituted, "How tall are you?"

"At least four inches shorter than Francine, if I am any judge. And you may stop looking at me like that. I can assure you, her gowns will not suit, and I would not wear them if they should."

Nicholas narrowed his eyes, mentally rearranged her bodice, loosened a few strands of her pitch black hair, and came to the same conclusion. "You are right. You should wear ruby or sapphire or emerald. We will look in the warehouse in the morning and see what is available."

Eavin's fingers clenched more tightly around her fork. "I will not go with you. I do not belong in society. Do not play me for a fool. Irish is not a synonym for stupid."

"You speak remarkably well for a bog maiden. Better than many of these Kaintucks who come down here posing as gentlemen. You are Jeannette's aunt. They must accept you as they must accept Jeannette in the future. If you wish to be the one to rear her, you must become acquainted with the society into which she is born."

That not only had the ring of finality to it, it had the ring of truth. Cursing and biting her tongue, Eavin offered no further protest. She could not imagine why the madman had suddenly decided she needed to meet the neighbors, particularly on such a formal occasion, but she was

in no position to argue with him. She had wanted to meet
people, but she hadn't imagined meeting those on the
same level as Saint-Just. Perhaps there were no in-
betweens here.

Before dinner was over, a sharp rap at the front door
intruded. A maid hurried to answer it, and remembering
the unpleasantness of the last intrusion, Eavin sent a
questioning look at her dinner companion. She didn't
think she could call him her employer any longer, but she
had not yet determined her status in his household. It was
still as a nonentity, she decided, when Nicholas merely
sipped his wine and waited for the maid to announce the
visitor.

"Nick, you're a damned elusive bast—"

The visitor halted suddenly at the sight of a woman at
the table. Swiping his tall hat from his head, he bowed
and apologized. "I beg your pardon, madam. I did not realize ... I ..." He turned to Nicholas for rescue.

Nicholas was smiling to himself as Jeremy looked from
him back to the prim female in black at his side. "Eavin,
Jeremy Howell; my sister-in-law, Eavin Dupré. His family is hosting the soiree of which I spoke."

A slight gentleman with sandy brown hair and a face
more friendly than handsome, he seemed torn between
surprise and pleasure, and was finally induced to take a
seat when Saint-Just kicked a chair out from under the table for him.

"I didn't mean to intrude, Mrs. Dupré. I just never
thought of Old Nick dining like everyone else. You will
be attending our entertainment on Friday?"

"She will," Nicholas answered firmly for her. "Eavin,
ma chère, since this will soon devolve into a business discussion, why don't you go check on Jeannette or something?"

For a brief moment Eavin contemplated what it would
be like to be someone like Francine, with all the wealth
and background to do anything she liked. At this moment
she would very much like to bring a plate of rice down
over this arrogant monster's head. Had she been Francine,
with her advantages, she would have. As it was, she
merely lifted her skirts and beat a hasty retreat, much as
his black mistress had earlier.

Once she was out of hearing, Jeremy returned to his

seat and glared at Nicholas. "Can't you leave your hands off any woman who comes in reach? My word, Nick, Francine's scarce been gone four months."

Saint-Just's lips lifted in small amusement. "My taste would have to have changed dramatically to offer carte blanche to an Irish mouse. We annoy each other, that is all."

"She cannot deserve what those angry wives will make of her should you introduce her to society now. Have some pity for a change, Nick. If you want to flout society, do it with someone better able to fight back. She couldn't be more than a child."

"Au contraire, mon frère. Mrs. Dupré has the calculating mind and sharp tongue of an adder. She is quite capable of setting a few clacking tongues back in place. She was quite admirable when Reyes and Brown appeared here."

Jeremy remained dubious. "I still think it unfair of you. She has no defense against the fact that she is living here with you without chaperonage. Where in hell is Madame Dupré?"

"One could only hope she is in hell," Nicholas replied with feeling. "I sent her packing after the funeral. And I don't need any more females clacking about the place, so don't push me on this, Jeremy. Eavin is the child's aunt. That is it and no more."

"You would have done better to send them both with your mother-in-law. If Reyes should ever get wind of your other occupation—"

"Shut up, Howell, you talk too much." Rising abruptly, Saint-Just stalked from the room.

Eavin had no intention of returning below for the rest of the night, but sometime after she heard the front door slam, the sound of boots on the stairs warned Nicholas wasn't going to leave her in peace. Standing over Jeannette's cradle, she was too far from her room to run toward its safety. She bent and tucked a straying strand of hair over the infant's ear.

"Howell's gone. You can come out of hiding now."

Eavin straightened and glared at the shadowy figure in the doorway. "I am quite content right here."

"Are you?" The shadow leaned against the door frame.

"That's most extraordinary. You have no friends, no one to talk to but a man you despise, and you consider yourself content. You cannot have led a very pleasant life, Mrs. Dupré."

"You used my name with enough familiarity earlier, why do you hesitate now? I did marry Dominic, you know. I have the papers to prove it." Against her better judgment Eavin moved toward the doorway. This was no place to hold an argument. It would give Jeannette nightmares.

Nicholas politely moved into the hall, out of her way, then appropriated her arm and led her toward the stairs, not slowing when she balked. "I have no doubt that you got precisely what you wanted, Irish. You are a very determined woman. Under your gentle auspices I have acquired a daughter to raise for the next twenty years and a nursemaid who does not always hold her tongue. To be fair, I've also been rescued from certain imprisonment because it did not suit your needs. I think it is time we get to know each other better."

"I think I know more than enough about you already. I fail to see why we should know each other at all."

"Because circumstances have thrown us in each other's way. Quit being so damned recalcitrant, Eavin. We don't have to be enemies." He threw open the door of the *petite salle* and escorted her to her chair.

"I think I would prefer just being Jeannette's nanny," Eavin said stiffly as she sat down.

"Then I would have to send you away in a few years and hire a governess and a duenna and who knows what other assorted females, which I refuse to do. Do you have any education at all?"

Eavin drew herself up irately. "I can read and write and do mathematics, if that is what you ask. My parents were Irish, not savages."

"Very well." Nicholas accepted that with aplomb, taking his comfortable chair and meeting her glare calmly. "That is more than any female around here knows. I would prefer that Jeannette at least knows how to write her name rather than just the usual etiquette and such. When I take you out in company, you will need to observe the other ladies to see how they go on. I would rather Jeannette did not grow up with the temper and manners of an Irish virago. You seem to possess the essential social skills. I suppose the Irish inherit them by birth?"

Eavin ignored his sarcasm. "My mother was a lady's maid before she came to America." Before she had been accused of theft would be more accurate, but he didn't deserve the full truth. She continued her defense. "Before he died, my father was a fairly wealthy builder. I am not ignorant of social skills." Nor of how her father had made some of his wealth. Still, he hadn't been any more dishonest than the rest, and some of the finest buildings in the new capital of Washington were standing because of Sean O'Flannery. She wouldn't blacken his memory.

"How very noble." Nicholas splashed some brandy into a waiting glass. "With such an aristocratic background, you should be planning on remarrying, not hiding in the backwoods for the rest of your life."

Eavin definitely wasn't stupid. She heard not only the implied criticism but the suspicion in Saint-Just's comment, and she bit back an angry retort in favor of a truthful one. "You have no need to worry about my intentions, sir." The words came out a trifle more angrily than she had intended. "I have no wish to marry again, and I certainly do not have my sights set on you. I could not think of a more certain way to invite misery."

Loosening his cravat, Nicholas gave her a long, thoughtful look. The amusement on his lips did not quite reach his eyes as he made himself comfortable. "The name is Nicholas. You have my permission to use it. Aside from the fact that even Francine would no doubt agree with you about my company, why would you denigrate marriage in general? I thought that was the state to which all women aspire."

Eavin looked away from the strong column of his throat exposed by the open neckcloth. "I am certain Francine never thought any such thing. And my reasons are none of your business."

He moved his chair closer to hers, leaning over the small table between them to fill another glass. The distance between them narrowed to a few inches, but she continued avoiding looking at him. "Have some brandy, Irish. It helps you sleep at night. Since I will have to give up the comfort of Jess's charms, I no doubt will find it difficult to find the escape of easy slumber. But I suppose with your late husband out playing at war most of your married life, you are more accustomed to an empty bed than I."

Not only scandalized but furious, Eavin swung to face him, only to discover Nicholas was far closer than she had thought. His hand with the brandy glass hovered dangerously near her lips. She suppressed a nervous gasp and pushed herself farther back in her chair.

"I do not need strong spirits to help me sleep. My conscience is clear. I think it is time that I retire. I have some experience with men in various states of inebriation, and I have no desire to repeat it."

Eavin couldn't rise until he moved his hand, and instead of cooperating, Nicholas caught her fingers and wrapped them around the stem of the glass. She felt a jolt of heat at his touch, and she jerked, sloshing the amber liquid, but he didn't seem to notice anything.

"You may take the glass with you, Irish. Just answer my question. Why do you think you will never marry again?"

Taking a deep breath and glaring at him, Eavin replied, "Because I cannot bear any more children."

When he moved back with a look of shock, she rose from her chair with offended dignity and escaped.

7

To hide his surprise at the sight drifting down the stairs, Nicholas narrowed his eyes and pretended cool indifference, sensing anything more would drive the little widow into flight back up the stairs.

He had suspected Eavin Dupré of concealing more beneath those witch's rags than met the eye, but the shape of a goddess was not what he had expected. In the modest gown she had fashioned from the lavender silk in his storehouse, she revealed an exquisite hour-glass shape that while not precisely fashionable, appealed blatantly to a man's baser instincts. Nicholas was almost thankful she had the good sense to cover herself when they were alone.

That thought jarred loose the answer to a few questions that had been hovering at the back of his mind. With great care Nicholas offered his arm to the approaching Venus, not lowering his gaze any farther than Eavin's face. He received his reward in the form of a shy smile and the slight relaxation of her grip on his coat sleeve.

He had just discovered the flaw in the Irish witch's defenses, but it was of little matter to him that his guest was afraid of men. He had no wish for another woman to complicate his life. He would use her as she used him, and that would be the extent of it.

But it did make things supremely more pleasant to arrive at the soiree with a vision of loveliness on his arm. Keeping his smug satisfaction to himself, Nicholas solemnly introduced his Irish sister-in-law to their hostess and left her in good hands.

"I am so pleased to finally make your acquaintance, Mrs. Dupré. Nicholas has kept you to himself for too long. It is time that you meet some of your neighbors. Come along and let me introduce you."

Eavin reluctantly accepted the guidance of the stately woman who had been introduced as Jeremy's mother. The gown she had hurriedly made from the silk Nicholas had given her seemed to cling indecently to her breasts as she walked. She had kept herself buried in heavy, over-large dresses so long she had forgotten what it felt like to appear in public in anything remotely fashionable. Gamely she tried to tell herself no one was staring, but she felt gazes scorching her skin as she traversed the room.

Cursing Nicholas's callous desertion, Eavin made a pleasant nod to Jeremy's sister Lucinda and the other young girls in her company as she was introduced. She didn't think she'd ever been that young, she mused as they chattered on about the various fashions circulating about the room. It was far too late now to learn how to indulge in idle chatter. She was beginning to think she would be an abysmal failure as Jeannette's aunt when the time came to bring her out into society.

Trying not to think such thoughts, Eavin excused herself and drifted through the crowd in search of a place where she could hide for a while. Not intentionally eavesdropping, she couldn't help but hear those snippets of conversation that applied to herself and Nicholas. They seemed to leap out from the general conversation as she walked by.

". . . he brought the pirate Lafitte to his mother's birthday ball just last week . . ."

She hadn't even known the monster had a mother, but she knew it was Nicholas of whom they spoke when they elbowed each other and grew silent as Eavin drew closer. Expressionless, she wandered on.

". . . living with him. It's scandalous. Even Madame Dupré . . ."

Eavin didn't need to see this couple to know they spoke of her relationship with Nicholas. Proper ladies did not live alone with gentlemen to whom they were not related. Even she knew that. But all she had wanted to be was a nursemaid. Nicholas was the madman who had made her come out in this.

"The blockade would destroy business were it not for the smugglers."

Eavin hesitated behind a potted plant at this piece of conversation. She recognized Jeremy's voice and wondered if Nicholas was with him. It seemed very much like the kind of conversation they had indulged in over the newspapers in the evenings. The men were around the corner from the plant, and she could see little more than their coats.

"Old Nick won't let the British keep the ladies from their laces," an unknown high-pitched voice giggled.

"I heard he's bringing in flour," Jeremy responded in evident disgust with this nonsense.

"Everyone knows the best money in smuggling is in slaves. Where do you think he got his wealth? Do not fool yourself, Howell. Saint-Just and the pirates are as thick as the thieves they are."

"And I suppose now you'll repeat that accursed rumor Reyes is spreading that Nick killed his wife and her child? Perhaps you ought to meet the man sometime instead of talking behind his back."

Jeremy stalked out of the alcove before Eavin had time to step back. They nearly ran into each other, and judging by the paleness of Eavin's cheeks, Jeremy swiftly ascertained that she had overheard some of the conversation. Catching her hand, he led her toward the main crowd of the ballroom.

"Sometimes I think men gossip more than women," he muttered as the music began to swell.

"Gossip is the product of idle minds," Eavin responded absently. Ahead, she could see Nicholas leaning over the hand of a strikingly lovely woman nearly as tall as him.

Jeremy followed her gaze. "The widow Mignon Dubois. They're old friends. Her reputation is as wicked as his." He looked up at Eavin's nervous start and grinned. "My mind is as idle as the next's. I apologize. Would you care to dance, Mrs. Dupré?"

"No, I do not dance, Mr. Howell. I'm sorry. Nicholas insisted that it was time to come out of my blacks, but I cannot bring myself to join in as I should. Would you mind finding me a cup of punch?"

He barely had time to reassure her and leave her in the company of Lucinda while he went to fetch the requested drink when Nicholas miraculously appeared out of the crowd.

As he made his bow before Lucinda and herself, Eavin wondered that such an aristocratically handsome man

could also have the gleam of the devil, but she could see
it in his eyes now. His lips twisted with unholy amusement as he met her disapproving gaze.

"Come now, Mrs. Dupré. I cannot have scandalized
you so thoroughly so early in the evening. Lucinda, will
you excuse us? Your mother has insisted that I must join
the dancing, and I have told her I will only do so with my
sister-in-law's approval and accompaniment."

Eavin's horror quickly communicated itself, and Nicholas glanced at her with raised eyebrows. "You object?"

"I cannot," she stated uneasily. "I had not thought you
would join the dancing so soon after ..." She switched
directions as the scowl began to appear between his eyes.
"If you must dance, take Lucinda. I will be quite content
watching."

Nicholas made a nod of acknowledgment to Jeremy's
blond younger sister, but turned the bulk of his wrath on
Eavin. "Jeremy would call me out should I sully Lucinda
with my attentions. I have told you before that I am not
in the habit of devouring innocent females. I mean only
to dance once to meet my obligations. I cannot think that
cause for consternation."

For a moment Eavin almost felt a flow of empathy between them, a knowledge of hurt and anger and something else as he waited for her to give him her hand so
they might face the crowd together. But then she saw the
tightening of his jaw, the dangerous coldness of his eyes,
and realized her foolishness in thinking him inclined toward the same vulnerability as she. Taking a deep breath,
she replied, "I cannot dance, Nicholas. I am sorry."

He did not look particularly appeased by the apology.
"Cannot or will not? Never mind, I shall look elsewhere."

When he turned and walked away, Eavin felt something go out of her, and she had to draw herself up
straight and face the room to keep from running after
him. Odd, how she feared and wanted his presence at the
same time. Facing Nicholas seemed much easier than
standing on her own in this cold crowd. But she couldn't
dance and she had no right to rely on Nicholas. She
would learn to face these people by herself.

On the sidelines sometime later, watching Eavin's hair
curl around her face in the heat of the crowded room as
she promenaded the perimeter on the arm of Clyde

Brown, Nicholas felt a disgust he wasn't certain was for her or for himself. Of course, she belonged with the likes of Clyde Brown. To think just because he had taken her into his household made her something she was not was the work of a fool. And why should he want her to be any more or less than she was? She was no more than the child's nursemaid.

But her rejection rankled, and the sight of that petite figure he had just discovered existed in another man's arms irked him endlessly. She had a woman's body, and every man in the room had noticed it by now. While he had been admiring her sharp tongue and quick intelligence, she had been hiding sultry charms and laughing eyes behind those damned black dresses. *Mon dieu,* but Francine's death must truly have made him blind.

Remembering the child and the closeness of the quarters in which they lived, Nicholas reluctantly admitted to himself that it was better this way. He didn't need another woman in his life right now. Watching as the crowd near the entrance parted and the hum of tongues flapping increased, Nicholas found a new object for his irritation.

Reyes was not a tall man, but neither was he particularly old or weak. Nicholas was well aware that only the fact that Reyes's fingers were crippled with rheumatism kept him from challenging him as his son had. Nicholas could sympathize with the man's plight, but he didn't have to fall victim to his lies.

When the music and dancing came to its natural stop, the room suddenly seemed very quiet. The crowd had made a pathway between the two men, and everyone waited expectantly for the confrontation to come. The Howells rushed to interfere, but Reyes brushed aside his host while Nicholas politely handed his hostess over to her son. He despised scenes like this one, but he wasn't going to run from it, either. "Good evening, *señor,* I believe you owe me an apology."

Reyes refused to be put on the defensive. "I believe you owe me your life. An eye for an eye, the Bible says. You will pay, Saint-Just."

"If I had killed your son, Reyes, you can be certain that I would have dumped his rotten carcass on your doorstep. He cost me more than his wretched life was worth."

A gasp went up from those nearest, and whispers

formed a wave carrying the insult to the back of the room along with the speculation that accompanied it.

Before Reyes could do more than lift his gloved hand to strike the insolent Frenchman standing before him, Clyde Brown caught his arm and pulled it down.

"Carry your grievances elsewhere, Reyes. This is a respectable private party and no place for fighting."

The men who had arrived in Reyes's company flanked him now, but the older man waved them off with disdain. Narrowed eyes focused only on Nicholas, he made a curt bow. "A life for a life, Saint-Just. You will pay." With that reminder he turned and stalked out again.

Nicholas turned to find Eavin at his side, her green eyes wide and startled as she followed the old man's path. The face earlier flushed with excitement had paled, and he instinctively pulled her hand into the crook of his elbow. Wide eyes turned up to him, and he noticed her lashes were so thick and long as to appear almost velvet against the whiteness of her skin. Then she recovered herself, and the lashes lowered to hide the raw fear in her eyes.

At this sign of her concern, Nicholas felt a jolt of something beyond the icy emptiness that had engulfed him since Francine's death. Softly he said, "I am sorry, Irish. Would you prefer to go now?"

Eavin's fingers clenched as she watched the crowd close around the Spaniard. "He wouldn't harm Jeannette, would he?"

With a touch of bitterness at this response, Nicholas responded in kind, "No, he wouldn't hurt Jeannette," and holding his shoulders stiffly, he turned and walked away.

8

Pacing the hall floor in much the same manner as Nicholas, Eavin repeated all her arguments to herself, reinforcing her courage. She had to talk with him. Christmas was just a month away, and it was a sin to go on as they were. Perhaps Nicholas had surrendered his religion, but she had not. She had not been to confession or mass since Dominic's death, and she had always attended Christmas mass. Jeannette must learn her faith sometime. She was too young now, but how would she learn later if neither of the adults in her life attended church?

Eavin swung on her heel and marched toward the back stairs. For Jeannette's good and her own soul, she must confront Nicholas.

The only obstacle was the distance between them. The sugarcane harvest had taken all his time since the night of the Howells' soiree. Eavin had contemplated waiting up for him, but he was so late entering every night that she suspected he had been with Jess or another woman, and she couldn't face him again like that. And he was gone in the mornings before she could tend to Jeannette and get herself dressed. She didn't think she amounted to enough in his life for Nicholas to avoid her, but the result was much the same. So if she were going to confront him with anything, it would have to be on his grounds.

Unfortunately, his grounds consisted of miles of cultivated fields and acres of swamp, and she had never learned to ride. But Annie had informed her that the men were working in the refinery today, and that was within walking distance. Eavin glanced at the building on the horizon and prayed that was the refinery as she set her feet to the hard-packed dirt of the road leading in that direction. She was a child of the city. She knew how to avoid reckless carriages and drunken sailors and running

sewage in the gutters. She knew absolutely nothing about
the dangers inhabiting cane-stubbled fields and deceptive
cypress forests except what the servants had told her, and
those tales made her shiver.

She hugged her woolen shawl closer and tried to keep
both hands inside as she trudged along the path, repeating
her litany of arguments. The December day was compara-
tively mild, but her thin slippers didn't keep out the damp
from low-lying places in the ground, and the chill wind
whipped through the fine material of her gown. She had
been a fool to accept Nicholas's generous offer of the contents of his warehouse. Her femininity might crave the
lovely silver-gray cashmere, but common sense should
have kept her to her own heavy black bombazine.

Eavin almost turned back when she arrived at the
building she had hoped was the refinery only to be told
by the man in charge that the place she sought was still
farther down the road and across a field. She had the feeling that the buck-toothed overseer was enjoying her dismay as he spoke, but she refused to acknowledge his
mockery. Gazing at the distant structure, Eavin summoned all her resources and told herself that she had
come this far, there was no use in turning back. The black
field hands looked at her with curiosity, but her only fear
was of her own ignorance. She knew nothing of this
country in which she walked. She had heard the tales of
fearsome alligators and poisonous snakes and giant spiders, but surely these things slept or went away or something in the winter.

Reassuring herself that there was nothing to fear, Eavin
marched on. It was almost pleasant to be out of the house
for a change, if she weren't quite so chilly. Nicholas had
taken her nowhere since the Howells', and she had no
means of transportation on her own. She was isolated out
here, entirely reliant on Nicholas, and she wasn't at all
certain that she liked it that way. Nicholas wasn't precisely the sort of man on whom she wished to rely. She
didn't think any such man existed.

But if she had to rely on just herself, then she must
have the courage to seek what she wanted, and she
wanted to attend Christmas mass. Lifting her chin, Eavin
delicately set one foot on the muddy field, felt it squish
beneath her slippers, and wrinkling her nose in distaste,

lifted her skirts, and set out across the stubble to the refinery.

She sighed with relief as her feet found a grassy strip at the edge of the field. The refinery was only a short distance away, and she could see Nicholas mounting his horse as he spoke to a group of black men gathered outside. She prayed he would see her before he rode away. She would most assuredly kill him if he rode off before she had a chance to speak with him.

One of the men pointed in her direction, and Eavin could almost feel the waves of fury emanating from the man on the horse as he swung toward her. Coldness crept around her heart, but her own temper kept her moving forward. She had done nothing to deserve this abandonment. Even the slaves were allowed a day off every week. There was no reason in the world that she shouldn't ask to be taken to mass.

Eavin knew Nicholas was shouting, but she couldn't hear the words and made no attempt to. Tightening her lips and pulling her shawl closer, Eavin grimly continued her pilgrimage through the thick grass. Did he think she was fool enough to turn around and go back now? The sight of the whip he suddenly brandished caused her to hesitate, however. She had known he was a violent man, but had he taken leave of his senses?

The whine of the whip froze Eavin where Nicholas's shouts hadn't. She could see him more clearly now and remembered the dangerous narrowing of amber eyes full well. Although garbed in the long frock coat of a gentleman, he displayed the raw masculinity of a riverboat man as he urged his huge mount into a gallop directly toward her. She could see the fallen shock of wheat-colored hair against the weathered darkness of his brow and the angry lines cutting into his jaw as he clenched his teeth, and she had the sudden desire to turn and run, but something in his fury froze her in place.

The whip struck again, and the grass not inches from Eavin's feet began to ripple. Too startled to scream, Eavin glanced up again to Nicholas, only to find herself looking down the barrel of his pistol. The weapon exploded before she had time to register its direction.

Her hand flew from her shawl to her mouth as a frantic bellow split the air and the grass thrashed and writhed.

Blood erupted from a monster beast not inches away, splattering her new gown, but Eavin was unconscious of anything except her battle to remain upright as her breath locked in her throat and her head spun. Nicholas was upon her in seconds, dragging her back, cursing in more languages than Eavin knew existed as she kept her horrified gaze on the dying struggles of the monster. When her gaze finally focused on the viscera pouring from the gaping hole in the animal's hide, Eavin turned abruptly in Nicholas's arms, leaned over the cane-stubbled field, and heaved the contents of her breakfast upon the mud.

"Mon dieu, I'll have someone keelhauled for this. Have you not a lick of sense in your silly head? What in the name of the Holy Mother of God possessed you to come out here?" Another string of curses followed as Nicholas discovered her mud-caked shoes and castigated her for her lack of boots as well as sense.

Grabbing his offered handkerchief, Eavin tried to pull away, but at this demonstration of her ability to stand on her own, Nicholas jerked her back toward his horse.

"Did no one tell you this land crawls with 'gators and snakes and spiders as big as your hand? Did you not believe them? Or did you think you could walk on water like the saints? What . . ." His string of adjectives were almost entirely French, and Eavin made no attempt to translate them. ". . . bastard told you where I was?"

Nicholas seemed to be waiting for some response to this furious jumble of words, but Eavin was more concerned with the huge animal suddenly looming before her. She had never sat on a horse before, and she wasn't at all certain that she meant to start now. The animal turned his head and flared his nostrils in certain disapproval, and Eavin stepped backward, directly into Nicholas.

Without waiting for permission, he caught her waist and flung her upward, holding her firmly to the saddle while Eavin grabbed for any support she could find. His sharp curse stopped the stallion from sidling away, and grabbing the reins, he held the horse while she found the pommel and clung for dear life.

"Nicholas, I can't ride." Eavin's teeth chattered with the cold and fear as she looked down and saw the distance to the ground.

"That is evident." With a look of disgust Nicholas

brought the reins over the horse's head and began to lead it forward. "Just hang on, unless you want me to join you."

Impossibly, Eavin did want him to join her. She would feel a good deal more secure if there was another human body up here beside her. But she was seated on the saddle sideways and clinging to anything her hands could reach, and she didn't see how it would be humanly possible for him to fit anywhere.

It was better if she closed her eyes. Sighing, Eavin felt the sway of the horse and heard Nicholas's mutters and began to gather her shattered senses again. "What was that creature?" she asked once she had the tongue to utter the words.

"Alligator. Every damned man on this plantation knew that beast was there. I was just going out to get rid of it. What in hell possessed you to cross that field?"

"That's where they told me I'd find you." She sounded defensive and hated it, but she was doing well to answer at all.

"*Who* told you?"

The sharp command of Nicholas's voice did not bode well for someone, but Eavin felt no sympathy for the grinning idiot who had sent her across that field. Without remorse she replied, "The buck-toothed man, your overseer."

"Jenkins. That does it. I've put up with that bumpkin as long as I intend to. Can you hang on a little longer? I have a stop I want to make before we return to the house."

Eavin opened her eyes long enough to look down at Nicholas. His low-crowned hat prevented her from seeing his eyes, but she could read the furious set of his jaw well enough. No one would mistake him for a gentleman right now. She couldn't imagine why she had thought him part of the languid, genteel society he frequented. That indolent image was a masquerade. The real man was clenching the reins with fists of steel.

"Why would he send me out there if he knew there was an alligator? That doesn't make sense, Nicholas. You had better wait until your temper cools."

A mocking grin flashed across his lips as he turned his head slightly to regard her, but there was nothing of humor in his eyes. "The blacks believe alligators are the tools of devils. I rather suspect that idiot Jenkins thinks the same, only I'm the devil in his mind. We had a rather rousing quarrel this morning. I imagine he thought it would be amusing to see if the devil could save his own woman from the teeth of the beast. It has nothing to do with you."

Nothing to do with her! Eavin wanted to spit in his face, but she jerked her head up and stared ahead with as much dignity as she could muster. "Sure, and I'll tear his eyeballs out if he's after thinking I'm your woman. I'm the one he near to got killed. Let me deal with him."

Nicholas grimaced at the fierce lilt of Eavin's language. He really ought to set the two of them in a room together and see which one came out alive, but he still had some remnants of civilization clinging to him. He ignored her demand as he approached the storage shed.

Jenkins was nowhere in sight, but that didn't deter Nicholas. The field hands loitering in the road wouldn't have been there if Jenkins were out doing his job. He had a good idea of what the man was doing and where. Throwing a glance upward to the proper Irish prude in the saddle, Nicholas wished she weren't with him, but this was something that had to be done now.

With a jerk of his head, he indicated the storage shed as he commanded the man nearest him. "Drag Jenkins out here."

He knew he was setting the fox among the chickens. He'd seen enough hatred and slaughter in Santa Domingue to know better than to give a slave permission to lay hands on a white man, but he had too close an empathy for the slaves' plight to deny them this opportunity. He had never caught Jenkins in a transgression of any sort, but Nicholas was aware of the hatred between his slaves and the overseer, and couldn't pretend something wasn't going on. He had the excuse he needed now to get rid of the man.

Eavin jerked at the sound of a woman's screams as the shed door was thrown open. A man's furious yells followed, and then there were the unpleasant thuds of fists and bodies, and she wished she could close her eyes again. She had thrown herself into enough of her brother's fights to recognize those sounds. She could only be grateful she wasn't close enough to hear the crunch of bones.

Jenkins came flying out headfirst several moments later. As he staggered to his feet, the burly field hands came out after him, and he didn't attempt to go farther. One of the kitchen servants appeared in the doorway, her cotton dress torn and pulled down off one shoulder, her nappy hair studded with wheat chaff. She watched dispassionately as the men shoved Jenkins toward Nicholas.

Leaving Eavin to manage the horse on her own, Nicholas strode rapidly toward the little gathering. She gasped at the suddenness with which he struck. The crack of bone against bone and Jenkins went sprawling backward in the dirt. When Jenkins rose again, fists raised, Nicholas caught him in the midsection, dealing two furious blows that bent the man in two. Astounded by Nicholas's unleashed violence, Eavin could only stare as he spoke in low tones she couldn't have heard if she wanted. Although she knew what Nicholas was, she had never seen him in any other guise than that of gentleman. Seeing him now, shoulders straining at his shirt, hands on narrow hips, she had some glimpse of the man beneath the elegance of silk.

She had to be realistic. She knew Nicholas wasn't defending her. He was protecting his property and using her as the excuse he needed to get rid of a man he didn't like. But Eavin's shattered nerves needed the reassurance, and she allowed herself a small feeling of security at the thought that some of Nicholas's rage was in her behalf. She had spent the better part of a lifetime protecting herself. Her brother occasionally had come to her rescue, but she had been as likely to come to his as the other way around. It was somehow satisfying to think that a man like Nicholas would come to her defense when necessary.

She would have to leave it at that. Despite the violence unveiled before her, her body was beginning to wake from the numbness of fear and remember how it felt to have Nicholas's hands on her. It had been nearly a year since a man had held her, but she hadn't felt any need for such until now. It wouldn't do to dredge up those memories, after all this time.

Jenkins wasn't fool enough to argue with a man with a whip, a powerful punch, and two brawny slaves at his side. Muttering threats, he spat at the ground and limped off in the direction of the house when Nicholas turned his back on him. Eavin could read nothing in Saint-Just's expression as he approached. She wondered how Francine had ever got close enough to him to win his heart. It didn't seem possible that Nicholas had one. The violence simmering so close to his surface must have replaced it.

They returned to the house in relative silence. Only when they reached the stable and Nicholas lifted Eavin from the saddle did he break the truce.

"You will tell me now why it is you went to the fields today."

Eavin didn't trust the man at the best of times. She trusted him even less when his easy English gave way to the stilted French accents of his youth. Pulling from the strong hands encompassing her waist, Eavin met Nicholas's dark eyes with a bravery she didn't feel.

"I want to go to Christmas mass."

A muscle in his jaw twitched. His hand went up to pull his hat off and wipe his brow, releasing the wild mane of his hair. His eyes narrowed slightly as he glared at her. Then recovering himself, sweeping his gaze over her petite stature and blood-splattered clothing, returning it to rest on the disheveled mass of her curls, Nicholas asked with a slight drawl, "You wish me to take you to New Orleans?"

"I wish to go to mass."

Undaunted, he replied, "Mass is in New Orleans."

With the truth suddenly dawning on her, Eavin gave a cry of frustration and ran for the house.

This godforsaken, alligator-ridden, swampy hell didn't even have a church.

9

"The harvest is in. I can take you to New Orleans now if you require."

"No, I don't wish to endanger Jeannette in this weather."

Nicholas gave the dark head bent over her sewing a disbelieving glance as he poured his brandy.

"And that is the reason you did not go with Jeremy to his church?"

"His church is not mine." Eavin bit her lip to keep from saying more. Nicholas in this mood was worse than no Nicholas at all. When he had nothing else to occupy his time, his energy strained at the seams of the old house until it rubbed everything and everyone within his reach raw.

"And your excuse for not accompanying Clyde Brown to the American Christmas festivities?"

"Is none of your business," she replied firmly, snapping off a piece of thread with her teeth.

Nicholas threw himself into his usual chair, propping his feet on the fireplace fender as he sipped from his glass. Lifting his brows in her direction, he inquired politely, "What are you afraid of?"

"Snakes and alligators," Eavin answered promptly, threading another needle.

Nicholas grunted at the quickness of her wit. "Brown and Howell are many things, but they're not snakes or alligators. You are afraid of men. Admit it." He had studied on this topic since the night of the Howells' soiree. Unaccustomed to women who shied from his presence, he had considered the possibility that it was himself she feared. Careful observation of late had brought about a different conclusion. Except in the company of others, the widow kept her distance from all men.

"I've been married," Eavin reminded him. "I'm not eager to repeat the experience."

"Your behavior is unnatural," Nicholas persisted. "You are a young, healthy woman who should enjoy the company of the opposite sex." Their evening conversations had gone entirely out of hand that he could say such things, but he could tell from the fact that Eavin expressed no shock that he had worn away her scruples on the subject. To be able to approach a woman intellectually instead of physically was a new experience. "No one ever said you had to marry any of them. You could just enjoy yourself."

That was the typical Gallic irreverency Eavin was coming to expect in this place. The French were an extremely poor influence on public morals. She had even seen Governor Claiborne quoted as saying that in the papers.

"I am enjoying myself. You have no idea how good it is to have a house this size with only you and Jeannette to look after. Even after Dominic and I married, I had to stay and help in my mother's boardinghouse. There was no place to go where I could be alone for more than a few minutes."

Nicholas sent her shapeless clothing a speculative glance. So that was it. Boardinghouses meant men. He didn't think her protective camouflage would have worked very well for very long. He had seen Eavin in an evening gown and was well aware of the figure she tried to conceal. Men she lived with on a daily basis would not be blind forever. "Your mother didn't leave you alone with her boarders, did she?" he found himself asking more sharply than he intended.

Eavin glanced up in surprise, then away as the intensity of Nicholas's eyes revealed he saw more than she had meant him to. "She could not be everywhere at once. I learned to defend myself. Dominic got all that he bargained for when we married."

"But that's why you married," Nicholas denounced her triumphantly, finally divining one of the secrets that had obsessed him lately. "You thought gallant Dominic would protect you from those lecherous bastards. And then when you were widowed, you were open game for every man in the house, so you came here."

"I came here because I thought Dominic's family

would wish to have his child with them," she answered stiffly, ignoring his triumph.

"And because you thought they could support you in comfort and because you're afraid of men. You've been frightened by men once too many times and so have written us all off as being reprehensible in nature. Is that any better than assuming all the Irish drink whiskey?"

Eavin made an impatient gesture. If she was truthful with herself, she had to admit that Nicholas terrified her more than any man she'd ever met. Perhaps because he was more man than any man she'd ever known. He wasn't just taller or broader or more handsome; actually, she thought her brother outfavored Nicholas in some of those aspects. It was just that Nicholas exuded some virile male confidence that must be part of his nature.

"What difference can it make to anyone whether or not I am afraid of men? Call me cold if you like. I'm certain if Dominic were here, he would agree. What does it matter? I can never marry, and I'm not after wanting to be a man's mistress, which is all your friends see in me. So your curiosity may go wanting, sir."

Her Irish was really up for her to allow the accent to creep in. Nicholas shrugged laconically. "You would make the ideal mistress, at that. Pardon me for not thinking of it sooner. A man loves his mistress a great deal more than his wife, you know. He has to marry where name and fortune require, but he can choose a mistress to his liking. And if you cannot have children, you would save him the expense and the occasional embarrassment of raising bastards along with his legitimate progeny. Who told you that you couldn't have children, by the way? You were carrying a child when you came to us. I am not so ignorant as to not know that."

The anger evaporated and Eavin turned away before Nicholas could see the tears forming in her eyes. "The doctor told me. After I lost . . . There was an infection, you see. It did something to me, and he said I would never bear another child. Nicholas, stop it. I don't want to talk about this anymore."

"I'm sorry, *chère amie.*" His mood suddenly changed and he lifted an apologetic hand. "I didn't mean to distress you. I know about pain, but sometimes if you keep it all inside you, it festers and grows worse. I would not have Jeannette's lovely aunt turn into a bitter, angry woman with time."

Eavin wasn't so quick to accept the apology. "Is that why you challenged Raphael? Because it was better than keeping the anger in?"

She felt Nicholas stiffen, but to her surprise he replied. His voice was low and thoughtful and far from the angry wild man she had seen before.

"Perhaps. But more because he deserved to die. He seduced Francine, knowing full well he would never marry her. That killed her more certainly than childbirth. If he still lives, I will try to kill him again for that."

Eavin shuddered at the menace in his quiet voice. She had been right in her first judgment. Nicholas Saint-Just was a violent, dangerous man.

"I was under the impression that you and Francine had been married for years. I don't mean to pry, but someday Jeannette will be old enough to ask questions. Is Raphael truly her father?"

Bitterness flared briefly in the amber of his eyes, but then Nicholas rose and crossed to the dying fire and began prodding it into flame again. "Francine and I knew each other very well, too well perhaps. Her family knew mine, knew where they came from and what became of them. Although the name Saint-Just is old and dates back to France and some illustrious titles, my father managed to besmirch what little glitter it might have retained, and we didn't have wealth to make up for it. Francine's family did not consider me suitable. So I went away for a long time. When I came back, it was to find Francine inconsolable. The brave and gallant Raphael had left town one step ahead of the warrants for his debts, leaving Francine carrying his child."

Nicholas clanked the metal poker back onto its stand and swirled around to catch Eavin's wide-eyed sorrow. "You needn't look like that. I wanted Francine bad enough to take her any way that I could have her. We married quietly and let the story go about that we had been married all along, that I had just left her long enough to make my fortune. Everyone loved Francine, and they were eager to accept any tale we told. And when it became apparent that I had indeed returned with wealth, they were even more eager to accept us. Had

Raphael not returned when he did, no one would think any differently even now."

"I see." And astonishingly, she did. Had Raphael stayed away, Nicholas would have allowed the world to believe that Jeannette was his daughter, just because she was Francine's child. But his anger and his pride would not allow Raphael to escape unscathed when he returned to the scene of his crime. His sense of honor demanded no less than revenge. As different as their cultures were, Eavin understood the need for revenge.

Nicholas smiled grudgingly at her admission. "I imagine you do, Irish. Perhaps it would be more fitting that I teach you to fence than to make love."

"Is that what you mean to do?" Eavin met his gaze calmly, thinking he jested.

"Most certainly, *chère amie,* sooner or later. I can do no less."

He stood before the fire, all bronze and gold, exuding masculine confidence, the aristocratic angles of his face shadowed by the light, and Eavin knew he meant what he said.

Shivering slightly, she hid her fear behind her words. "Then I suggest you teach me to shoot instead. I can see a great deal more use for guns."

He threw back his head and laughed and although the warmth of that unusual sound flowed through her veins like mellow liquor, Eavin knew the battle had just been joined.

After a quiet Christmas, Eavin accepted the rains of January with a previously unknown serenity. Five-month-old Jeannette was sitting up now, becoming more of a personality with every day. She threw up her hands and laughed when she heard Nicholas's voice, for he invariably lifted her to his shoulder and swung her around when he entered the nursery. Their two heads together could not be more unalike, Jeannette's crop of black curls and pale face next to Nicholas's golden hair and sun-browned visage, but they accepted each other, and that was all Eavin could ask.

If she was more aware of Nicholas as a man now, she didn't let it show. He still ignored her a great deal of the time, but she was aware of the effort he had made to see that she accompanied him to the various Christmas festivities. He didn't stay at her side long enough to cause talk, but he was always there to lead her onto the dance floor—after she agreed to learn the steps—to catch her elbow and introduce her to newcomers, to bring her supper, and to wrap her cloak around her when they departed. To Eavin, these constant niceties were almost as wearing as the abrupt and quickly ended crudities of her mother's boarders.

She knew what he was doing. She no longer ran away when he entered a room. She didn't jump in startlement when he touched her. She could sit in a closed carriage with him without fear. But his words never left her mind. Their highly improper conversations had stirred something that couldn't easily be set to rest. She didn't know how or when it would happen, but the confrontation to come was inevitable.

Eavin pressed her head against the glass of the doors leading out onto the gallery and watched the rain streak the panes, smearing the old oak trees into a gray blur. She didn't want what Nicholas wanted. The thought that he had been Francine's husband wasn't what deterred her. She knew he had loved Francine, and that his wife had returned some affection, but what was happening between herself and Nicholas had nothing to do with love. It had more to do with the fact that he had given up his black mistress and couldn't get to New Orleans enough to relieve his male needs. She had been married. She knew about these things. But try as she might as she lay in her lonely bed at night, Eavin couldn't imagine herself occupying the place beside Nicholas in his bed.

So she quietly hoped he would find some new outlet for his restlessness before the inevitable happened. She was just beginning to realize how much she owed him. Should he ever come to her demanding payment, she would be in no position to refuse. She was quite certain that she wouldn't refuse. She wanted to stay too much. She loved this quiet life she had found. To leave Jeannette would be like cutting off her arm. She couldn't do it. But Nicholas never played upon any of these arguments. He merely looked at her with smoldering fires, touched her arm to help her in and out of chairs, and talked with her as if her opinion counted.

It was a devastatingly effective seduction. She was standing here waiting to see his horse arrive along the lane. He had been in New Orleans these last few days, and she missed him to an extent that she wouldn't dare admit. The house wouldn't come alive until the door slammed open and he strode into the hall, flinging his dripping cloak onto the nearest piece of furniture, yelling for a fire and brandy, permeating the house with his vibrancy. So she waited and felt her heart beat excitedly at the first sight of a horse walking between the ancient oaks.

It took a moment before Eavin could eradicate the hope that it was Nicholas. Nicholas had never walked a horse in his life. Wind and rain and mud wouldn't halt him from flying down the lane as if the devil was on his tail. Eavin strained to discern the soaked figure from this distance, but she couldn't recognize him.

Whoever it was would be wet and cold. Eavin ordered a fire made up in what Nicholas called the *petite salle* and sent someone to begin a hot toddy. She couldn't imagine any good reason for someone to come out in this downpour, and she waited anxiously as the man rode up to the house and tethered his horse below the gallery.

He seemed uncertain about approaching the stairs to the upper story, and Eavin wondered if she should send someone to show him through the storeroom if he preferred not to come into the house. But he finally threw back his shoulders and marched up the stairs with an insouciance she recognized at once.

Michael!

Eavin raced to the door, stifling a scream of excitement only as she realized that he would never be here if trouble weren't far behind. She had always idolized her older brother, and he had always treated her with laughter and love, but she had known from an early age that Michael was incapable of civilized behavior. He had a temper to match Nicholas's any time, and a propensity for whiskey and gambling that had caused their father to heave him out of the house more than once. By the time their father had died, Michael had found a life of his own, and Eavin had seldom seen him except at holidays and when he was in trouble.

His arrival here was not a good sign at all. She braced

herself as she threw open the door to welcome him. He wasn't even wearing a cloak or rain slicker but came in soaked to the bone and dripping, a huge grin on his face as he recognized his sister.

"Ahh, my beautiful colleen, a sight for sore eyes you be, indeed! Will you not come and give your long-lost brother a hug?"

"I'd sooner hug a drowned dog. Don't use your blarney on me, Michael, it won't work and you know it. Start getting those wet things off. I'll send for dry ones."

Striding off to summon a maid, Eavin felt torn between joy and despair. She had never admitted to herself how homesick she was for her family, such as they might be. Michael's appearance here, for whatever reason, sent happiness singing through her veins. But what would happen when Nicholas discovered Michael's identity was entirely another story. There would be no question of seduction while her brother was present, that was for certain. Michael would rip Nicholas's head from his shoulders.

Once Michael had time to change out of his wet clothes into some old ones of Nicholas's that were too long in the legs and arms and too tight at the waist, Eavin seated him in front of the fire with his toddy and began her interrogation.

"How was Mum when you left her?" she demanded first.

"Same as ever, far as I know. She's got a gentleman friend now to treat her fancy. She's not likely to be missing us."

Eavin hadn't worried for a minute about that. Their mother was an independent person and expected her two children to be the same. "And the war? Is there any sign they'll open the ports again?"

"Sure, and you must be bored to ask a thing like that, colleen. What difference will it be makin' to the likes of us if the rich can get their brandy and the like? Is that what living in this grandeur has done to ye?" He gestured around the comfortable salon.

Annoyed, Eavin sat back in her chair and examined the changes in her brother. There was a line or two more on his brow than she remembered, and black circles beneath his eyes that spoke of many sleepless nights. He looked older and less carefree than the brother she remembered, and it was time to quit avoiding the question.

"What brings ye here, Michael? What have ye done now?" The accents of her youth intruded without her knowing.

"Aye, and that's a long story, colleen. We needn't go into that now. And where's the loving family you came to join, love? Mam told me about the babe. I'm sorry to hear it, but perhaps it's for the best. Bringing up a child in this world without a man at your side isn't the life I'd have for you."

Eavin remembered Michael's charm, but not his habit of diverting the subject so brilliantly. Or perhaps she was just old enough now to recognize a humbug when she saw one. Taking a sip from the hot tea she had ordered for herself, she collected her wits.

"Dominic's sister died giving birth. I'm taking care of the child now. Now, tell me what brings you here so I know what to say before Nicholas comes home."

"Nicholas, is it?" Michael's eyes narrowed with suspicion. "You're living here alone with a man named Nicholas?"

There it was, the anger that boiled up so fast and furious that it got him into trouble every time. Eavin sighed and attempted to defuse the situation. "He is Jeannette's father, and I am Jeannette's aunt, and if you haven't noticed, we're scarcely alone with a house full of servants. Now, I think it's time you tell me what brought you here. No more evading the subject, Michael."

"If he's another of those Frenchies like Dominic—"

Eavin stood up and glared at him. "This is my home now, Michael. If you cannot treat me with respect in it, you may leave. I've heard the likes of this before, and I'll not be hearin' it from you again. Tell me why you've come."

Michael managed to look a trifle sheepish as he drained his cup and gestured for her to sit down. "You've grown up, little sister. I'll not be questioning you anymore. From the looks of that rag you wear, the man hasn't been tempting you with worldly goods."

Eavin sat, but the look of determination remained on her face. "Your reason, Michael. It's good to see you again, but I'll know what's in store for me if you stay."

He sighed and looked tired again. "I'm startin' all over,

colleen. I heard the West was the place to do that. I took a ship to New Orleans to see you first, then I thought I'd make my way into Texas."

"That's a very commendable attitude. I'm certain there are any number of people in Baltimore who would be relieved to hear that. But I'd like you to stay awhile, and I want to know if the sheriff's likely to come to the door after you if you do."

Michael's grin was rueful as he watched his baby sister in the firelight. He'd never seen her look quite so beautiful. The pinched lines of worry had left her face, and there was a new serenity to her that became her well. For a while he'd thought she would turn into a harpy at an early age, but though she nagged at him like one now, it was with an assurance that she had not possessed before. Whatever had happened to her in this strange place, it was for the better.

"Word doesn't travel that swiftly, but I'll be grateful to you if you would introduce me as Michael Rourke to your new family. Call me a cousin if you like. If I'm to start anew, it would best be with a new name."

Eavin gave him a look of despair. "Have you been after murtherin' someone to give up your name for it?"

"Well, and there was a bit of a fight, you see. I just defended myself. But the law never looks kindly on the Irish, and the other man had a name for himself. So I thought it wisest to look for a new life."

That was far more than Eavin wanted to know. She supposed it wasn't any different than Nicholas killing a man in a duel, although she rather suspected the argument Michael had ended had little to do with honor. "'Tis a bother you are, Michael O'Flannery, but you're welcome to stay. There's few to talk to in these parts, and I've been a mite homesick. Perhaps Nicholas will know of a place for you hereabouts. Then there'd be two of us against the world."

Michael grinned at that, but the sound of the front door slamming open halted whatever he meant to say. Eavin's heart tightened as the expected summons rang through the wide hall.

"Eavin, where the hell is the blasted maid! It's damned cold out here . . ." Nicholas halted in the doorway of the *petite salle*. Eavin's cheeks were flushed and her eyes glittered with excitement, and the cause was obviously the handsome man in the chair beside her, his chair, to be exact. A frown began to form on his brow as he entered the room, oblivious to his dripping cloak.

Eavin leapt to her feet. "Get that wet thing off, Nicholas." She signaled to the servant hurriedly entering behind him. "Clemmie, take this downstairs and send someone up with another toddy."

"I don't want a damned toddy. Vile drink. Just give me some brandy." Ill humor emanated from Nicholas in waves as he glared at the intruder.

Michael had risen from the offending chair, but the laughter in his eyes had died and anger was rapidly replacing it.

Eavin hastily came between the two men to perform the introductions, stumbling over the name "Rourke" but recovering sufficiently to explain that Michael was her cousin.

Nicholas remained suspicious, but he held out his hand. "Any family of Eavin's is welcome. What brings you to these parts?"

Eavin held a sigh of relief as the two men settled into the chairs with the brandy bottle between them while she went to order another place for dinner. The quietness of these last months had finally broken. She had needed the time to heal, and she regretted the loss, but it was better this way. She would have to persuade Nicholas to allow Michael to stay. It would be her only salvation.

Nicholas wasn't thrilled with the idea, but as he watched Michael and Eavin at the table together, he had to admit that it was his own selfishness standing in the way. The Irishman had spun a tale of being Eavin's first cousin, and while Nicholas fully intended to verify it, he could see for himself that Eavin didn't fear this man. He couldn't deny the laughter that Rourke brought to her eyes, but he could damn well resent the man's coming between Eavin and his plans for her.

He was relieved when the man took the hint and followed one of the servants out to the *garçonnière* after dinner, leaving them alone. Nicholas was still a little shocked at his reaction to this unexpected guest. So when Eavin asked that night if a place could be found for her cousin somewhere in the area, Nicholas found himself offering the vacant position of overseer and wondering what in hell he was doing.

10

"Fleming, as you are perfectly aware, I don't have to store my cotton in your warehouses. I can build my own or ship the damn bales to China if I so choose. I do not have to endure your insult or your blackmail. Have you lost your mind, man?"

Nicholas violently smacked his riding crop against one of the offending bales as he waited for the warehouse owner to reply. The man was little more than a weasel, cringing in the face of any loud noise or strong wind. Nicholas's desire to hit someone didn't extend to slaughtering the weak.

For the hundredth time Nicholas vowed to build his own warehouses. The impermanence of the seas had always been his life, and in the back of his mind he'd thought he would be returning to them. The commitment of building went against his nature, but it might be time to consider it, before he had to strangle the cringing bastard in front of him.

Michael leaned against a stack of bales and watched this confrontation with unmitigated interest. Surprisingly, he'd come to admire his hotheaded employer. Beneath their widely disparate surfaces they had much in common. Of course, Michael observed, he would have simply punched Fleming's ugly nose for the insult rather than threaten him, but Saint-Just had appearances to keep up. Aristocrats didn't indulge in fisticuffs.

"Now, Saint-Just, I got a business to run just like anyone else. There's been threats made, and I can't afford to just ignore them. I don't rightly know if I can afford to take the risk as it is. If they burn my building, I'll be bankrupt, and you'll not be in any position to pay what you owe with your cotton in cinders. I need some insurance up front to make it worth the risk."

"People who burn buildings don't give warnings, you fool," Nicholas gritted out between clenched teeth. "If they meant to burn it, they'd have done so by now. If you're so concerned about your building, I'll take my business elsewhere. How many other planters do you have on your list with the funds for indefinite storage?"

Knowing full well there were none, the man cringed at this threat. "Now, look, Saint-Just, I just mean to get a bit up front, just enough for insurance, you see." He straightened himself a little more belligerently at another thought. "And ain't anyone else in these parts gonna take your cotton without the same. The rumor's out all over. You've got yourself some powerful enemies, Saint-Just. It don't pay to make enemies."

"It doesn't pay to make friends with snakes, either. I'll pay you one month's rent in advance every month until the cotton is shipped, but I want a discount on the rent since you'll have the money in your hand earlier than if you had to wait until fall. That's the best I can do for you."

Michael watched the man's scheming mind turn the offer over and knew when the definite threat of an empty warehouse won over the indefinite threat of a possible disaster. He wondered what kind of enemies a man like Saint-Just could make, but he had to admire his employer's guts. From what he'd seen, he doubted that there was another warehouse available to hold this much cotton.

As they left, Michael speculated out loud: "I suppose building a warehouse of your own would be prohibitive until after the cotton is sold?"

Still furious, Nicholas threw his overseer a searing look, but he had already learned that Michael Rourke had skin a foot thick when he chose. There were certain things he could say to raise his Irish temper, but filthy looks and general insults bounced off him like water off a duck.

"I can do it, if I want to," he grudgingly admitted. "It's a damned nuisance, but if I stay in the business, it would be more profitable, doubly so if this blockade continues any longer."

From that, Michael deduced that Saint-Just had doubts about staying with the plantation, and that raised his brows a little. Why would anyone give up the lucrative business of planting? Since his own and Eavin's future depended on the answer, he risked pushing further.

"I thought the plantation seemed successful. Is there some reason you wouldn't stay with it?"

Nicholas found his horse and mounted, forcing his temper under control. "Is there some reason why I should? I can think of any number of more interesting enterprises, and none of them require the indecency of owning slaves."

That radical admission from a southerner brought Michael's eyebrows up to his hairline. "I thought the public policy was that those were your people, like your family, and you take care of them just like you take care of family. I'm after thinkin', Mr. Saint-Just, there's a reason so many people in these parts want to stone you."

Nicholas had to grin at the insolent Irishman's tone. "The hell they're my people. My people come from France, not Africa. The damned slaves came with the house, just like some of the furniture. I took the lot in payment for a debt. I never said I wanted them."

"But you couldn't run the plantation without them. And now you've got a family to raise, and you're stuck." Michael summed up the situation knowledgeably.

"Something to the effect, I suppose." Nicholas thought back to the time when he had imagined turning the old house into the kind of mansion that Francine deserved, filling it with their children, entertaining guests and family. The dream had died with Francine. If it hadn't been for Eavin and Jeannette, he would no doubt have sold the place long ago. But Eavin was right. Jeannette was Francine's daughter, and she deserved the kind of upbringing that Francine had had. He just hadn't thought any further than that.

"Where are we going now?" Satisfied he'd got all the answers he was going to get, Michael turned his attention to their direction. New Orleans was very definitely not Baltimore. He caught the attention of a colorfully dressed mulatto and winked when she smiled back.

Catching the exchange, Nicholas replied wryly, "Somewhere I'm sure you'll appreciate. Since I haven't paid you any wages yet, the treat's on me."

As Nicholas introduced his new overseer to the occupants of the tastefully decorated bordello and watched him led away, he breathed a sigh of relief. Having an observer around could be extremely inconvenient at times, especially when that observer was related to someone as perspicacious as Eavin. But Michael would be well taken care of for the rest of the night. Nicholas shook his head at the offer of the young woman waiting patiently on him, put his hat back on his head, and strode out with the gait of a man who knew precisely where he was going and why.

"Why don't I write an editorial on the unlawful power of men like Reyes who can threaten the livelihoods of honest working men like Fleming?"

The speaker was a long-legged Kentuckian with uncombed curls the color of radishes and ears that stuck out at odd angles from his head. Despite his appearance, the man knew the printing business and had a way with words that more educated men never mastered. Nicholas held him in respect, but he shook his head negatively.

"Reyes is an old man, Daniel, and this thing with Raphael has bent his mind. He has a wife and younger son I would not insult. There will be no name calling. But I think we should begin questioning the safety of the warehouses and what protection is offered for the owners of the contents. As past fires have proved, our fire brigade is useless, yet the docks are covered with unprotected cotton and half the buildings in the area are still timber, and in the present economy, insuring those bales is beyond the pockets of most planters."

"To what point?" Daniel watched the elegant Frenchman with suspicion. Nicholas Saint-Just wore the tailored frock coats, ruffles, and high hats of a gentleman, but he had a mind like a steel trap. One of Daniel's goals in life was to stay out of that trap.

"To the point that they demand brick warehouses with tile roofs, of course," Nicholas replied smoothly, pulling on his gloves. "Ones like I mean to build."

Daniel choked, coughed, then managed a grudging laugh. "No one ever said a paper had to be entirely altruistic, I suppose. Does this mean I can write my article chastising Congress for not developing a standing army?"

"Only if you also chastise the states for not providing their volunteer armies on longer terms. Did they really think Napoleon would have got as far as he did if he let his troops go home after two months?"

"Now wait a minute! We don't want to go conquering other territories—"

"But we'd damned well better start defending this one, or we'll see a king ruling us again. And you know as well as I do that we're losing this war because we have no one to fight it."

"That's fine for you to say. You can buy your way out of any draft. My talents are with words, not guns. This volunteer business is shit. We need a real army, one that gets paid for doing the work of an army, made up of men who are willing to kill to protect our country."

"Men who are willing to kill for a living—the prospect is daunting. And who would pay for this army? You just said you can't afford to pay someone to take your place. Do you think it would be any less expensive if Congress took over the task?"

Daniel glared at him. "Have you ever heard of a government yet that couldn't think of a way to tax their constituents? I'm just hoping they'll figure out how to tax you and not me."

Nicholas laughed. "I've got someone at home you really ought to meet. She said almost the exact same thing the other night. The two of you together would be dangerous." He picked up his riding crop and started for the door.

"Why don't you bring her by next time? Maybe the two of us together can bring you around to the right way of thinking."

Standing in the doorway, Nicholas turned back to look into the dimness of the shop. "Over my dead body," he said pleasantly. "I'm keeping this one to myself."

11

Eavin brushed a splatter of mud from the yellow petal of the daffodil, then in a fit of longing for spring, she plucked the fat green stem. The open blue of the sky held promise of warm days and short nights, but the winter wind still cut through the wool of her old coat. The single yellow flower was the only hint of spring to be found in the mud flat that was the yard.

Imagining how the old house would look with banks of azaleas along its foundation as she had seen elsewhere, Eavin didn't notice the rider until he was almost upon her. Expecting his arrival, she turned with a welcoming smile as Jeremy Howell leapt from the saddle and approached with an eager step.

In his hand he carried a huge bouquet of daffodils to dwarf the single yellow bloom she held.

"Jeremy, how lovely! Come in out of the wind and let me find a vase. I want to show them to Jeannette. It's still too wet for her to go outside."

Jeremy made a wry face behind her back as he followed her up the stairs. However he approached Eavin Dupré, she always managed to divert him to the nursery. He felt exceedingly awkward courting a woman over the gurgles of a child too young to walk.

"How is your mother? I've been meaning to visit, but Nicholas won't let me out when the rains start. He says the road floods too quickly."

"Unfortunately, he is right. That is why everyone else is in New Orleans, where they can dance and visit all within a few blocks of each other. But for a change, I am not annoyed with my father for not finding us a house there."

Eavin inserted the flowers in the vase that Clemmie brought, carefully ignoring the innuendo behind Jeremy's words. She was learning to be very good at avoiding the charming habit of these Louisiana men of sprinkling their conversations with blatant flattery. She still felt the personal references to be embarrassing, and she merely smiled and led him toward the nursery.

Jeannette cooed and babbled and batted the flowers with her hands before turning expectantly to the man entering the room. Eavin laughed at Jeremy's helplessness when the babe waved her hands at him.

"Nicholas spoils her terribly. She already thinks all men ought to bow before her and give her everything she wants."

"I never pictured Old Nick as a family man. The image still fails me. I guess I shall have to linger and watch him in action. It's time I started learning such paternal duties."

Eavin glanced up in surprise. "You are planning to marry?" He seemed much too young, although she supposed he must be several years her senior.

Jeremy's look was wry as he caught her tone. The sight of those two ebony heads together twisted inside him, and he couldn't keep his tongue away from the words that had haunted him these months since she had come into his life.

"I thought I had made my intention clear. I know Alfonso has been calling regularly, but I didn't think he had engaged your affections. I had hoped you would see that we suited much better."

"Jeremy!" Astonished, Eavin returned the flowers to a table and sat Jeannette in her crib to play with her toys. The homely functions gave her time to think before she had to face her caller again. She had recovered herself to some extent by the time she was forced to turn and meet his gaze. "I'm sorry. I just thought you were being polite by coming to keep me company when Nicholas is away. I didn't think . . ."

Jeremy touched a gentle hand to Eavin's brow, brushing away a stray strand of hair. "It's been a year since Dominic died. I didn't think it was too soon for you to start thinking of what you wish to do now. Surely you can't mean to wait until Nick marries to turn over your guardian duties to someone else."

The thought of Nicholas marrying had never occurred to her. Eavin's eyes widened as the thought struck her now. Of course he would, eventually. And then Jeannette would have a real mother instead of just an aunt. The idea tore at her heart, but she disguised the pain with a swift smile as she took Jeremy's arm and led him from the nursery.

"I admit to not having given it any thought at all, Mr. Howell. The past year has been a terrible one for me. You'll have to excuse me for burying my head beneath the pillows. Perhaps it has been a little too soon for me to start thinking about anyone else."

Jeremy stopped her in the shadows of the stairs. He was several inches taller, and his light brown hair fell in his face as he bent earnestly over her. "You're not like these French girls around here, Eavin. I may call you Eavin, please? They make me feel like an ill-mannered hillbilly. You make me feel as if I'm as strong and experienced as Old Nick. Say you'll consider my suit. I don't want any other but you."

Before Eavin could offer a word of warning, Jeremy bent his head closer and closed his lips over hers. The sensation was quite pleasant. His grip on her arm was strong and secure. She felt none of the panic or fear she was accustomed to feeling when approached suddenly like this. His mouth was like a warm caress, and she didn't offer the proper objection when he finally lifted his head and looked down at her questioningly.

"You're very persuasive, Mr. Howell, but we scarcely know anything of each other." Eavin met his gaze more firmly. "Before you decide anything rash, I suggest you talk to Nicholas. You're a good friend ... Jeremy. I would like to see you stay that way."

A slamming of a door at the rear of the house indicated someone entering, and they quickly stepped apart, coming down the stairs just as Michael erupted into the hall below.

Michael narrowed his eyes suspiciously at the man holding his sister's arm and descending from the upper-story bedrooms, but there wasn't time to indulge in arguments. He spoke his message curtly. "The river's reaching the top of the levee. Nick said to get everyone out when it does. Grab some clothes and round up the servants while I have the carriage and wagon hitched up."

"Were are we going?" Eavin yelled after him.

"To New Orleans" was the drifting reply as Michael strode out the front door and out of sight.

The rain had begun again by the time the caravan of wagons and carriage arrived in the city. Teething, Jeannette was fretful in Eavin's arms, and the damp cold penetrated every layer of clothing to make everyone miserable. Rather than awed at this first glimpse of the graceful city beyond the dock, Eavin was only relieved at the thought of the proximity of dry rooms and fires.

The carriage halted outside a lovely town house wider than its neighbors while the wagons rattled down a passageway through the courtyard and back to the servants' quarters. Nervously, Eavin gazed up at the closed shutters and wished Nicholas were here. Michael was already scrambling down from the carriage and giving the driver instructions, and filled with trepidation, Eavin allowed someone to help her from the interior into the shelter of an overhanging gallery.

Black servants hastened her inside, with Michael following on her heels. Jeannette was openly weeping now, and Annie took her in her arms, patiently rocking her while they waited for their hostess to appear. It took a moment before Eavin realized the elegant woman languidly approaching had to be Nicholas's mother. It was rather difficult to imagine Nicholas having a mother, but this was certainly the type that he would have.

Scarcely giving her sodden guests a second look, Madame Saint-Just directed the servants with a careless wave of her beringed hand.

"Take the child and her nurse to the old nursery, Maudine, and show her companion to the room next to it. Have a brazier carried down. The rooms will be cool. You, sir," she turned to Michael, "may take the rooms in the *garçonnière*. Rufus will show you the way."

No word of welcome or introduction, no acknowledgment beyond the dispatch of a bored general. Eavin had the feeling of being firmly set in her place. Had she not been damp and chilled and worried about Jeannette, she might have had a word to say about this summary dismissal, but the argument seemed too trivial to pursue under these conditions. She was the child's nanny, no matter what face Nicholas tried to put on it.

Refusing to allow the misery of this day to seep into her bones like the cold, Eavin followed Annie through endless corridors and stairs to the servants' rooms assigned them. The damp clung to the walls beneath the endless patter of rain, and the braziers the servants carried in did little to relieve the chill. If she had felt firmly put in her place by her greeting, her quarters now gave no uncertain indication of where she stood. She was a servant with only slightly better status than the slaves in the attached building beyond this one.

This was the position she had undertaken when first she had approached Nicholas about staying. She should not complain about her treatment now just because Nicholas had odd ideas about squiring her to parties to avoid becoming entangled with marriage-minded females. This was her place, and she should be happy with it. It had to be better than returning to Baltimore.

She helped Annie unpack Jeannette's clothes and linens. While Jeannette nursed, Eavin cleaned off the dusty crib and laid it out with clean sheets while she told herself this was much better than waiting for the river to overflow and wash them away. She ought to be accustomed to the damp by now. Baltimore certainly wasn't one of the driest cities in the world.

But she couldn't help feeling relief when she finally heard Nicholas's steps along the corridor.

Handing the waiting servant his cloak and shaking the water droplets from his hair, succeeding only in disheveling it to a wild mane, Nicholas gave his mother's imperturbable features an impatient glance, then started for the stairway. "Where did you put Eavin and Jeannette?"

Coming in from the back entrance, Michael entered the hallway from the rear in time to catch Madame Saint-Just's reply.

"You mean the Reyes bastard and her nurse? Where do you think? I am not totally inhumane. I'll not put a child out in the cold. They're in the other wing, of course."

Nicholas's fist clenched the polished rosewood of the banister as he turned to stare down at his lovely, cold mother. "Jeannette is my daughter and Mrs. Dupré is her aunt. They are to be given all due respect as such. This is my house, *maman,* and my wishes are to be obeyed. I will

see my child and her aunt treated as members of the
household. I assume you at least put Mrs. Dupré in
the rose room."

"Mrs. Dupré? You mean that common Irish tart the
foolish Dupré boy ran off and married? Is that who she
is? Nicholas, you have taken leave of your senses."

Michael crossed his arms over his chest and lifted his
gaze to see how his employer would take this direct as-
sault. Nicholas growled and swung around to take a different direction, disappearing down a connecting hall
with a furious tread that did not bode well for someone.
When the crisply elegant Madame Saint-Just turned to
discover him there, Michael offered a wolfish grin and
said nothing.

Hair still damp and flowing wildly over his open collar,
Nicholas stormed into the tiny nursery with the force of
a hurricane wind. Speaking to a servant scurrying behind
him, he pointed at the assorted trunks and boxes in the
corner. "Take the lady's trunk up to the rose room. Have
someone start a fire in the grate. Send up hot water and
a maid to help the lady change for dinner. We ought to
have enough damned servants in this house now to see it
done immediately."

Having just reconciled herself to her fate, Eavin wasn't
ready to be thrown arbitrarily into the world inhabited by
her enemies at the hands of this madman who thought her
world was his to command. Without giving half a thought
to what she was doing, she promptly sat down on her
trunk and glared at the man who had ordered it removed.

"What in hell do you think you're doing?" Already furious, Nicholas didn't need more fuel added to the fires of
his temper. He glared at the slender figure garbed in hid-
eous black perched like a malevolent crow on the trunk
and dared her to defy him.

Which she promptly did. "This is my trunk and my
room, and you're not welcome here. I suggest you leave
if all you can do is order me about as if I'm a piece of
furniture."

"It's my damned trunk and my house, and you're
damned well going wherever I tell you to!" Nicholas exploded. "Now get your pretty *derrière* off that trunk and
upstairs where it belongs."

"I'm your child's nurse and I'm staying here where I belong." Eavin crossed her arms across her chest in a manner reminiscent of her brother's.

With a muttered expletive, Nicholas crossed the small room in two strides. Before Eavin was aware of his intentions, he caught her by the waist, heaved her over his shoulder, and slammed out of the nursery with the fury of a man pushed beyond his limits.

Eavin's screams of outrage carried down lengthy hallways to the two people waiting above. Madame Saint-Just stiffened and sniffed suspiciously. Michael gave her a disbelieving look, then shoved around her to take the steps at the same speed as Nicholas had earlier. Behind him he heard the rustle of satin petticoats following.

"Nicholas, you bastard, you put me down right now!" Eavin screamed as she clutched the back of his coat and swung her feet in a blatant attempt to maim him. His arm only tightened around her thighs, and she screamed again as her position became more precarious.

Taking a different path than their concerned relatives, Nicholas dropped Eavin unceremoniously to her feet when they reached his destination. Hands on hips, he glared down at her. "Don't ever defy me again, Eavin O'Flannery Dupré. I've suffered more than my share of bitches in this lifetime, and I'll not endure another. Get ready for dinner. I'll be back in half an hour."

Before he could turn to escape, Eavin launched herself at him with both fists. She had learned to defend herself in Michael's days of street fighting, and the knowledge came back to her with the instinct for survival. But before she could land even the first blow, Nicholas caught her in his arms and crushed her against his hard chest, rendering her helpless.

And when his mouth closed over hers, she found herself rendered speechless also.

The kiss was searing and regrettably brief. The heat of Nicholas's lips burned like the fire of brandy down Eavin's throat and through her middle before the sound of flying feet down the hallway intruded. With swift sureness Nicholas released her and stepped away, but the amber of his eyes glowed with the demons of hell as they met hers. Eavin brought the back of her hand up to her mouth to wipe away the brand of his kiss, but she felt it searing through her soul like poisonous venom, and the look in his eyes told her that he knew it.

When Michael slammed into the room, they were glaring at each other like two cats in a cage, but both seemed singularly unharmed by the battle. His gaze flew to his sister, but she didn't look any more disheveled than she had when she arrived earlier. Color flooded her cheeks, but it did that when the temper was on her, and Michael almost felt sorry for the poor bastard who had aroused her fury. Eavin in a temper had the viciousness of a cornered animal.

Nicholas seemed to have endured her fury remarkably well. He calmly brushed off the arm of his rumpled coat, made a polite bow to the woman he had just molested, and turned to greet his overseer and nod at his mother following close behind.

"We have had a minor disagreement over the arrangement of rooms. Everything is settled now. Maudine, you may bring in that water." Stepping toward the door, Nicholas forced their audience backward into the hall so the black servant could carry in the pail of hot water, leaving Eavin trapped in the room behind him.

And such was the force of his personality that no one questioned him.

12

"The rain may go on for weeks or it may stop tomorrow. You may as well take advantage of the opportunity to have your wardrobe improved. Surely it has been over a year since your husband died."

The woman at the end of the table spoke woodenly, as if it were an effort to maintain a polite conversation. Only the presence of her glowering son at the far end could have forced her to broach the subject.

Eavin set her lips and made no reply. She had no intention of spending her hard-earned coins on fripperies of no use to her in the backwaters of civilization. Someday she might need those coins to survive. She couldn't politely say that out loud, no more than she could say that she refused to have Nicholas buy the clothes for her. Faced with two impossible alternatives, she wisely remained silent.

Nicholas answered for her. "I will send a seamstress over in the morning. In the press of business I have neglected my responsibilities."

Eavin seethed. Providing a wardrobe for his daughter's aunt or nanny or whatever she was wasn't part of his responsibility. She was beginning to have a very good idea of what position entailed that particular responsibility, however. The burning taste of his kiss had not yet left her.

"That won't be necessary, *monsieur*," she replied with the sweetness she had heard employed by the likes of Mignon Dubois. "I have no wish to come out of mourning. If we are here long enough, I will inquire about having a gray one made so I will not shame Jeannette."

Eavin sensed that only the presence of Madame Saint-Just and Michael brought this topic to a draw. She could feel the glitter of Nicholas's eyes as he neither agreed nor disagreed with her response but turned the conversation to a less volatile subject. Why should it be that in this large house filled with more people than had ever been present in the other, she suddenly felt confined more intimately with this man than before?

His closeness grated on Eavin's nerves. Even though she retired after dinner to the nursery in the servants' quarters, she was aware that Nicholas and Michael lingered over brandy two floors away. The despised servants' rooms suddenly became a haven when she eventually realized that now her room would be on the same level with Nicholas. It was with great reluctance after leaving the nursery that she entered the charming room Nicholas had so demonstratively assigned to her. Although she was certain he hadn't come upstairs yet, she could almost feel him in one of the rooms nearby.

The rose-velvet-draped tester bed enveloped in clouds of netting was something out of her dreams and not meant for the reality of her world. Eavin touched the lush fabric longingly, then retreated to the window to look out over the rain-swamped courtyard below. Something strange was happening to her in this foreign place. She lived in far more comfort and ease than she had ever known before, but she felt more uncertain of herself than she could ever remember being. When times were hard and her frustration enormous, she had been able to fight and claw and strike out at the forces holding her down until she attained some measure of satisfaction. But now she was engulfed in this cloud of cotton gauze with nothing concrete to fight, nothing more than these odd sensations that kept twisting her around until she was too dizzy to know whether she were standing or crawling.

Two men had kissed her this day. One had been gentle and loving and honorable. The other had been demanding and passionate and intent on dishonor. Why was it that last kiss she remembered so clearly and not the first? And why would she respond to any kiss when her husband's had stirred nothing in her at all?

Those were topics better not tested. Undressing without calling for a maid, Eavin dismissed both men from her thoughts. Jeremy would have to be told that she was unsuitable as a wife. Surely Nicholas could find some way of doing that politely without her having to spell it out. Then she and Jeremy could remain friends without the pain of embarrassment between them. Addressing the topic of Nicholas was akin to talking about the weather. The permutations were manifold, but all the talk would have no control over the outcome. Nicholas was a force unto himself.

As Eavin had expected, the seamstress arrived the next day to take her measurements whether she wished it or not. The woman made no inquiries as to Eavin's preferences, showed her no pattern books, merely took notes and departed. Eavin gave a sigh of exasperation and prepared herself for another confrontation with Nicholas.

When he arrived, it was in the company of a gangly stranger with red hair and an awkward accent who purportedly wanted the views of an easterner on the escalating war with England. Michael was called upon to offer his viewpoints while Eavin watched suspiciously from a corner. The man's questions were leading to an extreme, and she glared at Nicholas, who sat smugly behind his desk listening to the interrogation. She had gathered enough from the talk at parties to know that Nicholas's politics were diametrically opposed to the society around him, but that was to be expected from his contrary nature. He didn't have to draw her brother in after him.

When the man suddenly turned a question to her, Eavin was unprepared. She merely stared at him until he repeated himself.

"I didn't mean to startle you, ma'am. But women always have a different outlook than we menfolk. What is your opinion on this war with England?"

"My opinion is that men aren't happy unless they're fighting," she snapped. "But if they're going to fight, they ought to do it with the intention of winning. Sitting back and asking to be whipped is the work of fools."

To her surprise, the red-haired man grinned and threw a triumphant look at Nicholas. "You're right, Saint-Just, she's smarter than you are. Pity I can't take her back with me."

Nicholas's eyes narrowed as Michael rose belligerently to stand beside Eavin's chair, but he responded with cool control. "That's enough, Daniel. One dangerous hothead in this town is sufficient. Setting Mrs. Dupré loose on the populace would be unfair in the extreme. You will keep names out of this story, you understand."

"Story?" Both Michael and Eavin responded in unison, but it was too late. Nicholas was already ushering the other man out of the study with vague reassurances, ignoring the questioning looks behind him.

Eavin knew better than Michael what was happening here, and she shot dagger looks at Nicholas when he re-entered the room. "You're feeding information to that radical newspaper, aren't you?" she demanded as soon as the door closed.

"Daniel always likes to interview newcomers to the city," he replied smoothly. "There will be an article on the charming widow of Dominic Dupré visiting our fair city which will intrigue all the ladies and send them into debating whether or not they ought to call. Had you been French, they would have been at your door immediately. As it is, the Americans will pursue all their dubious connections to see if they can arrange a meeting, and the French will debate into eternity whether or not to recognize you. It will be your duty to open both segments of society for Jeannette's sake."

He was good. He was too good. Eavin wished she wore the taffeta and starch of Madame Saint-Just so she could rustle indignantly when she stood up. As it was, she could only send him a look that ought to let him know she saw through his charade. "And you will tell me there will be no story about a 'distinguished gentleman from the East who disparages our country's inability to produce either army or navy to defend our populace in these desperate times'? And where will I fit into this story if you wish to protect Jeannette's chaperone from public outcry? Shall I be the 'gentleman's lady'? Will I be 'weeping over the deaths of our poor boys'? You are a low-down, conniving, good-for-nothing spalpeen of the worst sort, Nicholas Saint-Just!"

With that, she swept out of the room, leaving the two men to stare at each other. Michael's lips began to twitch first as he watched the elegant Frenchman struggling to restrain his temper and his urge to rage after her. "She's used to saying what she thinks, Saint-Just. Don't be expectin' to make a silk purse out of a sow's ear."

"With flattery like that, it's a wonder the Irish marry at all," Nicholas replied sourly, rising belatedly from his chair.

"Ah, well now, she's family, and we don't mind what we say among family. Her opinion of me will be less than flattering should you ask. Are you sartin you wish to let the mite loose on society?"

A light suddenly flared in Nicholas's eyes as he strode for the door. "I can't wait."

If Nicholas expected fireworks, he was to be sorely disappointed. Eavin warily accepted the arrival of a gray silk gown as being the proper attire for a child's guardian and not the kind of gift for a mistress. She wore it when Madame Dupré arrived to pay her respects, and sat silently while the two widows politely bared their teeth and neatly began slicing each other into ribbons. The arrival of several more society matrons of her acquaintance enlivened the proceedings suitably, particularly when one of them was Mignon Dubois. Since Nicholas wasn't present, the widow entertained the company with tales of rustic life that made Eavin appear the ideal of every bumpkin in the countryside.

If Mignon thought to annoy Eavin, she found the wrong target. With none of the vanity of the rarefied society around her, Eavin found the company of the disparaged Jeremy Howell and Clyde Brown to be more edifying than that of the idle fops who called on the Widow Dubois. She merely smiled at the stories and stabbed her needle into her embroidery. She was beginning to have serious doubts whether or not it was worth bringing Jeannette out in this society. Perhaps she ought to leave that to Nicholas's future wife.

That thought didn't help Eavin's mood any. Perhaps she ought to consider Jeremy's proposal seriously. Or perhaps she ought to look around for a man who already had children and needed a wife. That was an appealing idea— much better than imagining Nicholas marrying and his new wife taking over the raising of Jeannette. Just the thought of sharing a house with someone like Mignon Dubois made Eavin's insides curdle. She must have been half mad when she had offered to be Jeannette's nanny.

But when Eavin went downstairs later, after everyone was gone, to find Jeannette laughing and holding her hands out to her, she knew why she had done it and would do it all over again. Because Jeannette needed her.

The child had no one, and she needed the love that Eavin had in quantities to spare. Mignon Dubois would never love her as Eavin did. Whatever the future held, she could not see herself parted from the child who was as much part of her heart as the child who had died.

So when Nicholas sent up orders that she wear one of the evening gowns he had bought her to dinner, Eavin made no protest. Whatever else he was, Nicholas played the part of Jeannette's father well, and she would do whatever was necessary to keep him happy so she could stay.

When she arrived downstairs, she discovered a package set beside her place and his mother's. The men were already at the table discussing the spring planting, but Nicholas turned expectantly when both women arrived almost simultaneously.

Gesturing toward the boxes, he said, "I am making my apologies for my earlier behavior. I would see you in new gowns made up with that. I fancy the ladies of New Orleans will be green with envy shortly."

Eavin opened the lid to a froth of delicate lace and stifled a gasp. Madame Saint-Just opened her box, sniffed, and gave her son a look of loathing.

"Valenciennes," she muttered, as if the one word contained her gratitude.

Having no idea what the word meant, Eavin could only murmur startled thanks and look with bewilderment to her brother, who said nothing. Since he didn't seem to approve or disapprove, she assumed there was no more to the gift than Nicholas had said. Glancing at him, he seemed to have already dismissed the matter and gone back to his earlier discussion.

It wasn't until several days later, after she had sent the lace to the dressmaker and found it returned as a trim on an elegant morning gown of ice-blue kerseymere, that Eavin began to suspect the origin of the gift.

She hated the necessity of wearing the restrictive corset the slender silhouette of the gown demanded, but she thought the lace a lovely touch to disguise what she considered to be a rather décolleté neckline for a morning gown. It wasn't until the very first of their callers to the very last exclaimed over the "Valenciennes" that Eavin began to understand the rarity of the lace.

"However did you come by it?" Madame Dupré gushed with more boldness than the others would be permitted as she jealously fingered the fine stitching.

Giving Madame Saint-Just's stony expression a swift look, Eavin defiantly settled for a lie. If this lace was as valuable as their callers seemed to assume, she wasn't about to admit to its source. "It is a family heirloom," she murmured as she had heard other of these women do over jewels and other objects of interest.

A glance at Madame Saint-Just revealed a reluctant gleam of approval from that lady's eyes, and despite the protests of disappointment from the other ladies, Eavin felt satisfied with her leap of this hurdle. Since Nicholas's mother showed no evidence of having followed his orders in having her lace made up, she could only wonder at the source of the acquisition.

The question was resolved to some extent a while later as Nicholas arrived with the departure of the last of their guests. Tall and suavely handsome in his navy frock coat, he made his bows to the departing guests, smiling at Mignon Dubois's hovering attentions but resisting her overtures, revealing none of his impatience as the ladies finally carried their chatter outside and closed the door behind them.

When they were gone, he eyed the froth of lace on Eavin's gown with approval, and she felt as if his gaze saw through it to what she would have concealed. Feeling a sudden burning in the vicinity where his gaze lingered, she diverted the sensation by taking the offensive.

"What is this Valenciennes that they so covet it?" she demanded.

Nicholas's lips turned up enigmatically as his mother launched irately into the subject before he could reply.

"Smuggled, is what it is! It's from France, and no ship is supposed to deal with France. My son means to see us all in prison."

Nicholas showed no evidence of disapproval but merely smiled at his parent before returning his gaze once again to the object of their discussion, or to the one wearing it. "You do not object to the goods that smuggling can buy, *ma mère*. Eavin has only advertised the fact that the lace has arrived. No doubt every woman who left here this morning is on her way to the dressmakers to demand that the shipment be located. The law is a foolish one made to be broken. How did you explain your adornment, *ma petite*?"

Madame Saint-Just smiled triumphantly. "She said it was a family heirloom. I do believe Madame Dupré thought Francine's clothes were the contributing source."

Nicholas frowned slightly at his mother, but the smile he gave Eavin was sufficient to melt her bones had she been innocent enough to believe it. As it was, her heart pounded faster than was good for it, even though she knew his smile never reached his eyes.

"You are a clever liar, Mrs. Dupré, but your story will fool no one. Come, let us see how Jeannette fares." Nicholas held out his arm for Eavin to take.

She took it reluctantly, all too aware that once they went down the stairs there was no one to come between them but a child and her nurse, and they were no protection at all. Still, she had no reason to believe that she needed protection from Nicholas, and she followed him obediently out of his mother's sight and hearing.

"I have had a letter from Jeremy saying he wishes to talk to me about you. Do you have any knowledge of what this is about?"

His voice was smooth, without any edge to indicate his feelings. Eavin cursed the sophistication that allowed Nicholas to hide his thoughts while all she felt appeared instantaneously to the astute observer. She prayed he didn't know her breasts still tingled where his gaze had rested or that his masculine proximity in the narrow landing aroused unwarranted emotions. Damn the man, but where any other man's touch left her cold, just his look made her hot.

"I do," she stated flatly, not meeting his eyes but attempting to continue down the stairs.

Nicholas's hold on her arm didn't permit it. When he said nothing, Eavin was forced to look up and meet his gaze. The muscle over his cheek was pulled tight, and she would swear that the amber of his eyes glowed in the dark, but she felt none of the menace or alarm that this same situation would have caused had he been another man. He had very effectively disarmed all her defenses.

"He wishes to marry me." Eavin didn't try to interpret the slight flaring of his nostrils at this news. "I have told him he would do better to talk with you before addressing me." She lowered her eyes, unable to face him with her plea. "I would ask that you explain to him the circumstances. I'm not certain that I can."

Nicholas's grip on her arm relaxed. "Jeremy is a good friend. I would not see him hurt. He is a cherished only son, and his family expects him to marry well and produce many heirs to their property. I will speak with him."

"Thank you." Annoyed at the gratitude in her voice, Eavin started for the stairs again. She had just flung away her only chance of ever leaving this arrogant man; why in heaven's name she should be grateful was beyond her capacity to understand.

Nicholas pulled her back to his side. "That does not mean you must never marry." Her startled gaze whipped up to him and he smiled grimly. "If it is a husband you wish, I will introduce you to several good men who already have children. It is not always easy for a man to find a good mother for his children. Most women prefer their own, and this causes dissension when there is wealth to be divided."

Her heart was pounding erratically again, but Eavin couldn't place the blame anywhere in particular. The intensity in Nicholas's eyes wasn't unusual and had no meaning. The stair was narrow and she had to stand close. The hated corset pushed her breasts upward too prominently, and she felt as if she were rubbing against his waistcoat as they stood there. There was no reason she should feel the tension mounting between them. He had just made a generous offer, and she was about to refuse him. Why should that send her heart to pounding like a jungle drum?

"Your kindness is appreciated," she replied stiffly, "but I have no intention of marrying ever again."

With that, she shoved past him and proceeded down the stairs, the back of her narrow gown swaying softly as his gaze followed.

13

The damp wind blew Eavin's curls loosely as she straightened her new bonnet and tried to keep the straying strands covered. She loved the elegant velvet of the spencer and only wished it could be that daring wine color she had seen in the shop window instead of the more modest dark green. But in a city where married women seemed to adopt black for the rest of their lives, she felt exotic enough in green.

The bells of the cathedral tolled overhead, and she relished the sound as she took Michael's arm and followed his lead. As a city, New Orleans might seem foreign, but mass had the same familiar sound as home, and she felt better for having gone. Making confession to a French-speaking priest had been awkward, but the familiar Latin phrases had served her well, and she had survived the ordeal better than she had expected. Perhaps the priest had not understood her admission of sins of lust. Her penance had been extraordinarily light.

Michael apparently had other plans besides lingering among the well-dressed crowd to greet acquaintances and gossip. He led her through the Place d'Armes to avoid the congestion, and Eavin turned her admiration toward the parade of people along the levee.

It was Sunday, and even the slaves had earned a day of rest. Elegant gentlemen in beaver hats and frock coats walked side by side with Africans in homespun and riverboat men in earrings and braided hair. Elegant ladies with parasols contrasted with free women of color in their bright *tignons*. In the distance she could hear the pounding of drums, and she ached to follow the sound. The music of New Orleans was a constant source of delight, almost as exhilarating as the improbable combinations of people.

Eavin's grip on Michael's arm tightened as she thought she saw the sun strike against the glitter of golden hair as a gentleman doffed his hat in greeting to one of the women of color. Few in this city had hair the color of Nicholas, and only he would be eccentric enough to doff his hat to a woman not considered to be a lady. Curiosity kept her gaze fastened on the sight as Michael unknowingly led her closer.

The woman had the graceful posture of a queen as she smiled and tapped her fan lightly on the gentleman's coat. The *tignon,* meant to make her less attractive than the ladies in their beribboned and feathered hats, had the opposite effect, emphasizing her high cheekbones and accenting her creamy complexion while its exotic colors matched her fashionable gown. When the gentleman turned slightly to take her arm, Eavin could see for certain that it was Nicholas.

Eavin's grip on his arm made Michael look ahead, and with a growl of irritation he immediately swung his sister down the next street rather than continuing the promenade.

"Is that his mistress?" she asked calmly as they entered the shadowed street between three-story buildings.

Michael turned his irritation toward her. "You're not supposed to know about such things."

"Don't be ridiculous. What else do you think the ladies talk about when they're together? I know all about a certain newlywed gentleman who refuses to give up his mistress on Rampart Street. It is an enormous scandal and has produced any number of fascinating stories. Apparently it is considered quite acceptable for an unmarried man to keep a woman of color. I suppose that makes them think their precious daughters are safer if men have other outlets."

Michael's brotherly scowl had no effect on his sister's serene demeanor. "I ought to send you back home. This whole damned city is an immoral woman, and you're becoming too much like her. I hold Nicholas to blame. He's too free in his speech with you."

"Michael, I've been married." Temper rising, Eavin jerked her hand from her brother's arm. "It's not as if I don't know what goes on between men and women. And after some of the suggestions that were made to me in

Baltimore, I cannot believe the men of New Orleans are any worse. I have not received one improper proposal since arriving."

Michael cursed and grabbed her arm, restoring it to its former position. "That doesn't mean one won't be forthcoming. Keep away from Saint-Just, colleen. He's a man without scruples."

"I know that. I'm not a fool. But I cannot see that I have anything to fear if that woman back there is his mistress. I could not begin to compare with anyone so fascinating. I am just curious, that's all."

"Well, you can remain curious. I've never seen her before. Nicholas has a closed mouth and secretive ways. He's not likely to let mere employees know his business."

Seeing the red-haired newspaper editor heading their way, Eavin smiled and ignored Michael's sarcastic remark. The article on an "eastern" point of view had been remarkably vivid. She had another suggestion or so she wished to make.

"Fire! There is fire at the docks!" The voice echoed up the stairwell as Eavin came from the nursery after settling a fretful Jeannette to sleep. She watched as Nicholas's bedroom door exploded open and he raced into the hall, pulling on his coat over his partially opened shirt. He had obviously just been preparing for bed, although she was quite certain it must be after midnight.

He didn't see her on the back stairs but ran down to question the messenger. Eavin crept to the top of the stairs leading into the entryway and openly listened as the small black boy excitedly poured out his story to the old servant guarding the door and to the master of the household. Nicholas's face was livid as he gave orders sending both boy and old man scurrying. Before she could offer help, he was gone, striding out the front door with none of the languid air of the gentleman he occasionally purported to be.

It was the middle of the night, and she was wearing naught but her gown and robe. She couldn't follow. There was nothing she could do if she did. But she couldn't go to bed, either.

She found a window overlooking the courtyard and watched as Michael raced down from his room to load the male slaves into a wagon with whatever implements could be located in the shed. This was a city house with little use for the hoes and shovels of the plantation. The selection was limited.

She admired the way Michael efficiently handled the half-asleep servants. The wagon was trundling out of the courtyard within minutes of the warning. She had always known that her older brother was an intelligent man, but she had doubted his ambition. She would never have thought him capable of taking on the job as overseer. But somehow the relationship between Michael and Nicholas had given him the confidence that he needed to prove himself. Eavin didn't understand it, but she was grateful that Nicholas had given him the chance.

She had reason to be grateful to Nicholas for many things. The man was a smuggler, probably little better than a pirate if his conversation with his mother meant anything. He had no doubt killed Raphael Reyes for dallying with his wife. He slept with his slaves and no doubt any other woman who crossed his path. In the eyes of the church and the law, Nicholas was a totally reprehensible criminal. But to Eavin, he was a man who loved his wife's child, who took his sister-in-law in when no one else would, who provided her brother employment not only without recommendation but without knowing he was her brother. That wasn't the mark of a criminal in her eyes.

Eavin sent the house servants aroused by the noise to begin making pots of hot coffee, boiling water, and biscuits, while sending others searching for warm blankets and dry clothes. She knew very little about fighting fires except that it required lots of water, and on a night as cold as this one, it would be a thankless, unpleasant task.

Perhaps having a father who manipulated the law and a mother with few morals made her a poor judge of character, Eavin pondered idly as she waited for some sign that the fire had been doused. She had seen honest, churchgoing men beat their wives into a pulp on Saturday nights. She had watched children starve in the streets because their parents were too drunk to work. She had seen little of the finer side of life, the life of Nicholas's society, where men were supposed to be morally upright and monogamous and women were supposed to be chaste and obedient. But Nicholas had told her what had happened to Francine, and she had seen for herself the way these "moral" gentlemen behaved when they consumed too much alcohol. Perhaps they had enough wealth to keep their children from starving in the streets, but she didn't think their manners were so much different from the men she knew beyond that.

There were good men among the rich and the poor, she knew. Clyde Brown and Jeremy Howell and Dominic were proof of that. She didn't think they engaged in any of the dissipations of Nicholas and her brother, but then, perhaps they never had to. From what little she understood, Nicholas came from an aristocratic family, but his father had squandered what little they had. Like herself and Michael, he'd had to make his own life. He could have married a fortune, but he had fallen in love with a woman who had as little as he. Who could blame him for doing whatever was necessary to make the wealth Francine's status required?

Eavin didn't understand the law that made smuggling illegal any more than she understood the law that made her father's bid-rigging notorious. They were both making a life for their families. But she did know that her father had eventually paid for his cost-cutting with his life, and Nicholas would inevitably do the same if he continued.

For Jeannette's sake, she hoped Madame Saint-Just's accusations were untrue. Nicholas couldn't have sailed the ship that brought in that lace. He had been here all the time. But he very well could have owned that ship. Did that make a difference?

The fire fighters straggled in some hours later, drenched by the downpour of rain that had started some time earlier. Soaked to the bone, shivering, and covered with soot, they greeted the coffee and blankets and dry clothes with weary gratitude. Once she saw that Michael had returned safely and the servants were provided for, Eavin turned back to the house, only to be met by Nicholas in the doorway.

His frilled shirt was ruined with soot and damp, his coat was lost, and the filth on his face made the gold of his hair even more incongruous. Lines etched beside his mouth indicated the state of his mind, and Eavin gently pushed him to a bench in the back room while she summoned a maid to bring him coffee and a bowl in which to wash.

"What burned?" she asked bluntly as Nicholas spread a warm cloth over his face and scrubbed off the worst of the soot.

"Part of the warehouse where the cotton was stored. The rain will drench the other goods unless we get back there with tarps. Thanks for the coffee." He gulped the black brew hastily when it was handed to him, then set the mug aside and began to strip off his wet shirt. "Have someone find me some dry clothes. I've got to get back out there."

Remembering vividly the ridges of muscle beneath that shirt, Eavin escaped into the hallway to send someone upstairs for his clothes. How Madame Saint-Just slept through all this was beyond her comprehension, but someone had to look after Nicholas. She was beginning to wonder if anyone ever had.

He was rubbing himself down with a blanket when she returned behind the maid carrying his clothes. He nodded his thanks and started to drop the blanket until he realized Eavin was standing there; then he lifted his eyebrows warily.

"You have done enough, *ma chérie*. Return to bed. Jeannette will rise early, as always. She is your responsibility, not me."

"Have you ever considered what would happen to her if anything happened to you?" Eavin asked curtly, not even knowing the question had formed in her mind until it was out.

Nicholas looked startled, then smiled bleakly. "I had not. Thank you for reminding me. I will look into it in the morning. Nothing will happen to me before then, I assure you. Now go to bed."

Eavin had the oddest urge to go to him with a hug and a kiss, but she was well aware that was her fantasy and not his. She might wish that he needed her, but he did not, and the growing frown on his face proved it. With no other acknowledgment Eavin turned around and swept out.

Nicholas watched her go with a mixture of relief and regret. The sleepy look in her green eyes and her flushed color against a long, black braid had combined to give Eavin O'Flannery Dupré a seductive look of innocence he found hard to resist. Despite being cold and wet, his body had responded to her with a lust that he found remarkably irritating. He didn't mind seducing her when he had nothing better to do, but he'd be damned if he would have her seducing him.

Yet he knew, if he had taken her in his arms just then, she would have come willingly, and something in his insides ached for the little bit of comfort she could offer.

Growling at the thought of any woman offering more than trouble, Nicholas proceeded to throw aside the blanket and dress, ignoring the tittering maids behind him.

"Ship 'em before they rot. The new warehouse will never be done in time." Michael sipped his coffee and eyed his employer, who was in the blackest humor he had ever seen him in, and considering Saint-Just's temperament, that was saying something.

"They could as easily end up at the bottom of the sea that way. With Napoleon defeated, the British will be turning their navy full force on us. I don't wish to lose my ships and men as well as the cotton."

"You're not getting any money out of either of them the way things stand," Michael reminded him practically. "And if it comes to a sea battle, you're just as likely to lose your ships defending the city as in shipping cotton."

"And you'd have no need to defend the city if your cotton was already gone," Eavin interrupted cynically, sitting down at the table with her toast.

Michael gave her a distrustful look, but Nicholas smiled humorlessly. "That is so. They could shell it to pieces and I'd have nothing to lose but this house. Perhaps we could send out welcome signals to the next destroyer that sails by."

Understanding some of the pain in his sarcasm, Eavin gave him a shrewd look. "I'm certain society would expect it of you. Why disappoint them?"

"You're quite right. I must be getting soft in my old age. Ship the cotton, Michael. You know the procedure. I doubt if anyone will question if I move my cotton after a fire." With that bland statement Nicholas rose from the table and walked out, leaving brother and sister glaring at each other.

"You know what that means, don't you, oh brilliant sister of mine?" Michael stared at his plate with disgust.

"That he's willing to risk his ships and men for his cotton and not for the city," Eavin replied calmly.

Michael looked up sharply. "Perhaps you're not quite as brilliant as I assumed. It means I'll be loading his cotton aboard a smuggling ship and sending it out to dodge the blockade. They'll be lucky to find a friendly port once they manage that. The whole world's at war, in case you haven't noticed."

"So, what else is new?" But Eavin felt a sinking sensation in the pit of her stomach. Michael not only had confirmed her conjectures, but admitted his part in it. She had done him no favor by finding him work here.

She wondered once again if she hadn't been overly hasty in seeking what had appeared to be the security of Nicholas's protection. But as she settled Jeannette down for her nap later that day, she couldn't see how she could have done any differently. Touching the infant's dark curls, she turned around to find Nicholas in the doorway.

"From this morning's conversation, I ascertain that you are having second thoughts about your choice of homes." His voice was dry as he watched her visibly retreat from him.

"Everyone is entitled to contemplate his future upon occasion. I merely agreed with what you were already thinking. You have worked hard for your reputation as a scoundrel. Why should I be the one to reform you? I'm not Francine."

"No, you're not, but I have provided for you and Jeannette as if you were, so you need not worry about the future any longer. When my enemies grow tired of waiting for each other to do the deed and one of them finally cuts my throat, you will be a wealthy woman. Now you need only sit back and wait."

The glitter of emerald in Eavin's normally hazel eyes gave fair warning of the tempest to come. "How very generous of you. You wouldn't mind making that sooner than later? Somehow, I imagine it will be rather difficult to introduce Jeannette into a society that scorns her father. It will be made much easier if she is orphaned."

The grip on her arm was painful as Nicholas jerked her away from the crib and out of the room. Closing the nursery door softly, he leaned against it as he regarded her as if she were a viper.

"I could defend that same society single-handed, and they would still scorn me despite their smiling welcomes. I could buy half the women in this city, but they would never accept me as anything more than my father's son. I can't think of any particularly good reason why I should hold a high opinion of their concerns."

"No one asked you to. Most people naturally think the worst of everyone. Why should you care? Francine is dead. You don't need to win her anymore. You don't even owe her daughter any respect. There is no one to condemn or condone what you do but yourself. Your father has nothing at all to do with it."

Nicholas's eyes glittered in the gloom of the unlighted hall as he crossed his arms over his chest. "I shall remember that when we return to the plantation. Last night's rain didn't hurt the roads much. They will be dry in a day or two. Are you coming back with me or have you found New Orleans society more to your liking? I'll not stand in your way if you have."

Puzzled, Eavin backed away a step or two. "I go where Jeannette goes. Nothing has changed."

Nicholas had a bleak look at the future Jeannette would have with a smuggler for a father and an Irish maid for a companion, but he was too angry with himself and others to ponder the implications for long. He unfolded himself from the door and glared down at her. "Then begin packing your bags."

She nodded and started down the hall, but before she could reach the stairs, Nicholas called after her, making her turn. Putting his hands on the stair rail behind her, he pinned her against the newel post.

"Before you start putting on airs in Jeannette's name, you better know that my father was a drunkard and a gambler. He was shot for cheating at the table, and there are those who thought he should have been shot for cheating in other ways before then. I have a half brother that I know of by an octaroon down in the quarters, and I suspect two half sisters by prominent women you may have met in these last few weeks. My mother carefully warned me away from them without giving any reason. To my credit, I didn't instantly pursue them. It was only sometime later that I began to understand why their mothers whisked them out of my reach. Now you know why I have little care for my family name."

"Your father ruined his own name, not yours. And not Jeannette's. She is a Saint-Just to society, but she will be a beautiful woman of her own when she grows up. You can help her achieve that, or hurt her. That is your decision to make." Eavin fought against the panic of his closeness. She had nowhere to put her hands but on him, and that she would not do. She clenched her fingers behind her and waited for Nicholas to move.

"You are an innocent fool if that is all you think of society, but I will not disillusion you. You will learn on your own soon enough. In the meantime, I will do what I think is best for Jeannette's sake, and I wish to hear no criticism from you. Is that understood?"

"Of course. Did you hear me say anything else?" With a lifted eyebrow, Eavin indicated her displeasure.

Nicholas gave her a mocking look and stepped back. "Somehow I think our minds are much alike, Irish. You will do whatever is necessary for Jeannette's sake also, won't you?"

She didn't like the way he said that. There was nothing in his look but cool admiration, and nothing in his tone but more of the same. But he was right. Their minds were much alike, and she didn't like what hers was thinking.

"I suppose we'll see, won't we?" she inquired sweetly, stepping away from his encroaching arms. And before he could stop her, she lifted her skirts and hurried up the stairs.

His mocking laughter followed her up, and horribly, it sent a shiver of anticipation through her middle and added fuel to the fire that his kiss had already set alight.

14

"He is a most handsome man, is he not?" a husky voice behind her inquired.

Watching Nicholas walk away, Eavin cursed her foolishness in not bringing a maid with her. She would never grow accustomed to thinking of herself as a lady who needed the chaperonage of a maid, and obviously, neither would Nicholas. He had abandoned her here in front of the dressmaker's to go off on business of his own, leaving her an open target for forward strangers.

She swung around to confront the speaker, startled to discover a woman of color and not a gossip-prone man. She bit her tongue as she recognized the lovely features beneath the brilliant blue and silver of the *tignon*.

"I have met more handsome," Eavin replied stiffly.

"Yet none so exciting, *mais oui*?"

The woman was watching her with curiosity, studying her in the same way that Eavin was surreptitiously returning the gaze. Eavin opted for propriety in this unfamiliar situation. "I have errands to do. Was there some reason you wished to speak with me?"

The woman smiled with a trace of mockery at Eavin's naiveté. "I think we have the same interests and thought it wise to make your acquaintance."

Propriety seemed to be rapidly eluding her. Eavin felt the stares of strangers around them, but curiosity was ever stronger than her sense of propriety. Her reply was more cynical than the other woman obviously expected. "If you mean Nicholas's support, I suppose I must agree that our interests coincide, but I'm not certain why that makes it necessary to meet."

Dancing laughter leapt to chocolate eyes as the woman raised her parasol and prepared to leave. "Because we both wish to protect what we love most. My name is

Labelle Saint-Just. If you ever have need of me, you need only tell one of his servants. They will know where to find me."

She swept away before any could question her right to stop a white woman in the center of town. Eavin stared after her in confusion. Saint-Just? Surely Nicholas could not have married her. What was it he had said of his father's peccadilloes? There had been mention of a quadroon son and several daughters, but she had been under the impression that the daughters were white. Damn, but this city and its inhabitants were growing more complicated by the day.

She had to be insane to stay here. She had to be twice as mad to stay in the same establishment as Nicholas Saint-Just.

What was that the woman had said about love? Did this Labelle person have a child she loved as much as Eavin loved Jeannette?

Not wanting to contemplate any more complications, Eavin retreated into the dressmaker's shop, where only the profusion of goods could confuse her. It didn't help her day any to note the Valenciennes lace prominently displayed in the first case that she studied.

The man entering the *petite salle* was the picture of indolent elegance. His gray long-tailed frock coat rested in impeccable folds against a lean frame more long than broad. A maid whisked away his tall hat, and he gave her a charming smile and murmured French flattery that made her giggle.

Not until Nicholas was certain there was no one in the salon other than family did he allow any hint of his anger to show. "Where the hell were you? I've been scouring the damned town."

Nicholas's mother looked up in shock at these tones spoken in the presence of a lady, but the other occupant of the salon merely held her embroidery up to the waning afternoon light to examine it.

"I was admiring the quantity of goods in your local stores," Eavin mentioned calmly, as if he had said nothing and she were just giving a description of her day. Satisfied with her stitching, she lowered the needlework to her lap and jabbed the needle in again. "It is quite fascinating to note how many carry that exquisite lace now. And did you know that there are French perfumes and silk stockings available? At quite reasonable prices, lower I think, than in Baltimore before the war. And the market! Why, I saw the oddest men carrying in barrel after barrel of what I'm certain must be fine brandy. The people of New Orleans certainly do know how to live. I'm quite staggered by all these luxuries."

Still fuming but curious to know which way the wind blew, Nicholas strode into the room and poured himself some sherry, the strongest drink his mother allowed in the house. "You wandered down to the market by yourself, without an escort. How clever of you."

"Oh, no, by all means, no." Still seething after her afternoon encounters, Eavin was dying to mention the woman Labelle, but she didn't think it appropriate to bring the matter up in front of Madame Saint-Just. Instead she allowed her ire to escape in sarcasm. "I went to have a little chat with your newspaper friend, Mr. Fletcher, the red-haired man, remember?" She kept her smile to herself as Nicholas nodded impatiently, obviously gritting his teeth. "He escorted me around quite nicely, thank you."

"I see. And what did you and my red-haired friend have to discuss all this time while I was searching for your body in the river?"

Eavin couldn't keep from smiling at that. She looked up to find Madame Saint-Just staring at her with an odd look on her face, but she ignored the older woman's disapproval to smile sweetly at Nicholas. "Why, lots and lots of things. I'm certain you wouldn't be interested."

He really was going to have to strangle her. She sat there just as demure and innocent-looking as a milk-fed miss, but Nicholas knew damned good and well the wicked mind hiding behind those blinding green eyes. He wouldn't put it past her to know more about his business by now than he did himself. There wasn't a man in this town who had connected him with that American newspaper. Not even her cousin suspected. To Nicholas's surprise, his mother interrupted before he could find an appropriate response.

"I'm happy to know that you have enjoyed our city, Mrs. Dupré," Hélène Saint-Just said stiffly. "I was hoping to find some opportunity to ask you to stay with me when Nicholas returns to the plantation. It is lonesome here with no young people about."

Nicholas leaned his elbow against the mahogany secretaire and watched his mother with something akin to amazement. She was lying through her teeth. In private she still referred to Jeannette as "the bastard," and her opinion of Eavin was not much higher, although he had noticed a certain grudging respect these last weeks. Still, the woman who had stood in the shadows holding her tongue while his father had beat the hell out of him wasn't a woman to stand up to any other adversary, either. What was she doing inviting one to stay in the house? Out of curiosity he waited for Eavin's reply.

After a brief, startled silence when she waited for Nicholas to make some retort, Eavin spoke for herself. "That is a generous offer and one I am certain I will love to take up when Jeannette is a little older. But I find I prefer the country and would like to take advantage of it while I can, if you do not mind."

Hélène glanced up to her son. "Would it help if I insist?"

Nicholas met her eyes coldly. "Not at all. She returns with me."

"It is unfair of you to keep Madame Dupré's only grandchild from her."

Not liking this direction any better, Nicholas's lips twisted cynically. "She and her cronies never came here until Jeannette arrived. Surely you cannot still covet the society that has always turned its back on you?"

"And why should I not? It is the society to which I was born—less than the society to which I was born. You forget your grandfathers were of the nobility. You are entitled to return to France and seek the return of the marquesate if you so desire. Why should I not travel in the highest circles?"

He was aware of Eavin's shocked stare and her silent departure, but the argument was an old one, and Nicholas crossed his arms in boredom. "Because those circles turned their backs on you when you needed them. Your only true friends have been among the Americans. Why do you not cultivate them instead of the Madame Duprés of the world?"

Hélène Saint-Just drew her shoulders back proudly. "How can I discuss with them the finer things of life? Americans do not understand the opera. They do not know how to give a soiree. They know nothing of etiquette. All they understand is money. You are becoming desperately like them, Nicholas."

Growing impatient, he raised himself from the desk and started for the door. "Excellent. I admire their audacity and their ingenuity. They own this country now. The future is theirs. I will see my daughter grow with respect in their eyes."

"She is not your daughter!"

The words were almost a screech as Nicholas walked out of the room. He halted briefly, closed his eyes in an attempt to control his temper, then turned for one final word. Standing in the doorway, he said in a voice of exaggerated calm, "Jeannette is my daughter, *Maman*. You would be wise to remember that."

Turning back to the hallway, Nicholas met the gaze of the woman standing at the top of the stairs, her eyes wide with some emotion he did not care to investigate. With a nod, he retrieved his hat and stalked out.

As the wagons were loaded the next day, his conversation with his mother prompted Nicholas to examine his own life once again, and he didn't like what he was seeing. What little stability he had achieved by marriage to Francine was rapidly eroding. He was thirty-two years old, wealthy enough to have whatever he desired, and reluctant guardian of an infant he had sworn to protect. Yet he was still behaving as if he were two and twenty with no ties, no responsibilities, and no concerns beyond his own.

Soon he would have to consider marrying again. Francine had been the only woman he had ever come close to loving. He didn't expect to find that again. Perhaps he ought to choose an American wife this time. Watching the last sway of Eavin's skirt as she disappeared into the gallery overhead, Nicholas had to grin at how his thoughts had led him astray. With the warm sun on his back, the scent of flowers in the air, and trailing plants swinging gently in the breeze created by Eavin's passing, Nicholas felt the first stirrings of life since

Francine's death, and his thoughts turned lustful. If he was to take his rightful place in society for Jeannette's sake, he couldn't do it by marrying an Irish maid, even if she could bear the children he wanted. No, there were better places for women like Eavin Dupré, and his best friend's bed wasn't one of them.

Whistling to himself, realizing that he was actually glad to be returning to the plantation he had designated as his retreat from the society he despised, Nicholas strode through the house to supervise the packing of the wagons. He was looking forward to planting season. It had been a long time since he had looked forward to anything.

Eavin was highly suspicious of Nicholas's mood as the small caravan wound through cypress forests and over streams still swollen from spring rains. He frequently rode his restive stallion on ahead to check low places in the road and the passability of fords, and she very much thought he was behaving as restlessly as his stallion.

She watched as Nicholas set the prancing horse to ride toward them with another report, and she couldn't help noticing how the wind flattened his shirt against his chest, emphasizing not only his breadth but the fact that muscles and no fat lay beneath the fabric. Eavin reminded herself that his shirt was the silk of a wealthy man, adorned with the ruffles of society, and had no relation to the unadorned cotton of her brother's. She didn't know why he was displaying his grandeur, but she would have no part of it.

She said the same to herself again when Nicholas leaned over the carriage to inform her he was riding on to the Howells. The sun glinted off the wild mane of his hair, and Eavin couldn't help but think that Jeremy's shy sister was likely to faint at the sight of him. She pointedly handed him his coat and waistcoat, and the grin he gave her was as good as a reprimand.

She wanted to smack him. Her mood had soured as his had escalated. Michael gave her an odd look when she coldly ignored his employer's gallant farewell, but he had sense enough to stay silent. He had borne the brunt of her temper in the past and knew when silence served best.

Settling against the uncomfortable seat, Eavin scowled at the trees rolling by. She knew where Nicholas was going and why. He was making haste to see that Jeremy didn't repeat his mistaken overtures now that she had returned. He was only doing what she had asked. He didn't have to do it with such good humor. She was throwing away the opportunity of a lifetime, one even better than she had grabbed when she had married Dominic. Nicholas didn't have to be so damned happy about it.

Annie took the fussy infant from Eavin's arms and to her breast, leaving Eavin with nothing better to do than watch the passing countryside. The new green of the leaves colored the expectant hush of the swampy forest. Birdsong dwindled as the wagons and horses passed by, but it lingered on the warm breeze, promising the joys of spring. Wildflowers sprang out of the moss and new fern fronds unfurled before her eyes, and Eavin couldn't retain her anger and suspicion for long under the influence of the countryside.

She loved it here, she realized. She had hated the noise and the filth and the closeness of the clapboard houses and crowds of the city. Out here she could almost imagine she had been reborn into a whole new world, a world she could shape as she wished, not one shaped by her parents before her. It was exciting and challenging, and for the first time since Dominic had died, she began to feel as if she might have some control over her life.

It had been her decision to reject Jeremy, and it was the right decision. She had been unhappy with Dominic, even though he had been gentler and probably more malleable than Jeremy. It was apparent she wasn't meant for marriage. Not all the men in her mother's boardinghouse had been poor or cruel or unpleasant. Some had been promising lawyers. One had gone on to be elected to Congress. She hadn't found one of them attractive or interesting in the ways her friends found their husbands and boyfriends. Their attentions had horrified and revolted her until she had resorted to disguising herself in an attempt to divert their interest. So it was quite obvious that she would only be unhappy if she married.

In which case, finding a home and a child to raise was a lucky piece of work on her part. If her employer sometimes looked at her in the same way as her mother's boarders, Eavin had matured enough to understand that men did that but didn't necessarily mean anything by it. Nicholas had a rash temper, but she certainly knew how to deal with that. She didn't think he would ever harm her, and with Michael nearby, she could be quite certain of it. All was finally right in her world. It was up to her to see that it stayed that way.

So when the caravan arrived at the plantation to find Nicholas and Jeremy already waiting, Eavin managed a pleasant smile and left them to their own devices while she saw Jeannette settled in the nursery.

A month's worth of dust had accumulated on the furniture and floors upstairs, and Jeremy's lovely bouquet of daffodils had dried to pitiful skeletons. As soon as Jeannette was settled in her bed, Eavin set the servants to cleaning up the debris from the flood while she began on the upper floors.

Below, Nicholas watched Jeremy's nervous pacing as the sounds of activity sprang to life throughout the house. The click-click of a feminine step set the younger man turning toward the door, but the sound went by without stopping. He frowned at his friend's fidgeting and poured a glass of brandy.

"Drink this and stop pacing, for pity's sake," Nicholas said in disgust, passing the glass to Jeremy. "It's time you went into New Orleans and got some of this out of your system. I'll not let you make my daughter's aunt into your mistress, so you might as well start looking for another one."

Jeremy swished the liquid in his glass angrily, and Nicholas thought he might expect it in his face at any minute, but Howell had more control over his temper than Nicholas.

"There's no knowing for certain that she can't have children," he said coldly, as if that had been the topic all along. "You know Doc Johnson is half blind and half senile. He's the one who pronounced Raphael dead, and you know as well as I do that the scoundrel's out there alive somewhere. If it's his word she's taking, there could be a mistake."

Nicholas shrugged this off as irrelevant. "There's every chance that he's right, but even so, you know Eavin isn't suitable. Dominic was a weakling alone for the first time in his life and no doubt scared half out of his wits. He married her because he couldn't have her any other way and he needed someone to cling to. As much as I admire

Eavin, she's not our sort, and your family would agree if
you tried to bring her home. You haven't seen her in the
devil of a temper like I have, or you would agree."

"I daresay I've seen you in worse moods, and I haven't
shot you yet," Jeremy replied angrily, slamming his glass
down. "So she's Irish. What has that to say to anything?"

Patiently, Nicholas poured himself a glass. "From
things that Eavin has said, I rather suspect that her family
stayed one step ahead of the law. Her mother was a lady's
maid in Ireland, Howell. And if my intuition is right, that
cousin of hers is hiding behind her skirts from something
neither of them is telling. I've made a few inquiries, but
it will be a while before they're returned. Eavin asked me
to tell you these things, Jeremy. It's not as if I'm talking
out of turn. She knows you're not suited, but she wants to
remain friends. Don't embarrass her by asking for more."

"Damnation!" Jeremy picked up the discarded glass
and swallowed the contents with a gulp that nearly
choked him. Recovering, he discovered Nicholas leaning
one elbow against a bookcase and staring overhead where
the sound of an Irish lullaby could be heard. Suspicion
raised its ugly head. "You want her for yourself, don't
you?"

Nicholas slanted him a look through half-closed eyes.
"You will curb your tongue in my presence, Jeremy.
Friend or not, I have sliced hastier tongues for less than
that. Eavin is here because Francine wanted her to be and
because Jeannette needs her. You would do well to stifle
any further speculation."

Effectively chastised, Jeremy grimaced and wandered
to the window, empty glass in hand. "Perhaps I will go
into New Orleans. My father is thinking of building in the
new quarter. I can look for a location and begin inter-
viewing builders."

Nicholas nodded approvingly, but before he could
speak, a knock interrupted him. Both men lifted their
heads and turned as the door swung open.

"I don't mean to intrude. I just wanted to know if
Jeremy would stay for dinner." Gleaming masses of black
hair appeared around the corner of the door, crowning a
lively face of purest porcelain. She didn't even enter the
room, but the spring breeze coming through the doorway
smelled a little sweeter.

Before Jeremy could answer, Nicholas shook his head. "His family is expecting him. I've kept him too long. I think a cold collation would suffice tonight under the circumstances."

Eavin nodded and disappeared, closing the door quietly after her. Nicholas watched with sympathy the torture plainly etched on his friend's face, but it was in everyone's best interest that the break be made now. He didn't bend to the naked plea in Jeremy's eyes.

Seeing the stubborn refusal in Nicholas's expression, Jeremy set his glass down and held out his hand. "You're probably right. She doesn't even know I exist. I'll be going now."

They shook and he departed, leaving Nicholas to contemplate the walls of his study with a certain amount of satisfaction. He had done nothing that she hadn't asked him to. His conscience was thoroughly clear on that point.

15

"I would rather not go, Nicholas," Eavin said stiffly as she bent over the needlework in her lap. She was making a gown for Jeannette's first birthday, although the event was several months away. Sewing had never been one of her better talents, but she was learning rapidly.

The evening was early and the sun still illuminated the western sky, but the draperies were drawn against the damaging rays, and the lantern had already been lit on the table beside Eavin. Nicholas studied her bent head with curiosity before reaching for the book he had left on the mantel.

"Don't be foolish. The Howells are good friends, of yours as well as mine. They would be insulted if you did not go."

Eavin had studied the problem from every angle, and this was the only suitable conclusion she could draw. She didn't like having her decision questioned. Unsmiling, she looked up to meet his gaze. "I am a grown woman, Nicholas. You needn't remind me of my responsibilities. I am quite capable of speaking with Mrs. Howell on my own, so you needn't worry about explaining it to her. I just feel that it's no longer suitable for me to continue attending these occasions with you."

A dangerous scowl began to form along Nicholas's brow as his fingers clenched the book, and he remained standing, towering over her. "I see. My reputation has become such that you no longer wish to associate with me."

Eavin looked at him with surprise. "That thought never occurred to me. I don't think I've ever heard anything so foolish. Have you quite taken leave of your senses?"

Nicholas scowled more ferociously, but when she did not retreat, a sliver of a smile appeared at the corner of his lips. "You've a damned wicked mind, Mrs. Dupré.

You are supposed to dither anxiously and wring your hands and swear you didn't mean a word of it and say of course you will do whatever I say."

Eavin flung her sewing aside and rose to cross the room to the desk, where she produced a sheaf of papers from beneath the blotter. "If you wish dithering, then I shall bring you one of the hens from the yard. And any woman who agrees to do whatever you say is a goose of the worst sort. Is that how you make your conquests, by scowling at them?"

Nicholas leaned against the mantel and watched as she sorted through the papers. Was it his imagination, or did she look thinner than he remembered? Perhaps it was those damned corsets. She didn't need one. The gown she was wearing was high-waisted and emphasized the lovely curve of her breasts, although the chemise beneath it covered all the more interesting aspects. Why she should bother restricting the natural softness of her body wasn't a subject he ought to dwell on.

"I've never considered seducing a woman with terror. Remind me to try it sometime; it sounds most amusing. Are you going to tell me just exactly what you are doing in my desk?"

"Organizing a rebuttal. I am not very good at arguing with you; I don't think quick enough and I get angry too easily. So I've put my arguments down on paper so you can peruse them at will. I find I can be very effective with pen in hand." Satisfied that everything was where it should be, Eavin crossed the room and handed the sheaf of papers to Nicholas. Just his presence was somehow threatening, overwhelming. Even after a day of physical labor, he exuded a restless energy that could easily flare into a rage. Or passion, she suspected. But she didn't want to consider that.

When she turned to leave, Nicholas held the papers aside and watched her quizzically. "Where are you going?"

"To my room. I can sew just as well there as here."

He pointed at the chair she had just deserted. "Sit. I don't like one-sided arguments. I demand equal time."

Nervously, Eavin considered the chair, then the man waiting impatiently for her to take it. "I think it would be

better if we left the discussion to another time. Neither of
us is very sensible when in a temper."

Nicholas resisted a grin and kept his face stern. "Good.
Then you wouldn't wish to put me in a temper, would
you? Sit."

Eavin reluctantly took the chair and picked up her sewing as he began to read over the papers she had written.
She thought her arguments were quite compelling, but she
could tell by the frown forming over Nicholas's nose that
he might be of a different opinion. Restlessly she set the
sewing aside and rose to push back the draperies. She
wished to open the window and drink deeply of the evening air, but she had already learned that the punishment
for that was a thousand mosquito bites up her arms. She
wondered if mosquito netting could be tacked over the
window somehow so it could be opened at night. She let
her mind wander over anything but the reaction of the
man behind her to her declaration of independence.

She heard the rustle of the papers and what she suspected was a chuckle, followed by a sound that was most
definitely an irritated grumble. She knew precisely when
Nicholas was done. He slammed his hand on the mantel
with a thud that could have been heard outside.

"If I want a nursemaid for Jeannette, I will hire one."

Eavin was relieved that he came no closer. She continued staring out at the growing darkness. Now that the
trees were covered with leaves, she could no longer see
the river from this window. But she could almost see
Nicholas's reflection against the shadow of the trees.

"If you need someone to attend social functions with
you, hire Mignon Dubois," she retorted sarcastically.

"It is just such escort service that I wish to avoid. If
Mignon and her ilk know that you will be attending with
me, they will not press me into service."

Eavin swung around and glared at him, letting the
drapery drop. "Do you tell me that the great Nicholas
Saint-Just needs a woman to shield him?"

He crumpled one of the papers in his hand as he
stepped closer. "I am saying that I appreciate the conve-
nience of your presence."

"Even at the cost of pain to myself and others?" she
demanded, not backing away from his advance.

Nicholas flung the paper aside. "You said you had no

feeling for Jeremy. You told me to send him away. Are you telling me now that you regret it?"

"I am telling you that I will come to regret it. I am telling you that I am not suitable to the life you would have me lead. I am telling you that it hurts me to know that I cannot be what men expect me to be. Why won't you listen to my side of the story for a change?"

"Because it is garbage!" Nicholas flung his hand up and released the rest of the papers in a whirlwind that spun and fluttered and fell to the floor. He could read the defiance in her face, but he resisted the urge to reach out and strangle her. Strangling wasn't what he really had in mind. What he had in mind was the same thing that had been on his mind for quite some time now. It would be better if he had it over and done with.

"I will find you a husband," he stated flatly, staring down at her, daring her to defy him.

"That won't solve the problem." Eavin crossed her arms beneath her breasts and regretted it instantly. She knew at once when the focus of Nicholas's attention shifted.

"I don't see the problem. You have come out of your dowdy clothes and no one has molested you. You have been kissed and you haven't resisted. Unless Dominic or someone else was given to beating you, I cannot see what you fear. It is all in your head."

That wasn't the problem Eavin had referred to, but it was the underlying source of everything else. Leave it to Nicholas to go to the heart of the matter. Still, she couldn't let him see he had struck so close. "I am talking about the gossip. Buying me a husband won't halt the gossip. They will forget I exist if I stay in the nursery. Escort Mignon to these functions and the gossip will stop."

"No, it won't. And that is the garbage to which I refer. It isn't the gossip bothering you. It isn't my reputation bothering you. It's Jeremy. And Alphonso. And Clyde Brown. You're afraid of them. You're hiding behind your pretense of coldness. Hell, you're the least cold woman I've ever known. You've got a temper like a firestorm, and I venture to say a passion to match. Ladies like Francine and Lucinda are the cold ones. They have talked themselves into believing that lust is for animals, which consigns all men to being animals, I suppose. But you're not like that. I can touch you, and you ignite in a blaze. You don't turn your nose up in disgust."

"I do not," Eavin whispered defensively, knowing the argument was degenerating rapidly as it always did. "I don't like it when men touch me. I didn't like it when Dominic touched me, and he was my husband. And this argument is senseless. What difference does it make whether I want to be touched? The only purpose to marriage is to have children, and we both know that I can't."

"Everybody wants to be touched. It's human nature. Why do you think you hold Jeannette and caress her? Because she loves it and so do you. Life is empty without someone to share it. It doesn't have to be Jeremy or Clyde. Someone else will come along, but you'll never know it if you're hiding away in your room."

Tears sprang to Eavin's eyes as she tried to avoid his. "Nicholas, why can you not just take my word for it? Don't you think I'm old enough to know myself?"

Nicholas reached out and buried his hand in the thickness of Eavin's upswept tresses. She shivered beneath his touch, but he didn't believe she was afraid of him. Still, he pressed no further. "Let's experiment," he found himself saying.

Eavin held herself still and turned her head toward him warily. He wasn't laughing. Neither did he seem to be angry. There was a look of curiosity on his face, and something else. She supposed it was mischief, or lust. She wasn't certain, but it was much less fearful than anger. She offered a watery smile in return.

"Experiment? Like dropping a feather and a stone from the roof to see which lands first?"

"That sounds amusing, too, but it isn't what I had in mind. An experiment is designed to test a hypothesis." Nicholas released her hair and stepped backward, placing his hands behind his back as he observed her reaction.

Eavin surreptitiously wiped a tear from her eye and stood straighter, folding her hands in front of her and regarding him with expectation. Nicholas like this was a fascinating man. She had heard him expound upon the politics of the embargo and Napoleon, extol the merits of the cotton gin and the shift in production that would result, and denounce the system of slavery that would inevitably come of it. She waited now to be enlightened by the lecture on experimentation.

Satisfied with this reaction, Nicholas chose his words carefully, knowing his audience well. Eavin had been raised simply, her only concern the day-to-day matters of surviving. Although he had found her extremely intelligent and ready to grasp the most complex of topics, she was not accustomed to the convolutions of logic and philosophy that permeated the arguments of better-educated men. Had he asked her how many angels could dance on the head of a pin, she would have handed him a pin and told him to count them. So he eliminated all but the simplest of explanations.

"My experience tells me that: one, ladies of my class on the whole have been taught sex is only a distasteful means of procreation, and two, that women of other classes have been taught a more earthy appreciation of the attractions between men and women. You do nothing to disguise the fact that you are from a working-class Irish family who cannot claim any closer association with ladies than working for one. Therefore, I must conclude that you find yourself not suitable for marriage to someone of my class because you are not a lady, not because you are cold. My hypothesis is that you are perfectly capable of enjoying the marriage act, but for some reason you are afraid of it, and you are disguising your fear behind protestations of unsuitability."

Eavin wrinkled her nose up in concentration as she tried to follow this exercise in logic. "Not being a lady didn't keep me from marrying Dominic," she finally responded, not knowing where else to take the argument.

So much for the principles of logic. Nicholas threw in the towel and went straight to the point. "Being afraid of sex is keeping you from marrying anyone else."

Eavin stiffened and primly drew her lips tight. "I am not afraid. I simply do not like it."

"If you're not a lady, that's poppycock. You've just never been taught what making love is all about."

He stood there with his hands behind his back, the lamplight catching the golden strands of his hair, exuding male superiority. He had not thrown aside his coat yet, but it hung loose and unfastened from his wide shoulders as he waited confidently for her to fall into his trap.

Eavin's gaze fell on the opened collar of his shirt, and she had the urge to grab his cravat and strangle him with it. But that wasn't the only urge she was experiencing.

"You are an arrogant bastard," she whispered, almost to herself.

"But I'm right." Nicholas reached out to lift her chin until their gazes met. "Let me prove it."

16

Eavin stared at Nicholas as if he had just proposed that they rob a bank. The stark light emphasized the aristocratic hollows of his features, the elegant lines of his masculine frame, the intelligence gleaming behind his amber eyes. She couldn't think of a single reason in the world why he would make what she knew was a highly improper suggestion. He had everything. She had nothing. Why would he bother?

"You are making mock of me," she finally responded, twisting her chin from his grasp.

"I am not." Nicholas didn't touch her again but positioned himself so Eavin could not easily escape. "I am being perfectly sensible. We can look at this as a purely scientific exercise to prove my theory. That's all it has to be. No more, no less."

He was still speaking in the crisp tones of logic, and Eavin's mercurial temperament couldn't resist seeing the humor of the situation. "If I prove as cold as I think I am, will that make me a lady and suitable to marry one of your friends?"

Nicholas's mouth twisted upward on one side. "Alphonso perhaps? Reyes would be overwhelmed with my generosity."

"That's mean." Relieved that he was not taking this any more seriously than she, Eavin shoved Nicholas aside and escaped, grateful that he did not press her further. "Alphonso may be a trifle serious, but he is a gracious gentleman. Just because you and his brother never got along is no reason to single him out for your contempt."

Nicholas caught her arm before she could retreat to the door. "You're running away, Eavin. I know what it is to run away. Don't do it. Stand up to your fears and make them go away. You're only living half a life until you do."

Eavin jerked her arm free and glared at him. "I won't be your mistress, Nicholas. If that's the price of my staying here, I'll leave."

He ran his hand through his hair and offered a wry grin. "I'll admit, the proposition is tempting. There are damned few opportunities out here without causing tongues to wag all over the district, and it's been a long drought since I sent Jess packing. But you're right. As convenient as it might be in some ways, it would be suicide in others. I'm just talking one night, Eavin, one night to prove you have what it takes to be happy."

"That's ridiculous." Leaning over the table, she cornered him. "What would you get out of such an arrangement?"

Nicholas shoved his hands into his pockets and deliberately surveyed Eavin's lush figure from head to toe and back again. "Besides the obvious?" he asked arrogantly. Before she could throw the book her hand rested on at him, he added, "Proof of my theory. I like being right."

"You want to prove that I'm a whore because I'm Irish," she stated.

He winced. *"Touché.* You have a wicked tongue, Irish. If you applied it to pen, we would all be sliced to ribbons. But that isn't what I meant. Whores sell their wares but don't necessarily enjoy them. You have no need to sell anything."

"Thank you, then I shan't." Swirling around, Eavin marched out of the room before either of them could observe out loud that she had sold herself to Dominic. There was such a thing as too much honesty, and they were bordering dangerously near to it.

But Nicholas's words stayed with Eavin all the night. She swore at the closed windows and stuffy air as she tossed and turned in her cocoon of mosquito netting. She got up and opened the windows despite all the warnings she had received of the deadliness of the swamp miasmas. She returned to bed and kicked off the sheets, but the cool linen of her nightgown still twisted about her legs and stuck to her breasts until she was tempted to toss it aside, too. But the thought of lying naked in this bed that in all reality belonged to the man below kept her from any such freedom.

She didn't want to imagine Nicholas doing to her what Dominic had done in those few uncomfortable attempts in Baltimore. In the darkness her mind's eye strayed to her wedding night. She had tried to be calm when Dominic led her to the room she would share with him. He had kissed her before, and she had enjoyed it much more than the usual pawing caresses she had received in the past. Dominic was a gentleman. Eavin relied on that fact to bolster her confidence as he turned her into his arms as soon as the door was shut.

Her confidence faltered as soon as she realized this kiss wasn't going to be like his others. His teeth pressed against hers with urgent heat while his hand came up to twist her breast. When she opened her mouth to protest, he plunged his tongue down her throat, and Eavin could do little more than gag.

Even her mind's eye went blank when confronted with the rest of the scene. Only glimpses of those horrible minutes flashed through the curtain of time: Dominic pushing her back toward the bed, his hips already grinding against hers; the feeling of her skirt being jerked around her waist; the piercing pain and Dominic's cry of relief. Eavin stared at the canopy of netting over her head much as she had done those nights long ago when Dominic had repeated that performance time after time.

The pain had never quite gone away, as she had been led to expect. She had just endured it as the price of respectability and sighed in relief when Dominic finally sailed with his ship. The nuns had been quite right in teaching her that such things were best saved for marriage and only then when a child was wanted. The prospect of a child was the only reason Eavin would endure such an activity again, and that prospect didn't exist any longer. Why should she believe that with Nicholas things could be different?

But Nicholas made it so easy to believe. Just looking at him made her want to believe. He was the golden god every young girl believed in. She was too experienced to put her faith in white knights, and Nicholas would certainly never qualify for that designation, but just the fact that he was as human as she made it so much easier to believe in him. But she couldn't go any further than wishful thinking. Eavin knew the reality behind little-girl dreams of life after marriage.

When she finally fell into a restless slumber, her mind drew on the images left by Nicholas's brief kiss, twisting that one incident she had blocked from her memory into terrifying proportions, combining it with other, less pleasant, incidents, until she woke up, wide-eyed and sweating.

It was a terrible state to be in. She couldn't even get up and pace the room without taking the netting with her or closing out the first cool breezes of dawn. Other people had nightmares about floods and fires and disease. She had nightmares about kissing. She really was quite insane.

She couldn't differentiate between the groping hands of Nicholas and Dominic and the countless other men before them. She knew there were differences. Nicholas had been forceful, abrupt, and passionate. Dominic had been gentle but selfish. The others she wouldn't even think of. She still had mental images of the first man she had seen stumbling out of her mother's room. She had been little more than twelve but already developing a figure. He had still smelled of sex when he had twisted her tender breasts and slobbered over her lips. The shriek she had emitted then lingered on her tongue now.

Face her fears, he had said. Eavin made a disgruntled noise as she sat up in bed and refused to return to her nightmares. She faced her fears every day of her life. Her fears constituted half the population of the world.

She wondered what fears Nicholas could possibly have run away from. He didn't strike her as the sort to ever be afraid of anything. But he had to have been young once. She understood his childhood hadn't been a great deal better than hers. It was ironic that they could both come from poor and essentially dishonest backgrounds, but his French family and education made him an aristocrat while her Irish name and religious upbringing made her a servant.

But she wasn't a servant. She was in a brand-new country where the men outnumbered the women and the differences between the classes began to blur. Black slaves were servants here. She wasn't a slave, and she wasn't French, but she was something in between, something just as valuable as anyone else. She had to remember that. Nicholas might poke fun at her accent, but he treated her as an equal. He did it for Jeannette's sake, but that was enough. She could raise herself up as high as she wished to go if she wanted to bad enough.

The question was how high did she wish to go?

When dawn filled the room with light, Eavin leapt from the bed and began to dress. She didn't have to be just a nanny. She could be Jeannette's aunt and a valuable member of the community, once she figured out what a valuable member of the community did. Most women she knew were married or had been married and had homes of their own. They ran their households for their husbands and children, helped in the church societies, and entertained. Being a dependent relative, she could only do one of the three, but that was a start.

Eavin was surprised to find Nicholas already at the breakfast table. He usually kept later hours than she, but she made no comment as he looked up from his newspaper and greeted her calmly. It had to be yesterday's paper he was reading. Perhaps he hadn't had time to finish it last night.

Michael entered with a sheet of paper covered with numbers, and Eavin realized she was intruding on an impending business discussion. Picking up the cup of tea she had just poured, she started to beat a hasty retreat when Nicholas gestured her back to her seat.

"Don't let us interrupt. I just asked Michael to have breakfast with us before he runs off to the city."

Michael winked at his sister and helped himself to half a dozen *beignets* as he slid into his seat. "Want to go with me, colleen? I'll show you a side to New Orleans I bet this toplofty fellow hasn't shown you."

"I can imagine." As usual, Michael's presence both reassured and irritated Eavin. "You'd be much better off if you wouldn't do anything I wouldn't do."

Michael grinned. "The next time I look down and find I've become a woman, I'll remember that. Until then you'll have to let me be what I am."

"A stag in rut." Eavin smeared butter on her roll and ignored the rustle of paper and choking sound from the man at the head of the table.

Before Michael could retort, Nicholas threw his folded paper in Eavin's direction. "Now, children, behave," he admonished with a look that silenced Michael's tongue though not his grin. Turning to Eavin, Nicholas pointed at an article near the bottom of the page. "Since you've proved so good with arguing by pen, why don't you turn your talent on this idiot?"

Eavin thoughtfully chewed her roll as she scanned the article while the two men discussed the numbers Michael had produced. The newspaper was the American one that Nicholas had introduced to her, but the writer was obviously French and rebutting some earlier story. He was scathing in his denouncement of the uncouth Americans who would turn New Orleans into a giant marketplace and the theater into a pigsty. He went on to declare that Louisiana should secede from the Union and pledge allegiance to France now that Napoleon had abdicated. Why should New Orleans suffer the plague of war with England when France had settled its differences?

Eavin wasn't certain why Nicholas had given the article to her. She had never been to the theater, but she saw nothing wrong with opening more marketplaces. Would the merchants of New Orleans prefer to starve and go naked? Seceding from the Union was so much balderdash. She had seen enough of that kind of cry in Baltimore, only then it had been the New England states crying the same thing when Louisiana had been admitted as a slave state. Men were behaving like petulant children who refused to play when they couldn't get their own way.

That thought brought a sudden gleam to Eavin's eye. French Louisiana would be the snobbish little brat who wouldn't play with the others because she might get her hands dirty. The New England states resembled querulous brothers constantly bickering and kicking and fighting with one another, while ganging up on everyone else. Virginia—well, Virginia would have to be the older child who smiled smugly on the antics of the younger children while dabbling dangerously in waters too deep for her to swim in.

The possibilities were amusing. Eavin could see them coming to life now, and her fingers itched for an excuse to hold a pen. She scarcely noticed when Michael pecked her cheek in farewell, and Nicholas had to remove the paper from her hand when he tried to address her before she would respond.

"Well? What do you think? Can you argue with the man?"

Still lost in her thoughts, Eavin returned to reality only gradually, focusing on his voice before the question. When his words finally registered, she stared at Nicholas without comprehension. "Why should I? Who would care what I thought?"

"The same people who care what that idiot thinks. They don't print names, so you needn't worry about that. I haven't got time to answer the fool, or I would. I thought it might amuse you. Besides, the paper will pay for an article. You can add the coins to that little store under your mattress."

"I don't keep money under my mattress," Eavin replied frostily. "Any thief would know to look there."

Nicholas grinned. "But you're hiding it somewhere, aren't you? I never see you spend any of the money I give you. Do you think I'm going to throw you out on the street without a cent someday?"

Eavin primly removed a crumb stuck to the upper curve of her bodice, deciding she resembled a pouter pigeon in gray, before deigning to answer Nicholas's nonsensical question. "It's been known to happen. Or you could gamble everything away or lost it all in a flood, and I would be no better off than before. I'll not take that chance, thank you."

"I won't, you know." Serious now, Nicholas rose from the table. "But you're entitled to do as you will. I'd recommend putting the coins in a bank, though. They're not going to do you much good under the Mississippi if a flood is what you fear."

"Men run banks," she informed him calmly.

"So they do, but all men love wealthy widows. I will introduce you to some when we return to New Orleans." Without warning, Nicholas bent and placed a peck on her cheek in the identical place that Michael had earlier, then striding out on long legs, left Eavin to hold her reddened face in peace.

She was having difficulty keeping the rambunctious Kentucky child out of her elder sister Virginia's problems. Eavin was quite certain that this wasn't the kind of article that Nicholas had in mind when he had suggested that she write, but she didn't care a fig for his opinion. If she could earn coins from a newspaper article, it might as well be for one she wanted to write, and one that gave her great pleasure. From her observations, these New Orleans newspapers preferred trivia to news in any case.

She hated to set her pen aside when Clemmie announced she had a caller, but neighbors were so far and few that she couldn't refuse to greet one. Wiping her hands off on a rag she kept to clean up ink, Eavin hurried out to the hallway.

Hat in hand, Alphonso Reyes waited patiently for her appearance. Although he was not tall, his slenderness gave that appearance. His solemn dark features broke into a tentative smile at Eavin's greeting, and he made a courtly bow that left no strand of his ebony hair out of place. Eavin was quite certain that Nicholas would come up looking like a lion should he ever bend so low, but then, she couldn't see him bending that low for anyone. She held out her hand, and Alphonso immediately brought it to his lips to kiss it.

That particular habit of his disturbed her, but Eavin tried to be polite about it. She was a stranger in a foreign land, and she must get used to the local customs. "It's good to see you, Alphonso. Won't you come in the salon? I'll have Clemmie bring you something cool to drink. I'm sure the heat outside must be most oppressive."

Alphonso obediently followed her into the *petite salle,* but his concentration was evidently set on one object, and he ignored any distraction. "I have come to ask you to accompany me to the Howells' ball next week. It would give me great pleasure if you would say yes."

Startled by the intensity of his tone, Eavin evaded an immediate response by taking a seat. She was vaguely irritated that Alphonso did not follow suit, but she could understand nervousness. What she didn't understand was why he should be nervous with her.

"I am flattered, Alphonso, but I can't think that your father would approve. There are enough hard feelings between Nicholas and Señor Reyes without searching for ways to create more. Please sit, and let us just talk about pleasant things."

Alphonso obstinately remained standing, looming over her with what she could only identify as a noble Spanish frown.

"Nicholas should have no claim on what you do. I would halt these rumors now, before your reputation is irrevocably damaged."

Perhaps she should be flattered that he sought to protect her, but she didn't place much trust in the idea of male protection. She folded her hands in her lap and sought to remain polite. "What rumors, may I ask?" The Howells had dutifully informed her of the ridiculous slanders concerning Nicholas and Francine, and even Jeannette. One of the benefits of taking Jeannette to New Orleans had been to disprove the theory that Nicholas had murdered the child. But accompanying Alphonso anywhere wouldn't prove anything that she knew of.

Alphonso's face darkened. "You live here unchaperoned with a man of destructive nature. It is only natural that gossip should pair your name with his. I wish to put an end to such tales."

Eavin smiled wryly, remembering the prior night's argument. "That is generous of you, sir, but not necessary. Your intentions could only do more harm than good. If you truly wished to be helpful, you would find some way to reconcile your father and Nicholas, but I suppose only a saint could grant that."

A small smile glimmered at the edge of his thin lips. "Thank you for recognizing that I am no saint. Neither am I my brother. You will be safe in my company."

"Your father would come after me with a sword if I accompanied you. I have no name, no title, and no wealth, and I'm quite certain that's what your family intends for their remaining son—unless Raphael has returned from wherever he has disappeared?"

Alphonso sank onto the chair beside her and played with the edge of his hat. "It is true that they expect me to take his place, but I cannot. There is a betrothal contract binding Raphael to the daughter of a noble house in Spain. My father wishes me to stand in his stead, but I am not Raphael. I do not need title or wealth. I never expected either. I thought to be a priest until this happened with Raphael. I will acknowledge that it is now my duty to carry on the family name unless my brother returns, but I cannot go to Spain to find my future. I wish to remain here."

Eavin reached over to touch his hand in sympathy. "Families can sometimes make life difficult, but they only want what is best for us. It is just that we often disagree on what is best."

Alphonso's hand closed eagerly around hers, and he looked up as if ready to make some confession, but a movement in the doorway brought him to a frozen halt.

"How very touching. Alphonso, I suggest you leave before your father finds out where you are. I have a reputation to keep up, and it doesn't include dueling with children and old men."

"Nicholas!" Infuriated at this treatment of a gentle boy, Eavin jumped up, ready to do combat. "You have no right to insult my guests."

Alphonso rose with her and made a stiff nod to his host. "I did not think I had done anything to offend you. Pardon my misunderstanding if the rumors I have heard of you and Mrs. Dupré are true."

"Alphonso!" Now thoroughly outraged, Eavin swung around to confront this betrayal.

"Leave him alone, Eavin. He's only spewing the poison his father has fed him. You will know your real friends by the trust they have in you." Nicholas strode into the room carrying the scent of the horse he had just dismounted, his hair tangled and blown from the wind. Next to Alphonso's elegant slenderness, Nicholas appeared almost bestial, but his voice held the dangerously cool tones of an aristocrat.

"Then if there is naught between you, there is no reason Mrs. Dupré cannot accompany me to the Howells' ball," Alphonso stated emphatically, meeting his antagonist's gaze and ignoring the growing ire of the woman beside him.

"Sure, and there damned well is!" Eavin exploded. "I'm the reason I will not accompany you to the ball. Remember me? While the two of you glare daggers at each other, I shall be in the nursery. Let me know when you decide to be humans again."

Nicholas imagined he heard the rustle of ruffled feathers as Eavin flew by, but he made no attempt to stop her. He had nothing against Alphonso, but the treachery of the man's father could lead to anything, and he would have Eavin out of the way of it. When she was gone, he asked sardonically, "Does that mean she thinks we're animals?"

Alphonso's glare was still suspicious, but the tension in his clenched fists relaxed a degree. "I do not understand women well, but I think you are correct. Do all American women swear?"

"Women everywhere swear, just most of them try not to let us know it. I'll take you up to the nursery if you'd like, but she won't go to the ball with you. I have to twist her arm and hold a knife to her back to make her come with me."

Alphonso's frown deepened until he realized Nicholas was speaking metaphorically. "I do not understand. I thought women liked dancing."

Nicholas shrugged. "She likes dancing. She hates men."

Alphonso's eyebrows raised. "But she is so easy to . . . how you say it? To be with? To get to know? None of the other ladies are the same."

Nicholas grinned and leaned his shoulder against the door jamb. "You're right there, but that's no doubt because she was raised in a house full of men. All the more reason to hate them, I suspect. I'd recommend you go slowly with the Widow Dupré, *señor*. She's not at all what you think."

"But you will let me see her," Alphonso responded sternly, drawing himself up in defiance.

Nicholas backed from the doorway and swung his hand in the direction of the stairs. "Anytime you wish, my friend. Just make certain the lady wishes to see you."

Considering the temper in which she departed, Alphonso gave that some consideration. "Perhaps another time. Even in my family it is wisest not to speak to the women when they are . . . indisposed."

Upstairs, Eavin heard Nicholas's laugh, followed by the slamming of the door. One more suitor bites the dust, she decided gloomily as she changed Jeannette's diaper. Who said she was afraid of men? She only meant to drive them all away.

17

Lifting Jeannette to her shoulder, Eavin felt a prickle at the back of her neck that warned of someone watching. Steeling herself, she swung around to find Nicholas in a characteristic pose, leaning against the wall, arms crossed over his chest. When she had arrived here little more than a year ago, she had thought him an enigmatic stranger she would never understand. Now she was beginning to understand him a little too well. He was waiting for her to speak.

When she did, it wasn't anything she had planned to say.

"Do you still wish to test your theory?"

Nicholas watched through half-lowered eyes as he contemplated the woman garbed in drab gray holding the dark-haired infant over her shoulder. She had her hair pinned tightly against her head as always, but a few recalcitrant strands had escaped to soften the image. Despite Eavin's severe hairdo, there was nothing prim about the fullness of her mouth or the wide slant and sparkle of her black-lashed eyes. And if he allowed his gaze to fall lower, Nicholas knew he would find the full curve of a bosom meant for a man's caress. Since Francine's child had momentarily appropriated that tempting spot, he resisted the urge to investigate the folds of gray more closely.

"I do. I am ready anytime you are."

His tone was almost insolent, but Eavin was beyond blushing innocence. She would prove to him and to herself that she was incapable of finding anything pleasurable in a man's company, and that would be the end of the discussion. She had to know for certain that she was casting aside the possibility of the kind of life every woman craved with good reason. If she could find no pleasure with Nicholas, she could find it with no man.

When she didn't reply but continued staring at him as if he were a slug on a plate, Nicholas offered a self-deprecatory smile. "Would you prefer someone else, or will I be acceptable? Say, tonight after dinner?"

Jeannette struggled to get down, and Eavin bent to let her loose on the floor. The infant crowed, and with wobbly steps, she began a path toward her father. Eavin straightened and watched as Nicholas crouched down and held out his arms for the infant to catch.

"You are the expert," she said dryly, watching as Jeannette readily grabbed his strong hands and eagerly went into his arms. "I will leave the details to you."

The child still carried the scent of the woman who had held her, not the usual cloyingly sweet perfumes of the South, but a fresh, crisp scent that reminded Nicholas of pine forests. He snuggled Jeannette against his chest, kissed her neck until she giggled with glee, then released her to toddle about the room. Eavin had given him this child as surely as Francine had. He almost had the urge to bungle the lesson he meant to give her so she would be convinced she was meant to be the nun she pretended to be and remain here. But that would be an unfair payment for what she had done for him.

Nicholas looked up, and without smiling, replied, "Tonight, then."

Eavin nervously touched a hand to her hair and then straightened the folds of the rich emerald green of her gown for the hundredth time as she advanced before Nicholas into the parlor after the evening meal. The servants would be cleaning up, and she and Nicholas continued to behave as if this were any evening when they would retire to the salon to talk and read and sew.

But this wasn't just any night. Even Nicholas had dressed carefully. The frills on his shirt and cuffs were immaculate, without any sign that he had been down to the stable or out on the levee with one of the men, as he had often done before an evening out. His cravat still remained tied, and his exquisitely embroidered white-on-white waistcoat was fastened. He looked every inch the gentleman tonight, and more distant from her than ever.

As the salon door closed behind them, Eavin jumped, and Nicholas touched a hand to the wisps of hair at her nape.

"I only eat naughty little girls. Stop behaving as if I'm an ogre, Eavin, or I will be forced to send you to Clyde Brown for your lessons."

Eavin winced. If she thought of any of the men around here as a potential suitor, it was Clyde Brown. She had more in common with him than with these elegant gentlemen with their stiff manners and arrogant tempers. But why should she settle for the local lawman if she could truly be made to feel like other women? If marriage was the only occupation suitable for a woman, then she ought to make the best marriage possible, for Jeannette's sake as well as her own. She could give Jeannette a wealthy uncle to protect her against the whims of fate and Nicholas.

Building up her courage, Eavin turned around to face him. Nicholas was a head taller than she, and she had to look up to meet his eyes. "You don't have to go through with this. We can dismiss it as a jest and go on as before."

"You really don't have any idea at all what a man sees when he looks at you, do you?" Looking down at her now, with the lamplight dancing over her hair and sending shivering shadows down the cleft between her breasts, Nicholas had difficulty keeping his hands to himself. It seemed extraordinary that a woman with as much to offer as Eavin could not be aware of her charms. But he knew it was not that she wasn't aware of her charms, but that she thought them disadvantages, that gave her this lack of vanity.

Her gaze fell to the folds of his cravat. "I have the same assets as any other woman, I suppose."

"And a little something extra, something not so easily defined as the beauty of your hair or the purity of your skin or the loveliness of your figure. It's as if you have some perfume that draws men to you like bees to honey. We can't resist looking, touching. Not all women have it, Eavin. Some women have it only for a few men. Some women use it to their advantage. But you seem so totally unaware of your power that we succumb before we know what is happening. You're a dangerous lady. Even you should be aware of that by now."

"That is very lovely, Nicholas"—Eavin's lips formed a wry moue as she cupped her hands beneath her breasts—"but even I know this is what men see in me, nothing more. Please don't treat me as a complete innocent."

Nicholas caught his breath as she practically offered herself to him, and he gave a shaky laugh as his hand reached to cover hers, resting where he had imagined it more than once. "If blunt is the way you prefer it, then yes, perhaps this is what we see first." He grasped her hand firmly between his fingers and pulled it away from herself and to the crotch of his trousers. "But unless you are in the habit of judging all men by what you see here, you must understand that there are other factors involved."

The heat of him shocked her, and as if burned, Eavin jerked her hand away. She hadn't thought she was capable of blushing, but she could feel the warmth rise in her cheeks as she forced herself to look away from where he had forced her attention and upward to meet his eyes. "I should have known you would not hide behind gallant flattery."

"You are very perceptive." Before she had time to retreat, while the heat of awareness still flushed her face, Nicholas brought his mouth down to meet hers and captured her in his arms.

Eavin stiffened, but when he did no more than ply her lips with gentle kisses, she relaxed and tentatively allowed her hands to creep around the breadth of his back. His kiss deepened, and she could feel the flick of his tongue along the line of her lips. Something inside her stirred, something she had always denied and fought against, fearing the damnation to which it would lead. But she was determined to explore its depths this one night. For one night she would try to understand what it was that made women like her mother go to men, and then she would never have to wonder again.

Nicholas gasped with the sudden heat of desire exploding through him when Eavin finally relented and opened her mouth against his. It had been too long since he'd had a woman like this. With Jess it had just been a brief carnal release with none of the caresses, none of the aware-

ness of two individual people coming together for the
pleasure they found in each other. He had touched no
other lady after marrying Francine, not even Francine. At
the time, it had seemed the noble thing to do, but it had
been a long drought, and he was thirstier than he had
been aware. He gulped like a dying man at the sweetness
she held up to him.

Spreading his legs slightly to brace himself, Nicholas
pulled Eavin closer into his embrace, crushing her to him
so she could have no doubt as to the outcome of this evening. She resisted at first, but there was a fire in her kiss
that needed quenching as much as his did. It had been an
even longer drought for her, Nicholas surmised when she
finally pressed against him, her hips already seeking his.
The thought that he would be the first man to teach her
the secrets of her body increased his excitement. Un-
charted waters had always excited him.

Eavin was aware that she was crumpling the pleated
frill of Nicholas's shirt as first she tried to push away,
then grabbed it for support as her legs seemed to give out
beneath Nicholas's devouring kiss. She had never thought
it would come to this. She had never dreamed of clinging
to this man's shirt as his tongue and lips claimed un-
speakable intimacies, and she met and welcomed his every thrust. Her mind was whirling, unable to register what
the rest of her was doing. She felt as a drunk must do after too much brandy, and briefly she wondered if he'd
given her too much wine at dinner.

Nicholas's kiss wandered to Eavin's cheek and upward,
finding her ear and caressing it gravely while he gave her
time to compose herself. His hand slid between them to
lightly trace the curve of her breast as he whispered
against her ear, "If we continue like this, I'll take you
right here on the floor. Do you think they're done in the
other room? I want to see you naked in my bed."

He had taken her request for bluntness seriously. Eavin
twisted her head up to meet his eyes with a measure of
alarm, but the heat of desire she read there made her
quiver with something more than fear. She wanted to call
this all off, to tell him it was a mistake, that she wanted
to live forever as his daughter's spinster aunt, but she
couldn't speak if she tried.

Nicholas regarded her wide-eyed alarm wryly, then

bent to warm her with a lingering kiss that brought her shuddering back into his embrace again. He briefly contemplated taking her here, on the rug in the room where they had spent so many nights together, but if he were to have only this one night, he wished it to be as close to perfection as he could make it. Once freed of this obsession and the memory of Francine, he could take himself into New Orleans and indulge himself as he liked. Tonight he would do things properly.

Deciding to risk the observation of lingering servants, Nicholas caught Eavin by the waist and led her toward the door leading onto the gallery. There was less chance of anyone seeing them in the dark outside than in the lighted hallway of the house.

Sweetened by the orange scent of magnolias, the musky air of a May night engulfed them as they hurried down the moonlit gallery toward the doorway of the master suite. It was here that Francine had died and Jeannette had been born. The house was tainted with memories, but the moonlight bathed them clean.

Nicholas threw open one of the double doors and pushed Eavin through before either one of them could change their minds. When she turned to protest, he caught her up in his arms and, kicking the door shut, proceeded to quiet her with his kisses.

Eavin succumbed willingly, greedily wrapping her arms around Nicholas's neck and drawing his head down so she could taste more fully the passion he had taught her earlier. She was barely aware of her surroundings, of the draped windows and delicate chairs mixed with the towering heaviness of old wardrobes and masculine accouterments silhouetted in the moon's light. She only knew the silky texture of his hair, the crush of a hard male body beneath satin and silk, and the intoxicating battle of their mouths as his tongue plunged between her teeth.

Her gown suddenly gaped open at the back, and the tiny bodice fell forward, but the fragile chemise beneath protected her from the actual touch of Nicholas's hands. Eavin felt the caress of warm palms as they slid up and down her spine, slipped briefly lower, then rose slowly to span her waist. Her light corset kept her from feeling his touch, and she breathed easier as she felt the rest of her gown fall downward beneath his persistent pull. She was still securely covered. There was still time to retreat.

"Your hair. I want to see your hair down." Stepping back, Nicholas jerked a drapery to cover the door, then fumbled in the darkness for flints to light a candle. When the room flickered into view, he turned to find Eavin with her hands buried in her hair, searching for the pins. The sight of her there in thin chemise and corset, her breasts arched as if for his touch, nearly took his breath away.

Nicholas knew then that one night would never be enough, but he didn't tell that to the woman quaking before his lust, obediently releasing her hair at his command. She was still worried and uncertain, but she was courageously keeping to the letter of their agreement. He wouldn't disillusion her just yet.

"Allow me." Nicholas drew the pins from her hands and found the rest in the abundant ebony masses. Carefully setting the pins aside, he drew the thick curls down over her shoulders, spreading them across her arms and breasts in a curtain of silk.

"Turn around," he ordered, and she did, although her eyes were wide and questioning as she did so. His fingers had the corset unlaced and on the floor before Eavin knew what was happening, and his hands grazed unfettered up and down her sides, testing the smallness of her waist and the full curve of her hip. As he had suspected, she had no need of artificial contraptions to produce her womanly curves.

Nicholas impatiently threw off his coat and was working on his waistcoat before Eavin had the courage to turn around and face him again. She was working worriedly at her lower lip as her gaze went to his activities and her hands rose to cover her chemise-protected breasts.

"Don't," Nicholas warned as he flung his waistcoat to join the other. He could see the protest forming on her lips, and he hurriedly pressed a kiss there before she could speak. "Don't say a word," he whispered against her lips as his hands captured her waist. "Don't think. Don't do anything but what your body tells you. Let me do all the work."

He made it so very easy to agree. She didn't have to do anything but let his hands and lips work their magic. She didn't have to worry about whether she ought to wear a nightgown or not, whether she ought to climb in bed first or wait for him to take her, whether to touch him or just allow him to do as he willed until he was done. She didn't have to worry about whether she was doing the right thing, if he would find her displeasing, if he would blame her if he couldn't find his release. None of that mattered. All she had to do was fold her arms around his shoulders and glide off into a hazy world of his creation.

Eavin was aware when Nicholas carried her off to the bedroom. The heat of his powerful arm circling her thighs set off alarming sensations that she couldn't ignore. He lowered her to the turned-back sheets, and she found herself gazing up into the canopy that must have been the last thing Francine had seen before she died. But the knowledge that Nicholas was standing beside the bed, ripping off his shirt, distracted her from that morbid thought. She couldn't help staring as the shirt fell away to reveal the man beneath.

The candle in the other room gave only enough light to silhouette the width of his shoulders and the narrowness of his waist and hips, but Eavin clearly remembered the ridges of muscle and the light golden hairs forming a V from chest to navel. Her breath stopped in her lungs as he reached for the fastenings of his trousers.

Nicholas knew instantly when Eavin averted her face, and he stopped what he was doing to fall down on the bed beside her, cupping her chin and turning her face back to him so he could smother it with kisses. The warmth and softness of her curved so perfectly into his arms that he had difficulty remembering that the feeling might not be mutual.

Cursing the distraction of having to remove their various articles of clothing, Nicholas waited until he felt Eavin's excitement building again before sitting up and stating calmly, "I want to see you with your clothes off."

He saw the panic leap to her eyes, but with almost a gleam of mischief, he reached for her foot instead of her chemise.

Eavin scrambled to sit up and help him unlace the ribbons of her soft shoes, but Nicholas wouldn't let her touch her stockings. Gently he rolled them down one at a time, his hands circling her legs and pushing downward while he watched her face. He wasn't even looking at her legs but at her expression as he produced incredible sensations tingling up and down her limbs. When his hand cradled her foot in his palm, she nearly melted with the desire to have that hand do the same thing to the rest of her.

Then his hands were no longer safely on her foot but riding higher, stroking, caressing, learning, and possessing every inch of her skin as they moved inexorably upward. Eavin kept her gaze fixed on his and didn't stop him.

"Take the chemise off, Eavin," Nicholas murmured, his hand tugging the last remaining piece of fabric upward.

As if caught in a spell, Eavin did as told, lifting her hips with his aid until the garment slid over her shoulders and head and floated to the floor.

The light was too dim for him to discern much, and Eavin didn't feel the fear she had expected when Nicholas finally reached out to cup her breast. The sensation was gentle, loving, and not at all the hasty grabs and tugs she had experienced before. When he leaned forward to kiss her, she went into his embrace with an eagerness that surprised herself.

"You were made to be loved like this," Nicholas whispered as he laid her back against the pillows and leaned over her.

His hand continued its gentle explorations, circling, caressing, pressing into her until Eavin could scarcely heed his words. Breathlessly she met his kisses until the moment his fingers finally eased the ache of her nipple and her cry of relief was swallowed by his mouth.

From that point there was no return. Eavin clung to Nicholas's shoulders as he bent to suckle her breasts, arousing her to a peak of quivering desire she had not known was possible. She was scarcely aware when he unfastened his trousers and threw off the rest of his clothing. She held out her arms and welcomed his weight as he settled down beside her, his big legs covering hers and holding her still while his hands worked their incredible magic.

In the back of her mind Eavin knew what was going to happen. She felt the press of his hardness against her thighs and knew it for what it was. But she allowed herself to be carried away in the ecstasy of Nicholas's kisses, on the tide of sensation created by his hands and mouth upon her breasts, until she had no knowledge of what was happening to her lower body.

The flood of heat and pleasure spread downward until she was liquid and willing when he touched her there, but still she clenched her eyes closed and tensed when Nicholas moved over her. He halted what he was doing and bent to whisper kisses over her lips again.

"Don't, Eavin. I'm not going to hurt you. If there's any pain, just let me know and I'll stop. I promise. I just want to touch you there, if you'll let me."

His fingers were stroking knowingly again, spreading her gently until she relaxed her knees and let him do as he willed. The sensation began to build until she arched her hips upward to meet his finger when it entered her. His caresses quickly made her frantic, and this time when Nicholas moved over her and pressed her knees aside, Eavin surrendered.

18

Eavin's cries of pleasure still echoed in the air when Nicholas found himself quivering with the need for release. He tried to hold back, but when she arched to meet him and caught his hips with her soft hands to hold him there, he exploded with repressed desire.

His shout nearly drowned Eavin's cry of surprise, but then both sounds were swallowed as Nicholas pressed his mouth to hers and tasted the saltiness of tears and kissed her into senselessness.

When they came to, it could have been minutes or hours later. They were still joined, but Nicholas had rolled his greater weight to the side, allowing the night breezes from the window to blow over them. When the woman in his arms shivered and moved closer, he reluctantly bent to pull a sheet over her cooling skin. For himself, he could have steamed an arctic abode.

"Thank you," she murmured against his skin, and Nicholas stroked the curve of her upper arm, wondering how many times he had seen her lift Jeannette with these slender limbs without knowing the power to enthrall that they possessed.

He chose to accept her thank-you as more than gratitude for the cover of the sheet. Pressing a kiss to her brow, he answered, "Have I proved my theory?"

Eavin didn't want to think about it. She wanted to run her hands over the hair-roughened skin of his chest and arms. She wanted to press her breasts into his heat until he kissed her again. She wanted to kiss him until he took her all over, until her body finally had its fill of the sustenance it had craved for all these years without her knowing it. She moved her hips closer to his, finding that he was as ready as she.

"I'm not certain. Would you like to try again?" Boldly

she reached upward to kiss his lips and felt excitement when Nicholas wrapped his arm around her and pulled her closer rather than rejecting her advances.

The question was a foolish one. His body hadn't forgotten its place, and he was there again before she could renege on her offer.

This time Nicholas took her with all the lust he had held back the first time, driving hard and fast until Eavin was screaming his name and writhing with the waves of pleasure and pain he produced. But whatever Nicholas did to her, she regained in satisfaction when she brought him to the same pinnacle of ecstasy and pain that he had brought to her. Her body instinctively tightened to hold him as he lunged and shook and cried out his agony against her hair.

And it was agony that brought them together and held them as they drifted into sleep. It had been agony that had brought Eavin to this place, and agony of a different sort that had allowed Nicholas to keep her. It was a different kind of pain now, muted by time and distance, but still there, ready to awaken when they did.

Eavin woke to it first. Overhead, she heard Jeannette's waking babbles as dawn reddened the sky. Beside her, she felt the heat of a man not her husband as he slept, his arm curled possessively around her waist. And her heart sank to new lows as she imagined creeping from this bed, finding her clothing, and sneaking up the stairs to her room to wash before Annie came to feed the babe.

She had done a sinful thing, and she would pay for it sooner or later, but when she turned to see Nicholas's peaceful, sleeping face, she couldn't regret it just yet.

When Eavin tried to rise, Nicholas's arm tightened at her waist and drew her closer. She struggled against him, whispering his name frantically to wake him to their predicament. His eyes opened, and she could see they were an unholy gold in the morning light. They would have been frightening had she not known what she was doing to the rest of him with her struggles. She stopped wiggling and pressed knowingly against him.

"Not again, sir. Dawn is breaking and night is done. And your daughter will rouse the household at any moment."

Nicholas cursed beneath his breath and leaned over to

154 *Patricia Rice*

nibble at his captive's throat. His beard scraped her delicate skin and Eavin laughed low in her throat as he rubbed it against her, but she pushed him away when he would follow his instincts to the swelling curve of her breast.

"Damn! If I had known being a father entailed giving up my pleasures, I would never have got into this mess."

"Your pleasures eventually entail being a father in the normal run of things, might I remind you," Eavin informed him primly, struggling to remove herself from the temptation of his arms.

Before Nicholas could draw her into his arms again, an explosion of noise erupted in the hall outside.

"Saint-Just, where in the bejesus are you? There's a boat load of cutthroats comin' up the river path!"

"Sacrebleu!" Muttering curses in French, Nicholas leapt from the bed and grabbed trousers from the floor, tugging them on as he headed for the door. Michael wasn't supposed to be back from New Orleans so soon. That was enough of a problem without considering what his warning meant.

Holding the sheet to her breasts, Eavin watched Nicholas in fear and amazement. Nicholas unclothed was even more magnificent to her eyes than when fully garbed in fashion's finest. The dark gold of the hair on his chest and legs glimmered in the morning light, and she couldn't help but stare in disappointment as he covered first one, then the other as he pulled on the trousers and then the shirt he had worn last night. But his haste was sufficient to keep fear uppermost in her mind. Nicholas was never hasty.

She didn't dare halt him with questions but watched as he left the room with an expression of fury on his face. She was quite certain that the band of cutthroats, whoever they might be, were about to meet their maker. Nicholas looked fully capable of strangling them with his bare hands.

But she had not survived this long by placing reliance on others. As soon as he was gone, Eavin hurriedly dressed and prayed no one, particularly Michael, would be about as she made her way to her room wearing an evening gown.

Eavin could hear the clamor of voices outside as the

terrified servants congregated between their quarters and the house. Nicholas's roar drowned them out quickly enough, and somehow reassured, she darted from the bedroom into the hallway and up the stairs without seeing another soul.

She had to change her clothes before she went to the nursery. By the time she had made a hasty toilet, Annie was placing Jeannette in the crib and buttoning her blouse. The black woman turned a frightened glance her way, and Eavin tried to exude a calm she didn't feel.

"Master Nick is taking care of it. Why don't you stay here with Jeannette while I go down to the kitchen and see what's happening? I'll have someone bring something up for you."

The maid glanced toward the window and the lessening sound of voices, then rolled her eyes in agreement. The top floor of the big house seemed much safer than the old kitchen building out back.

Aware that she had not washed properly, feeling the aches left by unaccustomed lovemaking and the rubbing of her clothes against the irritated skin of her breasts, Eavin felt wholly uncomfortable in appearing in public. She felt as if her sin must be written across her forehead for all to see, but when she appeared in the yard, no one looked at her until she demanded to know what was happening.

Excited voices broke out all at once, giving Eavin time to note that Michael was not among them, nor were most of the field hands. It was possible the men were still in the fields, but it had very definitely been Michael carrying the warning. She glanced anxiously in the direction that the women pointed, but could see nothing other than the spreading oaks and muddy yard.

Deciding if there were a bloody battle being held on the other side of the trees, she would hear of it, Eavin gave orders for the women to return to the kitchen and the preparation of breakfast. Whatever the men were doing, it would involve healthy appetites afterward. She had learned that much at her mother's knee.

"What kind of bloody fool expedition is this?" Not having bothered to call for his horse, Nicholas stood at the forefront of his small army, sword in one hand, rifle in the other, contemplating the sight before him.

Arms and legs akimbo, Jean Lafitte grinned at Nicholas's obvious surprise. Behind him were the recognizable features of his cut-nose lieutenant and the eccentrically garbed and powerfully built bodies of several of his pirates. Although heavily armed, they brandished no weapons but looked laconically at the ragtag army of field hands with hoes and shovels standing behind their master.

"I have need of word with you, but your so charming *maman* would not oblige me by sending for you. It is a pleasant day, so I thought to visit you myself."

Disgruntled, Nicholas gestured toward the house while speaking to Michael. "Send the men back to the fields. Come join us when you're done. I'll see to our guests." The emphasis he placed on the last word was a sarcastic one.

Eavin nearly fainted when she caught sight of the motley band of pirates walking up the river road with Nicholas in the forefront. Bareheaded and stockingless, Nicholas appeared more a part of the pirate crew than the elegantly dressed man walking beside him. Deciding the Louisiana climate had rotted her brain to let her fall into the bed of a man like that, Eavin took a deep breath and hurried to order more table settings. Knowing Nicholas, he had every intention of bringing the crew of pirates directly to his table.

For they were pirates, she had no doubts about that. She had heard enough of the illicit society living among and apart from the rest of New Orleans to recognize them when she saw them. The pirates had their own island, their own village and homes, but they freely walked the streets of New Orleans whenever the notion took them. As she had discovered, the shops of the city were filled with the goods these men stole from Spanish ships. The slave auctions held right in the center of town were products of their illegal activities, although covered up by a charade of legality. As far as Eavin was aware, the pirates seldom dined at the tables of society, but she certainly wasn't going to stand in their way if that was where Nicholas wished to place them.

To her relief, all but the elegantly dressed man remained in the yard to help themselves from the kitchen when Nicholas led their leader upstairs. Her curiosity greater than her fear, Eavin came forward to greet them as they entered. She felt Nicholas's gaze sweeping over her as she approached, but her modest morning gown apparently passed inspection. In shirtsleeves and bare feet, he still managed the aristocratic air of host as he made the introductions.

"Eavin, Monsieur Jean Lafitte; Lafitte, my sister-in-law, Mrs. Eavin Dupré. *Ma chèrie,* if you will show the gentleman into the dining room, I will join you shortly. I would not shame you in my present garb."

Eavin avoided the look Nicholas sent her. She didn't wish to know whether it contained concern or possessiveness or some other emotion with which she wasn't equipped to deal. Just his presence reminded her of where she had been a few short minutes ago. She would have to blank that memory from her mind if she was to learn to deal with him normally.

The fact that she was being left in the company of a notorious pirate certainly made the task of forgetting everything else easier. As Eavin heard Nicholas striding off in the direction of his chambers, she nervously indicated the direction of the room where breakfast would be served.

"*Monsieur,* please have some coffee with me. Breakfast will arrive shortly."

Lafitte made a gallant bow and gestured for her to go before him. "My pleasure, *madame.*"

Uneasily, Eavin played the part of hostess. After a night of sin it seemed only fitting that she should be entertaining a pirate for breakfast. She rather thought her life in poverty had been slightly more moral than in this elevated society of Nicholas's. But Lafitte played the part of the perfect gentleman, and she relaxed slightly as they struck up a conversation on the suitability of striped silks for fashionable wear, brought on by the rather bold pattern of the pirate's waistcoat.

When Nicholas returned wearing shoes and stockings and a waistcoat and coat hastily pulled over his shirt, he raised an eyebrow at the sight of these two chatting amiably over the breakfast table. He frowned when Lafitte looked up and winked at him, but he had created this situation, and he would have to deal with it.

"You had a message of some importance?" Nicholas asked irascibly as the maid hurried to pour his coffee.

"I would not ruin the lady's digestion by discussing such matters at table," Lafitte responded smoothly, passing the platter of croissants, grinning when Nicholas crumbled his into pieces.

"Then I will ask the lady to take her meal elsewhere. I haven't time to play games." Having found a solution for removing Eavin from Lafitte's company, Nicholas turned expectantly to her.

She calmly poured herself another cup of tea and met his gaze directly. "Then you shouldn't have asked me to come in here in the first place, Nicholas. My digestion is quite strong. Please continue."

Not for the first time, Nicholas considered strangling her, but when his gaze came to rest on Eavin's lovely throat, he remembered how it had tasted beneath his kisses, and he jerked his gaze away, turning it to his guest. "I doubt that anyone can keep secrets hereabouts. She will hear whatever you have to say soon enough. Spill it, Lafitte."

As it was, they had to wait until the trays of hot ham and hominy and rolls were served along with the crystal jars of jellies and bowls of strawberries and cream before they could continue their conversation. Eavin tried to imagine the pirates below digging into the succulent strawberries with their knives, but the image failed her. After she dismissed the servants, she nodded politely to the pirate.

"Do you lack for anything, *monsieur*?"

Lafitte savored his coffee, threw a fuming Nicholas a grin, and leaned back in his chair. "Not now, *madame*. Could I only spirit you away from this place and home with me, I would not lack for anything ever. Nicholas is a most fortunate man."

That certainly sounded a little too suggestive after the night they had shared, and Eavin sent Nicholas a nervous glance. His expression had become ominously bland.

"I am, at that," he responded equitably, sipping his own coffee. "For I have friends who know better than to insult me or my family. You will please expound upon your reason for being here, *monsieur*?"

Having been reduced from friend to *monsieur*, Lafitte

quickly reined in his Gallic penchant for scandal and became a man of business again. "My men tell me there are more than the usual number of British ships in the port at Jamaica. They do not seem to be carrying anything of value, but there are those among us who are eager to test their strength."

"Why tell me of this? Claiborne should be the one to know, not that there is much he can do. We have no defenses. Merchant vessels and schooners cannot take on the royal navy."

Lafitte shrugged and slathered a croissant with jam. "Claiborne has a price set on my head. Why should I help him?"

Nicholas made an inelegant noise. "You set a higher price on his head. Posting that reward on our gallant governor really was a trifle rash, *mon ami*. You would do better to curry his favor by reporting British movements."

Lafitte scowled. "Do you have any idea how much it cost me to have those damned lawyers defend Pierre? And even then I will have to break him out. There is no justice in these Americans. They do not understand the meaning of helping each other."

Unconcerned, Nicholas reached for another roll. "You mean they tend to be abysmally honest and not easily corrupted. They are not a very old country. Give them time. Meanwhile, we must make what we can of them. I will pass the information on to Claiborne on your behalf, but as I said, there is little that he can do. You have a larger fleet than the American navy. When the time comes, they will have little choice but to turn to you. Play your advantages while you can."

Lafitte brightened at that thought. "Of course, you are right, *mon ami*. You have the mind of a true Frenchman. It is a pity you must cultivate these crude newcomers. Although I must admit, I find your friend's American news sheets *très amusant*. To read something other than *avertissements* for dog laxatives is refreshing."

Eavin coughed to hide her laughter and Nicholas gave her a sharp look, but a smile lingered in his eyes as he blandly dismissed the topic. "Daniel is merely an amusing acquaintance. We might make use of him someday. Eavin, is that Jeannette I hear?"

Excusing herself, Eavin left the room to see what was

happening in the nursery. Nicholas immediately turned, frowning at his guest.

"Now, what truly brings you here?"

The easy joviality left Lafitte's expression. "I have reason to believe your friend Raphael has returned. I thought you might wish to know."

Nicholas muttered a curse and glanced toward the doorway through which Eavin had departed. He should never have involved her in his life. Had he sent Eavin and Jeannette away, as had been his original intention, he would not be feeling so vulnerable to attack as he did now. On his own he could deal with Raphael. With a woman and a child to protect, he could only sit back and wait to see from which direction the attack would come.

"How do you know?"

"The woman he took with him is back. She is voluble in her displeasure, although she claims to know nothing of his whereabouts. I cannot believe she could find her way back here from Texas alone."

"Then it is possible he was here when the warehouse caught fire?"

Lafitte sipped his coffee, then nodded solemnly. "And when the owner was killed."

The curse Nicholas uttered would have made Eavin shiver had she heard it.

19

"Michael and I are going into the city for a few days. We will return in time to go to the Howells on Friday. I expect you to accompany me."

Eavin looked up from the cradle to stare at the man in the doorway. He had returned to the elegant autocrat she remembered after Francine's death. Impeccably dressed as he prepared to leave, Nicholas glowered at her from a distance, as if they had never shared the intimacies of the prior night. She supposed it ought to be a relief that he could so easily dismiss what they had done, but some small voice inside her raised a shriek of protest.

Still, she was not the type to weep and cling, and Eavin merely nodded her understanding. In his eyes, she no longer had any reason to avoid society. It did not matter that in her own she felt even less suitable than before. She was not his mistress, but the fact that she could easily fall into that role made her more like her mother and less like the honorable wife a gentleman would require. She had some deep soul-searching to do before Nicholas returned.

Nicholas turned away with vague disappointment that Eavin did not protest and general relief that it had been so easy. While he was in New Orleans, he would go through his list of acquaintances to find a rich widower with children who would appreciate a perfect wife. Surely he must know someone who would fit that description. Marrying his sister-in-law off would be the best thing he could do for everybody.

Eavin had little time to miss Nicholas's presence. The slight fever making Jeannette irritable, which she had attributed to teething, became higher as the evening approached, and she sent messengers to the neighbors and to the physician in search of advice.

The physician never appeared, but several of the neighbors sent possets and remedies to ward off the fever. During the course of the night, Eavin tried them all, but by morning the lively child of the previous day had become limp and lifeless and so hot to the touch that Eavin felt the first twinge of panic.

She called for ice to be placed in basins of water and sponged the infant until her skin cooled and her eyes opened. She coaxed water flavored with sugar and strawberry juice down her whenever she was awake, then returned to sponging her when she slept. Annie fretted and attempted to nurse her when she could, but Jeannette seemed to have no strength for the effort nursing required. Panic growing as the slaves recited the agonies of others who had died of the fever in this disease-prone climate, Eavin sent out more messengers in search of the elusive physician.

By the morning of the third day, Eavin could barely hold her head up and thinking seemed to be a waste of time. She didn't know why the neighbors didn't respond personally to her cries for help, and she didn't care to think about it. The vile rumors Alphonso had mentioned could have spread and multiplied. They could just fear the fever. Whatever the reason, Eavin endured the agony as best she could.

Cuddling a lifeless Jeannette in her arms, placing water between her lips a drop at a time, Eavin retained sense enough to realize she could not do this alone much longer. Handing the infant to Annie, she went down to Nicholas's desk and penned a message to his mother, sending it out by the carriage driver. Wherever Nicholas might be, Madame Saint-Just would undoubtedly find him.

And then she waited. Returning to the nursery and the monotonous tasks of changing sheets, sponge baths, and spoon-feeding, Eavin clung to the notion that Nicholas would come and make everything better. He had to. He would find the physician and force him to attend. He would know the right person to ask for a remedy. He would hold Jeannette and she would wake and babble his name.

When night fell, Eavin told herself that Nicholas could not possibly have received the message yet. There would be hours of delay while they located him. The distance between here and the city was great. It would take hours for the message to be delivered and for him to return. She couldn't calculate the time it would take for all this to happen. But Nicholas would come.

Eavin fell asleep rocking Jeannette in her arms. Annie woke her to put the infant in dry clothes. The moon was already falling toward the western sky, and still Nicholas didn't come.

He didn't arrive until dinnertime the next day, in time to prepare for the Howells' ball as planned. The sun was already falling into the river.

Eavin heard the clatter of his horse coming up the road, heard the slam of the door below, and waited. She had given up listening for his boots on the stairs. She reached for the sponge in the basin and brushed it over Jeannette's burning forehead. She had never felt so helpless in her life, and she no longer felt as if Nicholas could save the day. She was too tired to think he would even care. He hadn't come when she needed him. It was too late now.

When he finally burst into the room some time later, she didn't even lift her head to look at him.

Nicholas's strangled cry as he fell down on his knees beside the chair was the first thing that had roused Jeannette's interest in days. Her lashes lifted sleepily and she made a cooing sound that went straight through Eavin's heart. Then tossing restlessly in Eavin's arms, she drifted off again.

"My God, why didn't you send for me?" Pulling the child from Eavin, Nicholas brushed his hand across her brow, pushing back the limp locks of tangled dark hair and emitting a low groan when Jeannette didn't respond. "Where is the doctor? Why isn't anyone here? What do we do?"

Eavin wrung out the sponge and mercilessly handed it to him. "We wait. As I have waited for days. Your drunken doctor has not seen fit to put in an appearance. Your neighbors have no desire to come any closer. And I did sent word, but you didn't see fit to respond. Here, she must be kept cool with this. That is all I know to do."

For the first time Nicholas tore his gaze from the child and lifted it to the woman sitting woodenly in the chair.

He vaguely recollected that Eavin had worn that same dress when last he had seen her. But the lustrous piles of her hair hung now in limp tendrils about her throat, held only by pins she had absently shoved in to keep the strands out of her face. Her eyes were wide and filled with pain against the pallor of her face, and the fear he read in them went straight through his heart and made him want to weep.

This wasn't something that could be confronted with sword and pistol. Nicholas didn't know how to deal with death like this. Pleadingly he clasped the infant in his arms and met Eavin's eyes.

"There must be something else. There has to be. Help me."

Too tired to think, Eavin felt tears well up in her eyes at Nicholas's plea. She shook her head rather than speak, and the tears spilled over when she saw the despair form in his eyes.

"I cannot combat what I do not understand," she whispered. "I try to keep her from burning up in the fever, and I try to feed her liquids so she does not dry out. More than that I cannot do. Did your mother not get the message? I had hoped she would tell me what to do."

Nicholas stood up and went to the infant's crib, laying her down against the cool sheets and removing her wet gown. "I did not go to my mother's. Send one of the maids up here. I will send someone to look for the physician."

By that, Eavin had to assume he had gone to some other house, to one of those little houses on Rampart perhaps, perhaps to the woman called Labelle. She knew the men of this society often kept their women there, women by whom they frequently had children. She had thought Nicholas would have given up his mistress when he married Francine, but perhaps he thought it was time to renew his acquaintance.

Bowing her head in acceptance of this flaw in Nicholas's nature, Eavin went to call Annie. She couldn't struggle with her ambivalent feelings about Nicholas Saint-Just while Jeannette's life lay in danger. There were more important things to do.

Knowing her fears were shared by the man at her side seemed to ease the burden. They worked well together, one anticipating the other as Nicholas learned the tedious tasks that had kept his daughter alive this long. The physician still didn't arrive, and Eavin had discarded all the potions and possets as ineffective. There remained only the continuous ritual of bathing and feeding.

Some miles away, in a ballroom glittering with chandeliers and jewels, Jeremy Howell anxiously watched every new arrival for the one face he needed to see most. He had spent these last months putting his life in order, and he was prepared to proceed with the plans he had made, but first he needed the reassurance that he was doing the right thing.

From behind him, a feminine hand caught his arm, and a whisper of roses breathed around him. "Surely you do not look for the little peasant when your so lovely *enamorata* awaits?"

Jeremy didn't bother to look at Mignon as the door opened to a crush of new guests. "Your tongue will rot in your mouth one of these days, *madame*," he answered absently.

Mignon laughed. "You do not change, *mon ami*. Neither does Nicholas. You do not truly believe he keeps that lovely peasant for the sake of a child, do you? We have not seen her since he returned her here. If he does not bring her to greet your return, that says it all, does it not?"

Jeremy felt his heart freeze over. Giving Mignon a glare, he gave her a curt bow and walked away. He would seek other confirmation of that vicious insinuation before he would believe it. One did not bring a mistress to polite houses, Mignon was telling him. Though he believed Nicholas capable of anything, he did not believe Eavin would so lower herself.

Mignon shook her head in amusement as Jeremy walked straight into the grasp of one of the worst gossip-mongers in the parish. When the boy grew up, he would not look at her with such contempt. These Americans were tremendously slow about these things.

It was late and Eavin had the idle thought that the Howells' ball must be in full swing when she heard the furious shout of a man below. She looked up through bleary eyes as a frantic knocking at the door was quickly followed by a slam and a curse. Nicholas didn't even bother to rise from his place beside Jeannette. He merely replaced the old cloth with the new one Eavin handed him.

Eavin began to grow nervous as she heard the sound of boots running through the hall, followed by the frightened voice of Hattie, the downstairs maid. She glanced at Nicholas, but his jaw was set in grim lines, and the glitter in his eyes was too dangerous to question. Lifting Jeannette's head, she poured a small spoonful of honeyed water between the child's lips.

The sound of doors slamming made her wince, but Eavin didn't stir from her place. The boots soon found their way to the stairs, and a familiar voice bellowed upward.

"Saint-Just, I know you're back! So help me, if I find you anywhere near Eavin, you'd better have your weapon on you!"

Although his gaze was bleak, a wry smile twisted Nicholas's lips as he looked up to meet Eavin's startled glance. "Jeremy," he murmured, almost apologetically.

Apparently guided by the light in the nursery, the furious intruder found them almost at the same time as his name was uttered. He stopped short in the doorway when the light of a single candle revealed the tableau inside.

Nicholas lifted the cloth from his daughter's brow and dipped it into the basin of ice water while regarding Jeremy coolly. They had found it easier to take turns holding Jeannette rather than bending over the cradle, and he was well aware that he was kneeling at Eavin's feet, close enough to run his hands up her skirt had that been his inclination. He didn't think any man in his right senses would make that assumption under the circumstances.

Feeling her hand shake, Eavin set the spoon aside and looked up to meet Jeremy's startled gaze. She hadn't seen him in months, and he looked particularly well tonight, garbed in his finest coat and trousers, his hair neatly barbered and slicked back. She thought she saw pain in his eyes when he met hers, but there was nothing that she could say.

"It was generous of you to leave your homecoming

ball to visit the sick, Howell," Nicholas offered sarcastically from his position on the floor. "Might I inquire as to your haste?"

Struck by guilt, Jeremy advanced slowly into the room without saying anything. He didn't have to repeat the rumors that had brought him here. He had made that clear when he came up the stairs. Gazing on the weary innocence of Eavin's face, he felt shame creeping through him. She didn't even look at him accusingly. For all he knew, she hadn't understood the monstrous assumption under which he had arrived. But Nicholas did. That was apparent in every stiff muscle of his back as he turned it on him.

"My mother was concerned that you hadn't arrived at her party. She had heard that there was illness here and she feared Eavin might have fallen victim to it. Newcomers often do."

The lie didn't come easily to Jeremy's tongue, but it brought a faint smile to Eavin's lips, if not her eyes, and he was momentarily reassured.

"Eavin's been here over a year, Howell. She had the fever last summer and recovered. Unless you know some remedy for infants, I suggest you go back and dally with your betrothed."

Eavin started, but she wasn't certain whether it was from the harshness in Nicholas's voice or the news that Jeremy was betrothed. Her gaze fell to the sleeping infant, and she imagined that Jeannette stirred at the sound of her father's voice.

"The announcement hasn't been made. You are a little premature in your congratulations," Jeremy said sourly. "I am an American, after all, scarcely suitable for the ladies of New Orleans."

By this time, aroused by the alarmed maids, Michael had arrived in the upper hallway. His eyebrows lifted at the sight of two grown men arguing in the nursery over his sister's head, but the infant in Eavin's lap made the scene innocuous enough. He shouldered his way past Jeremy to lay the back of his hand to Jeannette's cheek.

"Poor wee colleen. Have you tried a drop of the bitters in her water? Mam used to swear by it."

Michael's presence somehow defused the situation. He wasn't a tall man like Nicholas, but sturdy with a strong sense of self-assurance. Jeremy looked even more embarrassed that he could have suspected the worst while Eavin's more than competent cousin was in the household. When Michael turned his curious gaze his way, Jeremy backed toward the door.

"My mother has a maid who is good with fevers. I'll send her over. Eavin, I'm sorry . . ."

His behavior made it easy for Eavin to smile her farewells. Jeremy had been a pleasant companion in the past, and his protective instincts had won a piece of her heart, but she could see him more clearly now. He wasn't a strong man like Nicholas and Michael. He was nice, and he would make some woman a good husband, but that woman wasn't herself.

"Be careful, Jeremy. The road is dangerous this time of night. Wait until morning before you send anyone over."

Both Nicholas and Michael looked at her with suspicion at the softness of her tones, but Jeremy only flushed and bowed and turned away.

Michael looked at his employer next, and when he spoke, his voice held more command than question. "I'll send up one of the maids to see to the poor wee lassie. It looks as if Eavin could use some sleep."

Not intimidated by Michael's tone, Nicholas merely removed Jeannette from Eavin's arms and stood up. Holding out his hand to Eavin, he spoke to her and not her so-called cousin. "Go get some rest. I'll stay here and tell the maid what to do. You'll do no one any good by working yourself to exhaustion."

"And do you think I'll sleep while Jeannette lies like that?" Eavin asked crossly, rising stiffly from the chair. "I've been after seein' to her while the two of you played. Go about your business and leave me to her again."

There wasn't any good argument for that. Irritably, Nicholas shoved a hand through his hair, then glared at Michael. Reaching a decision, he lifted Jeannette to his shoulder and started for the door.

"Suit yourself, but I'm taking her downstairs, where it's cooler and where there's a bed large enough for resting in. Bring her paraphernalia with you if you're coming."

Eavin knew what he meant to do, and although she

knew her brother would be shocked at her acquiescence, she hurried to do as Nicholas ordered. It wasn't as if she were a stranger to Nicholas's bedroom. She had practically lived in it while Francine was alive. The master suite was one of the most spacious and comfortable rooms in the house. There was a small bed in the adjoining room where they could take turns lying down. There was room enough for any number of people to turn around without stumbling all over each other like in the nursery. And it was cooler.

Without a word, Michael picked up the basin of water and followed Eavin to the rooms below.

It was nearly dawn before the crisis came. Eavin lay fully clothed across Nicholas's bed, hugging Jeannette to her body as the infant shivered and cried pitifully. Nicholas had brought blankets to wrap around her and worriedly paced the floor. Michael fell asleep on the daybed in the adjoining room.

Jeannette's cries turned to whimpers as Eavin pressed her to her breast, hugging her closely and praying to the only God she knew. She could feel the dampness seeping through the layers of blankets, and she prayed more fervently. With a groan of anguish, Nicholas flung himself down beside them, gathering them both against him until Jeannette was huddled between their bodies, enveloped in their heat. Her shivering slackened, and moments later, she was lying peacefully in Eavin's arms.

Terrified, Eavin tore at the blankets, her fingers searching the tiny face and throat for some sign of life. Hair plastered to her brow with sweat, Jeannette murmured and smiled in her sleep as the blankets fell away.

Eyes swimming with tears, Eavin looked up to meet Nicholas's gaze, only to see him brush a hand at his face and turn away. With the child in between, she couldn't reach out to him, but she had the feeling that he needed a human touch even more than she did.

But she wasn't the one allowed to give it. With his name on her lips, Eavin curled around Jeannette and slept.

20

Jeannette's starving wails brought them all to wakeful-
ness at dawn.

The sound was music to Eavin's heart as she reached
for the infant. Her hand encountered another, and strong
fingers circled hers. She looked up with shock to meet
Nicholas's amber eyes staring from a bearded, sleep-
bleared face.

She had little time to register the difference in the
smoothly groomed gentleman she knew and the worried
father before Michael lurched into the doorway.

"Can't you do something for the lass, Eavin?" He staggered to a halt and brushed his eyes as he slowly took in
the couple on the bed with the wailing child between
them. Suspicion began to dawn as Eavin hastily curled
Jeannette into her arms and began to rise.

Nicholas stretched his long length over the bed and in-
solently propped himself against the bed's head before
greeting his overseer. With careful regard to the woman
waiting fearfully at the bed's edge, Nicholas offered Michael an outlet from the impending confrontation. "Welcome to the charms of being a father, Rourke."

True to character, Michael refused the escape. "I'm
after thinkin' there's more to these rumors than I gave
credit to." His tone was low out of respect for the woman
and child, but his black expression was clear enough.
"Get your things, Eavin. I'll be takin' you into New Orleans this day."

Eavin started to protest, but Nicholas overrode her
words. "And I'm after thinkin', *monsieur*—he mimicked
Michael's furious accents with a new twist of his own—
"that I don't need men around me I can't trust. You can
stay or go to hell as you choose, O'Flannery, but Eavin
stays here."

The use of his real name didn't escape Michael or his sister. He whitened a shade as he threw her a furious look, but she could only stare at Nicholas in surprise.

Noting this exchange, Nicholas growled and swung his long legs over the bed's edge. "*Mon dieu,* you are a surly bastard in the mornings. Your sister has not been whispering love secrets in my ear. Did you think me fool enough to hire a man just on her recommendation? Or to throw him out for the same reason? You can believe what you will, but if you're going to work for me, you'd better have a damned higher opinion than that of me."

Ignoring Eavin, Nicholas splashed water into the washbowl from the pitcher and began unfastening his shirt. Eavin hastily turned her back on him and began changing Jeannette's clothes into the fresh ones brought down last night. Michael glared at both of them and then up at the black maid appearing in the hall doorway and watching the infant anxiously.

"The place is a bloody circus," Michael muttered as Eavin lifted the wailing infant and handed her over to a relieved Annie. He winced at the scowl his sister sent him as she sailed by with her nose in the air, and when both women disappeared in the direction of the stairs, he returned a defeated look to the man lathering his face. "You win this time, only because I know Eavin and how she feels about men. But so help me God, if you lay one hand on her against her wishes—and I know she's a temptation to a man to do so—"

Nicholas turned and lifted an insolent brow. "She is that, and there's a damn sight more men around these parts than me. I'll not ask you what happened between you and that man you killed, because I've killed before and know how it happens. But in return, I'm expecting you to keep that surly temper to yourself and away from Eavin. She's having a difficult enough time protecting herself without having to protect you, or herself from you."

Michael rubbed his hand through his rumpled curls and gave a nod of acknowledgment to the truth of that. "Sure, and you have the way of it there. I wasn't sartin if you knew Eavin wasn't as she seems, but you have a discerning eye, and I apologize. She's my baby sister, and I haven't done as I ought for her, but I'm tryin' to mend my ways."

"Good." Nicholas nodded curtly and returned to his mirror and razor. "Then I'll see you at breakfast. I'm thinking about buying more of that high ground farther up the river for cotton. We need to talk about it."

Nicholas heard the other man's affirmative and the sound of his departing footsteps as he applied the razor to his jaw. He had handled the situation with adeptness, but the man in the mirror exuded none of the confidence he should have felt.

Remembering the peculiar smokiness of long-lashed eyes as they woke from sleep, Nicholas cursed and wiped the trace of blood from his nicked chin.

"We has a mass ever' week with singin' and prayin' and our own priest in that church out back. Sometimes they come over from the other houses. Marster Nick don't mind. He's the one what done told us we can use that place. He's not like the old marster."

Annie was gently rocking the satisfied infant while Eavin made some attempt to return order out of the chaos created by the last few days in the nursery. She had grown fond of the young black "mammy," as Annie referred to herself, and this discussion had come about from their mutual wish to offer thanks to God for Jeannette's recovery.

Eavin had learned early on that the slaves considered Nicholas a godsend after their previous owner, but she had not heard of his donation of a church before. She lifted a questioning brow as she added another linen to the growing basket of laundry.

"He's given you a church and priest? I've never seen the man attend mass himself."

"Oh, he comes now and then." Annie cautiously lifted the sleeping infant to return her to the crib. "They's several white folks done come. It don' make no matter. You can come too iffen you want."

Eavin didn't have to ask why Nicholas had never told her of the black church. She was quite certain it wasn't a place that white ladies attended. But she wasn't a lady, and she had a sin on her soul that needed cleansing as well as a gratefulness to a God who hadn't punished her with Jeannette's innocent life. It wasn't a moment's work to make her decision.

"Do you think we could get Clemmie to watch Jeannette while we go to church tomorrow?"

It was scarcely the same as attending a cathedral, but Eavin hadn't expected it to be. The small whitewashed building had no windows, and the seating consisted of split logs on legs, but the overall aspect was the same.

There was an open space at the far end of the building for the priest and a split log raised higher than the rest for an altar. Untutored hands had drawn and painted symbols of religious significance on the stucco walls, and interspersed between these were various icons of some meaning to the persons hanging them there. Eavin didn't attempt to go closer to examine them, for she felt they might be more pagan than sacred, and she preferred her illusions.

The slaves filling the seats wore a proper holy mien, but Eavin noted they whispered and nudged one another and threw looks over their shoulders just as in any church she had ever known. Annie made room next to her, and Eavin was surprised to find Jess coming to sit on her other side. Caught between the two black women in their Sunday-best cottons and bright *tignons* in imitation of the women in the city, Eavin had no chance of escape even if she wanted to.

As an elderly black man strode solemnly to the front of the room, followed by a string of younger people Eavin assumed to be a choir or attendants, she heard a rustling in the back of the room and turned to watch as did everyone.

Her eyes met Nicholas's as he bent his head and removed his hat to enter the doorway. She felt her heart give a jolt, and she turned to face the front again before she could recognize the message in his eyes.

They had spent the last day and night avoiding each other. Eavin prayed that he was here for the same reason as she was—to cleanse his soul from their sin and the temptation to repeat it. Her body ached even now with the memory of his touch. She wouldn't allow herself to think of what else she ached for.

She turned her concentration to the man at the front of

the room. He didn't speak in the Latin phrases with which she was familiar but in the heavy patois of Santa Domingue. The mixture of French and African with a hint of English was as untranslatable as Latin, but the people around her seemed to understand. They murmured and exclaimed and gradually began to rock as the choir chanted to the beat of a crude drum fashioned from a hollow log.

A few tallow candles smoked on the altar, providing the room's only illumination. The scent of the candles mixed with the stench of unwashed bodies and lye soap and cheap rosewater. The heat of a May sun cooked the wooden roof and mingled the smell of resin into the growing cauldron of fumes.

Eavin began to fan herself with the palmetto leaf that Annie had warned her to bring. She wore a new gown of thin muslin, but the long sleeves seemed to cling to her arms as her chemise stuck to her back. Out of respect, she had worn her light stays, but she wished them to the devil right now.

The priest's chant caused the choir to sing louder as they competed for attention, and Eavin's breathing seemed to constrict in her lungs. The crowd swayed to the rhythmical beat of the drums, and she felt compelled to move with them. A fire on the earth floor near the altar generated little heat, but the smoke climbing with the air currents added to the general miasma until Eavin's head spun with the noise, the fumes, and the swaying.

The choir began to move their feet as the priest threw herbs on the fire to make it flare. An excited cry from somewhere in the audience was repeated in several places throughout the smoky room. Eavin's dizziness became something else, something more elemental as the drums throbbed and the heat and the fumes and the droning chant drew the crowd into a single being.

She realized the people at the front of the room were dancing, but it didn't seem in the least strange. She felt the need to move drumming through her own veins. Annie's voice rang out next to her, and Eavin wished she knew the words so she could join in. The smoke hovering in a cloud overhead became thicker and lower, snaking around the room's inhabitants with the will of a live thing.

People began to rise from their seats and rumble the ground with the pounding of their feet as the chanting and the drums grew more intoxicating. Jess grabbed Eavin's arm and pulled her upward, but this change in altitude had the effect of separating her from the rest, making her uneasy.

Rather than cleansing her soul of temptation, the drums and the strange fumes were sending other messages to her body. Eavin was totally aware of Nicholas in the rear of the room, could feel his gaze crawl over every inch of her skin. As she watched the impassioned dancing of the men and women at the front, she became aware of the sexuality of their movements and felt the needs flowing through their veins echoing the excitement in her own.

A man turned to Annie, grasping her by the waist as he writhed closer with the beat. Annie slipped from his grasp, but Jess pushed Eavin forward. She stumbled and fell into his arms, but before black hands could catch her up, a pair of rough brown ones caught her from behind and pulled her out of reach.

"It's time to leave, *madame,*" Nicholas whispered in her ear as he dragged her backward through the swaying, writhing crowd in the aisle.

Eavin caught a glimpse of Jess laughing, flashing her white teeth as she stepped generously into a man's arms and continued the rhythm of the dance, and then the crowd closed around them, and Nicholas was her only anchor.

His body was necessarily close to hers as he pushed a path toward the back of the church. Even through the sweet fumes of smoke Eavin was aware of his masculine scent, and the beat of the drums echoed that of their heartbeats as Nicholas pulled her against him when he reached for the door.

Their eyes met briefly before the door opened. Eavin read the amber glow easily, felt the taut tension of his lean body as he held her, saw the trickle of sweat on the brown column of his throat, and she could not look away.

Then the door opened to blinding sunshine and he shoved her through.

Eavin recognized his French curses for what they were as she stumbled slightly over a patch of weeds and righted herself. Nicholas had released her as soon as they were outside, but they might as well have been in an illicit embrace for all the difference it made. She could feel him as surely as if they were in bed together, and she didn't dare turn around to face him.

"Undoubtedly one of his better sermons," she heard him say dryly from behind her. "Rather like adding manure to the corn crop to make things grow. The place will be burgeoning with life nine months from now."

That brought things down to a saner level. Covering her barren womb with one hand, Eavin raised the other to wipe the perspiration from her brow. The fierce sun burned away any lingering fumes from inside. She was aware of Nicholas right behind her, knew how close his hand had come to touching her waist when she had stumbled, felt his need as she did her own.

"I thought Annie said it was a church." She was surprised by her horrified whisper, but Nicholas seemed to accept it as he had accepted her presence there without question.

"To them it is. They are reaching another plane they consider higher than the daily toil of living. Man tries to get closer to God by whatever means he has available. I can think of a lot worse."

Nicholas had his hands in his pockets as he began to stride toward the house. Eavin wasn't fooled by the gesture. He had made her aware of how to look at a man and recognize the physical evidence of desire. She looked now and was ashamed of herself for doing so. She hurried to keep pace with him. At least she hadn't been the only one foolish enough to be affected.

"I don't think I wish to be enlightened any further by asking for examples."

Nicholas slanted her a cynical smile as he finally dared turn his gaze to her. "I suppose you feel holier surrounded by expensive incense and organ music in the light of stained glass windows that undoubtedly cost the fortunes and lives of hundreds of working men."

Sarcasm didn't offend her. "It's easier to think of God in those surroundings. I'm not certain anyone was considering God back there."

Nicholas stopped abruptly and caught Eavin by the shoulders, swinging her to face him. "No, they were thinking of lying naked in the grass and making love all afternoon under the sun. How much closer to God can you get?"

Eavin didn't know whether his words or his touch shocked her more. The hands gripping her shoulders were a more passionate embrace than she had ever suffered in her husband's care. One step forward and she would be in Nicholas's arms, finding out what it meant to lie naked in the grass and make love. The tension between them was that strong. His eyes held hers, and Eavin felt the power of their language. A shiver coursed through her as she realized she had the same power over him as he held over her. A flicker in his eyes revealed his recognition of the same.

It was enough just to know. Eavin stepped backward at the same time as Nicholas lifted his hands.

He shoved them back in his pockets and walked more slowly toward the house. "Daniel found your article most amusing. He means to run it in tomorrow's paper. I may have to put you on two payrolls."

Eavin had forgotten that hastily written sketch. She didn't even remember mailing it. In fact, she knew she hadn't mailed it. She sent Nicholas a suspicious glance. "I don't remember giving Mr. Fletcher any article."

"I did." He betrayed his confidence with his tone. "You left it on my desk, so I assumed it was safe to read. You're quite good, even if your pen is a trifle poisonous. Daniel wants to hire you on a regular basis. He sent several suggestions for future satires."

Eavin didn't know whether to feel betrayed, angry, or delighted. She sent Nicholas an anxious glance, but there was none of a man's usual repugnance for a woman who spoke out of turn. She supposed a gentleman who defied convention by owning radical newspapers and smuggling ships might have a slightly different outlook than most.

"You are not offended?" she asked curiously.

Nicholas heard her tone but refused to look down at her again. He could see the flash of those green eyes behind smoky lashes in his sleep and didn't need to embed them more deeply in his memory. Instead he took her question intellectually and tossed it around. Had Francine written that article, he would have been infuriated. Astonished, too, for few women of his society could even read, and Francine hadn't been much better than her contemporaries. But he would have been furious that a woman of his would expose herself to the public in such a common manner as a newspaper. Like the men he had grown up with, he would have sliced out the tongue of any man daring to mention a woman of his family in public gossip, whether the gossip was good or bad.

Yet he had not only encouraged Eavin to write the article, he was the one who had carried it to the paper and not she. He had been damned proud of her wit and pleased to show it off. Perhaps his mother was right. He was becoming more American every day, more American than was good for him, or for Eavin. Perhaps he ought to send her back to New Orleans.

But the summer fever season was starting, and no one went to the city now unless they had to. And he wasn't about to bring his mother out here to make him crazy just to provide chaperonage. Not yet, anyway.

"If I had been offended, I wouldn't have taken the article to Daniel," Nicholas answered reasonably. "You are capable of making your own decisions. If you wish to write for him, that is your choice. Just see that your name is in no way connected with him. It would be an unpardonable sin and would bar all the doors of society to you."

In Eavin's mind, that wouldn't be a half-bad idea, but she had to remember that Nicholas's only purpose in keeping her here was to someday help Jeannette enter that society. She would do well to play the assigned role of widowed aunt in the black robes of mourning, shrinking into the background of his life, coming forward only to shepherd Jeannette into the world.

"I will endeavor to remember my place," she replied wryly, earning her a wary look as they entered the house.

If she could just remember she was supposed to be one of those black crows who inevitably haunted the salons of the best houses in New Orleans, she would do very well for herself, Eavin decided as she hurriedly returned to the nursery and out of Nicholas's sight.

Perhaps then Nicholas would forget the night she had lain naked in his bed, and he would go in search of a proper wife.

21

"What the hell are you doing wearing that damnable black again?" Nicholas roared as Eavin started down the stairs to where he and Michael waited.

"I am being the proper maiden aunt required for Jeannette's sake," she replied, not at all surprised at her sarcastic tone. She hated the black as much as he, and denying herself the pretty things she had only come to know these last few months had her temper on edge.

"Don't play games with me, Eavin O'Flannery. Get yourself back up there and put on something suitable. We are going to a dance, not a funeral."

Leaning against the wall, arms crossed over his chest, Michael watched this argument with a mixture of amusement and suspicion. His sister's continued defiance of the lordly Saint-Just was what he expected of her, but there was an undercurrent to this argument that he didn't like. Deciding it was time to put on his brotherly shoes, Michael stood up and placed himself between the two combatants.

"I don't think it's your place to tell my sister what to wear, Saint-Just."

Nicholas favored the broad-shouldered Irishman with a look of disgust. "Then it's your place to tell her she looks like an old crone of fifty years determined to mourn the dead clear into eternity. The disguise doesn't fool anybody, it just depresses the hell out of them."

"I am only trying to be what you want me to be!" Infuriated by the argument, Eavin placed her hands on her hips, unintentionally drawing the fabric of the gown tighter and revealing the frailty of her disguise. "If even Michael has heard those awful rumors, I have to do something or Jeannette will never be accepted into the best society."

Nicholas drew in a deep breath as the gown outlined Eavin's full breasts and slender waist, and a sudden mental image of what lay beneath the gown flared in his mind. He could feel Michael looking to him for a reply, and he gritted his teeth to banish the image. "I will see to the end of those rumors. You will go upstairs and put on the green gown with the lace. You have five minutes."

In actuality, it was another half hour before they left for the plantation downriver. Carondelet had only recently been built on land that had once been part of the plantation that Nicholas now owned. The acreage had been parceled out as the original owner's debts increased, and the one piece of high ground along the river had gone to a French Creole and his Spanish wife. Although Carondelet was close, the only route to it was a treacherous drive through the swamps had it not been for the river.

Arriving by keelboat wasn't the most elegant mode of travel, but it was the most practical. The river current carried them downstream effortlessly, and the slaves traveling with them would enjoy the visit to their neighbors before poling back upstream when the night was done. If it weren't for the ever present mosquitoes, Eavin decided, she would travel like this all the time.

Inside the cabin, listening to Nicholas and Michael discuss the future of steamboats, she let her mind drift. For the first time in her life she felt comfortable. The sound of men's voices gave her a feeling of security instead of anxiety. The gentle lapping of the river relaxed her, and the low murmur of the crew had a hypnotic sound that made her want to close her eyes and smile. Times like this were rare, and Eavin wished the boat never had to stop.

Carondelet's dock came all too soon. As she felt the pitching and heard the calls indicating they were tying up, Eavin felt the force of Nicholas's gaze on her, and she opened her eyes to find herself alone with him. They had left several lamps smoking to combat mosquitoes, and in their dull glow his face was shadowed into angles and planes. She recognized the danger of his expression, and shuddered at her innocence in feeling secure in his presence. Whatever Nicholas Saint-Just might be in the familiar surroundings of his home, outside of it he was a dangerous man, one capable of elemental passions that could explode at any time.

She wished she knew more about him, wished she had some understanding of the forces that had turned a pampered aristocratic Creole gentleman into a sheathed sword of rage, but he wasn't likely to tell her. Taking his hand, Eavin allowed Nicholas to lead her out on deck and to the safety of the dock, where a carriage waited for them. She had no need to wonder what he was thinking. The look in his eyes now was no different from that of all the other men who had turned their desires in her direction.

She had made an immense mistake in allowing Nicholas to take her to bed. At the time it had felt right. He was an experienced man, and he had taught her wonders that she never would have known existed. But at the same time she had made him aware of herself, and years of experience had taught her that was always a mistake.

The fact that Eavin was now more aware of Nicholas than ever wasn't exceedingly helpful. She had been able to look away from the golden glow of his eyes before, and without knowledge of the taste of his skin she could ignore the sight of his sun-bronzed throat. But now even the touch of his hand caused shivers of expectation, and Eavin had to will herself to remember the infant in the nursery and the disaster that would come if she succumbed to these feelings.

Eavin entered the brilliance of Carondelet's salons with relief and allowed the eddies of the crowd to carry her away from Nicholas. The farther she stayed from him, the better off they both would be.

The crowd here tonight was more aristocratic than the guests usually attending the Howells' gatherings. Unlike Nicholas's family, who had come over from Santa Domingue just prior to the turn of the century, the family of Carondelet's owner had lived here since the early days of New Orleans. Many of his guests were the elite of society, and French flowed like fine wine around Eavin as she greeted those few of the crowd whom she knew.

With uneasiness she noted the prevalence of the rapier-like short swords called *colchemardes* favored by the gentlemen of society. Eavin had never attended one of the winter balls in New Orleans, but she had heard of the frequency of disputes and their inevitable outcomes in the

hands of these volatile men. Her gaze unconsciously
sought Nicholas, his fair hair easily located in this sea of
dark, and she realized edgily that he had not worn a
sword. Like the Americans, he was more inclined to favor
a pistol, but she was quite certain he had not worn one of
those, either.

Perhaps it was better that way. Gentlemen would not
attack an unarmed man, and these were gentlemen here
tonight. Insulated by his arrogant confidence, Nicholas
was quite capable of turning down a challenge with a
wicked word or two. The insult wouldn't make him any
better liked, but he didn't seem overly concerned with the
opinions of other people.

As if to confirm her thoughts, Eavin watched in horror
as Nicholas flung the contents of his wineglass at a
Spanish-looking gentleman near the buffet table. She had
not realized she had wandered so close, but she could
hear his words clearly in the silence that suddenly fell
over the salon.

"That should cool your tongue until your brain has
time to catch up with it, Marquez. I suggest you carry the
insult back to Reyes, where it belongs. Let him know I'll
not tolerate this bandying of names of members of my
household in public."

Nicholas strode off while the other man was still wiping his face with a handkerchief, and Eavin froze as she
heard him muttering about issuing a challenge. Saner
heads prevailed, however, and she uttered prayers of relief as she heard Jeremy enter the altercation.

"He's looking to kill someone, Marquez, and you know
it isn't you. He can't challenge Reyes because the man's
a cripple, but he'll accept anyone in his place. For the
sake of your new wife, don't get involved in their quarrel."

Behind her, Eavin heard the familiar voice of Clyde
Brown before she felt his hand on her elbow. "Saint-Just
could kill him blindfolded, and Marquez knows it.
They'll talk him out of it if they don't see you here. Go
to the powder room, Mrs. Dupré, and pretend you never
heard any of this."

Hastily she did as told, realizing belatedly that all the
other ladies in the room had found some way of averting
their eyes and ears from the altercation. Feeling heat rise

to her cheeks, Eavin escaped through a nearby set of doors and wished to heaven that she had never come.

She found herself on a torch-smoked gallery, but someone else was there before her. In horror she recognized Nicholas's broad shoulders as he bent to kiss the woman in his arms, and she fled back to the crowded ballroom without watching more. She didn't need to watch more. The scent of Mignon Dubois's heavy perfume filled the air behind her.

"You've been a naughty boy again, *mon chéri.*"

The husky voice whispered against Nicholas's lips as they brushed Mignon's. Once upon a time they would have sent a sensual thrill through his loins, but they did nothing for him now. As a widow, Mignon had sampled most of the men in the room behind them at one time or another. Once that fact had given Nicholas the freedom to do with her as he would without fear of the consequences. Now it only gave him a vague repugnance for the deliberate way she swayed into his arms and pressed her hips to his.

"I have a reputation to maintain." Nicholas shrugged off her chastisement with an insouciance he no longer felt. He had wanted to strangle Marquez. At one time he would have goaded him to a duel. But he suddenly found himself torn by conflicting emotions that he had never experienced before. He—of all people—was well aware that Eavin Dupré was not a lady whose reputation need be defended as one of his own. Yet he found it uncannily easy to go into a rage when he heard her name on the lips of another man. At the same time, he was quite certain that Eavin not only wouldn't appreciate the honor, but would be furious with him for endangering himself as well as another over such a trivial cause.

Why in hell he should care what Eavin Dupré thought was beyond his comprehension. Which was the reason he had come out here with Mignon, to assuage some of this confusion with pure, simple lust. He wasn't succeeding to any degree, but at least he was out of the press of bodies inside.

"You are in dire peril of losing that reputation, *mon chéri,*" Mignon whispered as her hands roamed across his chest. "There has been no rumor of duels or adulterous liaisons for months. Why don't you turn their tongues away from your Irish paramour and to more interesting subjects?"

The suggestion in her tone was blatant, but Nicholas pushed her away with distaste. "She's my daughter's aunt, and it was a comment like that which got me out here in the first place. Why don't you circulate more interesting gossip like why Raphael is hiding on the docks of New Orleans instead of showing his face like an honest man?"

Unaccustomed to being treated so rudely, Mignon brushed herself off with a huff and glared at the handsome man in the shadows. "Everyone knows he died in the swamps without even a proper funeral because of you, Saint-Just. Don't start pretending you're something you're not because of that bastard child. Go find your paramour and lie to her some more. I'm certain she'll believe every word of it."

As a lady, she couldn't repeat the rest of the insult, but the implication was clear enough as she stormed off. "Since her brain's between her legs" was a phrase he had heard before, and Nicholas wondered where Mignon might have heard it. She certainly didn't know Eavin very well if that was what she thought.

Staring out over the shrubbery-studded lawns to the trees blowing along the river, Nicholas thought it might be preferable to be an American right now. He had tasted their whiskey and tobacco in private and thought they might add a touch of comfort to this loneliness enveloping him, but he had a public standard to maintain, so he turned back to the lights and the crowd and started for the door.

The sound of booted feet along the gallery halted him. A shadow emerged from the darkness, and Nicholas recognized an acquaintance of his from New Orleans. A dedicated bachelor with a reputation as a dandy and a rake, the other man made a cynical bow and an offhand gesture to the shrubbery below. "There is a rogue below wishing a word with you, *monsieur*. From the looks of him, I am not so certain I would meet him unarmed."

Thinking a great number of the men he worked with fell into that category, Nicholas shrugged off the warning. He knew how to handle riffraff. It was the gentlemen with their codes of honor and guns and swords who required weaponry. With a curt nod of thanks, he took himself off to the lawn with almost a relief at not having to return to the salon.

The first slicing lash of the whip caught him off guard. Ripping through the fine material of his coat and shirt, it stung with a memory more painful than the actual wound. Enraged, Nicholas grabbed the flailing leather before it could strike again, only to find himself assailed from a second direction.

Nicholas gave a roar of fury as the whip sliced through to his cheekbone. Blood coursed down his face as he swung to meet this second attacker, while he was beset again by the devil behind him.

The lashes were no more than the sting of nettles as, blinded by fury, Nicholas flung himself on the first attacker foolish enough to get within reach. No stranger to pain, Nicholas made no attempt to avoid it but plunged toward the one inflicting it with all the anger repressed by time and circumstance.

The man's screams as Nicholas's fist connected with a soft belly only brought more lashes from still a third direction. Nicholas knew the pain now, recognized it for what it was as his clothing shredded and the sharp leather carved into his back, but he had no intention of running or crying from it. That had been beat out of him a long time ago. The need to kill had not.

Nicholas swung his feet at the man closest, using his other hand to grab for the flailing weapon, attempting to wrench it from his assailant's grasp. Showered by blows from three sides, he was given no time to think, and his mind retreated to an earlier haze.

He could hear the screams, feminine screeches that silenced after a few furious words. In his mind Nicholas heard the familiar taunt of his father's voice, and he struck out now as he had never struck out then.

"A marquis doesn't read poetry to coloreds! He swives them or beats them like a man. You're going to be a marquis someday, and you're going to learn to do it proper. Are you going to let some sissified Englishman beat you at fencing? Your grandfather would see you hung for that!"

The relentless chant of criticism echoed in his head as

Nicholas swung from one attacker to the next, kicking as he had learned to do among the dishonorable thieves and pirates he had sailed with, striking out with fists when he came close enough to injure. But the relentless lash of the whips went on, tearing into his flesh as the cane had once rained blows on him to accompany the chant.

"Puling milksop! Can't even hold your wine! You'll be a man when I'm done with you, or I'll know the reason why." Wham! Wham! The cane sliced across his back and buttocks and anywhere else it could reach. Stumbling to his knees with the force of the blows, Nicholas roared with impotent rage and lurched forward, bringing his head up until it connected with a crack beneath one attacker's chin.

The man cried out and dropped back, and Nicholas swung in the direction of the next lash, blood running in his eyes as he aimed his foot with deadly precision and caught the second man between his legs. He heard screams, but they weren't his own. Swinging, he tried to catch the third man, but he was grabbed from behind, both arms caught in vise-like grips as a large man stepped out of the shadows and swung a powerful arm into his abdomen.

Nicholas kicked and found his arm jerked backward with a noise he recognized. Pain brought sweat to his brow, but fury worked harder. He lunged forward, catching his captors by surprise, but the shouts and screams were coming closer. With one last blow to his ribs, they let him drop to the grass before blending into the night and disappearing ahead of the crowd.

With his last conscious thought, Nicholas wished he could have killed his father.

22

Eavin paced her room long after the sounds below had slipped into the silence of sleep.

They had kept her from Nicholas during all but the return trip. Michael and her hostess and the others had in all probability been correct to maintain propriety by keeping her worrying and fretting in the outer rooms while a physician and older, more experienced women tended to his wounds, but that did not make the ache any less.

Whatever the doctor had given Nicholas had kept him unconscious most of the journey home. There had been nothing Eavin could do but hold his head and try to keep him steady while the slaves carried them upstream. The long gash down his cheek had made her shiver, but the other wounds had been covered by the light silk of a shirt someone had given him—for propriety's sake, of course. The dislocated shoulder had been reset and would be fine Michael had told her, but seeing Nicholas's arm bound tightly as he tossed in restless sleep did not relieve her fears.

She wasn't at all certain what her fears were. Nicholas wasn't likely to die of a whipping. Eavin knew that in her mind, but as she paced her room now, something in her heart warned there were worse things than dying. The memory of Nicholas as he had been after Francine's death was still clear in her mind. That man had not been the same one who had swabbed Jeannette's head when she was ill or laughed and carried her around when she was not. Somewhere inside Nicholas Saint-Just lay a monster waiting to get out, and she couldn't help but think an incident like this would be sufficient to loose it.

The nighttime was the worst for fears like that. The scent of Francine's jasmine perfume suddenly seemed to permeate the air as Eavin stood indecisively before her wardrobe. That scent jarred her into action, making her choice perfectly clear. She knew what Francine would want her to do.

Pulling on her wrapper, Eavin stepped into the silent hallway. Only the call of some night bird and the incessant hum of insects could be heard as she walked toward the stairs. She would go by way of the gallery, peek in to be certain Nicholas slept. Francine would have wanted that. No one should be left alone after such an experience, but that wouldn't occur to Michael or the servants. Once satisfied Nicholas was all right, she would be able to sleep.

The pain of his injuries didn't wake him. Another ache, a dull roar somewhere in his midsection had his eyes open and staring at the prison of mosquito netting.

He was aware of the throbbing in his cheek, the tight bandage holding his arm in place, and the pain that kept him from lying on his back. Long ago he had learned to ignore those kinds of pains, to mentally step outside of them. But he had never learned to conquer the rage in his heart.

Closing his eyes, Nicholas tried to find sleep. He knew the futility of fighting the past. A child had few choices in this world. He had made the best of what he had been given and escaped as soon as he was able. It had never been enough, but it should have been. He had made something of himself. He was a wealthy, respected landowner. He had married a lady of grace and beauty loved by all society. He had thrown off the shackles of poverty, overcome the shame of constant abuse, and raised himself to his rightful place in the world. As his mother had said, he could return to France now that Bonaparte was gone and claim the title of marquis, and there would be none the wiser.

But he couldn't kill the child of rage inside him. Once he had longed for just a kind word, a soft caress, an expression of sympathy so he could release the rage, but there had been no one to offer even that. Logically, Nicholas couldn't blame his mother for being terrified of his father when he was in that state, but logic had nothing to do with the pain simmering inside.

Kicking back the netting, Nicholas wrapped a sheet

around his hips and went to stand by the French doors overlooking the acreage of his plantation. He was thirty-two years old and well beyond the need for mothering. Since he had left home at fifteen, he had found countless women who would have mothered him had he wanted it, but their attentions had never held him. Francine had been the only one he had ever wanted for something beyond her body, but in the end that had been denied him, too. Nicholas wasn't at all certain that there was anything else in the relationship between men and women but the desires of the body, yet he kept searching for more. Perhaps children were the secret. He had found something in Jeannette's innocent acceptance that he had never found elsewhere in this world.

But loneliness still burned in him. Mixed with rage, it was a volatile fuel, and Nicholas's fists clenched as he summoned Raphael's face to mind. The traitorous bastard was behind tonight's attack; Nicholas had no doubt of that. Señor Reyes might be a furious old man, half mad with grief, but even he wouldn't stoop to something so dishonorable as a blind attack of three against one. This was the work of Raphael. It was time he took an active role in bringing the *canaille* to his knees.

It felt better to let the anger boil and bubble and come to the top, blocking out the emptiness. He knew how to deal with anger. A dangerous half smile reached his lips as he contemplated what he would do with Raphael when he found him. A subject like that could keep him occupied for hours.

Before the first ghoulish torture could come to mind, a white wraith appeared on the moonlit gallery, and Nicholas held his breath as it blew along the boards toward him. He had no illusions of Francine returning from the dead to comfort him. Francine hadn't had that kind of courage when alive. But the woman in that delicate linen robe would.

Silently, Nicholas opened the door to the moonlight and let her in. Not hesitating, Eavin stepped through, her gaze flying to his injured face, bathed in the silver light. Her hand lifted of its own free will to caress the broken skin. With a groan Nicholas caught her in his arms and pulled her against him, and his head dipped to plunder her mouth with his.

Nicholas felt Eavin's resistance with that first kiss, knew he was pushing her over some edge that had stood between them, but he couldn't let her go. His soul craved what she had to offer, and he demanded that she relinquish it. The hesitation was there, in her touch, in her kiss, but Nicholas reached beyond it, reached deep down inside of her where their souls met, and ignited the flames of passion with the fuels of his rage and loneliness.

Eavin surrendered to that need. Her fingers curled in the thick hair at his nape, and her other hand found the road to destruction in the smooth heat of his flesh. She shuddered as Nicholas's kiss deepened, but she was the one who helped him remove her wrapper, which slipped into a puddle of moonlight. With only the slightest of pressures, she willingly fell into his bed. When his free hand pushed aside the bodice of her nightshift to caress her breast, she melted into a malleable clay he could do with as he wished.

He didn't have to force her to anything. Eavin was well aware that Nicholas's injuries prevented him from using his dangerous strength in any way. She was the one voluntarily removing her shift, wrapping herself around him, positioning herself to accommodate his needs with a care to his wounded back and arm. She was the one wholly responsible for opening herself to whatever happened next.

And she didn't care. She gave a cry of ecstasy as Nicholas entered her, and his muffled groan of reply burned a path through her as surely as his physical possession. The days of tension and denial erupted and spewed forth with an urgency they were both pushed to command. The surge of Nicholas's body inside hers brought Eavin quickly to a quivering peak from which there was no return. Nicholas took her mouth with his as he brought them up and over, and her cries were lost as they floated downward in each other's arms.

Sometime later, when her senses returned enough to know the weight of him pressing her into the mattress, the rasp of his hair against her thighs, the bruised pain of his hasty entrance, Eavin knew what she had done but continued to deny it. Nicholas shifted his weight to a more comfortable position, and his fingers wrapped caressingly around her breasts, easing her nipples to sensitive peaks even when they knew they were both momentarily satiated.

"*Merci, ma petite,*" Nicholas murmured against her ear.

The flow of French after that went on by her, but Eavin recognized that first phrase. Thank you. It was an odd thing to say, but in some way it warmed her heart, and she stroked his face and hair until she felt his breathing level into that of sleep.

She lay awake memorizing the scent and feel of Nicholas in her arms. He was a big man, much bigger than Dominic. She knew the strength of the muscles clasped around her, but it wasn't his physical strength that would keep her bound. It was his need for her. She wanted to be needed, craved it, and couldn't resist it when offered. Right now she was swollen with pride that Nicholas Saint-Just had turned to her in his hour of need.

She would recover from that soon enough, she supposed as she untangled herself from his sleeping possession. Once Nicholas was on his feet again, he would return to the arrogant man who didn't need anyone. And she would curse his arrogance and her own foolishness and cry herself to sleep at night. But she couldn't help being weak enough to crave just a little of this balm to her self-esteem. Tomorrow would be soon enough to castigate her stupidity.

Leaving Nicholas safely in the healing grip of slumber, Eavin slipped from his bed and back to her own.

Birdsong filled the darkness before dawn. Having given herself up to the sensuality of Nicholas's loving, Eavin had felt no shame in divesting herself of the encumbering lengths of material that were her nightclothes when she returned to bed short hours ago. Naked now, she stretched against the linen sheets and reached for a sturdy warmth that was not there.

The old floorboards outside her door creaked, and the door swung open just as she pushed up out of the haze of sleep. Blinking her eyes awake, Eavin felt rather than saw the shadow ease into her room. Before she could register anything more, he stripped himself of his breeches, and the shadow became the rock-solid frame of a man slipping in beside her.

"Shhh," Nicholas whispered against her mouth before she could open it to protest.

And then she was caught in the maelstrom of his kiss, and there was nothing else to do but succumb to the waywardness of the winds. His nakedness pinned her to the mattress, and she reveled in the familiarity of his touch. Sin became an abstract notion when she realized Nicholas had unbound his arm so he could touch her more thoroughly. Joy—wild, unfettered joy—was her only emotion as Nicholas took charge of her body and her passions, and molded them into a vessel that would accept him eagerly and without restraint.

He was already a part of her before he came into her. Eavin exulted in the physical recognition of what had already gone before. Their needs were such that nothing less could have sufficed, and she rocked against him with all the pleasure and vulnerability he had opened in her. She was his for the taking, and as Nicholas ground himself into her, Eavin was at peace with that knowledge.

Afterward, with the moisture of their bodies rubbed and blended into a soothing lotion across their skins, Nicholas turned on his side and pulled Eavin into his arms. His kisses whispered across her face, and his hands massaged and caressed her back to take away any lingering consciousness of their plight.

"Don't ever slip away from my bed like that again," he murmured into her hair. "I want you beside me when I wake. Promise me that."

The man was quite insane, but Eavin could deny him nothing. She had spent a lifetime denying herself pleasure. In just a few short hours Nicholas had taught her what life could really be like. She would pay for this someday, but not right now.

Touching him gently, exploring the curves and planes of his chest, lingering at the torn places in his flesh, Eavin nodded acquiescence. If she had her way, she would never leave his bed. Impossible thought, but she smiled at it just the same.

Pleased with the ease of her surrender, Nicholas stroked her cheek and pressed a kiss there. "Does Jeannette always wake babbling?"

The sound of the infant in the other room woke Eavin to reality, and she stared into Nicholas's face with a panic she could not hide. The gash across his cheek had hardened into a bloody crust. Combined with the wild mane of his hair, he looked the part of pirate or worse, but his smile was extraordinarily gentle as he read her expression well.

"Go to her. I'll meet you later downstairs. I have an interest in preserving your good name, too."

And so he would. Rising from the bed, terribly conscious of her nakedness and Nicholas's smiling scrutiny, Eavin reached for her nightclothes. Getting dressed would have to wait until she had warm water with which to wash. She couldn't go to breakfast with the scent of Nicholas still on her.

Rather liking the idea of being stained with his lovemaking, Eavin smoothed the loose material over her breasts, understanding for the first time the sensuality of her response to the caress of cloth. She had despised her body as a nuisance to be hidden from the grasping hands of men. Nicholas had taught her to appreciate the way she was made, and a hot flush rose to her skin as she recognized his masculine response when she turned back toward the bed.

Nicholas chuckled and pulled himself to a sitting position as Eavin hastily tied her wrapper and ran out. He'd never had a shy mistress before, but he thought Eavin would soon overcome that particular trait. He enjoyed teaching her the pleasures of her body, but he was rather looking forward to the wantonness that he would soon release.

Eavin didn't come out of the nursery until she was certain that Nicholas was gone. She had done a terrible thing last night and given him ideas that should never have been placed in his head. She remembered all too well their conversation when he had called her the ideal mistress. But she wasn't the ideal mistress. For Jeannette's sake, she had to keep her reputation. And for Michael's sake, she had to stay away from Nicholas.

But after washing and dressing and coming down to join the men for breakfast, Eavin could see that at least one of these obstacles was about to be removed.

"The cane can take care of itself this time of year. I need you to keep an eye on those cotton fields I bought last summer. There's accommodations of a sort there already, enough for you and the field hands. I think it's safe to sink our initial profits in making improvements while you're there. Let me know what you need after you arrive, and I'll see to it that you get it. I'll have to go into New Orleans in your place to look after the warehouse, so it ought to all fall into place."

Michael sipped his coffee and studied his employer without seeming to do so. By all rights the man ought to still be in bed. He had seen the bruises and the flailed flesh and knew the agony of a dislocated shoulder. But Nicholas sat there with his arm in a sling and his jaw bruised and scarred as if these were the latest fashions. Michael raised an eyebrow at Eavin's timid entrance, but his fascination was with his employer at the moment, and he ignored his sister.

"Don't you think I ought to wait a week or two until you feel more like riding the fields yourself? The cotton isn't going anywhere just yet."

Nicholas pulled his eyebrows together in a formidable frown. "I've got work to do that won't allow me to wallow in pity for any length of time. I'll be out the rest of the day, so you'd better tell me if you need me for anything else before you leave."

Eavin gave a squeak of surprise and protest, but the men were caught up in a contest of wills now and took no notice.

"If you're going after whoever did that to you, you need someone at your side. There's no call to go after a son of a bitch like that by yourself. Three against one calls for war where I come from."

"I don't need an army to take care of him," Nicholas replied smoothly, but the ominous undertone belied his affable smile. "But I'll employ one to find him. You just worry about the cotton. The last shipment must have made it clear of the blockade. I think we've planted enough acres to double the profit with this next one."

Michael gritted his teeth, turned to Eavin as if for support, then gave up in disgust when she only stared at them both as if they spoke a foreign language. Shoving his chair back, he rose from the table.

"I think the heat down here makes you all insane. But I'm after thinkin' the alligators would toss you back if they ever got a hold of you, so I'll be damned if I'll spend my time worryin'. Eavin, colleen, keep a pistol under your pillow and blow the head off any man who comes near you. I'll be happy to come back in time to clean up the remains."

Eavin frowned at this disparaging remark, but she knew Michael meant it as his idea of a parting pleasantry. He kissed the top of her head and strode out without another look back, leaving her to avoid the eyes of the man who had so thoroughly enslaved her body only a few hours before.

"I don't intend to get killed, you know," Nicholas said pleasantly as he rose from the table. "I have too many things I wish to do in this lifetime to allow a snake like Raphael to stop me."

He walked off without waiting for a reply. Eavin idled over her tea as she considered his words. The man was quite capable of turning a band of pirates loose on New Orleans to achieve his goal. Why should she worry about the perverse creature?

Her only concern had better be her own self-preservation. She had the quite distinct and unmistakable feeling that Nicholas now considered her one of his possessions, like the cotton fields.

23

The clatter and laughter and sound of feet in the normally empty room across the hall finally drove Eavin out of the nursery to investigate.

She caught Clemmie leaving the room with her arms full of musty draperies and Jess coming up the stairs ahead of two men carrying a trunk. Puzzled, Eavin inquired about the activity.

Clemmie laughed and raised a cloud of dust as she shook the heavy material in her hands. "Marster Nick done got tired of the ghosts downstairs and is movin' in up here. He's gonna have them rooms down there done all over. Said it was that or burn the place down and start again. Maybe he finally got some sense whupped into him. Those rooms down there are a plumb disgrace."

The house was old and perhaps some of the plaster was cracking, and the walls certainly could use a good scrubbing and painting, but Eavin didn't think those niceties were the cause of Nicholas's sudden distaste for the decor. Stepping across the hall, she watched as the maids scrubbed down the floors while workmen set up a wider bed than had previously adorned this unused chamber. Jess was already unpacking the trunk and sorting through Nicholas's clothes to place them in the empty wardrobe. The room was considerably smaller than the one Nicholas was used to. Eavin didn't think he was sacrificing all that magnificence below stairs for the sake of a new decor. He had every intention of exchanging one pleasure for another, and she could very well guess which one he had in mind.

But when she went in search of him, he was nowhere to be found. Cursing her stupidity, heart pounding erratically at the thought of how far Nicholas would go to get what he wanted, Eavin threw herself down at his desk and thought of a dozen scathing diatribes she would like to unleash on him.

Instead she found herself perusing the list of suggestions Daniel Fletcher had sent for another satire. The hypocrisy of the gentlemen attending balls in the white theater while slipping out to meet their mistresses at the colored ball across the street had a certain appeal, but Eavin didn't think it was a topic to grace the pages of a newspaper. If the ladies of New Orleans could tolerate men who would treat them that way, it was their problem. She had enough of her own.

The slave auctions were an entirely different kettle of fish. Everyone knew there was a law against importing slaves. Maspero's Exchange would scarcely do half its present business if not for the suspiciously foreign-speaking slaves sold there. The pirates were responsible for the contraband, but the merchants and the government were responsible for turning their backs on the legal circles that put the slaves on the block. If the militia didn't "capture" the slaves and sell them as contraband, there would be no market at all. She could certainly put her heart into a story like that.

Writing gave Eavin an outlet for her anger. Instead of raging at Nicholas for taking her acquiescence for granted, she could scorn the hypocrisies and cruelties of the revolting practice of slave trading. She doubted that her anger would have any effect in either case, but at least the article to the paper would produce a few coins to store away in her growing hoard.

Someday she wouldn't be reliant on any man for her living. It might take years, but that was better than an entire lifetime at the beck and call of men.

Writing made her feel better, and Eavin began to smile as she mentally counted the coins this excuse to scream in outrage would produce. She really was going to have to thank Nicholas for opening this opportunity. To be paid for what she wanted to do seemed almost a sin. Perhaps she had better consult with him about that bank account. She didn't trust men or banks, but she couldn't be certain her cache of coins would survive flood or fire or thieves, either. When she had enough saved, perhaps she could put half in the bank and keep half with her. There was no sense in putting all her eggs in one basket.

All that self-satisfaction fled the moment Nicholas walked into the study, slammed the door, and drew Eavin into his arms.

He made it impossible to fight. Even with the gash across his cheek, he was so handsome he took her breath away. Or perhaps handsome wasn't the word. Virile. Eavin's mind raced crazily for suitable synonyms as Nicholas's mouth crushed hers. If she could only distance herself . . .

But she couldn't. The strong arm around her waist reminded her all too clearly of how he had held her naked not so many hours ago. The pounding of his heart beat in time with hers, and when she put her hand up to push him away, she encountered the sling and remembered his agony, and there was no escaping the need swirling through them.

She gave in to the kiss, melted in his arms, and allowed nature to take its course.

Satisfied, Nicholas stepped back and gazed at her through eyes darkened with desire. "I didn't want you to forget. I'm going downriver for a while, and I won't be back until late. Keep the bed warm for me."

Eavin's fingers wrapped in his sling, preventing his convenient escape. "Nicholas, you assume too much. We must talk."

A rakish smile tilted one corner of his mouth, a smile that had not been there with any frequency this past year. Even the lust that drove it did not detract from the charm it added to his harsh face.

"Write me an argument, *chère amie*. I promise to read it, but I don't promise to fight fair. Your place is in my bed, whether you admit it or not."

She wanted to hit him but could not for fear of opening one of his wounds. He had made it perfectly clear that physical violence was not effective, anyway. Glaring at the insolent assurance on his masculine face, Eavin released her grip and stepped away. "I hope the alligators eat you," she retorted childishly.

He took that with a smile as he strode toward the door. "You and Jeannette will be very rich women if one does, but just think how you'll miss me."

He walked out to the sound of an inkwell crashing against the wall.

* * *

Eavin heard the long clock on the landing chime midnight before she heard Nicholas's boots on the stairs. It had suited her to have him safely tucked in the opposite wing of the house below, where she could not hear his comings and goings. Having him upstairs with her was going to be upsetting to the equilibrium.

His appearance in her room at every hour of the night and day was going to be even more upsetting. As her door swung open, Eavin cursed the builder who had neglected locks or latches or bolts on any of the doors. She simply didn't have the proper pioneer spirit. She wanted that door bolted.

"The bed in my room is bigger," Nicholas commented genially as he began unfastening his shirt. "I could carry you there, I suppose, but I'm in a hurry to get this arm healed and that might not be conducive to the process."

Eavin gave up pretending to sleep and sat up to glare at his silhouette in the darkened room. "Neither will coming in here in the middle of the night, uninvited."

The shirt fell to the floor and Nicholas started on his trouser buttons. "I'll take my chances. I think what I have in mind will be very conducive to healing. The only question is whether it will be here or there."

"If you think I'm going to meekly follow you into your bed, you have seriously underestimated me." Eavin heard the lie in her words even as she said them. She was avidly watching the process of Nicholas undressing himself and wondering how soon he would reach for her. She knew how it would feel when he did, and she knew she wouldn't be able to fight him. Words were her only hope.

"Don't get your Irish up." He chuckled softly as he sat at the bed's edge to remove his boots. "A good woman would help me take these things off, you realize. I ache all over and my arm hurts like hell. I can make love to you much better if I don't have to strain myself removing these damned boots."

"I'm not your whore, Nicholas," Eavin muttered in ominous undertones.

Nicholas succeeded in pulling off one boot, letting it fall to the floor as he turned to pin the sheets on either side of her. Face to face, he met her uncertain gaze. "I don't have need of whores, *ma petite*. I need a woman who wants what I have to offer. I may not be much compared to the pampered Jeremys and Alphonsos of this world, but I think I can give you what you need. And I think you can give me the same in return. It's a mutual arrangement, *chèrie*. Why not give it a try?"

Eavin had no easy answer to that. The fear of pregnancy that had kept her chaste until marriage was gone. Now that she had a better understanding of marriage, she had no desire to enter into it again anymore than Nicholas did. To be permanently tied to a man's whims and desires while he did as he pleased held no appeal at all. If what Nicholas said about his will was true, she had no more to gain financially by marrying him than living with him. Of course, there was always the chance that he would grow tired of her and throw her out, but she didn't think Nicholas would be that totally dishonorable. Even the men who took mistresses among the women of color set them up handsomely before they left them. Eavin was beginning to understand that that was an eminently practical arrangement. All the world knew men tired of having just one woman. Why be tied to one and watch as he philandered his life away? It was much more reasonable to take what he had to offer while he wished to offer it, and still maintain her independence.

The other boot dropped to the floor. Nicholas held out his hand, and wordlessly Eavin took it.

Together they crossed the hall to the freshly made bed of masculine proportions that Nicholas had had set up for them to share. In a way, Eavin mused as she stepped into Nicholas's welcoming arms, it was almost like being married. Only the "death do us part" was missing. She raised her lips for Nicholas's kiss and clasped her hands behind his neck with almost a sense of pride. For whatever reason, her trust in Nicholas Saint-Just was unbreachable. By handing herself into his care, she was admitting that she trusted him to treat her with all the respect due a wife. Perhaps others would call her mad, but she had seen the man behind the mask and knew his pain as well as her own. She was willing to take her chances.

And Nicholas certainly made the gamble worth it. Eavin closed her eyes in ecstasy as his lips moved to cover her breasts with kisses and to suckle gently at the tips. If any man could teach her the joys of love, Nicholas could.

They woke to the blinding glare of a June dawn and Jeannette's contented chatter in the nursery. Eavin's lashes fluttered open to meet the amber glow of Nicholas's eyes and the breathtaking warmth of his slow smile. She gradually became aware of those places on her body that had received his most urgent attentions last night, but the aches and scrapes were well worth it. She returned his smile with one of her own.

Nicholas breathed a sigh of relief and kissed her nose. "I was afraid you would change your mind again with the crow of the cock. You are not an easy person to second-guess, Irish."

"I didn't think you had any doubts," Eavin answered wryly.

"It is always better to pretend one doesn't, I have found. Would you have come with me last night had I asked instead of commanded?" Nicholas slipped his hand into the thick richness of her ebony hair, lifting the soft curls over her shoulder to better see her breasts. The points were puckered and ripe and ready for plucking, and his loins stirred at the knowledge.

Eavin tried to regard this question sensibly, but what he was doing to her insides made her incapable of coherent thought. Somehow he had talked her into agreeing to be his mistress. She ought to be ashamed, but she couldn't summon the emotion as the sun poured light across their skin and the infant blessed the silence with her coos.

"I don't know what I would have done," she confessed. "But I had better leave here before Annie comes upstairs. It is human nature to gossip, and there is no point in adding proof to the rumors."

"I told Annie I would call her when I wanted her to come up. Jeannette is old enough to wait a while for breakfast. How soon can she be weaned?"

His decisive means of settling all problems left Eavin bemused, and she stared at him in amazement. "She's terribly young . . ." She hesitated beneath Nicholas's questioning gaze. He would accept any answer she gave him, she realized. A relationship like theirs was beset with problems from the start, but they would only multiply should their trust in each other be lost. She had never trusted a man before, not even Michael, but for some odd reason she was trusting this one. She might as well give him reason to make the feeling mutual. "I don't know for certain, but she's eating a little food now that she has some teeth. It will be difficult to persuade Annie."

Nicholas looked satisfied. "I'll persuade her. Keeping Annie out won't stop all speculation, but there will be no one to say otherwise, either."

He was quite right. She had never got out of the habit of making her own bed. The servants would never know if she didn't sleep in it. Without Annie in the nursery, no one would have any right to be up here until they called. It was their word against rumor, as it had been all along. She lost nothing by the arrangement, and she had gained more. She looked up into Nicholas's face, saw that he was waiting for her to realize how simple he had made it, and for the first time in her life Eavin reached out to hold a man.

The first day of her new life as a man's mistress ran more smoothly than her first day as a wife. The day after she had married Dominic she had spent in constant fear and revulsion of the night to come. In her nervousness, Eavin had argued with Dominic and burned his oatmeal and smacked one of the boarders when he had made a lewd comment about the marriage bed. All in all, she had been perfectly miserable. Nicholas was succeeding in wiping out that memory.

He had a magnolia blossom floating in a bowl of water at her place at the table for breakfast. He arrived at the noon meal with a bouquet of roses, and when Eavin informed him she would rather have the bush, he gave her the name of a man to write to request whatever shrub she would like. Instead of politely keeping his hands to himself during the day as Dominic had been prone to do, Nicholas never missed an opportunity to kiss her when they were alone, inspiring a desire for the night to come instead of dread.

That didn't mean the arrangement was idyllic. When Eavin protested at his insistence on driving himself physically when it was obvious that he was in pain, Nicholas ignored her arguments. When she noted one of Lafitte's scurrilous pirates loitering in the yard and inquired about his presence, Nicholas refused to tell her. He kept his business to himself and left her to her woman's work, which maddened her but gave her no room for argument.

Physical intimacy did not mean intimacy in all areas of their lives; Nicholas made that perfectly clear. Eavin chafed at the restriction, but she could find no satisfactory way around it. He would be the same with a wife. In her own family there were no secrets. They had yelled and screamed and argued the house down over every topic of the other's life. But Nicholas came from a different culture, and she would have to learn to accept it. Gritting her teeth, she flung a paper wad at the door from which he had just departed. Arrogant bastard that he was, he thought himself invincible. Who was she to tell him otherwise?

No surprise awaited her at their evening meal, but Eavin could tell from Nicholas's smug expression that he had something in store. They discussed the highlights of their day with their usual politeness while the servants were about, but expectation began to curl in Eavin's stomach as soon as the meal was done.

Nicholas retreated to his desk to deal with correspondence, as he often did in the evenings, and Eavin went up to the nursery to tuck Jeannette into bed. Already learning to walk, the toddler wasn't eager to part with Eavin's attention, but eventually she wearied and fell asleep. By that time Annie had retired to her own room out back, and Eavin was prepared to spend the remainder of the evening reading. Instead she found Nicholas in the nursery doorway, waiting for her.

Drawing her into his room across the hall, he closed the door and pulled her into his arms. It seemed like eternity instead of hours since they had been alone like this, and Eavin eagerly stepped into his embrace, turning her head for his kiss and stretching to thread her hands through his hair and press herself against him. Nicholas groaned against her mouth and crushed her closer, then stepped away and began to unfasten the front of her bodice.

She would never grow accustomed to the liberties he took with her person. Before she could do more than shiver at the touch of his fingers inside the thin muslin, Nicholas released her to reach into his pocket.

"Close your eyes," he commanded as she stared up at him with bewilderment.

Doing as told, Eavin felt the brush of something cold against her skin. He had untied the drawstring of her chemise, leaving her naked to his gaze, and she felt her nipples pucker against the material that barely clung there.

"Open them."

Eavin looked at Nicholas first, then down at herself. A ruby teardrop encircled with tiny diamonds hung from an intricate silver chain between her breasts, and her hand involuntarily reached to cover it. Just the touch of her own hand against the sensitive flesh made her aware of the man who had placed the jewel there, and she clutched the pendant as fury welled up in her at the same time as her breast ached for his touch.

"You agreed I am not your whore. You said this was a mutually beneficial arrangement! How dare you pay me with jewels for what I freely gave? Why don't you give this to your colored mistress? She would appreciate it more." Eavin struggled to find the clasp so she could throw the necklace at him.

Nicholas caught her hand and jerked it down, pulling her gown from her shoulders as he did so. "Don't try my temper, Eavin. It won't work. If I want to give you jewels, I will. I would do the same for a wife. It pleases me to see you wear things I have bought for you. Had I the right, I would brand you for all to see, but I don't have that right. So allow me what little I can."

"Little?" Eavin glanced down at the costly pendant and the place where Nicholas's brown hand rested, and tears formed in her eyes. "This necklace must be worth more than I have ever worn on my back in all my lifetime. How can you call it little? And I have nothing to give you in return. I can't accept it, Nicholas, can't you see?"

Slowly he began unfastening the remainder of her buttons and bows. "It is but a pirate's bauble, *ma chèrie.* How can it compare to the joy you bring me every time I hear Jeannette laugh? Do not argue the value of our gifts for each other; that is for merchants. It has naught to do with life."

Nor love. Eavin shuddered as Nicholas bent his lips to

her breast, seducing her in the way he knew best. And it was seduction, she knew. What was between them had no more to do with love than the jewel hanging about her neck. It was desire, pure and simple, and she gave herself up to it as easily as she accepted his claim.

It was more than she had ever known before.

24

"Ahh, my poor *chéri,* is worse than I thought." A creamy hand caressed the sun-browned cheek beside the healing gash. "You should have come to me. This may scar your pretty face."

Nicholas smiled gently, kissed her palm, and set her hand aside. "I have been assured that a scar will only improve my miserable attractions."

Dark eyes lit with amusement as the woman studied his satisfied expression. Wearing a gown of gold-and-cream-striped silk that would have appeared gaudy on any other, but suited her black hair and magnolia complexion to perfection, she swayed with the smooth grace of a gazelle as she turned away from him. Stopping effectively in the lace-curtained window through which the sun poured, she faced him once again.

"*La petite mademoiselle* with the green eyes?"

Not surprised by Labelle's knowledge of all his secrets, Nicholas grinned and poured himself a glass of wine. "She has a wicked tongue," he agreed.

"I can think of more than one way to apply that expression," Labelle replied suggestively. "Whatever it is she does, she does it well. I cannot remember seeing you so . . ." she hesitated over the word, "content. She is good for you, I think."

"She is a stubborn, hotheaded, argumentative little witch," Nicholas said calmly. "But I did not come here to enlighten you with my personal life."

"You should not come here at all." Labelle stepped back from the curtain and walked to the wine decanter to help herself. "You have a house of your own. Why do you not go there?"

Nicholas stiffened but continued sipping his wine. "Do I get in the way of your latest lover?"

Labelle gave him the closest thing she had to a scowl: a slightly miffed expression involving raising her delicately plucked eyebrows. "When and if I wish to take lovers, they will not tell me who I may entertain in my own home."

Nicholas relaxed and leaned against a set of shelves lined with books. "You should marry, Belle. You should have gone with Henrí to France. You would be courted by the wealthiest and most powerful men in the country once Henrí establishes his credentials."

"Your credentials, you mean." Belle drifted to a chair and floated into it. "I am certain you find it *très amusant* to send a man of color to take the title of marquis in your place. Just think of the generations to come, so proud of their blue blood, not knowing it is tinted with black. You are a cynical bastard, Nicholas, and you have the nerve to ask me why I do not marry?"

"He could not get into any more trouble over there than he was about to here, and after all these years of hearing it pounded into my brain, you can be certain I have no wish to ever hear the title again. Henrí has the same noble blood in his veins as I do."

"Not quite the same," she said wryly. "Your noble mother would dispute the fact vehemently. Can you still hold a grudge against her after all these years? Why do you not go to her when you come to town instead of here?"

Nicholas shifted his shoulder against the shelf, then straightened and paced restlessly to the window. "There has never been anything between us but my father, and I wouldn't exactly call him a glue to bind the family. You and Henrí are the family I've never had. Let it go at that. You still have not told me why you object to marriage and did not go with Henrí. Why do you stay here when you can be little more than an invisible woman among society?"

Belle pouted with a sensual bow of her lips. "Ahh, big brother, have you no more eyes than that? An invisible woman has much power. I can do things you cannot do. I can pull invisible strings and bring men tumbling to the ground or make them disappear in a puff of smoke. Why should I give all that up to any man?"

Nicholas scowled as he glared at his half sister. "Don't

play the priestess with me, Belle. That voodoo superstition is beneath you. You are an educated woman and far more intelligent than most. Why do you waste yourself playing these games?"

"Because I am useful." Her abrupt tone was distinctly different from the languid ones of earlier. "Do not underestimate me, Nicholas, and do not question too thoroughly. You have come here for help in finding Raphael, have you not? You are quite correct in assuming he hired those men to attack you. You would do well to keep someone at your back at all times. He knows he cannot win in any honest fight with you, and he knows you mean to kill him. He has nothing to lose by making you suffer before he moves in for the final blow."

"I'm fully aware of that. Why does he not let his father know he is alive? The old man is grieving himself into madness."

"Snakes don't recognize their parents," she replied scornfully. "He has all the warmth of a copperhead, and the same skills. You will not find him, Nicholas. He is in the bayous. Even if I gave you his direction, he would see you coming and be gone before you got there. Let me take care of him for you."

Nicholas could tell his half sister would relish the task, and perhaps in her mind she thought the deed would repay him for what he had done for her in the past, but he still retained some thread of honor, and he shook his head. "There is no satisfaction in that. If anything, I would have him delivered in one piece to his father's doorstep, but I am aware that is a more difficult request than death. I will wait. He has to come out of hiding sometime."

"But not when you expect it. The child is his, and he is capable of using her if he chooses. A snake does not carry a sword, Nicholas. Poison is his choice of weapons."

A flush of anger darkened Nicholas's skin. "If you hear anything of that sort, you have my permission to take whatever action is necessary. Jeannette means more than honor to me."

"And the lady with the green eyes?" The mischievous tone returned to her voice as she regarded her older brother.

"There is no reason he should harm her." Nicholas dismissed the topic with a languid gesture.

"No? You think Raphael does not believe the rumors his father is spreading? Your dear *maman* is in a state of apoplexy trying to quench all the fires of gossip. Why do you think she stays so late in the city this year?"

Nicholas ran his hand through his hair in exasperation. "You are determined to send me home, are you not?"

Belle answered with the patience of a teacher to her student. "She could not help you when you were young, *chéri*. She tries to make up for it now. When will you learn to forgive her?"

Nicholas finished his wine with gulp. "The past is done. Leave it be."

"My *maman* could run and hide. We were used to starving. Yours could not, Nicholas. She did not know how to survive without her man. You judge her too harshly by the laws of your strength. There are different laws for women. Someday, before it is too late, you must realize that."

Remembering how he had found his half sister and half brother, living on the streets, practicing every trade known to mankind to keep clothes on their back and food in their stomachs, Nicholas clenched his teeth. He had pulled them out of the gutter, sent them to school with what little he could beg, borrow, and steal from the world he lived in. But there had been no one to do the same for him or his mother had their positions been reversed. He had grown up in the lap of pampered society and learned strength from abuse. Belle's mother had courageously given up Nicholas's father to protect her children from his malicious temper. She could not have known that she would die before her children were old enough to protect themselves; that had been the cruelty of fate.

"What you say may be right, but it cannot change how I feel. She is a weak woman who thought of herself as much as she did me. There had to be somewhere she could have gone, something she could have done, but she did not. As long as my father gave her a noble name so she could hold her head up in society and could run up debts to keep us in style, she would never leave him. It is too late to change any of that."

"Perhaps so, but perhaps someday you could listen to

her side of the story. Did you know he beat her, too?" Belle asked pleasantly, as if discussing the weather.

Nicholas sent her a livid look and strode toward the door. "I can see there is no talking with you today. I shall go humble myself before my mother and accept her reluctant hospitality in a house that belongs to me. One of these days I'm going to find a man who will teach you better uses for your mouth than nagging."

"Next time, bring Mrs. Dupré," Belle called happily after him. "She will sweeten your temper, no doubt."

The door slammed on her tinkling laughter.

"Nicholas! What are you doing here?" Hélène Saint-Just looked over her son's broad shoulder somewhat apprehensively, as if expecting to find him towing Eavin and child and sundry other undesirables.

Nicholas didn't miss the look, and he scowled at this confirmation of his expectations. "You needn't worry. I left Jeannette at home. I simply had some business to conduct and thought to stay the night, with your permission, of course. I didn't think you would stay so late in the city."

His mother waved her fan a little faster than was customary as she stood aside to allow Nicholas to enter the *petite salle*. "I had much to do here. And you know you are always welcome." A little less promptly, she added, "And your daughter, too."

Nicholas raised a cynical brow as he waited for his mother to take her seat. "That is gracious of you, thank you. We will wait until the weather cools, however. You do have plans to leave the city, do you not? I would not have you here if the fever strikes again."

"Yes, yes, of course. I have several invitations. I just haven't chosen which to accept. Do sit down, Nicholas. Your hovering makes me nervous."

Judging from his mother's tone that she was still hoping for an invitation more to her liking than the ones she had received, Nicholas refused to worry any longer about it. He had no intention of inviting her to invade the privacy of his home. The plantation was his refuge, the only place in the world where he could be himself, and with Eavin safely installed as his mistress, he had no compunction about keeping the rest of the world out.

"I don't have time to visit just yet, *maman*. I'll be back later this evening. I only wished to be certain you are well and would not be disadvantaged by my presence."

Madame Saint-Just drew herself up regally in her chair. "Of course I would not be 'disadvantaged,' as you say. You are always welcome. Perhaps I should arrange a small dinner party. Your year of mourning is almost ended, Nicholas, and I understand you have been attending social functions. It is time for you to begin looking for another wife."

Nicholas sighed and returned his hat to his head as he strode toward the door. "Whatever you say, *maman*. I will return later."

Much later. In general, good Creoles did not drink to excess, but Nicholas figured he had been given excuse enough to indulge just this one night. Nagged by his family, apart from Eavin for the first night in weeks, and still aching from that brutal beating, he allowed himself to be drawn into Daniel's carousing. He was even missing Michael's stubborn Irish company, he reflected with less than sobriety as he raised a glass of the American's abominable whiskey and took a gulp. He should have arranged for his overseer to meet him here. Michael would have loved this place.

Swinging away from the polished bar to admire the gaudily dressed dancing girls at the front of the room, Nicholas decided American tastes were a little raw for his palate, but they had an elemental nature that could be appealing when he was drunk enough.

His gaze wandered over the sea of keelboatmen and other river lowlives that inhabited a place like this, and he began to grin drunkenly. The Americans who poured into the city daily loved to drink and gamble and have a good time. He'd never owned a saloon before. Wouldn't the good people of New Orleans have rolling fits if they found out he meant to buy one?

Daniel watched his employer's hard-eyed grin with a mixture of wariness and camaraderie. Nicholas Saint-Just was a fair man. He'd known that before he brought him here. He just hadn't thought a citified French Creole would be happy about investing money in this kind of venture. But Nicholas was the only man Daniel knew with enough money to help finance the purchase, and he was ambitious enough to try anything once. A glow of satisfaction enveloped him as he lifted the bottle in another toast to their incipient partnership.

"Here's to the smartest damn man in the city of New Orleans!" Daniel's tongue was having a little trouble getting the word out clearly, but his companion wasn't hearing any better than he was speaking.

Glassy-eyed, Nicholas held out his glass for a refill.

"And here's to the prettiest little newspaper writer this world has ever seen!" Daniel lifted his glass to his lips only to find the point of a *colchemarde* suddenly at his throat.

He gulped, and Nicholas pressed the point a little deeper. "You do not speak of my woman in public, Fletcher. Is that understood?"

His reflexes must be growing stale to allow the elegant Frenchman to pull a weapon on him so fast he didn't see it coming. Nodding carefully, Daniel breathed a sigh of relief as the sword pulled back. The noisy crowd around them had scarcely noticed the contretemps, and he shuddered at how easily life could be shed in a place like this.

"I apologize, Saint-Just. I did not realize the lady was yours. Shall I offer you congratulations?"

Nicholas ignored the question. "If you are to do business in this city, *monsieur,* you must learn the manners. One does not mention a lady in public. That is why I shall never see her name on one of those articles, *comprenez-vous?*"

The sword disappeared just as quickly as it had appeared when Daniel nodded obediently.

"I cannot say that she is talented?" he inquired nervously.

"Not to anyone but me." Feeling quite well with the world, Nicholas rose from the table without staggering and issued a general invitation with a gesture of his hand. "You will come home with me? I think a meal is in order."

Daniel considered something in the stomach just what both of them needed, and pushing himself to his feet with the aid of the table, he imitated his employer's graceful retreat to the best of his abilities, bumping into only chairs and a dancing girl on the way out.

* * *

Their grand entrance into the Saint-Just dining room in the middle of the dinner party brought consternation and outrage from around the table as Nicholas pulled up abruptly and made a drunken salute with his cane while Daniel bumped into his back and nearly knocked him down.

As his mother frowned, Nicholas calmly and with much aplomb took his place at the head of the table and signaled one of the servants to set another plate. Daniel wavered slightly at being placed between a nervous miss and an amused old French gentleman, but the smell of food overcame his reluctance, and with a definite lack of grace, he fell into the offered chair.

All in all, it was a fitting ending to a perfect day, Nicholas mused as one of the ladies assisted his mother from the room. He leered blatantly at the terrified miss on his left and accepted her hasty retreat from the table with a certain satisfaction.

That should put an end to his mother's matrimonial plans.

25

"Nicholas, what are you doing?" Eavin rose from the desk as Nicholas slammed the door and threw home the newly installed bolt.

She gasped as he crossed to her in two strides and yanked her into his arms, but it was too good to see him again to protest. Throwing her arms around him in welcome, she returned his resounding kiss with eagerness. But when he began pulling up her dress and carrying her toward the sofa, she wriggled frantically in his grasp.

"Nicholas, put me down! Have you gone mad? What on earth do you think . . ." She completed that question with a cry as he dropped her to the cushions and sprawled on top of her.

"You must be drunk. Nicholas, stop that . . ." Whatever she meant to say disappeared from her tongue as he closed his mouth over hers and began to ravish it thoroughly. Eavin arched against him, pulling his head closer, releasing the desire kept pent up with these days of abstinence.

"So that story has spread already," Nicholas murmured as he turned his attention to the vulnerable hollow of her throat. "I am not so fond of the results of hard liquor that I mean to try it often, *ma chérie*. You have no need to worry of that. I am only eager to make up for lost time. Open to me, Eavin. I have need of you right now."

"Nicholas, not here! Not now. Someone will come," she protested even as she lifted her hips to accommodate his roving hands.

"They can't get in, *ma petite*. You need only to hush those delectable cries and no one will know the better. I thank the gods that you are no lady, for I am discovering numerous ungentlemanly urges."

"Discovering?" The sarcasm was modified by her kisses as Eavin parted his shirt and found his bare chest.

"Of course, Irish, do you doubt me?" Pushing himself up so he could see the sparkle of her emerald eyes, Nicholas grinned. He was home. To prove it wasn't an instant's work. As he unfastened his buttons and her eyes widened, he felt a rush of relief that had nothing to do with the physical release he was about to achieve.

Eavin stored her doubts for another time. He hadn't come to her like this without a reason, and the stories she had heard of the drunken dinner party needed further exploration, but the need between them now was too great for any other thought than how to get around their clothes. With impatience she helped him pull at her skirt and petticoat, and when his hand finally found her, she muffled her cries against his coat.

"I think we should give a soiree, *ma chérie*." Nicholas leaned over to straighten the lace at Eavin's throat, smoothing the fabric over her breasts with definite pleasure as he did so. "It is time we returned everyone's kind hospitality."

Eavin smacked his hand away and reached into her tumbled hair for some fragment of the pins that had once been there. She glanced at him anxiously. "It is not too soon? It has not quite been a year . . ."

Nicholas brushed her objection away with a gesture of his hand. "We will celebrate July Fourth. It is the patriotic thing to do. No one could object. You will come to understand we are much more generous in our ways than your countrymen." He did not tell her of his dual purpose in this celebration. If gossip was spreading all the way to New Orleans about his relationship with Eavin, she would soon be ostracized by the society he meant for her to live in. He would not have her relegated to a backstreet row house like Belle, not if there were any way to prevent it.

Anxiety was replaced by a frown of concentration as Eavin contemplated the logistics of coordinating a large party in two weeks' time. She had never given the sort of elegant balls that she had attended since coming here. She had next to no knowledge of the procedure, but she was certain the help of Mrs. Howell would be invaluable.

Ruthlessly pulling her hair into a tight roll, she nodded agreement.

"You will have to provide a list of whom to invite," she replied absently through a mouthful of pins.

Smiling at the distant expression appearing in those devilish eyes, Nicholas carefully removed the pins and set them on the table, then wrecked all her handiwork by shoving his hands into her hair and bringing it tumbling down about her shoulders.

"I must find you a lady's maid skilled in dressing hair. It is a sin to wear it hidden."

Eavin's astonishment melted beneath his kiss. As practical as she tried to be about this arrangement, she could not help her romantic nature from succumbing to Nicholas's practiced charm. She could almost believe his flattery when he took her in his arms as he did now, kissing her lovingly even after he had taken what he wanted. Closing her eyes and holding him close, she gladly accepted what he offered.

The coming ball was another matter entirely. Eavin frantically began making lists as soon as Nicholas took himself off to the fields. She dashed a note off to Mrs. Howell, and by the next morning she and Lucinda were in the *petite salle* with her, adding their notes to the already lengthy lists.

The names Nicholas provided brought a moan of envy to Mrs. Howell's lips. "Marigny? Surely he will not come so far. And Villeré? Eavin, these are people we could not hope to meet in New Orleans. Mr. Howell works with Governor Claiborne and we can expect the best Americans, but this list is the cream of Creole society. And Nicholas has both on here. Even if he knows all these people, the Creoles will not come if they know the Americans are invited."

Eavin looked up from her desk with curiosity. "You have entertained American and French and Spanish. I know there are differences, but they seem to get along well enough in your house. Why should Nicholas have any difficulty?"

"It is not Nicholas, it is these people." Mrs. Howell waved the invitation list. "The people you have met at our dinners have been neighbors and people who curry some favor with the government. Nicholas has been very helpful in getting us accepted by people like the Dubois. But the Creoles on this list are too wealthy and powerful to have any need to curry favors. They do not even acknowledge our existence."

"Because you are American? How extremely odd." Eavin took the list and scanned it. She choked as she came to several names toward the bottom. "I see Nicholas is being extremely democratic in his hospitality. You will not only be dancing with the elite of Creole society, but with the best pirates, too."

Lucinda gave a half scream and grabbed the list, finding the notorious names easily. Giggling, she handed the paper back to her mother. "I think this is one Fourth of July celebration that will bring its own fireworks. I have heard Jeremy talk, Mama. Nicholas is considered quite a catch in all circles. Every family on that list with a daughter to present will be here, regardless of the company. I think this shall be the most exciting night of my life."

"I think your father will insist you stay home if there are to be pirates." Mrs. Howell sniffed as she glared at the offending names. "Governor Claiborne is furious with those bandits."

"You and Lucinda will be almost the only ones I know. Please do not abandon me." Eavin sent a reassuring look to the crestfallen girl before Mrs. Howell looked up.

Satisfied with this excuse, the older woman nodded curtly. "I shall explain it like that to my husband. We could not let a good neighbor down."

The preparations went smoothly, if often hectically, after that. It was difficult enough to undertake the massive housecleaning and extensive refurbishing and repairs the old house needed before it could be presentable to such a large assembly, but the constant stream of visitors often took hours out of every day.

Eavin began to dread the times Nicholas came riding in from the fields to hastily wash and change into clean linen, for that meant someone had warned him that a boat or a carriage or horses were arriving. Had he been the idle Creole gentleman he wished to portray, his overseer would be out in the fields and Nicholas would be lounging over lemonade and cards in the salon. Playing two parts had to be wearing on him, and Eavin wondered at his excess of amiability.

But when it became apparent that the constant stream of visitors often had unwed daughters to introduce, Eavin remembered Lucinda's words, and she didn't know whether to sigh with exasperation or be afraid. Nicholas was unfailingly polite to all, and he made certain that she was introduced as Jeannette's aunt and treated with all due respect, but she could not see him taking any interest in the lovely young things fluttering their fans and eye-lashes at him. Actually, she didn't think any of the young women lifted their eyes long enough to look at him. They seemed determined to study the floor for any speck of dust or to locate their reflections in the polish, Eavin wasn't certain which. Only the daughters of the Ameri-cans were bold enough to flirt, but Nicholas didn't seem to notice that they were doing so.

It took nearly two weeks of this behavior before Eavin conquered her qualms and dared to broach the subject. She couldn't do it in the bright light of the supper table, when he might see the fear in her eyes. She waited until one night in bed, after their lovemaking, when it was too hot to sleep and they both lay contentedly awake in each other's arms.

"Nicholas, do you mean to find a wife among these girls that keep parading through here?"

Smoking one of the cheroots he had taken up since Mi-chael had sent him a box, Nicholas chomped the end, lifted a rakish eyebrow in her direction, then removed the tobacco from his mouth and set it aside. "Ahh, the plump little one in the red stripes has you worried, does she? She's ripe as a peach, but don't you think that high-pitched giggle would drive me to distraction after a while? Do you think Jeannette would learn to imitate it?"

Eavin curled her fingers in the fine hairs of his chest and tugged. "The good Lord knows I may be giving you too much credit, but I should hope you could do better than that."

Nicholas winced, grabbed Eavin's hand and twisted it to her side, and pushed her back to the mattress. Leaning over her, he nibbled at her throat and ears. "Do you tire of me so quickly that you wish to marry me off?"

"Never, but Nicholas . . ." Eavin grabbed his hair as he bent to bite at her breast.

"Let us hear no more of it then." With deliberation Nicholas sank his teeth into the tender flesh just enough to make her writhe beneath him. The topic was not one he wished to consider, but neither could he explain his reasons for opening up the sacred privacy of his home to these hordes of guests. It would only worry her to know he did it for her sake and her sake alone.

The night of the ball, Eavin stood in front of Nicholas's mirror and grimaced at her reflection. She wasn't at all certain that was the real Eavin Dupré standing there in a wisp of silver silk that revealed more of her breasts than any man should see. Violet ribbons tied beneath her breasts only served to emphasize the narrowness of her bodice, but Nicholas had assured her that the gown was a model of propriety by current standards. She dubiously eyed the matching ribbons threaded through her ebony curls by the Howells' experienced hairdresser. Wisps and tendrils already escaped about her face and throat. She shuddered to think how it would look in a few hours.

"This place isn't big enough to entertain overnight guests," Eavin fretted as she twisted herself nervously in an attempt to finish fastening the back of her gown.

Nicholas took the task from her hands, competently arranging all the tapes and hooks until the silk lay smoothly in a thin layer over the fine muslin of her chemise. Both materials were so thin as to make Eavin nearly naked, and his fingers idly tested his theory as he caressed her through her bodice.

"They are aware this is essentially a bachelor establishment. Carondelet will hold the families wishing to stay and visit. The gentlemen wishing to stay can go to the *garçonnière*. Do not worry that I will let anyone interfere with our arrangement. I know how to be discreet."

Eavin shivered as Nicholas's long fingers found her breast and teased it into responding to him. She bent her head back against his shoulder and relaxed into his arms, letting the strength of his body flow into hers. She needed that reassurance before facing the night ahead.

"I do not worry about you, Nicholas. I worry about myself. I'm not used to mixing in society, and although

I've been working with Mrs. Howell, I still don't know enough French to converse intelligently. Sometimes I really do think it would have been better if you had just left me to be Jeannette's nurse."

"No." His reply was firm and irrevocable as he swung her around to face him. Amber eyes glowed as they devoured the radiance of her simple beauty. Rather than offer the flattery that was on his tongue, Nicholas attempted to explain. "This United States is made up of many sorts of people. When my daughter is old enough to go out into society, I wish it to be in one that will accept her aunt for who she is and not for where she came from. It is a small thing, Eavin, but it has to start somewhere." Hesitantly, studying her expression for some sign of understanding, he continued, "I have already lost a brother and sister to the constraints of society. I would not lose more."

The sound of a carriage arriving below and Clemmie calling to one of the maids warned they had dawdled too long. Eavin wanted to know more, but when Nicholas kissed her cheek and set her gently aside, she knew the discussion was ended for now. There would be time enough to finish it later. Reaching to touch his jaw, where only a thin line gave evidence of the earlier injury, Eavin pulled his head down so she could kiss him, and then lifting her skirt, she fled the room to the chaos forming below.

The violins and flute could be heard over the dull roar of conversation as Eavin escaped the *grand salle* with Lucinda for the less crowded hall and *petite salle*, where conversational gatherings could be found.

"I cannot believe I just met the mythical Bernard Marigny!" Lucinda was chattering excitedly. "The tales I have heard about his wealth . . . why, he was just as charming as Nicholas."

Unfortunately, the woman with him had not been, Eavin mused as she greeted one guest and gestured for a maid to serve another. Marigny's haughty companion had spewed a river of angry French and flounced off, leaving Eavin feeling smaller than the lowliest slave. She had not understood the words, but she had understood the gist of her tone. Monsieur Marigny had to shrug and apologize for his companion's refusal to be introduced to an American. Eavin could only be thankful that Lucinda had been too excited to understand the exchange.

The late arrival of another boat load of guests from Carondelet brought another influx of chatter and gay laughter. All the doors and windows facing the gallery had been opened to circulate air through the crowded rooms, but the July heat and humidity easily won any battle with the night breeze. The torches burning along the railing outside to fend off mosquitoes sent a tarry odor drifting in with the newcomers, and Eavin fanned it away as she stepped forward to welcome the guests. She froze as the crowd shifted and two familiar formidable figures emerged.

"Madame Saint-Just and Madame Dupré!" Clutching Lucinda's arm for support and donning a brave smile, Eavin advanced upon the newcomers.

"Eavin, how good it is to see you again. I hope you will allow us a peek at our granddaughter before we join the company. Have you met . . ." Hélène Saint-Just began the introductions, drawing Eavin in with a proprietary hand.

Amazed at the woman's sudden about-face, Eavin fixed a smile on her lips and attempted to memorize the onslaught of names. Madame Saint-Just's obvious approval of her son's supposed paramour and Madame Dupré's intimate acceptance of her daughter-in-law eased this first stage, and those who spoke only French did so slowly, allowing Eavin to reply in kind. Perhaps it was the mention of the granddaughter that allayed their suspicions so swiftly, for the other women asked to be shown the nursery, too.

Jeannette was sound asleep when they entered, but the grandmothers insisted on holding her. Eavin felt a creeping selfishness that she and Nicholas had kept Jeannette from them so deliberately. Perhaps Madame Saint-Just had learned to accept the circumstances of Jeannette's birth, and the child was all Madame Dupré had left of her daughter. It had been cruel to keep them away.

When the women had all admired the sleepy infant and complimented Eavin on her care of her, they retreated to Eavin's room to repair their *toilettes* before descending to the hallway, chattering about the quaintness of Nicholas's living quarters. Madame Dupré insisted on taking them

downstairs to show them the intricately inlaid secretaire
that Nicholas had given Francine, and they all swarmed
into the master chamber to ooh and ahh over the new
construction. Once they had snooped sufficiently, they
prepared to join the others, quite content that everything
was as it should be.

Nicholas caught them as they came out of his chamber,
and Eavin had to stifle a giggle as she read the lifted eyebrow and glitter in his eye. He sent her an admonishing
look that warned her she had better not make him laugh,
before bowing over the hand of the eldest lady and moving on to compliment the next with the easy charm of his
nature.

Actually feeling almost accepted for the first time since
her arrival, Eavin rejoiced in the company as they returned to the hall. Madame Dupré was murmuring to her
about some embroidered dresses she had seen that would
suit Jeannette to perfection. Madame Saint-Just was re-
galing one of the other women with her son's plans to improve the house. Nicholas was leaning over to hear the
whispers of a pale girl whose hand rested on his arm. It
felt comfortable and familiar somehow, and Eavin had no
resentment for the other girl's proprietary hold, for she
knew Nicholas was only exhibiting the politeness he had
been taught from an early age.

Eavin heard the galloping hoofbeats first. Over the
noise of conversation and music, the sound was more a
vibration, and she looked up to see if any other heard.
She caught Nicholas's eye, and her hand instinctively
reached for his arm. He squeezed it there but made no
move to approach the front door as he exchanged some
pleasantry with his mother.

The sound of boots clattering up the wooden stairs
turned several heads, but no one was prepared for the furious appearance of the large Irishman in the doorway, his
angry gaze sweeping the crowd until he located the one
head lighter and taller than the rest. With a roar he
launched himself through the throng.

"Unhand my sister, you bloody son of a bitch!" Michael's punch landed squarely on Nicholas's jaw.

26

"Michael!" Eavin screamed, but both men were already beyond hearing.

As the circle of women scattered, Nicholas returned the punch, and the two were soon rolling on the floor in the kind of battle most Creole gentlemen considered unseemly.

"Fletcher told me what you said, you bastard," Michael ground out as he avoided Nicholas's pinning hold to throw him over. "You'll not make a whore out of my sister. Eavin's the marrying kind."

"I'm going to wring your neck when I get my hands around it," Nicholas growled, dodging Michael's kick and leaping to his feet to feint with his left and strike flesh with his right. "That Irish temper of yours is going to get you killed this time."

The blows grew more vicious as the threats progressed. Blood spurted from a cut above Michael's eye, and Nicholas's lip cracked and split under a well-aimed punch. The crowd in the hallway began to grow and change in mood. Men now filled most of the places where women had stood. No one looked at Eavin.

Clyde Brown was the first to arrive at Eavin's side. She had seen Jeremy lead his mother and sister into another room, and excused his absence. Alphonso had yet to put in an appearance. She knew next to nothing of any of the other men calmly watching the two men tear each other to pieces along with her reputation. She looked up at the lawman with relief. Before he could speak, she jerked out the gun hidden in the pocket of his coat.

A general gasp circled the room as Eavin took the stairs and pointed the pistol in the direction of the brawling men on the floor. The sudden silence marked only with the crack of bone against flesh did not catch the at-

tention of the combatants, but Eavin's voice brought their
heads up.

"My aim is good enough to know I'll hit one of you,
and at this minute I don't give a damn which one it is."

Nicholas deflected Michael's blow with his hand, shoving him off and forcing him to look up at Eavin.

"I'm almost sorry that you stopped. I would have enjoyed shooting something. Michael, I wish you would go
to your room and wash your mouth out with soap before
you return to the company." Eavin stalked down the stairs
and slapped the pistol into Clyde's palm. She sent Nicholas a scathing glare. "And you, I'm ashamed to know."
With a furious flounce of silk ruffles, she sailed out of the
hallway and into the *grand salle,* where the musicians
had stopped playing at the sudden exodus of male occupants.

Guests were preparing to leave. Eavin could see them
signaling to the servants or their escorts, gathering up
fans and shawls. Grimly refusing to allow the evening to
be destroyed by Michael's misplaced grand gesture, she
grabbed the arm of the pale young girl who had arrived
with Madame Saint-Just. Guiding her toward the gallery
doorway, she murmured confidentially, "Nicholas will
kill me if I reveal his surprise for the evening, but you
will not get the best place unless you find it early. Let us
leave the men to their play."

Eyes wide with fear and excitement, the girl glanced
over her shoulder toward the rumble of male voices in the
hall, then up at the elegant young woman over whom the
men were fighting. "Do you mean fireworks? I have
never seen fireworks," she answered in a voice heavily
accented with Spanish.

Excitement overcame her fear as she hurriedly followed her hostess. Much to Eavin's satisfaction, the girl's
evident pleasure turned questioning glances their way.
Nicholas's mother hurried in their direction, with her
nemesis not far in her wake.

"Go on and find a place while I speak with Madame
Saint-Just," Eavin whispered. The dangerous calm she
felt overtake her as the girl hurried off to whisper to another of her friends was not natural, but Nicholas's
mother would not know the source of the bitter gleam in
her eye.

"This is a disgrace." Hélène caught Eavin's arm and tried to lead her toward an exit. "We must get you out of here. Fetch Jeannette and I will call for a carriage."

Smiling, Eavin watched over the other woman's shoulder as a group of young girls began tugging protestingly at the arms of their parents, eager to follow their peers out onto the gallery. She turned a determined gaze on her former mother-in-law as that lady arrived and waited until both women had stopped talking to reply.

"If you have any feelings for Nicholas whatsoever, you will help me set this ball to rights again. It is still a little early yet for fireworks, but I will send someone to have them begin. The musicians must play something patriotic, I think. It had best be American first, then perhaps French. Let the men fight as they wish, but I would prefer it if the ladies would keep them calm. Are you with me or against me?"

Both women looked stricken at her audacity, but when it became obvious that Eavin would move off to do it on her own, they quickly caved in, Madame Saint-Just first.

"For Nicholas, I will do this," she hissed, "not for you, and not for the child, do you understand?"

"I understand quite well," Eavin replied with the same unnatural calm of earlier. "I would do the same in your place."

That piece of ambivalent information did not necessarily appease her, but Hélène moved off into the crowd, catching an aristocratic old lady before she could sail out of the room, whispering something cajoling in her ear, causing the woman to turn expectantly toward the wide bank of glass.

Madame Dupré, not to be outdone, repeated the same maneuver with two other women on the point of leaving. Assured that the competition between the two women would work in Nicholas's favor for a change, Eavin hurried across the floor toward the musicians while signaling to one of the servants. It was almost dark enough for fireworks. Who said one had to end a ball with them instead of beginning one? Perhaps she would start a new rage.

But it was an old rage burning in her breast while she ordered the musicians to a resounding "Yankee Doodle" and watched the crowd hesitate and turn back into the room. The men were coming in from outside, finding their ladies, and scowling or smiling as the American music echoed through the large room. The sound of the first explosion of gunpowder outside made them turn their attention in that direction.

The young people on the gallery cheered gallantly at the display of colored light against the night sky. The music soared louder, and drawn by the sounds, more people edged toward the windows. More gunpowder exploded and the cheers went wild. The musicians broke into the "Marseillaise," and even the crowd inside yelled their approval. An American, provoked by the French anthem or strong drink, crashed a chair against a wall. A Frenchman with sword drawn responded. But miraculously, a woman's soft voice cajoled one while the companions of the other pulled the combatants apart. The musicians, swelled with their success, attempted a Spanish theme.

The exploding reds and blues and golds lit the interior, fragmenting off the crystal chandeliers and captured in gilded mirrors. Almost a mystical atmosphere settled over the guests, and Eavin was certain it was Francine's gentle ghost prompting the musicians to settle into an elegant waltz. Few of the Americans knew the dance, but the Creoles seemed to know it by osmosis. The wealthy Monsieur Marigny led his partner onto the floor, followed by several of the more cosmopolitan residents of New Orleans. Before long, the *grand salle* filled with floating figures in silks and satins, and the crisis was ended.

Eavin knew the instant that Nicholas returned to the room. She knew he had to return, just as she had been forced to continue the ball. Appearance was everything to this society. She had done her part. Now let him do his.

Finding Clyde Brown, Eavin persuaded him to join her for the next dance. The fireworks ended and the young people filtered back into the room, providing a satisfactory crush. She didn't even have to look at Nicholas if she didn't want to. And she was too furious to want to. She was ready to explode with fury. It was much better that she keep moving and hold the anger in.

Nicholas watched as Eavin turned her back on him as soon as he entered the room and knew he had made a major tactical error. He had known it when he was doing it, but he had allowed too many insults to slide by in these last months of domestic life, and this one had set the rage inside him loose. He wasn't in the least bit sorry for breaking Michael's nose, the ass had deserved that, but Nicholas was genuinely sorry for what he had done to Eavin.

There was little he could do to make it up to her now, or possibly ever. Watching as she gaily slipped from Clyde Brown to Jeremy, not once looking in his direction, he realized how far she had come in this past year and how far she could have gone if tonight hadn't destroyed all her chances. But after tonight she would join the ranks of Mignon Dubois or worse, for Eavin didn't have the advantage of prestigious family or Creole ancestry to support her.

Avoiding the conflicting emotions that thought produced, Nicholas bowed over the hand of the nearest wallflower and proceeded to join the throng of dancers. Odd, that no matter how badly he behaved, it was no reflection on his reputation. Society excused men almost any indiscretion, but a woman had to be without flaw. Perhaps that was a way of admitting that men were weak and without character, Nicholas mused wryly. And he had a feeling that he wasn't going to prove anything different in these next few hours. The further Eavin moved away from him, the more determined he became to bring her back.

The gathering didn't break up until the wee hours of the morning. Nicholas stood in the doorway alone to see his guests off. Eavin had disappeared some time earlier, making it obvious that she was not hostess here. With the help of the servants he saw that the more drunken gentlemen were settled into the *garçonnière* for the night while the others were properly escorted to carriages and boats. He adamantly refused his mother's and mother-in-law's offer to stay for "appearances." They held their noses up and sniffed in disapproval and went off arm in arm for the first time in their lives.

When the last guest departed, Nicholas sighed in relief and shut the door. There was still one task left undone before he could seek the company of the one person he wished to see right now. With deliberation he headed for the small study and the man he had left pouring his sorrow into a whiskey glass.

Michael brought his head up with a jerk when Nicholas

slammed the study door behind him. A bruise was beginning to form beneath one eye, and the icepack he'd been holding to his nose was a melted puddle on the desk. He glared at his employer through bleary eyes and poured another drink.

The bottle was half empty, Nicholas noted as he swung himself into the nearest chair, but Michael didn't seem much worse for the drink. His glare sharpened as it focused on Nicholas, and the anger in him wasn't mellowed, just less concentrated than earlier. Perhaps it was better that way.

"You do realize you have just denounced your sister in front of all society," Nicholas began without preamble.

"Is that worse than what you've been doing?" Arrogantly, Michael filled a second glass and shoved it toward Nicholas.

"In the eyes of society, yes." Nicholas calmly lifted the glass and took a drink. The whiskey was potent and burned all the way down, but it was what he needed right now. "You don't understand the rules here. It was against the rules for Eavin and myself to live here unchaperoned, but with your presence and Jeannette's and the approval of our families, it could be excused as eccentric but not immoral. They might think the worst, but no one would ever say it. You, however, said it. In their eyes, that made it real. Nothing I can do now is ever going to remove the taint."

"Bullshit." Michael sat back in the desk chair and glared at Nicholas. "You could marry her. That is what any decent man would do."

That was a solution that had never really occurred to Nicholas. It was impractical, of course. Eavin wasn't Francine. Society would never accept her or her story. But it wasn't just society that stood in the way. Neither of them wanted the ties of marriage, and even if they did, it wouldn't be to each other. Eavin wanted children, and she would have to marry a man with a family already made to have them. Someday he would have to have an heir, and Eavin couldn't provide one. Marriage to each other was out of the question, but if it would settle this conflict looming between Eavin and her brother and himself, then he would put it to the test. Nicholas knew the answer before Eavin could give it, but Michael wouldn't be satisfied until he heard it from her lips.

"I think you mistake your sister's feelings, O'Flannery, but I will not speak for her. Send someone to bring her down."

Michael hurried to do just that. Standing in the hallway, he heard Eavin's refusal clearly when the servant knocked on her door, and he crossed to the stairs and yelled upward. "Get yourself down here now, little sister, or I'm coming up after you!"

The angry silence that followed foretold the unpleasantness to come, but he was only doing what was best for her. Satisfied that she would respond, Michael returned to the study and glared at his imperturbable employer while they waited.

Wrapped in a light linen robe, Eavin appeared in the doorway. Her hair tumbled down about her shoulders in a manner that should have emphasized her seductive femininity, but the furious glitter of her eyes and lift of her chin distracted from such thoughts. She was glorious in her fury, but the fact that she didn't even look at him assured Nicholas of the outcome of this little charade.

"Well?" Michael lifted a demanding eyebrow in their direction.

Nicholas had stood up when Eavin entered, now he gestured toward a chair. "I have a question to ask of you. Would you care to take a seat?"

"I've no wish to be speaking to the likes of either of you," Eavin replied coldly. "Have what you want to say and be done with it."

"You don't make it easy, you realize." Nicholas loomed over her, aware of every curve and swell of her body with the intimate knowledge of weeks of lovemaking. He wanted to touch her but dared not. Not yet.

"My heart bleeds." She smiled sweetly.

"After tonight, your brother thinks we should marry. It is the only solution to repair the damage that has been done."

Nicholas didn't know how anxiously he awaited her answer until Eavin made him stand there, the glitter of her eyes telling him exactly what she thought of this callous proposal before her words could make her decision public.

"Well, I wish the two of you happy. I'll be returning to my bed, then. Jeannette is up early in the mornings." She swung around and was almost out of the door before Michael could recover himself long enough to shout after her.

"Eavin Marie O'Flannery, you get yourself back here!"

Eavin swung around again, her hair flying around her shoulders as she did so. "You go back to whatever hell you came from, Michael O'Flannery. I'll not be taking orders from the likes of you!"

This time when she stalked out, no one tried to stop her. Nicholas continued standing, a wry smile twisting his lips as he watched every swaying movement. He decided she was more compact than stately as she marched up the stairs, but she carried herself with the proud fury of an Irish queen. He wanted her with a passion that he had some difficulty disguising.

Turning around, Nicholas gazed enigmatically at his overseer. "Have you any more suggestions?"

"She always was one to try the patience of a saint." Michael shook his head morosely as he stared into his glass. "Perhaps she'll cool off tomorrow."

"And perhaps it will snow, too. She has her reasons, O'Flannery. You'd best let her be the judge of what she wants; she's in a position to know more than you."

Michael glanced up at the cool Frenchman in the doorway. He supposed women found Nicholas Saint-Just attractive even though he sported a cracked lip and a hairline scar down the side of his cheek. But what he saw was a man made of fine-honed steel, too hard and unbendable for the likes of his vulnerable sister. Perhaps she was right. She didn't belong with a man like this.

Decisively, Michael answered, "Then I'll be taking her from here on the morrow."

The expression on Saint-Just's face was far from pleasant as he replied, "Over my dead body," and walked away.

27

As much as Nicholas longed to go to Eavin that night, he knew better than to compound one error with another. It was late and they both needed a good night's sleep, not another confrontation. Seeing Eavin's door firmly closed and probably blocked by half the furniture in the room, he turned to his own bed and contemplation of how best to handle the morrow.

But when Nicholas went downstairs the next day, he wasn't prepared for walking in on a moving scene between his mistress and the brother of the man he had sworn to kill.

Eavin virtually ignored Nicholas's entrance as she stood up and demanded that Alphonso do the same.

"This isn't appropriate, sir," she remonstrated, backing away so he couldn't touch her hem. "I know you do me an honor, but it isn't necessary. Please do behave, Alphonso."

The Spaniard rose gracefully, his pale face taut with emotion as he clasped Eavin's hand. "How would you have me behave? I will do whatever you ask, just let me take you away from this place. It is not fitting that you should suffer for his behavior."

Nicholas didn't even give Eavin a chance to reply to that insult. Grabbing the boy's collar, he shoved him toward the doorway. "Out, Reyes. If you wish to be of help to Mrs. Dupré, then cut out your father's tongue and see your brother hanged. You'll find Raphael skulking in the bayous."

Alphonso recovered his balance and grabbed the door frame, turning to face his opponent. "I will send my seconds," he said stiffly.

"You can send thirds and fourths for all I care. My quarrel isn't with you but with Raphael. Send him out, and I'll accept the challenge." Nicholas folded his arms across his chest and glared at the younger man.

"Raphael is dead, and you killed him. You cannot tell me otherwise. I will send my seconds, and if you refuse them, you will be scorned by all."

Nicholas shrugged. "What else is new? Go home, Alphonso, and don't come back or I won't bother with the formalities. I'll just cut your ears off."

Insulted, Alphonso strode out without another look back. Restraining a sigh of impatience, Nicholas swung around to capture Eavin before she could escape through another door.

"Don't you dare leave," he ordered in a voice that brooked no denial.

Eavin picked up her sewing and continued toward the far door.

"If you want a scene, I'll give you one, but you aren't going to like it." Nicholas leaned against the door, blocking this escape route.

Eavin stopped to face him. "Then say what you have to say and be done with it."

"I want an end to these strutting suitors of yours. You're mine and we both know it. There's no use in continuing the pretense." That wasn't at all what Nicholas had intended to say, but the words were out of his mouth before he could take them back. He had spent a miserable night longing for her welcoming arms, hating the arguments that kept them apart. He had meant to put an end to all argument, but this wasn't how he had meant to do it. Still, they were words that needed to be said in one way or another.

"Is that all you have to say?" Eavin raised her eyebrows inquiringly.

That was when Nicholas knew he was sitting on a powder keg. A calm Eavin was unnatural, like the silence of the swamp when a stranger intrudes. He had given her enough ammunition to blow his head off, and she was choosing her moment. The thought chilled him, and he moved in to defuse the situation.

"No, there are many things I would like to say, but these are not the best surroundings in which to say them." Nicholas caught her arm before she could realize his intent. "Come with me. It is time you learned to ride."

That caught her off guard. Eavin turned and stared at him rather than fighting his grip. She was growing accustomed to seeing Nicholas's face battered and bruised, and she did not allow sympathy to stand in her way. "I think not. Besides, I don't have the appropriate attire."

"I will buy you whatever you need later. For now, have Clemmie fetch you one of Francine's habits. The skirt should fit in everything but length, and there is none but me to see you."

Eavin hesitated. She was still furious, but Nicholas had somehow removed the target for her anger. Had he shouted at her, she could have shouted back. Had he ignored her, she could have got even in any number of ways. Confronting her calmly was beyond any expected behavior that she knew how to deal with.

There wasn't any sense in postponing the fight they both spoiled for, but Eavin wasn't at all certain that taking it outside the house was a wise idea. Remembering the toddler upstairs who knew their voices well, she supposed it would be better to carry this particular argument out of hearing.

"I'll be ready shortly." Coldly she eyed the hand on her arm until Nicholas released her. When she walked out, it was with the knowledge that his gaze was upon her. He'd called her *his*! Of all the bloody nerve . . .

She didn't keep him waiting as he had expected. Obviously having worked up to a full head of steam again, Eavin sailed down the stairs, disdaining his offered arm as she stormed toward the door. Nicholas followed, attempting to hide his smile as he watched the flash of her stockinged ankles beneath the long skirt she held up and admired the smallness of her waist and the curve of her hip in the revealing cut. Once they got the storm out of the way and laid a few ground rules around here, he was going to enjoy removing that particular article of clothing.

The horses he had ordered saddled were waiting. Eavin didn't have any choice but to accept Nicholas's help in gaining her seat. His hands were strong and familiar around her waist, but she resisted their temptation. Anger provided an armor against the sins of the body.

They rode slowly, Nicholas giving her instructions as they went, occasionally stopping her and adjusting her

hands or the way she sat, explaining what the horse expected as he did so. It was early yet, and there was none
to see their progress but the slaves in the fields. Their
guests had not risen after the night's debaucheries, and
the household servants would take care of their needs
when they did. The stickiness of the July heat and humidity had not yet reached unbearable proportions, and Eavin
endured the onslaught of Nicholas's attentions with surprising fortitude.

When they reached a high point, some distance from
the river but providing a spectacular view, Nicholas
halted the horses and swung down. The spot he had chosen was shaded by a sprawling oak and cooled by the
breeze off the river. When he brought her down to the
ground, Eavin could see that a natural dip in the top of
the hillock would provide privacy for anyone taking advantage of it. That point had not gone unnoticed by Nicholas, who spread a blanket over the tufts of grass in the
hollow and led her toward it.

"I don't see why we have any need to sit down for this
discussion." Eavin resisted his tug, refusing to lower herself to the blanket.

"I don't see any reason why we shouldn't. I don't see
any reason why we shouldn't lie down if we like. We've
gone beyond the need to be coy with each other, Irish.
Sit, and let us discuss this reasonably."

Irritated, Eavin sat, flouncing Francine's skirt around
her. She felt out of her realm right now. She wore a skirt
that belonged to another woman, had ridden a beast she
had never thought to ride, and was sitting in a savage
land that was beyond anything she had ever known. And
worst of all, the man beside her was so far from the ele-
ments of culture with which she was familiar that he
made her feel little more than a heathen. As Nicholas
lowered his elegant frame gracefully beside her, she was
tempted to pick up her skirt and run.

At least he wasn't wearing the formal frock coat and
cravat of last night. His shirt was open at the neck as she
had been accustomed to, and his hair was falling down in
his eyes, eyes that were as puffy with lack of sleep as her
own. That gave her some satisfaction. Reaching for a
handful of the coarse grass, Eavin tugged it.

"What is there to discuss? You and Michael behaved

abominably. You ruined everything. How can we discuss that away?"

"We can't. What's done is done. We have to realize that and go forward from there. I'm sorry for my part in it, if that makes any difference to you. I shouldn't have lost my temper."

Eavin felt his hand come to rest behind her, and she stiffened but didn't move away. If she allowed herself to be reasonable, she would recognize that Nicholas had endured any number of insults on her behalf for months, and he had gallantly resisted calling anyone out. But to accept that would be to accept that it was reasonable to kill someone for spreading gossip. That might be what society expected, but it was a stupid rule.

"No, you shouldn't have. If you had laughed him off, taken him outside, done anything but create a scene, the whole thing would have gone practically unnoticed. Now I am condemned forever." Eavin had tried not to think about what that meant, but the horror on the faces of the women around her when Michael had made his mad declaration haunted her thoughts. They had rallied for Nicholas's sake and because scandal was something to live on, but she would never be invited to polite homes again. The world knew her as she was now. Perhaps she could face it for her own sake, but there was still Jeannette to consider. She couldn't ruin Jeannette's future.

"Condemned? Is that how you feel about what is between us?" Nicholas touched her shoulder lightly, hoping to bring her to face him.

"What is between us?" she asked bitterly. "There is nothing between us but what animals do in the barnyard. There is no need to sugar-coat things for me, Nicholas. My mother has done the same since my father's death. She derives some pleasure from the company, I suppose, and our household finances always needed the help. I just never saw myself repeating her mistakes."

Nicholas knew no way of making it easier. Leaning back on his elbow, he gazed up at the canopy of dusty oak leaves and wished life could be arranged in a more orderly fashion. His gaze drifted to the delicate line of Eavin's nose, the soft curve of her cheek, and the maddeningly thick black lashes that rested there. She wouldn't even look at him.

"I'll not give you up to a succession of men like your mother has endured, Eavin." He wanted to sound reassuring, but his proposition was anything but honorable. "What we have is nothing like that. We have a relationship that extends beyond the bedroom door. You are my friend, Eavin. Is it so impossible to think of me in that way?"

It was. Eavin looked up at the ground rising ahead of her. Just on the other side was the view of the river. If she stood and turned her head slightly to the right, she could see the house. His house. With his daughter inside it. Not hers. Perhaps that was what rankled. She would never have a home of her own now. Tears coming to her eyes, she still refused to look at him.

"Yes. Yes, it is. I am your employee as much as Michael is. You can send me away anytime you wish to. I'm thinkin' it would be better if I left on my own before that happens."

"That's what I was afraid you were thinking." Throwing aside patience as not being conducive to his cause, Nicholas grabbed her shoulders and pulled her down beside him, catching her head in the curve of his shoulder and holding her waist until she was sprawled along the length of him. Her eyes condemned him for his treachery, but he would win this battle with every means at hand.

"I'll not allow you to leave," Nicholas informed her firmly. When Eavin began to struggle, he rolled her over and pinned her lightly against the ground, forcing her gaze to meet his. His loins responded eagerly to this position, but he ignored the demands of his body. "I'll build you a house of your own, give you title to it. Then I can never send you away. You will belong here as much as I do."

"You have taken leave of your senses." Eavin tried to retain her firm control, but already her heart was beating foolishly at the feel of Nicholas's body pressing into hers. She didn't know where her anger had gone, but it had been replaced by an overwhelming sorrow as she gazed up into Nicholas's intent expression. She had been wrong when she had declared there was no more between them than animals in the barnyard. There was something here much greater than that, and it terrified her.

Sensing some of her capitulation, Nicholas moved

slowly, forcing her to accept the logic of his desires. "No, it is the perfect solution. We will have separate households and in the eyes of society we will be perfectly moral. And you will know that you will always have a home of your own, no matter what the future brings." His eyes grew dark as they held hers. "But between us it is understood, I do not wish to share you with anyone but Jeannette."

The blood pounding through Eavin's veins almost drowned out the warning bells in her brain. What he was saying wasn't precisely what she desired, but so much closer than she could ever have believed possible that she wanted to shout yes without any further consideration. But she hadn't survived for twenty-four years by ignoring her common sense. With her shoulders pinned to the ground, Eavin couldn't reach to touch his face, but the tension drained out of them as she gave the answer he didn't want.

"Then you would own me as surely as if we were married, Nicholas. It won't work, you know. You can't buy me and keep me here as your slave. What we have won't last, can't last. Don't make it any harder than it will have to be."

Stunned at this rejection of what he had been certain would convince her, Nicholas did not reply with words. Instead he found his answer in the taste of her lips, heard what he wanted to hear in the arching of her body into his, and accepted the reply of her welcoming arms as he enfolded her in his embrace. One way or another, she would have her house and he would keep her here. For now, it was enough to know that she would stay a while longer.

When they rode back toward the house some time later, Eavin's clothes were rumpled and her hair was in disarray and her cheeks were flushed with the pleasure of lovemaking. Nicholas thought she looked perfectly enchanting, but a glance toward the drive, where a carriage waited, warned there were others who might not be so taken with her present appearance.

Halting the horses in the stable yard, he lifted her down and brushed a kiss against her hair before releasing her.

"Go up the back stairs, *ma chérie*. I will distract our visitors until you can change."

At this moment, feeling the passion Nicholas had poured into her, Eavin would have confronted the world with her pride in his possession, but that was never to be. She must learn to keep this feeling between them a secret, but it would be a very difficult thing to do when she felt it on her face every time she looked at him.

As if understanding some of her struggle, Nicholas brushed a kiss across her cheek and walked off, leaving her to deal with it out of his presence.

Inside, he halted at the doorway to the dining room to greet those of his guests who had managed to rise and avail themselves of the brunch the servants had laid out. The sound of his voice drew the visitors from the salon, as he had hoped. The confrontation to come would be much easier in public.

"Nicholas! Where have you been? You shouldn't desert your guests like this. We've been waiting and waiting."

He was sipping the coffee one of the younger men had handed him, and the sound of the woman's voice brought sympathetic grins from around the table. With an expressive shrug Nicholas returned his cup to the sideboard and turned to greet his mother.

With carefully concealed dismay he noted his mother-in-law trailing behind her, towing a young fair-haired child in her wake. There ought to be a limit to the number of battles a man must fight in a day, particularly in his own home. Stiffening his resolve, he made a polite bow.

"And good morning to you, *maman, madame,*"—he nodded in Madame Dupré's direction. "What brings me the pleasure of your presence here today?"

Ignoring his lightly veiled sarcasm, Hélène announced, "We have come to ask you to take us to Villeré, Nicholas. We cannot impose on our hosts for such a long journey, so I have told them you will be delighted to see us there. You are invited, too. You have been working too hard. It is time you rested and enjoyed yourself a little. Why, look at you now! You have already been out in the fields. There is grass all over your shirt."

The snicker behind him made Nicholas stiffen, but he had learned his lesson last night. The men at the table could think what they wished; he would not verify it for them. Extending his elbow for his mother to take, he replied, "I am much too busy for a prolonged visit, but I will be delighted to see to your transportation. Come, let us discuss the details elsewhere."

Instead of accepting his proposal, Hélène sniffed and went to inspect the sideboard. "Then offer us a bite to eat, Nicholas. You have adopted too many of a bachelor's habits to neglect your hospitality so. What on earth is this terrible stuff?"

Resigned, Nicholas signaled a servant to assist the ladies with plates while he pulled out a chair for the retiring miss whose name he seemed to have misplaced. "That is Irish soda bread, *maman*. Eavin and Michael prefer it for breakfast. Eavin has taught the cook to make it. Try some, it is quite good."

"Ugh. Peasant bread. No, thank you. I'll just have some of these *beignets*. They are a trifle greasy, are they not, Louisa?"

Until now Madame Dupré had remained silent. Beside Hélène's stately, gray-haired presence, she was little more than a small, dark shadow. But she nodded in serene agreement. "Francine would never have allowed the kitchen to be reduced to such a state."

"Francine taught the cook how to make *beignets*. Sure, and you can be sartin I never did."

The fox was in the chickens now, Nicholas groaned to himself as Eavin sailed into the room, all flags flying.

28

Eavin helped herself to a large portion of soda bread, slathered it lavishly with butter, and placed herself boldly at the end of the table. A servant hastened to fill her cup with the tea she preferred. As several of the young gentlemen began to hastily make their excuses, she waved them back to their seats.

"Do sit down, sirs, and finish your meal. I have asked Hattie to bring up some of the champagne Nicholas keeps hidden in the wine cellar. A sip of champagne with those glorious peaches is just what the day calls for. Raoul, please pour the lady beside you some coffee. Gentlemen, you are grown much too lax in your manners."

Nicholas smothered a grin as Eavin managed to imitate the pompous manner of his mother while softening it with a seductive smile that had the young men falling all over themselves. It was hard to believe that just minutes ago her cheeks had been flushed with his kisses and her hair strewn with the grass of their illicit encounter. Although not pinned in the tight bun she had first worn, her hair was still arranged in a respectable chignon, with only twists of curls escaping in charming disarray. She had daringly abandoned the long sleeves of her daytime chemise for the coolness of a puffed sleeve gown. Nicholas did not dare contemplate what she wore—or did not wear—under it. His gaze could scarcely move from the shockingly low bodice with just a hint of gauze to disguise what he would keep hidden from all eyes but his own.

Eavin turned her gaze sweetly to the two older women. "How thoughtful of you to come all this way to pay your respects, ladies. I am certain Nicholas is pleased with the honor you do him. Please, why don't you take a seat and let Hattie serve you?"

Seeing that Eavin had neatly arranged an audience, Hélène could do no more than acquiesce, understanding quite rightly that the men weren't going to leave the table until they had received the promised champagne. Had she her way, she would have refused to sit at the same table with the wanton hussy, but one glance at her son's wicked expression put an end to that thought. He would allow her to leave without a word of protest.

Sighing to herself over the tribulations of ungrateful offspring, she took a chair and sipped the surprisingly good coffee. "We cannot stay long," she announced formally. "We have only come to ask Nicholas to accompany us to Villeré. It is time he had some rest and relaxation with his own kind."

Eavin could feel the men waiting expectantly for her reply. Even Nicholas calmly took his coffee and found his seat at the head of the table. It would have been so much easier if she had just kept her place in the nursery, but if this was what was required to keep Nicholas, she knew how to fight. Madame Saint-Just didn't stand a chance. She almost felt sorry for the woman.

Eavin allowed a knowing smile to spread across her face. "Rest and relaxation? How novel!" She turned that look on Nicholas, who nearly choked on his coffee. "I know you are considerably older than I am, dear Nicholas, but I never meant to tire you. Forgive me for not understanding."

The suggestive implications of her words and look had all the men desperately trying to hide their laughter while Hélène fumed and the other two ladies managed to appear bewildered. Nicholas just grinned and saluted her with his coffee cup.

"Fear not, *ma chérie*. If I was any more relaxed, I would be asleep. You missed the point. It is 'my own kind' with whom I am supposed to relax. Do you think Mignon would care to join us?"

"I think Lafitte would be more appropriate," Eavin replied dryly at his good humor. As long as her reputation was in tatters, she might as well enjoy the advantage of it, but Nicholas didn't have to take it so easily. She and every man at the table knew what he meant when he referred to being relaxed enough to sleep. Had the table not been so long, she would have kicked him.

Uncharacteristically, Isabel Dupré stepped into the breach. "I don't believe Lafitte appears in public any longer," she said vaguely, crumbling a croissant on her plate. "The governor is extremely put out with him, although I heard Jean danced with the governor's wife recently. Still, I don't think he would be an appropriate escort. Dear Gabriella looks quite pale at the prospect. No, I'm afraid it will have to be Nicholas who escorts us."

This was said in heavily accented English so that Eavin could not fail to understand. Remembering this was Francine's mother, Eavin nodded respectfully at this admonition. "You are quite right, *madame*. I was only twisting Nicholas's arm a little bit. He is much too certain of himself, is he not?"

Pleased that her daughter-in-law had replied in stiff but perfectly correct French, Isabel Dupré dared a small smile of agreement before darting a look at Nicholas, who terrified her more than she would admit. "You have more courage than I do, *ma petite*," she murmured.

"She has more courage than is good for her." Nicholas lifted his freshly filled glass of champagne. "To the Irish, who have more courage than sense sometimes, but who always overcome the fault with looks and charm."

A cheer went up around the table as the young men lifted their glasses, and the girl named Gabriella looked even more bewildered. Eavin gave Nicholas a look of disdain and, when the noise settled, lifted her own glass.

"To the French, who have enough charm to make sense an unnecessary trait."

Laughter followed this riposte, and the male guests eagerly drank to this toast, anxious to gain their hostess's favor. Grimly deciding he'd had enough of their admiration, Nicholas put an abrupt end to the odd affray.

"This insensible Frenchman has business to complete with a certain Irish charmer, if she will accompany me to the study." Turning to his mother, he informed her, "I cannot find the time to accompany you to Villeré right now, *maman*, but I will gladly send Michael with you. He has business in New Orleans he can conduct, so it will not be so very far out of his way."

There was that in his voice that could not be protested, and since he rose immediately and peremptorily held out his hand to Eavin, nothing more could be said. His rudeness effectively dashed all hope of argument.

Unaffected by Nicholas's moods, Eavin stood up and stuck her tongue out at him. Then with a wink, she murmured an aside to the company, "Do you think he's after sending me to my room with bread and water or to be paddling me?"

Since she made it very plain that she preferred the latter with a slight wiggle of her hips and a winning look as she took Nicholas's arm, she left their male guests laughing appreciatively as she sallied out.

"I have half a mind to give that warm little bottom a paddling," Nicholas growled in an undertone as he dragged Eavin into the *petite salle* and shut the door behind them. "Was there some meaning to that performance?"

Eavin disengaged her arm and met his gaze boldly. "I am your mistress; everyone knows it. You have said you do not wish to share me with others. I have just made it plain that I am taken."

"To everyone including my mother! *Mon dieu,* but you are either a clever brat or a wanton woman. I could not applaud your performance for my need to keep from dragging you to my bed right there and then. I think I have unleashed a monster."

"You may very well have," Eavin replied calmly, meeting his gaze with the same longing that she saw there. "It works both ways, you know. Irish peasant that I am, I cannot look at you without wanting to touch. It is not a very pleasant experience when I am confined by the behavior expected of me. Who is that very young woman your mother is hauling about?"

Nicholas shrugged and reached for her. "Who knows? Perhaps she has dredged up some unknown cousin to harass. I will give her the pleasure of it. Come here and kiss me before I die of starvation."

With a furious look at the couple standing much too close together as they waved farewell from the gallery, Michael ordered the driver to set the horses moving on the first leg of their journey. Eavin's refusal to leave her immoral position had left him in a quandary. His first urge was to leave rather than condone what she did. His second urge was much more uncomfortable. Knowing his sister was heading straight for a downfall, he wanted to stay and catch her before she hurt herself too badly. It was not the kind of urge he was used to following, but this time it was necessary, for the health of his own soul as well as Eavin's.

Not caring to dwell on Michael's decision to remain in Nicholas's employ even after her refusal to leave with him, Eavin accepted Nicholas's hand and entered the shade of the old house. She knew where he was taking her. She knew the servants were watching and whispering. And she no longer cared.

After that, Nicholas was bombarded with letters from his mother, which he read impatiently and then took great relish in burning over a candle flame, after which he would drag Eavin off to whatever bedroom caught his fancy.

Lying half dressed in his bed after one of these sessions, wishing some miracle would occur to prove the physician wrong about her ability to conceive but facing the fact that it hadn't, Eavin straightened her disarranged chemise and turned to the man beside her.

Nicholas was propped against the headboard, one hand behind his head as he smoked his cheroot. When Eavin touched her hand to his bare chest, he reached down to lift it to his lips and kiss the palm.

"It is not right to despise your mother so much, Nicholas. If not for her, you would not be here. Even I cannot find it in my heart to despise my mother, and she is far from being as proper a lady as yours."

"Your mother is at least honest about what she is. I cannot approve of the situation she created for you, but it is evident that she never pretended to be what she was not. I detest hypocrisy." Nicholas set his cheroot aside and pulled Eavin up against him.

"Don't be ridiculous. This world survives on hypocrisy. Just look at New Orleans. The Creoles pretend that they are still French and that the rest of the United States does not exist. The Americans pretend that they have no wish to enter Creole society. They each look at what the other has and pretend they want no part of it when, in truth, it is just the opposite."

His lips twisted wryly as he wrapped his hand in her hair. "I see another article in the making. I think Daniel Fletcher is half in love with you. I'm not certain that I should allow you to write anymore."

"You can't stop me." Eavin tweaked his chest hairs, then darted a kiss under his arm to put an end to his depredations. "Besides, my reputation has become so scandalous that even the revelation that I write for the newspaper will not bring me lower. This is off the subject. I want to talk about your mother."

"And I don't." Looking down, Nicholas tugged the bodice of her chemise until it revealed the full swell of her breasts. He caressed a tip as a means of ending the subject. "We know our true friends, *ma chérie.* The Howells still accept us. Even Jeremy has come to acknowledge our relationship. When we go into New Orleans, I will introduce you to others who will be happy to make your acquaintance."

When, not if. Eavin sighed as the tingling sensation created by his skilled fingers began to seep through her. Wriggling closer, she tried to put an end to this distraction. "I cannot stay in your mother's house, Nicholas. You will have to go alone."

"It is my house, Irish, and you will go with me. My mother has no say in the matter."

"She's your *mother,* Nicholas. You owe her respect. That is what I have been trying to tell you."

"I owe her nothing." Grimly, Nicholas jerked Eavin onto his lap where he could meet her eyes. "I will tell you this only once, so listen carefully. That ever so proper lady you admire, this granddaughter of a marquis, wife in the noble house of Saint-Just, is not only a whore, but one so weak-willed as to watch her own son beaten nearly half to death without raising a hand to stop it. I owe her nothing. She is lucky to have a roof over her head."

His words didn't shock Eavin as much as the bitterness with which he said them. A furious Nicholas she understood. He had reacted to Francine's death with fury, but never bitterness. The pain of this old hurt must have entered deep and festered for years. This, then, was what he had once warned her of. Eavin curled into his shoulder and ran her hand slowly up and down his chest, exploring each ridge and curve as she did so.

"How is she a whore?" she asked quietly, knowing this was not the subject that was painful but not daring to touch the other.

"My father bought her. Every time he whipped one of us, he would go out and come back with some bauble to appease her. I had barely regained consciousness one time when he came back with a young quadroon and offered her to my mother as the maid she had been asking for. It didn't matter to her when he turned around and made the girl his mistress a few weeks later. The night we fled Santa Domingue because his *petite amie* warned us of the uprising before it could find us, they had to carry me on board the ship. I'd broken my leg when he chased me down the stairs with his cane. When we arrived in New Orleans, he bought my mother the largest house he could find, and she forgave him again."

"I thought there was no money." Again, Eavin questioned around the most painful topic. The thought of the proud boy Nicholas must have been chased through the house by a madman with a cane twisted her insides. She didn't want to think what it must be doing to him. Somehow she would have to draw the distress out of him, but it wouldn't be by forcing the subject.

Nicholas seldom talked about his boyhood. There were certain people who knew of it, but even with them he didn't discuss details. Those memories were buried deep inside, where he didn't have to acknowledge their existence. But with Eavin, it seemed somehow necessary to have them out again, to discard them, and in so doing, make her understand what he was. He wasn't at all certain that he knew himself, but Eavin made it so easy to share this heavy burden that he had kept within for so long.

"There was money in Santa Domingue. It would have been difficult to lose money with the plantation. But when we left, we left almost everything behind. We lived off the valuables we were able to carry and credit. My father was very good at persuading people to give him credit."

"I can imagine," Eavin responded wryly. Nicholas

must have inherited his charm from his father. He certainly hadn't got it from his mother. But that wasn't the boil that needed lancing right now. "Then your mother had nothing of her own here: no family, no wealth, not even friends?"

"She was not the only one. Hundreds fled the rebellion. Do not make excuses for her. Had he killed me, she would have slept in his bed that night."

"As I sleep in yours, even knowing what it makes of me." Eavin propped her elbows on his chest and met Nicholas's eyes. "You are not a woman, Nicholas. You will never understand what it means to be a woman. This is a man's world. We are given very few choices in it. We can marry without love and the world calls us respectable. Or we can love and live in sin and be closed out from the friends and family we crave. We can pray our husbands die so we can live quietly and respectably on our own. Very few are wealthy and lucky enough to have the funds to live without a man's support. Your mother made her choice when she married your father. If he was anything like you, at one time she probably loved him very much. It must have been torture for her to be torn between the man she once loved and the child of her body. But to keep a roof over your head and food in your stomach, she suffered that torture. It would have done you no good if she had interfered and been beaten, too. There was literally no other choice that she could make."

Nicholas caught Eavin's wrists and turned her on her back, covering her with his body. Amber eyes darkened to almost black as he glared down at her. "Is that the choice you would have made?"

"Would you have me choose between you and Jeannette?" she asked quietly.

Anguish welled in his eyes, and then he buried his lips against her throat and his body into the haven of hers, and there were no more words between them.

29

"Nicholas, I believe we have a visitor."

It was the first of September, but heat still clung to the skin and depressed even the oaks into drooping. Eavin stood on the gallery, fanning herself and pretending there was a breeze off the river in hopes that the thought would cool her. Sinful woman that she was, she wore her bodice unbuttoned at the throat, but a trickle of perspiration still gathered at the hollow there. She didn't even turn toward the man appearing in the doorway. She knew he was there by the way the air moved around him.

He came to stand beside her and gave an angry growl at the sight of the rogue boldly walking up the river road. His greasy hair and earring glinting in the sunlight made his occupation clear even if his identity weren't.

"I've warned them not to come around here. Claiborne is about to hang every one of them. He'd love an excuse to plant militia on my levee."

"They don't seem to cause anybody harm. Lafitte is your friend, isn't he?"

"Don't fool yourself, *ma petite*. Lafitte can kill at the drop of a hat, just like his men. That's why they live by themselves on Barataria, in a place where the law doesn't touch them. Lafitte was a gentleman once and knows how to live among more civilized people. His merry band of men are no such creatures. Stay out of sight while I see what this one wants."

Eavin sent one of the young boys working in the store-room to fetch cooled wine for their visitor while Nicholas went to greet him. She had no objection to staying out of the pirate's way, but she wished she could hear what he had to say. Nicholas still wasn't remarkably informative about his business.

But his business wasn't hers, and she had no right to

intrude. It was not a concept she would have grasped readily when first she came here, but she was coming to understand Nicholas's need for privacy a little more every day. That he shared as much with her as he did was a revelation she didn't think even he understood. But her confidence in their relationship grew a little with each discovery.

She knew she loved him. She didn't think he loved her as he had Francine, but he needed her, and that was enough for now. She lived minute by minute, not trying to imagine the future. The future of the entire country was uncertain right now. Why should she worry about so insignificant a problem as her own?

So she set Jeannette down in the middle of the *petite salle* and sat down to edit the paper she had been working on. The toddler wore the lacy linen gown Eavin had made for her birthday and played with the cotton-stuffed doll Nicholas had given her. Her hair was growing in thicker now, but she was still tiny, appearing little more than an elf or leprechaun perched in the middle of the rug. Eavin smiled with love as the child pulled the doll's hair and crowed with laughter. Nicholas had given her far more than she could ever give him. It would be time enough to consider the future when it came.

She looked up when Nicholas entered the room later, but the scowl on his face made her heart thump with trepidation. Since they had isolated themselves here out of hearing of scandalous tongues, she hadn't seen that expression in months. It didn't bode well to see it now.

Laughing, Jeannette ran on uncertain legs to hug the man she called "papa." A gabble of words spilled from her tongue now, laced liberally with sounds of "papa" and "dolly" and "auntie" as Nicholas lifted her up and she displayed some fascinating characteristic of her doll to him. The scowl softened as Nicholas carried his daughter across the room and bent to place a kiss on Eavin's head.

"The news is not good," Eavin said in a voice as calm as she could make it, so as not to worry the child.

"No." Nicholas bounced Jeannette in his arms and spoke through her squeals. "The British are trying to negotiate with Lafitte. They are offering his crew full pardon and large sums of money in return for his aid. Claiborne has made such a clown of himself over the pirates living in Barataria, the offer must be very tempting. And if the governor hears that Lafitte has talked with the British, he'll go after the whole island. He's only been looking for an excuse."

"And what will you do?" Eavin held her arms out and allowed Nicholas to deposit his daughter in them. She knew without asking that he was leaving.

He looked relieved at her easy acceptance. "I won't know until I get there. If the British are so bold as to meet with Lafitte, they must be confident of their success. Eavin, we haven't even got a navy to hold them back. There's nothing to stop them without Lafitte. I've learned to live under many flags, but I'm not eager to accept a British one. I've got to go."

"I know." Eavin kissed Jeannette and returned her to the floor, then rose to stand beside Nicholas. "You don't have to hide your feelings from me. You're very good at pretending in front of everyone else, but I know how much you care about what happens to New Orleans, to your friends and family. I understand."

She didn't add "because I love you." She just went into Nicholas's arms and kissed him with a lingering farewell that promised much for when he returned. He had burdens enough to carry without adding another one. She not only knew what he wanted to eat, how he wanted his servants to behave, what he liked in bed, but she knew what he needed from her: acceptance, with no strings attached.

And Eavin gave it unequivocally. A woman in love was capable of strange things. She called for Clemmie to begin packing Nicholas's bags and sent Hattie to warn the stable boys to saddle a horse while Nicholas went to his study and gathered whatever papers he meant to carry with him. She didn't weep and bemoan the fact that she couldn't go with him. She didn't argue and throw fits over the possibility that Claiborne would have him arrested along with the pirates. And she didn't tell him she loved him. He carried enough on his shoulders without that kind of unnecessary emotional baggage.

Eavin kissed Nicholas good-bye and watched him ride away before fleeing to her room and pouring her tears into her pillow.

* * *

"I didn't think you would have returned to the city already."

"Obviously." Hélène gave her son's muddy boots and sweat-stained clothes a disdainful glance. Warily she asked, "Where's Mrs. Dupré?"

"At home, I'm here on business. I haven't come to socialize. I'm in something of a hurry, *maman*." Nicholas impatiently started up the stairs.

"Be careful, you will terrify Gabriella with that scowl," she called up after him.

Nicholas sent her an incredulous look and took the remaining steps two at a time.

He didn't come back to the house for three days, and when he did, it was as if they had been waiting for him. He hadn't bathed in two of those days, and he had spent the last one crawling through bayous and thickets fit for nothing but alligators and mosquitoes. Nicholas was extremely conscious of his ripe appearance when he entered the house and found the elegantly dressed assembly seemingly waiting for his arrival.

Governor Claiborne rose and nodded briefly at Nicholas. His young wife smiled boldly and with a hint of laughter in her eyes as her gaze swept over Nicholas's muddied attire. Madame Dupré lifted her eyes nervously and away again. The pale female at her side gasped and stared, and Hélène Saint-Just turned to give her son a disparaging glance before dismissing him.

"We will delay our meal another hour, Nicholas. Go and wash."

The command was very similar to one a mother would give a child, but his mother had never used that particular tone in her life. Usually her commands were given with a languid grace that made them sound like requests of indulgence. This curt tone did not bode well at all.

Nicholas sent the governor a suspicious glance, nodded and made polite excuses, and escaped to the upper story. He had half a mind to change and slip out the back stairs, but the fate of New Orleans could lie in his hands tonight. He would have to make Claiborne understand the urgency of the situation. And he would have to do it without frightening the ladies.

He took care with his attire, something he'd not had to

do in months. He made certain his cravat was snowy and simply arranged, that his tan frock coat lay smoothly over his shoulders, his trousers were neatly pressed, and his shoes shined to perfection. Then confident that the governor would look on him as the French gentleman he managed to portray when he was so inclined, Nicholas sauntered downstairs.

To his annoyance, Nicholas found himself leading Gabriella into dinner and sitting beside her at the table. He needed to converse with the governor, but patiently he listened to the girl's timid remarks, gallantly made her feel at ease, and bided his time. The smothered look of fury he sent his mother went right past her.

When it came time for the company to retire from the table, Nicholas casually abandoned the child and approached the governor with the promise of some brandy in his study. The American was shorter than Nicholas, but he carried himself with the dignity worthy of his office. He made a sound of denial and gestured toward the ladies entering the salon.

"I believe the words we have to exchange would best be done in there. Besides, I cannot condone smuggled brandy. You understand my position."

Nicholas lifted a sardonic brow at that remark as he glanced at the lace adorning Mrs. Claiborne's silk gown, but wisely, he held his tongue. Let the man think he was avoiding smuggled goods by denying himself good brandy. There wasn't any silk or lace in this town that hadn't been brought in by the pirates, and smuggling wasn't the only way they came by their goods. The Spanish combs Mrs. Claiborne was wearing could have come only from one place. Lafitte never politely bought Spanish goods.

"What I wish to say must be done in private, Governor. I do not wish to frighten the ladies."

Claiborne sent him an ill-concealed look of irritation. "Now is a fine time to develop sensibility. You don't think your rendezvous with the pirates was a secret, do you?"

Nicholas had, actually, but he didn't allow his surprise to be seen. He didn't know who had betrayed his presence on Barataria, but he could very well guess. Raphael had been relatively quiet these last months, but then, it would have been a trifle difficult for Raphael to reach him when he was isolated on the plantation with an army of slaves at his disposal. He should have known the *canaille* would have taken the time to cultivate spies.

"I have never made my dealings with Lafitte a secret," Nicholas replied stiffly, bowing slightly to indicate that the other gentleman enter the salon first. "He is a friend of mine, and would be a friend of yours if you would but listen to reason."

"I was not elected to make friends with criminals. My office requires that I uphold the law. I understand that there is a difference in our cultures, but there is a limit that every self-respecting man must draw somewhere. Mine is in dealing with pirates, thieves, and murderers." Claiborne threw his host a piercing look, then took a chair beside his wife.

Nicholas didn't like the tone of this conversation. He could hear the warnings but couldn't find the direction of the attack. With a charming smile he dispensed sherry to the ladies and poured a good madeira for himself, as if all was well and he was no more than an unexceptional host. He knew the role well, had used it frequently while at home in New Orleans, and he could be very convincing. People believed what they wanted to believe. He was born of good family, blessed with aristocratic good looks, and he was rich. It was much easier to forget that "Old Nick" had sailed with the navy and pirates alike and came by his fortune in ways too dubious to mention.

"Madame Saint-Just, Madame Dupré, perhaps you will allow me to broach the subject that is most on your minds." Pompously the governor drew attention to himself.

Nicholas raised his eyebrows and winked at the lovely Mrs. Claiborne as he sat down. That lady hid a smile behind her fan as her husband took the floor.

"Monsieur Saint-Just, I was prepared to sign a warrant for your arrest until I was approached by several citizens of the community assuring me that your intentions might be misguided but are not traitorous. I find myself doubting their assurances. Forgive me, ladies." He bowed in the direction of the two older women. "But the facts remain. Nicholas Saint-Just is a known smuggler, an associate of the pirates who even now are treating with the

British, and a man who has engaged in dueling resulting in death. His private morals do not withstand inspection. Nonetheless, I've been given to understand there were unfortunate circumstances involved, and that you are a man of honor. Would you say that of yourself, Saint-Just?"

"A man of honor does not speak for himself, Claiborne. His actions speak for him. If you wish to arrest me, please do. We have laws and courts in Louisiana. I am persuaded I can stand before any of them without a qualm." Nicholas calmly arranged his long legs before him and straightened the seam of his trousers. He kept his irritation well in check. Eavin would be proud.

"Good. I do not wish to give these good ladies undue concern. Women tend to allow their emotions to cloud their judgment. But as an honorable man, you will do the right thing, and I will recognize your intentions by your actions. I understand your feelings at your wife's unfortunate demise—I have lost two wives of my own—but it is time you returned to proper behavior. Your neighbors tell me you settled down appreciably when you married, and it is only since your wife's death that you have fallen from grace. I think, and the ladies agree with me, that the solution is in your remarrying."

Fury flew through him with the speed of lightning. Nicholas straightened, started to push himself from the chair, then remembering his pose, brutally bottled his temper and lounged casually against the seat back. Locking his fingers over his chest, he eyed the governor speculatively. "I didn't realize your duties included match-making, Governor. In France we allow old widows with nothing else to do to engage in that chore." He'd never been in France in his life, but he amused himself with the color purple straining at the other man's cheeks. While the governor was controlling his own temper, Nicholas sent his mother a scathing glance. She had been nagging him for months now. This was an example of her handiwork.

Somehow she managed to look repentant and nervous at the same time. With a grimace of disdain Nicholas returned an innocent gaze to his judge and jury.

"I'll ignore your insolence, Saint-Just. A man doesn't like to be told what to do, but I'm persuaded you do not know the situation and will be eager to make amends once you do."

Nicholas had a few French phrases he'd like to use to tell the old meddler what to do right now, but he smiled genially and sipped his wine. "Of course, if I can be of assistance . . . ?"

"By killing Raphael Reyes, you have caused a young girl to be thrown into a strange land without a home, without family, and without protection. She is not only any young girl, but she is a cousin of your wife's. It is your duty to see that she is protected, and the only way that can be done is to marry her."

With the certain knowledge of a condemned man, Nicholas turned to the pale young female clenching her hands in her lap and watched her blanch at his inspection. Her fair hair was the only resemblance he could discern to Francine. His gaze lifted to the two duplicitous old women wringing their hands in their laps. Why in hell did they hate him so much? What had he ever done to make their lives so miserable?

His unruly temper gathered and concentrated into a curled ball inside his gut. With an astonishing and deceptive calm Nicholas returned his gaze to Claiborne. "I was not aware of the relationship, nor do I understand your reference to Reyes. But most of all, I resent your interference in a highly personal matter. I am certain the young lady does not wish to be chosen as a pawn in a game beyond her understanding. I think it is time that we adjourn to my study, Governor, and discuss whatever is bothering you at length."

"I was betrothed to Raphael," the girl whispered into the angry silence.

Those words were followed by another lengthy pause in which Nicholas suffered the verdict of a jury of his peers and had the first glimpse of understanding. He had been judged and found guilty, and they were about to announce his sentence.

Confirming that thought, his mother broke the silence. "The governor means to have you arrested if we cannot assure your good behavior, Nicholas. If you will not agree to our wishes in this, then he knows our promises are nothing." Hélène sat stiffly, her spine never touching the gracefully curved back of the gilded chair. The fading gold of her hair still held a glint in the candlelight, but pain had etched lines in the once smooth fairness of her skin. Pain deepened those lines now.

A trap. A foolish trap with enough holes to ride a herd of horses through, but one sufficient to make him step warily. Nicholas sipped his wine and smiled genially.

"How interesting," he murmured to the company in general. And when they began to relax and talk among themselves, he threw back the rest of the wine and let the alcohol add fuel to his anger.

30

"Are you out of your damned bloody mind?" Michael gulped back the last swallow of whiskey in his glass and held it out for a refill. Daniel Fletcher obliged without a word. He, too, waited for some reply from the man at the table across from them.

"I sense a certain sort of irony in the situation, actually." Nicholas lifted his own glass, examining the contents carefully as if the quality of the drink was all that mattered at this point in time. The raucous noise of the tavern around them didn't seem to intrude on his reverie. "After all, she comes with a lucrative dowry that Reyes is watering at the mouth to have. That young fool Alphonso has chosen a terrible time to turn rebellious."

"You need her dowry like the Mississippi needs water." Daniel grimaced at his partner's insouciant attitude and took a swallow of his own drink. "There is more to this than meets the eye."

"There aren't going to be any eyes when I get finished punching them out," Michael growled, his fingers clenching the glass as he raised it to his lips, his gaze fastened intently on the elegant Frenchman looking so totally out of place in this noisy American bar. "The only satisfaction I can find in this is that Eavin will finally come to her senses and leave you."

Nicholas very gently set his glass on the table and leaned forward, speaking slowly and with great care. "No, *mon ami,* she will not. There will be no change, *comprenez-vous?*"

Michael's chair scraped back and he began to rise, hands clutched into fists. Daniel reached over and shoved him back down. Both men were drunk enough to tilt slightly off balance at their movements.

"He's not telling you everything." Daniel clipped the

words out with remarkable accuracy considering the state of his tongue. "Listen to what he isn't saying. That's the secret."

If it was, it was a drunken one. Michael continued glaring, but obediently he waited to hear what wasn't being said.

Nicholas chuckled a trifle grimly. "I need an heir, gentlemen, it is as simple as that. Would you begrudge me an heir?"

Not knowing of Eavin's inability to have children, both men continued watching him owlishly, waiting for the moment of revelation. Sighing, Nicholas sipped his whiskey, swirled it in the glass, and returned to contemplating its color. "Lafitte thinks Claiborne is considering his offer of neutrality. Claiborne won't even listen to me until this wedding is over. The British are practically knocking on our door. What would you have me do?"

That made some kind of drunken sense. Still fighting the inevitable, Michael suggested, "We can join the pirates."

Once, the thought would have appealed to Nicholas. Perhaps he was growing old. Perhaps family life was making him soft. If so, he did not regret it. He didn't want to go back to being alone, one man in a ship full of men. He knew what it was like to have a woman's welcoming embrace, a child's laughter, the trust and confidence of his neighbors. He didn't want to give them up. Standing, exhibiting none of the loss of balance of his companions, Nicholas shook his head regretfully. "Pirating is in its last days, gentlemen. We will all be good, honest Americans shortly. Or dead ones."

Nicholas strode off, leaving his companions to stare after him, waiting for some stumble to reveal he had drunk more than half the bottle on his own. His head never turned; his footsteps never faltered. Shaking their heads, even in their drunkenness, they could see the handwriting on the wall.

"There's someone to see you, Miss Eavin." Nervously Annie glanced over her shoulder as if expecting the visitor to appear in a spectral vision behind her.

Putting Jeannette in bed for her nap, Eavin replied patiently, "I will be right down. Just give me a minute."

"Not here, Miss Eavin. She won't come in here. Out by the oak grove, she said. You've got to go to her."

That didn't make any more sense than anything else had lately. Since Nicholas had left, there had been reports of pirates on the river and in the swamp at the edge of the fields, but none came to the house. The slaves had told her of bands of militia camping in the marsh. She'd even received some kind of drunken letter from Michael demanding that she pack her bags and be ready to leave. Another letter had come from Daniel Fletcher in which he had all but proposed to her, although she scarcely knew the man. Jeremy had ridden by to tell her his family would always consider her a friend and their home would always be open to her. But when pressed, he would tell her nothing more.

Something was wrong, but there was little she could do about it until she knew what it was. If she hadn't burned her bridges behind her, she could have ordered the carriage up and gone into New Orleans to see for herself, but she wouldn't scandalize Nicholas's mother by appearing on her doorstep. Besides, that would indicate some distrust in Nicholas, and she wouldn't do that for the world. She would wait for him to come to her.

But curiosity and fear were potent motivators. Leaving Jeannette in Annie's capable hands, Eavin located a parasol and set out on foot to the oak grove. She wasn't brave enough to ride a horse by herself, although an excellent riding habit had arrived from New Orleans. On her own, she was too accustomed to using her own two feet.

The humidity wasn't as severe as it had been, but the sun was still warm as Eavin crossed the lawn in the direction of the spreading oaks. Deep shadows lingered beneath the veils of hanging moss, and she shivered vaguely at the hint of evil in that concealment. Perhaps she was being foolish in coming here alone. Nicholas had warned her that the pirates weren't innocent. But Annie had said "she." She had nothing to worry about from a woman.

Until she saw the woman. Eavin came to an abrupt halt when the shadow melted from the trees to sway before her. She recognized her at once, but the circumstances were different. On a public street in New Orleans, with crowds of people around, that face looked like any other.

In the sensuous silence of the oaks with shadows playing across her exotic features, the same face reflected otherworldly knowledge. Had Eavin come face to face with a ghost, she couldn't have been more paralyzed.

"You remember me?" the husky voice murmured with the languid accents of Santa Domingue.

"Labelle." Eavin was surprised to discover that her tongue still worked. With its recovery she regained some of her common sense. She was superstitious enough to believe in ghosts and devils, but only ones that couldn't be seen. This woman was flesh and blood; she would stake her soul on that. "Am I supposed to be afraid of you?"

The woman shrugged. "White folks aren't afraid of niggers."

Curious, Eavin stepped closer. *Nigger* wasn't a word she applied to anyone, least of all a woman like this one. "Annie is afraid of you. Why?"

Labelle met her gaze with a hint of defiance. "Niggers are afraid of everything."

"That is ridiculous. You're not afraid of me." That statement became almost a question as the woman's delicately plucked eyebrows rose.

"Not for myself. For Nicholas," was her enigmatic reply.

"Nicholas isn't afraid of anything," Eavin answered adamantly and began to turn away. This was a ridiculous conversation.

"Nick is afraid of many things. Nick is afraid of ghosts," came the soft reply.

Eavin swung around again, feeling her heart pounding a little harder. The woman's words hit very close to a truth she hadn't recognized.

"You never spoke to Nicholas of me." Belle's tone was affirmative, not accusing as she moved forward, certain now that she had Eavin's full attention.

"I saw no reason to. Should I have?" The parasol felt awkward and unfamiliar in her hand, just as this conversation made her feel awkward and uneasy. Eavin set the parasol against a tree and wished for somewhere to sit. The woman across from her seemed perfectly at ease in this jungle paradise, although at their first meeting she had appeared a creature of the city. Today she wore dangling gold at her ears and loops of beads and crystals around her neck and wrists. Her elegance had become something else, something much more primitive and striking.

The woman's laughter tinkled in the unmoving air. "I see why Nicholas likes you. He is impatient with the old ways. He believes in directness. You possess that quality. There is not another woman in New Orleans who could say the same."

"I am certain there must be; she just wouldn't be among the crowd he knows. Why have you come here?"

"To be certain you are what Nicholas needs. He is a strong man, one so confident in his strength that he will do what he perceives as necessary even if it is the wrong thing. But even strong men have weaknesses. From things he has said, I think you know him well enough to destroy him. I would destroy you before I would let that happen. But if you can hurt him, you also have the power to help him, to drive away the ghosts. If you choose that road, I will stand by you in whatever way I can."

Puzzled, Eavin gestured toward the house. "Wouldn't it be better if we talked inside? I am not very good at riddles. Perhaps if we . . ."

Labelle smiled and moved farther away. "I will not taint my magic with yours. But I will give you this." She produced a small vial from somewhere in the folds of her skirt.

Eavin found it in her hands without realizing she had reached for it. Staring at it blankly, she looked back to the woman who seemed to be fading farther into the trees. "What do I do with it?"

"A pinch in your tea every morning. It will make you whole again. It will give you strength. I do this for Nicholas. Betray him, and you will regret it."

The words were said in such elegantly rounded tones that Eavin couldn't quite believe their threat, and she certainly didn't understand it. Fear mixed with anger to make her slow in reacting, and when she did, it was too late. The woman had gone.

Stepping forward to see if she could find the path Labelle had taken, Eavin found nothing but the undisturbed debris of innumerable seasons scuffling beneath her shoes. The trees were not so thick that she couldn't see between them, but she might as well have been talking to a ghost for all the indication of Labelle's presence that she could find.

More puzzled than alarmed, Eavin started back for the house. The vial in her hand reminded her that the woman actually existed and wasn't just another figment of her imagination. Opening the lid, she sniffed the ingredients, recognizing the scents of some of the herbs but not all of them. The Creoles used a variety of seasonings with which she wasn't familiar. Perhaps Labelle just meant to improve the flavor of her tea. Give her strength, indeed! For that she had the power of the Lord.

Annie looked at her fearfully when she returned upstairs. At the sight of the vial she flinched. "What that voodoo woman give you?"

"Voodoo?" Amused by this reference to some strange religion she had heard that some of the slaves practiced, Eavin set the vial on the chest of drawers. "She's a little odd, but I wouldn't call her that. She seems to think I'm weak and need strengthening. Either that, or she thinks my tea needs strengthening. Personally, I think she's had too much sun."

"What she say that for?" Annie nodded at the vial.

"To make me whole again." Eavin laughed and looked down at herself. "I don't think I'm missing any parts, do you? But a pinch a day is supposed to make me stronger. If I remember, I'll try it tomorrow. My mother always recommended chamomile, but I hate the stuff."

Annie looked relieved and nodded. "Voodoo woman take care of you, then. Do as she say, and everythin' be all right."

Eavin doubted that, and she promptly forgot the vial as soon as she went downstairs and back to her writing. She worried over Labelle's words about Nicholas, though. He did have weaknesses. His temper was a terrible weakness. And his bitterness toward his mother hid a child's desire for love. No one could entirely erase the need for a mother's love. That could be a weakness if Hélène wished to use it against him. If anyone could destroy Nicholas, it would be his mother. Praying the woman wasn't as insensitive as she seemed, Eavin gave up trying to analyze what she couldn't change and applied her mind to the article in her hands.

* * *

"She is too young, *maman*." Nicholas shoved his hands into his pockets and stared out at the brilliant blue of the sky over the roof of the house across the street. Odd, but he had thought it was raining.

"The banns have been declared, Nicholas. Do not humiliate her by changing your mind now. You had to marry someday."

That was the refrain that had been drummed through his mind these last few weeks. He had to marry someday. Now that he had ruined everything for Eavin, she couldn't be the one to bring Jeannette out in society. He would need a proper wife to do that, preferably a Creole who would be accepted by his peers. He and Eavin had both known that someday he would have to marry, if only to produce a son to bear his name. Or he thought Eavin knew that. It wasn't a topic that they had discussed.

He didn't know how to tell her. Never in his life had he been a coward, but these weeks had melted away and still he hadn't found the words. A letter wouldn't do. But Claiborne and his men watched him every minute, and a hasty ride home to break the news to his mistress would give them something to gossip about for months to come. He didn't like appearing to be the pawn of women, but no matter what he did, that was how it would seem.

So as he had these last weeks, Nicholas tried to think of the pale child he would take as bride. "I think I frighten her. Shouldn't she be given some choice? Claiborne is forcing us both into an untenable position."

"She is very young and will learn to be as you wish with time, Nicholas. Would you have preferred she married Raphael?"

That was his mother's first admission of the possibility that he might be innocent of Raphael's death, and even then, it was so muted as to be a part of his imagination. Nicholas turned and studied the woman who had given him birth.

"I doubt if it could have been much worse than being married to me. I don't remember Francine complaining of his having beat her. She loved him. Her cousin might do the same. The only difference is that Gabriella has a dowry and Francine didn't."

"But Raphael has not come to claim her, and his

brother refuses to do so. What other choice does she
have? Isabel doesn't have the household to present her to
society as she deserves, and I am not in a position to do
so unless she is married to you. It is the best thing for
both of you, and you know it. I do not fool myself into
thinking that you do this for me."

Nicholas saw the hurt in his mother's eyes before she
turned away. It did not seem possible. He had seen his father slap her until she fell to the ground, but when she got
up again, the only thing visible on her face would be her
pride. He had never seen her weep. Occasionally there
had been cries of pain, but never when he was around, or
sensible, whichever the case might be. He didn't think
anyone was capable of causing his mother pain, particularly not him.

"I do this for you as much as for anyone," he replied
wearily. "I cannot think of any other good reason to do it.
You will have the daughter you never had. You can present her to society. You can win back all your respectability, gain Madame Dupré's approval, go to balls again. I
will leave all that to you, *maman,* for I have no patience
with it. I will be going back to the plantation as soon as
this is over."

"You will have to take her with you for a while, Nicholas. It is expected." Hélène clasped her hands tightly in
her lap as she watched her son pace the room restlessly
like a caged animal. She truly had his own good in mind
in forcing this marriage. He would destroy himself and
the child he claimed as daughter if he persisted in his
scandalous career. She would save him in whatever way
she could, even if he hated her for it.

Which he was coming very close to doing, she could
see for herself. He grimaced with distaste and turned
away at her words. She wondered if he had sent his mistress packing yet. Many men did, but she didn't think
Nicholas would. He would find some other way to keep
her.

"I am not a young man, and I have been married before. I don't think the tradition of keeping us locked in
our room for a week is called for in this instance.
Gabriella is quite likely to pass out from fear if we did.
You can be assured I will treat her with all respect due to

a wife, but do not expect more. She would be better off remaining here with you."

"Not if the British are coming, Nicholas," she whispered in defiance.

And as if to seal the hands of fate, Michael barged through the doorway, his cheeks ruddy from his run, his hair wind-blown as he scanned the room for his employer. Finding him, he spoke in a tone slightly lower than a shout.

"Claiborne has sent a fleet against Barataria. They're shelling the island right now!"

31

She had no warning at all. Or perhaps she had dozens of warnings and heeded none of them. She certainly didn't think it when the carriage arrived and Nicholas escorted the young girl and his mother toward the stairs. Actually, she cursed the presence of others now that Nicholas had finally returned home. She was so glad to see his face again that she wanted to throw herself into his arms and make a spectacle of herself, but by waiting on the women below, Nicholas gave Eavin time to compose herself.

She was grateful for that composure a little while later when they entered the house. Gabriella clung to Nicholas's arm, looking thoroughly unsure of herself as she glanced around the wide hallway as if she had never seen it before. Hélène busied herself with her bonnet and ordering Hattie about. It was Nicholas to whom Eavin turned, and the dead look in his eyes told her more than she wanted to know.

"Eavin, you remember Gabriella, Francine's cousin. We were married this morning and I think she is a little tired from the journey. Could you send Clemmie to take her into my chamber?"

It was cruel. He had known it would be. But there was no kind way of telling her. Nicholas watched as Eavin paled and the golden glow on her face disappeared. There would be accusations in those wide eyes shortly, but right now there was only pain, extreme pain. He held his breath, waiting for that Irish temper to explode and carry him with it. He almost craved the outburst. But she was much stronger than Nicholas had believed. Life had taken the softness out of her. He had known that and counted on it. Eavin wasn't one to faint or cry or have the vapors another woman would have. Eavin would carve his heart out with her teeth, but at the time of her own choosing.

"What a charming surprise." Eavin's voice was flat and uninterested as she turned to the child clinging to Nicholas's arm. "I had no idea you were Francine's cousin. Does that makes us cousins-in-law? Do come with me, I'll see that you get some rest."

Nicholas didn't realize he was holding his breath until he saw Eavin leading Gabriella down the hallway to the newly redecorated master suite. Grinding his teeth, he swung to confront his mother. She met his glare calmly and removed her gloves. Not daring to speak, Nicholas stalked off to his study and the brandy he desperately needed.

Nicholas waited for Eavin to seek him out. He could hear the accusations ringing in his ears before she spoke them. He knew his arguments well—he'd rehearsed them a thousand times to convince himself these last weeks—but they sounded weak even to him in the face of Eavin's anguish. The brandy wasn't making his tongue feel any smoother. He would have to talk fast if he was going to make her understand. And he had to make her understand. To contemplate the alternative was to drive a stake through his heart.

That was a damned fool thing for a sensible man to think. Growling at his idiocy, Nicholas applied his considerable brain to the problem. He had one argument that Eavin couldn't refute. Turning his gaze upward, he decided it would be better to use that argument first, since it was growing increasingly obvious that Eavin was too furious to face him right now.

Ignoring his mother's call from the salon, Nicholas strode up the stairs in the direction of the nursery. Eavin wouldn't argue in front of Jeannette. He could make his case heard with some degree of sanity that way. Eavin would understand once she heard him out. She might not speak to him for a week. He would no doubt have to seduce her all over again. But in the end she would understand. He had to believe that. To believe otherwise would be to doubt all that he had begun to trust between them, and he desperately needed her trust.

The nursery was empty. Disbelieving, Nicholas scanned the room thoroughly; then with growing fear he stalked toward the next chamber. That door was closed, but he could hear the sound of voices from within. Reassured, he threw open Eavin's door.

The one pitiful trunk with which she had arrived was already full. Eavin still wore the light summer gown she had been wearing when he arrived, a gown totally unsuitable for traveling, but Nicholas didn't mistake her intentions. The feral gleam in her emerald eyes as they looked right through him at his entrance was sufficient to gauge the extent of her fury.

"Clemmie, get out of here," Nicholas calmly ordered. The already rattled black maid eagerly complied.

Eavin slammed the trunk closed and began to fasten the various latches.

"Where do you think you are going?"

Eavin gave him a scathing look. "Away." She turned to the small chest of drawers at the side of the table and began to search for any items left behind.

The drawers were already empty. It was amazing that in the year and a half since she had been here she had accumulated so little that it could fit within the space of a trunk. Seeing those empty drawers that had once spilled with the fragile laces and scents of sachets he had given her, Nicholas felt a band tighten around his chest.

"Not in my lifetime." He stepped forward, slamming the door shut and reaching for the trunk on the floor.

Eavin turned and hit him squarely in the midsection with a punch. For a woman, she packed a powerful wallop, but Nicholas only grunted and caught her wrist. With a movement as quick as a cat's, she brought her knee up and missed his groin by a fraction when he anticipated her reaction and moved backward.

"You aren't even giving me a chance," he growled, pushing her toward the bed, where he could hold her trapped against the frame.

"I gave you everything I had, and you didn't even have the decency to give me a warning. Let go of me, Nicholas, or I will scream the house down."

"Scream. There is nothing anyone can do. You will hear me out first."

"I'll see you in hell first." Twisting, Eavin sank her teeth into the hand holding hers captive.

Not even attempting to free his hand, Nicholas used it to push her backward into the feather mattress. Clouds of mosquito netting flew up and settled around them, and Eavin screamed more in fury than fear as she was caught by his heavier weight.

"I'll kill you for this, Nicholas! Get off. Let me up this instant," Eavin screamed as she kicked and squirmed in a vain attempt to throw him off.

"Not until you listen to reason." His sudden arousal infuriated him as much as her refusal to listen. She was walking out on him as if they were nothing to each other, and he wanted her so badly he couldn't stand up even if he wanted to.

"Listening to your reasons is what got me into this! Now get the hell off before your precious new wife hears us. Nicholas, stop that!" Eavin's screech was as much anguish as fury as his kisses found their mark on her throat.

Below, Nicholas's bellows of rage could be heard plainly, and all ears turned with interest as the confrontation escalated. Hélène stepped anxiously into the hallway, glancing up the stairs. The black servants lingered in doorways and behind stairs, their fingers twisting nervously in whatever task they pretended to do as the master's fury was met chord by chord by the lady's. Tension mounted with the screams, but they stood frozen, uncertain of their place in the scheme of things.

"It will be a cold day in hell afore I'm lettin' the likes of you touch me again, Nicholas Saint-Just! Get your blasphemous hands off me!" There was no mistaking the lady's words. Clemmie glanced to Annie, who had come back upstairs after leaving the child in the kitchen. Annie wrung her hands helplessly and stared upward.

"*Mon dieu,* you are a vicious witch! Get your claws out of me! You're not going anywhere, do you understand? Marriage changes nothing!"

The cry of fury that produced caused even Hélène to flinch. When she looked up to find the frail figure of Gabriella standing frightened in the hall, looking upward, she straightened her shoulders.

"Go back to your room, child. I'll take care of this." Hélène advanced toward the bottom of the stairs.

"Will he hurt her?" Gabriella pulled her robe more tightly closed, her fear evident in the whitening of her knuckles, but a certain note of defiance crept into her voice.

"He already has." Without another word of explanation Hélène proceeded upward.

When first she entered, she thought Nicholas was strangling his mistress, but it soon became evident that the two of them were locked in an equal battle of wills. Eavin was smaller, with much less strength, but Nicholas was forced to hold back his own greater size to keep from harming her. There was no winning such a battle, and Hélène gathered air into her lungs to override their curses.

"Nicholas!"

Both combatants jumped guiltily. Eavin's frantic struggles ceased as embarrassment flooded through her. Nicholas looked down into her flushed face stained with tears and had the urge to gather her into his arms. She would take his hide off first. Keeping her trapped between his body and the bed, Nicholas answered with annoyance.

"Get out of here, *maman*. You have caused enough trouble. This is between myself and Eavin."

"And the entire household. Get up from there and be sensible. Mrs. Dupré, you cannot think of leaving the child. I would suggest that you have your trunk moved out to the *garçonnière* along with Jeannette's belongings. Gabriella is much too young to know how to take care of an infant, and I'm certain she wouldn't dream of separating you from your niece. Nicholas, you had best go calm your wife. She will no doubt be in a state of hysterics shortly."

Satisfied that the battle had been brought to a standstill, Hélène turned on her heel and walked off.

Studying Eavin's face to be certain she would not launch herself at him again, Nicholas slowly rose, giving her the freedom to do the same. She wouldn't look at him but angrily wiped her face with the back of her hands.

"I will send one of the men to carry the trunk. You will need to make changes. The rooms have been neglected with lack of use. When I find Annie, I'll send her and Jeannette to you." Nicholas spoke stiffly, choosing his words by her lack of reaction.

Eavin said nothing, merely turned away, her cheeks flushed with shame.

Nicholas had the overwhelming urge to cry. The need to do so had been beaten out of him a long time ago and he did not give in to the urge now, but the pain ached in him, longing for release. She was so proud and beautiful, and he had brought her down to this. Why had it never occurred to him that humiliation was more powerful than logic?

There was nothing that could be said to make it better. Understanding that much, Nicholas turned and walked out, closing the door softly behind him.

Eavin didn't join them for dinner. Nicholas kept close watch on her through the servants to be certain she went no farther than the bachelor's quarters, but he stayed out of her way otherwise. She couldn't stay silent forever. Sometime she would come to him and unleash that formidable tongue. That would be his chance to make her see reason.

His original idea of building another house seemed more logical now. Eavin wouldn't accept the idea of his building one for her, but he could build a new one. He'd contemplated the thought for some time now, even had a location chosen. Once it was done, he would turn this house over to Eavin. She would see the suitability of it. This house was too small for entertaining, but it would be just right for Eavin and Jeannette. And for himself, once things were settled. Gabriella would be content to play house in a brand-new structure she could decorate to her heart's desire.

Once she learned how to run a household. Nicholas stared grimly at the burned concoction on his plate. The servants were declaring their allegiance to Eavin. He remembered a time before Eavin came when he had eaten this kind of mess daily. Francine had been too delicate to attend to the kitchen as she ought. And Gabriella was too young and frightened to establish her authority as yet. She would learn with time.

Nicholas rang for someone to come and take the unpalatable plate away. There was a crash on the backstairs but no other response. Hélène raised her eyebrows and rose to go in search of the culprits. Nicholas groaned inwardly. Of a certainty, his mother would use this opportunity to make herself at home. The new house would have to contain a wing just for her.

He turned his attention to the young girl at his right.

He would have to quit thinking of her as a child. He had
seen her birth date on the marriage records. She would be
eighteen shortly. Beneath the gauzy frills of her gown he
could see the curve of small breasts. She had much the
same sort of figure as Francine: long and delicate, with
fragile bones and little flesh. He had thought that the mark
of a lady once. Perhaps it was, but it wasn't the promise of
a woman.

Eavin was the opposite of what he had thought he
wanted. She had a peasant's healthy physique with wide
hips and full breasts and the strength to punch him hard
enough to cause pain. And a passion to match.

Sighing, Nicholas lifted his wineglass to his lips. He
had proved his theory. Eavin wasn't a cold lady but a passionate woman, just as he had predicted. He had thought
himself very clever in his choice of mistress. Would that
he could think himself equally clever in his choice of
wife.

Later, Gabriella dutifully trudged off to bed under the
tender auspices of Nicholas's mother. He watched them
go with a feeling of trepidation. Perhaps they should have
stayed in New Orleans for a few days after the wedding.
It might have been easier surrounded by crowds of well-
wishers. But traditionally, the newly married couple
weren't supposed to show their faces for some time after
the wedding, and it had seemed simpler to isolate himself
here where he felt at home. Where Eavin was.

Instinct urged Nicholas to go to Eavin now and not to
his newly acquired wife. Gabriella would be relieved not
to have to endure his presence. He didn't need instinct to
tell him that. She was terrified of him, and perhaps
rightly so after some of the performances he had given in
her presence. Gently bred in another country far from this
one, she had no notion of what it took to survive here.
She no doubt had her heart set on some effeminate young
man who would produce a lace-edged handkerchief
whenever she looked peaked, and who wouldn't have the
audacity to make constant demands on her in bed. It was
rather obvious that her new husband didn't fit that mold.

But the marriage had to be consummated sometime.
And after today's episode it would be best to do so tonight, or Gabriella and his mother would go crying back
to New Orleans. Claiborne had finally taken the time to

hear Nicholas's plea for recognition of Lafitte's offer. It might be a little too late, but there was still a chance that the pirates would prefer American rule to British, although the terms of their offer would probably be stiffer now that their island had been demolished. But if Gabriella went flying back to New Orleans for refuge, Nicholas's credibility and honor would be questioned and the treaty with the pirates would be lost. He'd made his bed. It was time he slept in it.

Reluctantly, Nicholas left his study at the sound of his mother's footsteps retreating into the interior of the house. Gabriella would be alone and expecting him. It had been so much simpler with Eavin. Although frightened, she had wanted his caresses. He didn't fool himself into thinking any such nonsense with Gabriella. She would despise what he would do to her tonight.

Shedding his coat, his cravat already long since removed, Nicholas began to undress in the sitting room outside the chamber where his wife waited. He hadn't worn a nightshirt since a child, but he would have to cover himself with some modicum of respectability tonight—although the way he felt at the moment, he had very little to hide.

Deciding to discard all but trousers and shirt, Nicholas approached the darkened chamber on quiet feet. Perhaps she slept and they could save the final act of this terrible day for morning. That would be preferable. They would both be rested and relaxed, and things wouldn't look quite as ominous as now. If they were to spend the rest of their lives together, it ought to be in some measure of peace.

Trying not to think of the woman sleeping in a strange bed in the house across the lawn, Nicholas crept into his bedroom as if he were the outsider. He had to remember that Gabriella was in a place strange to her also, but he could find no empathy with the silent child. She seemed to have no character, no thoughts of her own. Perhaps she was waiting for him to give her some.

Not relishing that thought, Nicholas bent over the bed to see if she was there.

"I thought you might not come," she whispered.

Nicholas could hear the quaver in her voice and tried to keep himself from scowling, though the room was dark enough to prevent her seeing. "We were married in the eyes of God and the church this morning," he reminded her. "I must make this a marriage in truth now." He sat down at the edge of the bed.

"I understand. Your mother explained things to me. I will lie very still and let you do what you like. But when there's a baby, will I need to do it anymore?"

Disgust rose in his throat and Nicholas reached to light a candle. He felt like a cradle robber as he looked down on her white face. Her high-necked gown covered everything, enveloping even her breasts in loose folds. She wore her pale hair pulled in a single tight braid that fell over her shoulder. Despite her brave words, terror widened her eyes to blue pools against the drawn skin of her face. Her lips looked cracked and dry, and he had a sudden vision of full, moist red ones quivering eagerly for his touch.

Nicholas fought the image. He reached to find Gabriella's breast, searching futilely among the folds of linen before he encountered the small mound. She whimpered when he touched her, and a glance told him she was biting her bottom lip. Disgust was turning into something more violent, and to head it off, Nicholas bent to kiss her unappealing lips.

He encountered the barrier of her teeth and something snapped. His hands closed vengefully over her shoulders as he pushed her roughly downward. He would not have another wife who refused him in bed. Prying at her mouth with his tongue, he reached to pull her gown upward. Only her childish cry of alarm restored his senses and his repulsion with himself.

Shoving himself from the bed, Nicholas strode for the door. "Go to sleep, Gabriella. I will speak with you in the morning."

He could almost feel her relief as he shut the door behind him.

32

Nicholas slept alone that night. He heard the drunken arrival of Eavin's brother and slipped out to the gallery to be certain she did not persuade Michael to take her away. Ignoring the mosquitoes, he sat with his legs propped on the railing, watching the *garçonnière* hungrily as lights moved from the lower salon to upper bed chambers. Then the lights went out, and all was peaceful again. She was staying, for now.

He would have to see that she stayed forever. Nicholas leaned back in the cane chair, drinking in the scent of the heavy night air, sipping his wine. He'd had mistresses before. He was a man who enjoyed physical pleasures. But he'd never had one who haunted his thoughts even when she wasn't there.

A breeze caressed his face, and Nicholas thought of Eavin's kisses. The perfume of the roses she had planted drifted upward, and her heavenly scent came back to him. He could hear her laughter in the call of the night birds. He could see her eyes sparkling in the lights of a boat drifting by on the river. He could see her walk in the movement of the willows in the wind. He longed for the sound of her voice whispering in his ear, but there was only silence.

He was dangerously near some cataclysm that he would fall into and never return from if he kept on this way. Nicholas didn't know the solution, but he recognized the danger. Considered logically, he didn't think he had done the wrong thing. But logic wasn't pulling at him now. Temptation was.

Tearing himself away from temptation, Nicholas rose and returned to the lonely room he had shared with Eavin. Even the pillows smelled of her perfume. He fell asleep hugging one to him.

In the morning, with only a few hours' fitful sleep behind him, Nicholas appeared downstairs before the ladies to find Michael in the dining room ahead of him. His overseer looked the worse for drink, but the stubborn glow of determination in his Irish eyes was much the same as Eavin's, and Nicholas reached for the coffee. He needed to be awake for this confrontation.

"Lafitte was in the bar looking for you last night." Michael produced a flask and added a swig of the contents to his coffee, then passed the flask to Nicholas. "I don't think he was amused that you married in order to save him. Daniel and I had a time pouring enough whiskey down him to keep him from taking the place apart single-handed."

"I'm surprised you hadn't already done it yourself." Nicholas splashed the liquor into his cup and grimaced as he tasted it.

"If it hadn't been for Daniel, I would have. I left him talking about shutting down the paper and buying you out of the bar so he wouldn't have to deal with you anymore."

"That's what a man likes, loyalty." Sitting down, Nicholas picked up a croissant and belligerently bit into it. "So, when are you leaving?"

"Today. One of the other things I learned last night was that the British claim their fleet attacked Baltimore and Washington. I'm going home."

The grayness inside his soul muffled any strong reaction to this news of the outside world, but it didn't stop Nicholas from contemplating the chain of events that would follow should the rumor be true. If the British were boldly attacking the cities on the East Coast, it could very well mean that their fleet in the Lakes had finally shut off those ports, fully capturing the north, and they were now moving southward to put an end to the war.

It didn't take much imagination to know that New Orleans was the key to the west. Conquer New Orleans, and the entire Mississippi and all the states and territories along it would be conquered. The New England states had been against the war all along; the British wouldn't risk arousing their ire by attacking there now that they claimed Maine. New Orleans was an entirely different matter. New Orleans with their pirates and privateers boldly thumbing their noses at the mighty British navy's blockade would be a satisfying target all around. The stockpiles of valuable cargo waiting for shipping would be an irresistible temptation to sailors starving for prize money. It had been inevitable from the start.

"There won't be any ships out," Nicholas stated calmly. "The only way back to Baltimore will be over the mountains. By the time you get there, we're likely to be British subjects. Our only hope in hell is to keep New Orleans out of their hands."

Michael looked at him in disbelief. "What do we have? Five miserable little ships collecting shrimp in the bay? Lafitte says the British have nearly fifty ships of the line in Jamaica, and Wellington's army is on its way. What are we going to do, set the alligators on them?"

"I don't know what you're going to do, but I'm going to offer my services to General Jackson. I've never fought a land war before, but my ship isn't here, so I don't have any other choice. Jackson is a tough man. I don't admire his politics, but he's our only hope."

Michael shook his head as he watched his employer sip coffee as if they were discussing the newspaper. "You have a house full of women here and cane and cotton ready for harvest. And you're going to up and march to Mobile?"

That brought a flicker of pain to his face, but Nicholas quickly erased it. "The British would have to sail all fifty ships up the river and ground them and walk from one to the other before they could reach this place. The city is where they'll attack, and they'll have to do that on foot. They'll not get frigates through the mud. As for the harvest, well, I know a man looking for work if you're not going to stay. I might still have a friend or two to call on. It will have to take care of itself beyond that. I don't know how Baltimore and Washington fought, but no self-respecting Creole is going to allow New Orleans to fall without a fight. The cane will have to wait."

Thinking of the fortunes in cotton and other goods stacked in warehouses and all along the docks of the city because of the blockade, Michael could understand that attitude, but he shivered to think of it. He had spent his life scratching for a living, and here was wealth unbounded going to waste in the fields. He didn't want to feel respect and admiration for the man next to him, but he couldn't despise him as he ought, either.

"I'm Irish. You can't hate the British any more than I do. If Jackson's the man to lead this fight, I'll be joining him."

Nicholas nodded. He hadn't expected any less from Eavin's feisty brother. Michael was looking for a battle, and Nicholas was only relieved that he had chosen this one and not one against himself. There would be no winning in a fight with Eavin's brother. Even if he beat Michael, Eavin would hate him forever. She wasn't going to appreciate his leading her brother to war, either, but women seldom appreciated these things.

"I suppose you better tell Eavin, then. She won't speak to me. I'll make the other arrangements." Resolutely, Nicholas rose from the table. This wasn't what he wanted, but he didn't see any alternative. He'd thought he'd returned from the fighting life when he had come here. But it seemed life was one kind of battle or another after all, the only difference being that war provided a more useful outlet for the rage boiling inside him than dueling or rape.

With a frown Michael watched the Frenchman walk away. All the electric energy that had driven Nicholas earlier seemed to have gone out of him. When Michael had first arrived here, Nicholas Saint-Just had appeared to be a golden warrior from King Arthur's days, and Michael hadn't been able to help admiring him. He couldn't fault Eavin for choosing a man like that. But the glitter seemed singularly tarnished now, and the warrior looked too tired to lift a sword. What had happened to make such a change?

Mindful of his sister's well-being, Michael returned to the room where Eavin had imprisoned herself. She met Michael's news with the same stony implacability as Nicholas. She continued combing Jeannette's hair and fastening a ribbon in it the whole time Michael told his tale. When he announced he was leaving, she merely nodded her head and set the child on the floor.

"Are you going to be here when I get back?" Michael finally demanded.

Eavin looked at him blankly. "Where else would I be going then?"

Throwing his hands up in disgust, Michael walked out. He would never understand women, and right at the moment he saw no purpose in trying.

Nicholas wasn't at all certain that he was achieving much more success with his wife, but he cared less than Michael. Finding Gabriella still in bed, he entered the chamber they were meant to share and paced the rug while she pulled the sheets around her and watched him with unmitigated terror.

"General Jackson will be needing experienced fighting men. It's my duty to offer my services. You will be safe here. There's no need to worry."

Gabriella watched him stalk up and down and didn't observe any of the lack of energy that Michael had. What Nicholas exuded now frightened her enough. Nervously she inquired, "When are you leaving?"

Nicholas favored her with a look of disgust. "Immediately. You are herewith relieved of your marital duties until I return. If you are having second thoughts about this marriage, I'd suggest you consult a priest about an annulment. It's still possible now. It won't be later, once I bed you."

If it was possible, Gabriella paled a shade whiter at this mention of what he would do when he returned. Her fingers clutched the sheet tighter as the room seemed to fill to bursting with his anger. She didn't know what she had done to make him angry, and tears began to seep from the corners of her eyes.

Nicholas saw the tears, and to his shame, he felt nothing for them. He was terrifying her, and he wasn't the least repentant. All he knew was the disgust welling up in him, that and the anger that made him want to shake her until her teeth rattled. He could have raped her last night. Today he would favor beating her. Such a violent reaction to someone he was meant to share his life with did not portend well for the future.

Since she seemed to have nothing else to say to a husband about to go off to war, Nicholas turned around and strode out. He should have known better than to expect anything else. He didn't even seek out his mother but began giving a list of instructions to the servants.

* * *

Eavin stared out the small window at the activity around the stable in the distance. Saddlebags of provisions were being loaded onto two sturdy field horses. Men were scrambling everywhere. She had seen several messengers ride out earlier. One of them had apparently already returned with Jeremy. She saw him now talking with Michael. She didn't see any sign of Nicholas.

She reached for the tea Annie had prepared for her earlier. It was cold now, but she sipped it without conscious thought. Annie had obviously liberally laced it with Labelle's herbs, but whiskey would have done more good. She needed something to warm her insides against this pervading cold.

Not that the weather had changed. It was still hot. Flies still buzzed along the gallery. Hummingbirds darted in and out of the honeysuckle. But there was a coldness in her middle just the same.

Perhaps this was what it was like to be dead and a ghost. If so, Eavin felt sorry for Francine. It was a horrible, helpless feeling watching life march on without her. Nicholas was married and going off to war. Her only brother was following behind him. And she was left to sit here and stare at four walls and wonder what there was left to do with her life after she had destroyed all her other options for a man who was about to turn his back on her.

Even thinking like that did not fire her fury. She truly must be dead inside. There just didn't seem to be any point in anything anymore.

Eavin didn't dare leave the room until Nicholas was gone. She was relieved that he was going. She didn't know how she would ever face the women in the house again, but she knew she could never face Nicholas. It would be better for all concerned if she packed and left, too, except for Jeannette. She couldn't leave Jeannette.

She stared at the child happily playing on the floor and wondered if she was wrong in that, too. Annie loved Jeannette and would take care of her. In a few months Jeannette wouldn't even remember Eavin existed. She had a new mother who could introduce her to society when the time came. Even this one last purpose was denied her.

Eavin hardened her heart against self-pity as a rap came at the door. Thinking it was Michael come to say his farewells, she absently called for him to enter and set her empty cup back on the tray. She would have to take the tray back to the kitchens. She couldn't expect Annie to wait on her hand and foot from now on.

When Nicholas entered, filling the small chamber with his height and the overpowering scents of horses and perspiring male flesh, Eavin stepped backward, grasping the windowsill as she stared up at him. He returned the stare. His gold mane of hair had recently been cut short and was damp now from exertion, but it still framed his sun-bronzed face, accenting its strengths. The faint hairline scar along his jaw was barely visible now. He hadn't spent much time with his wardrobe. Her gaze fell with fascination to the rivulet of sweat running down the *V* of his open shirt.

"I wanted to see Jeannette before I left," Nicholas said stiffly when Eavin said nothing. Despite his words, his gaze didn't fall to the infant but stayed fastened on the woman clinging to the windowsill. Black curls tumbled unhindered to shoulders covered by only the briefest puff of muslin. He didn't look lower but hungrily drank in the wide green of her eyes and the lush pout of her bottom lip before she drew it closed in a tight frown.

"Of course. I will leave you to say your good-byes." Eavin didn't offer to move. The bulk of Nicholas's body blocked her exit.

Since the child in question was now clinging to his trousers, calling to be picked up, Nicholas bent and lifted her into his arms. It kept them occupied and away from temptation. "I want you to promise to stay in the house while I am gone. I don't like you and Jeannette out here alone."

"I'll have Annie take Jeannette back to the nursery," Earvin agreed woodenly.

Nicholas's eyes narrowed and their amber flared briefly golden. "That house is your home. Do not let anyone drive you from it. I will build a new one for Gabriella when I return. Don't look at me like that!" he snapped when he easily read the angry refusal in her eyes. "I haven't had time to change my will. You and Jeannette are still the beneficiaries. I don't know what that means under the law, but if anything should happen to me, I ask that you look after my mother and Gabriella. If the will holds, they have nowhere else to go. Even the house in New Orleans will belong to Jeannette."

Anger faded to fear as Eavin's gaze flew to search Nicholas's face. He was going to war and there was every chance that he would never return. She could read that in his expression. He didn't want to return. He hugged Jeannette as if this were his last farewell. Tears stung her eyes for the second time that morning, tears that she hadn't shed in years and seemed to shed too easily anymore.

Refusing to give in to them, Eavin shook herself back to anger. "I'd recommend that you come back alive if you want to see your wishes carried out. I'll not promise to play rug to their feet."

A wistful smile crossed his lips as Nicholas watched the color rise to her cheeks. "I'm counting on you not to. I want Jeannette to grow up like you, not like Gabriella. Will you do that for me?"

"You're coming back!" she insisted angrily.

And as he watched Eavin bristle with life and fury, felt the flow of blood making her heart beat as strongly as his, and knew the heat of the emotions boiling beneath the womanly curves of breast and hip, Nicholas knew she was right. He was coming back, and when he did, she was going to be his again.

Nicholas didn't dwell on this discovery. He felt only the stirring of life where all had been dead, and read the same in Eavin's eyes. The caring that was so much a part of her was more than he had ever known before. With that thought he handed the child into her arms.

"I'll be back, then, and you'd better be in that house where you belong. *Comprends-tu?*"

"Oh, I'll be there all right," Eavin replied maliciously. "But I won't promise that your mousy little wife will be. I may just eat her for supper."

"That's what cats do," Nicholas responded calmly. "But you'd do better to sink your claws in me and not the innocent. I'm the one you want to punish."

"And so you are." Eavin straightened and glared at him. "Hurry back so I can see justice done."

"With pleasure." And with a mocking grin that did not quite reach his eyes, Nicholas tilted her chin and pecked her briefly on the mouth, and walked out before she could throw something at him.

33

Eavin didn't keep to the letter of her agreement. Nicholas might call the house hers, but the constant company of two helpless women kept it from being the haven it once was.

She compromised. During the day she brought Jeannette to the house to be pampered by her grandmother while Eavin commanded the servants in the day-to-day details of living. Jams and vegetables were put up from the gardens and orchards under her vigilance. The laundry was carried out regularly every Monday and boiled and scrubbed and hung out to dry. The ironing was done on Tuesdays. The cooking for the household and the field hands went on constantly. The new overseer brought squabbles among the slaves to Eavin since they seemed to respect her decisions over his own. She found herself diving into Nicholas's store of coins to provide shoes for everyone when a cobbler came to spend a week. The tasks of the day were seemingly endless.

But the night was hers. After the last meal of the day, Eavin packed Jeannette up and returned to the bachelor's quarters. The new overseer was a married man with a wife and children he installed in one of the small outlying cottages. The *garçonnière* was hers to do with as she would.

It was better than sitting in the salon doing needlework and listening to the complaints of Hélène and Gabriella. Eavin appropriated books from Nicholas's library and taught herself to read French from the phrases she learned daily. She sewed new curtains for the windows, decorated the tables with bouquets of autumn flowers, stole supplies from Nicholas's desk and installed them in a small escritoire she appropriated for her own use. She wrote articles for Daniel and sent them by any manner she could contrive. His replies contained all the news and gossip of the city, more than the newspapers ever revealed.

From the newspapers Eavin knew the legislature had convened to discuss raising militia and means of fortifying the city. Daniel's letters revealed they did nothing more than argue, fuss, and fight while accomplishing nothing. She read that Baltimore had bravely withstood the British attack, coming to little harm while their guns bombarded the mighty British navy mercilessly. Daniel reported that neither side could claim victory, but that in itself was a victory for the Americans. To hold their own with no navy or army to speak of against the mightiest war machine in the world was not something to be taken lightly. His reasonable explanations of the happenings around her reminded Eavin constantly of Nicholas and tore the hole in her heart a little wider, but she wouldn't do without those letters for the world.

For Nicholas didn't write. The women in the house waited daily for messengers from the outside world. Daniel's stream of letters to Eavin caused suspicion until she read a few aloud and they grew bored and left her alone. New Orleans went about its pleasure as usual, and invitations arrived with frequency, but unless someone offered to escort them, they were stranded. That made it even more imperative that they receive some word from Nicholas as to his return. But none came.

As much as Eavin wished for some word from Nicholas, she didn't expect it. He had left carrying a load of anger and bitterness with him. She didn't expect the trials of traveling to alleviate them in any way. Listening to Hélène and Gabriella, she was beginning to understand some of the pressures under which he had left, even if not all of them.

"He is a terrifying man. I do not know how you have suffered him," Gabriella confided in her soft Spanish accent. "I think he would blow me out the window if I stood up to him."

Patiently, Eavin replied in the French that Gabriella would have to learn if she meant to live here. "Did he ever hurt you?"

Gabriella's eyes widened in distress. "No, but he is so big." She held her hands out wide at the shoulders and then raised them to indicate height. "And he rages so. Is like a storm come into the house."

Eavin had to smile at that. Gabriella was quite correct there. The fault lay in fearing the storm. "Jeannette isn't afraid of him. You shouldn't be, either," she said firmly.

"You are right, of course." Gabriella sighed and turned back to her needlework. "Will you go with us to this American soiree tomorrow?"

The Howells' invitation was all that had been talked about these last few days. Eavin would have liked to see her friends again, but she felt uncomfortable appearing in public now that she was branded a fallen woman. The neighbors had been kind to her, coming to visit and treating her the same as Gabriella and Hélène, but it was different in a room full of people, half of whom could be strangers who knew nothing but the scandalous rumors.

"I would rather stay here. Jeannette seems to be coming down with a cold, and I'd like to keep an eye on her. You can tell me all about it later."

That seemed to satisfy Gabriella, but Hélène was a different matter. Coming upon Eavin directing an army of servants in cleaning the chandelier, she caught her by the arm and steered her into the *petite salle*.

"You must come with us to the Howells."

Bewildered, Eavin stared at her for a moment before she realized the command related to the invitations. Recovering, she removed her arm from the woman's grasp. "I think not." She started to return to the hall, but Hélène's voice halted her.

"Nicholas would want it. To stay away would only confirm the rumors."

Eavin gritted her teeth and turned to glare at the woman. "The rumors have been thoroughly confirmed already. I will not give them something to talk about all night."

Nicholas's mother drew herself up to her relatively tall stature. "What you and Nicholas did before he married no longer counts. You are a free woman. If you appear in our company, they will know there is nothing between you and Nicholas. It will all pass over. For Jeannette's sake, you must come."

"For Jeannette's sake I have sacrificed all that I am or

could be. Do not ask for more than that, for I have no more to give."

"It is we who will give to you," she replied coolly. "I cannot say that Gabriella will ever be a mother to the child, but she would be your friend. By restoring your name in exchange for all that you have done for Jeannette, we will be even."

Eavin was certain that made sense in some crazy Gallic way that she didn't hope to understand, but it didn't necessarily make the situation easier. She shook her head and walked out without answering.

In the end, it was Jeremy and his new betrothed who made the decision for her. They arrived to escort the Saint-Justs and refused to leave until Eavin got dressed and accompanied them.

It wasn't as horrible as it could have been. Mignon Dubois even greeted Eavin with graciousness and introduced her to a cousin of hers who immediately appropriated the first dance of the evening. Clyde Brown claimed her for his usual reel and stayed at her side until Alphonso came in and discovered them. The young Spaniard instantly named himself Eavin's protector and almost engaged in a duel over an imagined slight from one of the other guests until Eavin threatened to slap him if he didn't behave. After that, even Señor Reyes nodded a stiff acknowledgment in her direction, and she felt almost justified in dancing the rest of the night away.

Not that it made it any easier to sleep when she returned home. Although the weather was growing cooler, Eavin tossed restlessly beneath the covers, finally throwing them aside and getting up to open the window. The cool night air poured in around her and she breathed deeply of it, wondering if Nicholas was somewhere out there sleeping beneath the same stars she could see from here. It was a foolish thought, but it made her feel better to think of it. She could picture him wrapped in a blanket, his saddle beneath the rumpled gold of his hair, his broad shoulders resting on the ground as she had seen them so many times on her pillow. As she would never see them again.

Turning away, Eavin returned to her bed and deliberately shut off such thoughts. Tomorrow she needed to harvest the last of the herbs in the garden. She didn't know when the frost would come, but she meant to be prepared.

Annie laughed as Jeannette spun herself dizzily in circles until she fell down giggling. The slave's skin was the polished ebony of a true African, but her expression was that of any mother anywhere. Eavin looked up from her gardening to watch as Annie gently teased the child into learning to balance her uncertain footsteps along the brick walkways. Jeannette was nearly weaned now, and with Eavin to watch over her she really didn't need a "mammy," but there wasn't a chance that Eavin would separate the child from her nurse.

Eavin had heard the slaves described as little more than children, and perhaps in this world so far from their own they were. But even children learned, and Annie was learning rapidly. Eavin wasn't fooled by the woman's insisting on bringing her the morning meal on a tray, bending over backward to make life easier for her while virtually ignoring the women in the house. Annie knew that her connection with Jeannette was based on Eavin's favor and not Gabriella's or Hélène's. She was even learning to speak like Eavin, and the sound of *shenanigans* on Annie's lips brought laughter to Eavin's eyes.

"Annie, why do you not have children of your own?" The question was out before she could stop it. Children were very much on Eavin's mind, and watching Annie with Jeannette convinced her they were not far from the other woman's. Eavin might not be able to bear children, but Annie seemed healthy enough, and there was no shortage of men in the quarters. She had seen Annie walking with one of them in particular.

The slave looked up quickly at the question, then averted her eyes as was considered respectable. "Don' know, Miss Eavin."

Eavin could understand the feeling of sorrow that went with that answer, but it wasn't sorrow in Annie's voice, it was defiance. She put down her trowel and began pulling off her gloves. "Don't know or won't say? I've seen you walking out with that Jim. He's a handsome man. I'm sure Nicholas wouldn't mind if you were to marry."

A stubborn expression that she had seldom seen appeared on Annie's face. "Yes'm, Miss Eavin."

Exasperated, Eavin threw her gloves into the gardening basket and stood up. "If you don't want to talk about it, just say so. I certainly know how it feels to want something and not be able to have it. I just thought I could help if there was something standing in your way."

Annie looked up with an expression lost somewhere between fear and hope. "I'se a slave, Miss Eavin. If Marster Nick say marry, we do, but we wants to wait."

Eavin was no judge of ages, but she knew both Annie and Jim were young enough to want each other with the same kind of desperation she felt for Nicholas, and undoubtedly with the same lack of control. What could possibly interfere with their desire to marry?

"Why? You don't have to tell me. I just see you with Jeannette and think you ought to have children. I know what it feels like to lose a child. I would have thought you'd want to try again."

"That child warn't mine. It were Jenkins'. Me and Jim, we gonna wait until I'se thirty. Miss Belle gonna tell me when that day comes."

That didn't spread enlightenment but spurred curiosity. The fact that the child Annie had lost belonged to the misbegotten overseer that Nicholas had fired came as no surprise. But Labelle's name did. "Miss Belle? I thought you didn't like her. Why is she going to tell you when you're thirty? And how is she going to know?"

Definite defiance flared in Annie's eyes now as she looked up at Eavin. "Miss Belle knows things. She's dang'rous. She can stare a gator back to the swamp. But she he'ps us. Iffen we got 'nough coins when we gets to be thirty, we can buy our freedom. But iffen I have a child afore then, he still be a slave. So I'se got to wait."

Eavin's eyes widened at this piece of information. "Did Nicholas say that? I'll have a thing or two to say to him if that's true. That's awful! You mean you could be free, but he would keep your child?"

"Ain't Marster Nick's fault." Annie looked a little relieved that Eavin accepted her explanation without complaint. Some owners thought of their slaves as breeding machines expected to reproduce and replace themselves. The fact that she and Jim refused to do so could have had them whipped anywhere else. It had been the reason Jenkins had given for repeatedly raping her.

"It's the law, Miss Belle says. Marster Nick can't change the law. Them babies in the quarters all gonna belong to him until they'se thirty. Most of 'em gonna be slaves all their lives 'cause they ain't got gumption 'nough to make coins or keep 'em. But Jim, he's got most 'nough to buy me free when it comes time, and I been savin', too, just like you. We'll have babies then."

Annie seemed completely content with that plan. Eavin was horrified. Until now she had thought of the slaves more or less as servants, as she had been in her own house in Baltimore. People worked to live. It was a concept she understood well. People didn't necessarily choose to be servants, it was just their lot in life unless something else came along. But for most of these slaves, nothing else was ever going to come along. How could they possibly ever earn enough money to buy their freedom? And if they could find some way to earn money, how could they resist the temptation to spend it on the things that made their present lot a little easier? And there was nothing anyone could do about it even if they wanted to if the law wouldn't allow them to be free until they were thirty.

Eavin gasped as another thought occurred to her. "Belle's the daughter of a slave, isn't she? Does that mean she belongs to Nicholas?"

Annie thought about that a minute. "Reckon so. Don't reckon it's no different 'cause she's white. Her mama was a slave. She done tol' me so."

Belle was Nicholas's half sister, but she belonged to him in the eyes of the law. It defied the imagination. Eavin sat back down on the tree stump she had been using as a seat and stared out over the fields as she digested this information. Belle wasn't the only woman of color in Louisiana. There was a whole segment of society who looked like her. Many of them were free, having bought their freedom as Annie was planning on doing. But how many more must there be who would raise their children in slavery? Even now there were light-skinned children in the quarters, products of Jenkins and his ilk. Would Jenkins have sold his own children if he had remained?

"Something has to be done," she murmured, not realizing she said it aloud.

"Yes'm," Annie agreed. "Iffen you tell Marster Nick

how good I'se been when I turn thirty, maybe he won't ask too much for me. Then Jim can get out that much faster."

Eavin looked up with a glitter in her eyes that Nicholas would have recognized well. "Don't you worry about that, Annie. The day you turn thirty, you'll be free, and Jim as well. You just see if you aren't."

That was a reason to go on living. Somebody needed her, even if Nicholas didn't. With grim satisfaction Eavin picked up her basket and started back toward the house, her fingers itching for a pen.

34

"Hell, I think it would be easier to cross the damned mountains than these swamps." Michael swatted at another mosquito, then tossed a handful of dried leaves and humus on the fire to make it smoke more.

Their first night had not brought them much farther than the marshes on the other side of the city. It would be a long ride to Mobile. Despite his complaint, Michael was glad he had chosen this route. He wasn't much of one for walking, and Nicholas's horses made travel considerably easier. He would have had to have stolen one of the mounts if he had chosen Baltimore.

"Better get used to it unless you mean to head out for Texas." Unsympathetic, Nicholas crossed his hands behind his head and leaned back against his saddle. He had lived under the stars before. He preferred it to the filthy holds of ships. He could remember sleeping in a rotting hammock with the stenches and snores of a hundred men around him, vowing to own the damned ship one day so he could sleep in the captain's bunk. Once he'd had the right to the captain's bunk, he hadn't wanted it any longer. He had wanted a home. Now he had a home, and here he was back under the stars again. Perhaps he wasn't meant to be satisfied.

Michael whittled a point on the stick he meant to use to hold his portion of the frog legs they'd caught over the fire. Frog-eaters, he muttered to himself. There were worse words for these Frenchmen. If he stayed in their company much longer, he would become just like them. He gave the man sprawled in relaxation on the other side of the fire a spiteful look. The man had everything: looks, wealth, land, and aristocratic connections. Just for being born. And for that, he thought everything belonged to him. Well, he'd learn differently. Eavin would straighten

out while they were gone. The lass had a good head on
her shoulders even if she had a soft heart. She'd know
where her duty was. She would come with him to Texas
when it came time to go. And the Frenchman would be a
sorry bastard then.

"Texas sounds fair enough to me," he agreed bluntly.

"Better get in a little experience Indian fighting first."
Lying there staring at the stars, Nicholas could follow Michael's thoughts as well as his own. O'Flannery fully intended to take Eavin away. Nicholas didn't blame him.
That didn't mean he wouldn't fight him tooth and nail.

"Can't be much worse than a drunken German on Saturday night," Michael mused aloud. He was a city boy,
but he knew about fighting.

Nicholas chuckled. "And I suppose rattlesnakes aren't
much worse than an Irish priest on Sunday morning. How
do you mean to handle the Mexicans, who think that land
is still theirs?"

"Gently, very gently." The voice came out of the
thicket of cypress and not from Michael's mouth. Both
men turned to scan the landscape.

Belle drifted down the path as if it were the aisle to her
box seat at the theater. The swarming mosquitoes didn't
seem to bother her as she smiled languidly when Nicholas
leapt to his feet. Her light gown whispered in the breeze,
floating on the wind as if it were carrying her into the
clearing. The fragrance she wore arrived before she did,
an exotic scent with nothing of the floral in it. Reluctantly
following Nicholas's example, Michael stood up, too.

Her dark gaze swept with amusement to the Irishman.
As if Nicholas didn't exist, she drifted in Michael's direction, her hand reaching proprietarily to straighten his collar. "But you will not go to Texas, you foolish man. You
will stay here and raise many babies. When would you
like to start, hmmm?" She held her face up so that the
firelight flickered over her dusky skin, and Michael's
gaze was captured by the fine silk of her lips.

"Stop it, Belle. You've proved your point. Now sit
down and tell us why you've come." Irritated by his sister's advances toward Eavin's brother, Nicholas pointed
at a log by the fire.

Belle turned her enchanting smile in his direction and,
surprisingly, did as told. "Do you see, Nicholas? Really

see? I think not. But no matter. I have only come to tell you that Raphael is no longer in the bayou. He left when the militia shelled Barataria."

Her words meant nothing to Michael. He watched in a daze as she perched on the rotten log as if she were queen of the fairies on her throne. He had never seen a woman like her. Oh, he had. He'd been to the quadroons' ball in New Orleans. He knew what she was. But this one was different. This one was magical, like something from the old country. He could feel the spell she was weaving even as she spoke to Nicholas. Why didn't Nicholas see it?

Nicholas muttered a pithy French curse and threw more sticks on the fire. "I don't suppose you know where he went, do you?"

"Not yet, but I think even you can summon that knowledge without my poor help." Belle's tone was mocking as she watched her brother scowl.

"Once he learns I'm gone, he'll go home. That should make Señor Reyes deliriously happy."

"And Alphonso," Belle murmured wickedly. "He is head over heels, that one. I don't think he means to be a priest any longer."

Nicholas's scowl deepened, and her laughter chimed as she turned back to Michael. She held out her long fingers and a glint of gold caught in the firelight. "You have something I might drink, *non*?"

"*Oui.*" Grinning foolishly, Michael drew a bottle of wine from his saddle bag. He'd been saving it for something special. He couldn't think of anything more special than this.

Delighted, Belle accepted the tin cup of wine as if it were crystal. "You are a good man, I think. You will keep Nicholas out of trouble. He has a hasty temper and is a stupid, stupid man sometimes. I leave him to you."

Nicholas's eyes narrowed. Belle might tantalize other men into thinking she was charming and witty and dangerously knowledgeable, but he had known her since she was a child. Right now she was just being damned catty.

"If you came here to chastise me for my choice of wives, you are wasting your time, Belle. There are some things you don't know, and it isn't any of your business knowing."

Dark, almond-shaped eyes turned unblinkingly in his

direction. "Ahh, Nickie, you are all man, and that is why you are so incredibly stupid. Perhaps you should listen to your Irish friend more. He understands there is more to this world than can be seen."

Nicholas noted Michael's idiotic grin with irritation. One more down for the count. Belle was very good at knocking the pedestals from other people. "Go put your voodoo to good use, little sister. Find Raphael and put a hex on him until I get back."

Belle smiled gently and rose, floating to her brother's side and pressing a kiss on his golden hair. "You are being purposefully obtuse. Go fight your silly man's war. Raphael will still be here when you get back. And he won't have changed."

She set her cup down and started back toward the forest without a word of farewell. Before Michael could jump up, she had disappeared into the shadows. Giving Nicholas a threatening frown, Michael ran toward the horses. "You can't let her go back in there alone! For God's sake, man, we've got to take her back to the city."

Nicholas remained sprawled where he was. "You'd not find her again if you searched all night. Sit down and relax. Belle walks on alligators. She probably has a tribe of pygmies waiting to carry her on their shoulders back to whatever witch's cave she's inhabiting now. She'll laugh herself silly if you try to follow her. And the worst of it is, you'll hear her laugh, and you'll still not find her."

Perplexed, Michael stopped his efforts to saddle the horse and turned to stare at his ex-employer. "You speak with the voice of experience."

Nicholas's smile was tight as he glared at the fire. "I do. She would have you believe she is superhuman. I think she halfway believes it herself. But I will grant her this much, she has an uncanny ability to navigate the bayous. As a child she used to run away and hide in them. I've tried to follow her, track her down, been right on her damned heels, and still not found her. To this day, I've never been able to find Belle when she takes to the bayou. It's a waste of time. She will get through better than you."

Still uncertain, Michael hesitated. He hadn't been born a gentleman. He wasn't necessarily compelled to act as one, but the idea of a woman alone in this treacherous landscape gave him the shudders. "Who is she?" he demanded.

Nicholas shrugged. "My sister. My half sister, to be perfectly correct."

Michael knew all about sisters. Unwillingly he lowered the saddle to the ground and returned to the fire. "She's colored," he stated flatly.

The expression on Nicholas's face wasn't pleasant. "You're Irish."

That riposte wasn't sufficient. Michael returned his glare. "Irish is good enough for colored."

"She could have had a damned marquis if she weren't so stubborn." Nicholas reached for the flask lying on its side.

"My sister's had a damned marquis, and I don't see that it's improved her any." Michael reached and grabbed the silver flask away, taking a deep drink.

Nicholas laughed hollowly and rubbed his hand over his face. "Oh, hell, what difference does it make? They're going to do what they want anyway. The days when the man of the household makes the decisions seem to be gone."

"They never existed." Michael handed the flask back. "Men only thought they did. It was women who made the decisions, then twisted their men into believing it was their own thoughts. Seen it many a time. When did you ever see a woman do something she didn't want to?"

Nicholas closed his eyes to shut out the painful images. He had. He knew that he had. But it took violence to do it. Men could rule by violence. He had learned that lesson well. He had almost unleashed that propensity on Gabriella. Belle was quite right. He was a stupid, stupid man.

"You drink all that tea now. Since Marster Nick's been gone, you been lookin' puny. Miss Belle's potion will put you right." Annie fussed around the small room, dusting off the shelves, primping the new curtains while Eavin lay propped against her pillows sipping her breakfast.

Eavin didn't know if the tea made her feel any better. She certainly didn't feel any stronger. Actually, she rather thought she was growing weaker. The nights were filled with dreams of Nicholas until she woke up sweating, feeling his body inside hers, certain that he had come to her during the night. She literally ached with the need for him. She had never known such uncontrollable urges, but she didn't think Belle's tea had much to do with it. A month of abstinence was the more likely culprit.

"I think it's going to take something stronger than tea to face Gabriella this morning. I trust last night's callers have finally departed?"

Annie nodded solemnly. "Them gen'muns be awful sweet to a married lady. But they ain't gonna take kindly to you a'throwin' them out."

Eavin drained her tea and set it aside and prepared to get up and face the day. She really couldn't believe the effrontery of Raphael Reyes appearing on their doorstep. She hadn't known him when he arrived and had allowed him to enter with Alphonso, but she would have liked to have thrown him out on his ear when he was introduced. Instead she had simply risen and calmly told Gabriella that it was inappropriate for them to entertain the gentleman. When Gabriella had refused to leave the room, Eavin had turned to Hélène for assistance, but the older woman had oddly refused to concur.

It hadn't been a pleasant situation. Eavin had walked out, but Raphael had remained. She had successfully prevented the servants from bringing their guests refreshments. She had stationed Annie's Jim and several of the largest men available in strategic places, some of them openly visible to their guests, but they hadn't taken the hint. They had remained for hours, making the timid Gabriella laugh and giggle and talk with their flow of Spanish as she hadn't done since she'd come here. And Hélène Saint-Just had sat there and allowed it.

Nicholas would have heart failure if he knew his first wife's lover was now entertaining his second wife. It didn't matter that Gabriella had once been betrothed to Raphael. She was married now, and her loyalty should be with her husband. Perhaps Gabriella didn't understand the situation. Eavin would have to explain it to her this morning.

The thought wasn't a pleasant one. It would mean exposing Jeannette's heritage. Perhaps she could avoid that part. People could speculate, but they would never know that Jeannette wasn't Nicholas's child unless Nicholas came right out and told them. And he would never do that. It would be better to remain silent about that part—and keep Raphael far away from Jeannette.

In the days that followed, that thought became a futile one. Raphael returned regularly, sometimes with and sometimes without his brother, and Gabriella continued to accept him even after the situation was explained.

Eavin cornered Alphonso alone one day, practically poking her finger at his chest as she demanded, "Why are you doing this? You know how it must look. When Nicholas returns, he will have to call your brother out. Surely your father cannot want that."

The young man looked dejected, but holding his hat in his hand, he twisted it as he spoke. "My father wants satisfaction. He believes Nicholas left Raphael to die in the swamp. He knows Raphael is the better duelist, and some trickery must have been involved for Nicholas to injure him enough to make him helpless. He thinks it was Nicholas's plot all along to claim Gabriella for his own. She rightly belongs to Raphael. Even you must see that."

Ignoring the fact that the girl seemed thoroughly enchanted with the dapper, charming Spaniard, Eavin stuck to her point. "Do you believe Nicholas is capable of such base trickery?"

"Raphael is my brother," Alphonso replied simply. "I see no reason for him to lie. You are blinded by your woman's emotions. I wish you would see what is right before you. Nicholas shamed you, then married a woman who could bring him a better dowry. Is that the work of an honest man?"

There was no easy answer to that question. She could try to explain about children and Nicholas's need for acceptance and his place in society and hers. She could even talk about pirates and saving New Orleans and all the other excuses that Nicholas had undoubtedly used when he had married Gabriella. The fact of the matter remained that Nicholas didn't love her enough to marry her. He wanted her in his bed and not on his arm. Eavin might understand that, but she wasn't about to try to explain it to this innocent boy, who still believed in honor and all the rest of the lies that men told themselves.

"Yes, that is the work of an honest man. Nicholas never made a promise he couldn't keep, but I don't expect you to understand that. The question here has nothing to do with Nicholas. Gabriella is another man's wife. Your brother is courting immorality by courting Gabriella. How can you support that, you who would have been a priest?"

Alphonso held himself stiffly. "I am not keeper of my brother's soul. He tells me there is some chance that the marriage can be annulled. I must believe he is telling the truth."

Eavin had heard nothing of that. Alarm clamored through her as she left Alphonso standing in the hall to seek out the lovers. She didn't know a lot about annulments, but she didn't think a consummated marriage could be annulled. Perhaps she was wrong. Perhaps she wasn't. Perhaps Gabriella was still a virgin. If so, she wouldn't remain so long in Raphael's company. That point had been proven already.

Desperate for aid in this matter, Eavin turned to Hélène for some explanation of her role. The older woman only looked at her sadly, then gazed out at the gallery, where Gabriella and Raphael were strolling despite the increasingly inclement weather.

"Everything I have ever done has been wrong. Perhaps if I do nothing, something right will happen," was her only reply.

"You would destroy your own son," Eavin pleaded. "What do you think this will do to Nicholas? He already has one child of Raphael's in the nursery. What if the next is a boy?"

Hélène looked at her without curiosity. "Nicholas is strong. Life has made him strong, much stronger than I am. He will know what to do."

The woman whose approval or disapproval she had so feared had given up in defeat. Eavin stared at her a moment longer, not understanding what could be going through her mind. It suddenly occurred to her that Hélène was only a shell of a woman, her brittle exterior easily manipulated by the direction of the wind. Deciding Nicholas's mother was no longer a factor in this battle, Eavin turned around and headed for Nicholas's desk. With no one else to rely on, she would take matters in her own hands.

What she actually took was a pistol into her hands. It

was heavy and awkward, but she knew its uses. A woman with a gun put the fear of God in men. Smiling grimly, Eavin walked down the hall and onto the gallery.

The loving couple looked up in surprise at Eavin's approach. And then Gabriella screamed and Raphael pushed her behind him as Eavin raised the pistol and aimed it at his heart.

"You have worn out your welcome, *señor*," she informed him in dangerously soft tones. "I suggest you leave now. I have given the overseer permission to shoot you the next time he sees you on this property. And do not think I will hesitate to do the same if I see you first."

Raphael advanced slowly toward her, holding out his hand. "Give me the gun, *señora*. There is nothing you can do. I have already told my father the child in your nursery is mine. He will demand her return should anything happen to me."

Fear swamped Eavin, fear so devastatingly piercing that it turned to anger on the spot. She had never thought so quickly in her life as she did now, with Jeannette's well-being at stake. Holding the gun steady, Eavin gave a chilling smile. "All the more excuse to be rid of you then, *señor*. Without you, it is only your father's word against mine and Nicholas's. Do not mistake me. I have shot one of these before; I will not hesitate to do so again."

His bluff called, Raphael shrugged and started for the stairs. "I will go, but do not think this is the last of me. Saint-Just has stolen all that I have ever had. I'll not allow him to steal any more."

Eavin kept the gun trained on the Spaniard as he mounted his horse and rode out of range. She heard Gabriella weeping hysterically behind her, but the sobs of a woman who would choose a snake over Nicholas did not touch her. Her first thought was to protect Jeannette. How could she save Jeannette if Raphael returned with his father and the law and a band of men to take her away?

When Gabriella launched herself at Eavin, grabbing for the gun, Eavin merely turned and slapped the silly child.

"You wanted a husband, now you have one. I'd suggest you think twice before going after another one." Leaving Gabriella to wail wildly, Eavin returned to the house.

35

"I have hired lawyers. They will take written testimony from you and Madame Dupré that Jeannette is Francine's child, born during her marriage to Nicholas. When Nicholas returns, he can sign a similar testimony. It will be filed with the court. There is not a thing that Raphael can do. A child born during a marriage belongs to the husband unless Nicholas disclaims her. Quit worrying, Eavin, you are pacing the floor worse than Nicholas."

Jeremy stood by the window, hat in hand as Eavin walked the length of the rug and back, her hands twisting nervously. She never looked at him but occasionally looked up as if hearing something outside that made her nervous.

"Thank you, Jeremy, you are a good friend. I wish . . ." She didn't finish the statement but looked up again at a sound from across the hall.

Jeremy caught her hand and followed the direction of her gaze but could see nothing. This close, he could smell the scent of her light perfume, and his gaze returned to the cloud of her ebony hair. "There are things I could wish, too," he murmured, "but wishing will not make them come true. What is bothering you, Eavin? Can I help?"

Eavin turned to him with tears in her eyes, clasping his generous hands in her own. "You have helped, Jeremy. Jeannette is everything to me. You have relieved my mind considerably. I cannot believe Raphael would truly want her, but he would take her out of spite. What makes people behave that way?"

"There is no good answer to that. There has been bad blood between Nicholas and Raphael for years. Nicholas is very good at ignoring things that annoy him, but Raphael has gone beyond that now. If you know how to reach Nicholas, you should summon him home."

There hadn't been a word from Nicholas and Michael since they left. Mail was uncertain at best, and if they were on the trail, there wouldn't be much opportunity to write. Eavin shook her head. "I cannot call him away for this, even if I had the power to do so. I will handle it."

"Damnation, Eavin, you shouldn't have to do it! You're Jeannette's aunt, not Gabriella's keeper. Let Nicholas worry over his pitiful choice of a wife. You have your hands full as it is."

"She's just a child, Jeremy. She's young and scared, and Raphael is obviously an experienced seducer. I hold Nicholas as much to blame as anyone for walking out on her like that. She needs to go to the theater and parties and out in society to meet people. Instead she is dumped out here, where she is not wanted or needed and left to entertain herself. Perhaps I have been lax by not seeing that she got out more and had more to do."

"Save me from the saints of this world," Jeremy exclaimed with disgust, dropping Eavin's hands and walking back toward the window. "Gabriella is a spoiled, weak-willed little brat. Nicholas couldn't have made a worse match if he had deliberately tried. His devotion to Francine has gone beyond the mark if that is his excuse for marrying her cousin."

Outside the salon door, a slight figure in bonnet and pelisse hesitated. She had been drawn by the sound of voices. After hearing this diatribe, she paled and hurriedly lifted her skirt to hasten down the hall, staying in the shadows of twilight left by unlit sconces. Soon someone would be around to light them. But not just yet.

Eavin shivered as a cold draft wrapped around her. She pulled her shawl closer and went to light a candle on the table. The fire's meager light was no longer sufficient in the winter gloom. An insistent tug at her consciousness made her glance toward the window, but it was too dark to see. She felt as fretful and nervous as a cat over water, but she could discern no particular reason. Jeremy's solid presence should have been reassuring. Instead she wished he would go. Something was wrong, and she couldn't go looking until he left.

"What's done can't be undone, Jeremy. I have asked

Madame Dupré to write Gabriella's parents. I cannot imagine them sending a girl that age over here without proper chaperonage beyond that one seasick maid who refuses to leave the city. She has a brother, I believe. She needs someone of her own here. When Nicholas returns, there will be time to make the marriage work. I don't think she's a bad girl, just inexperienced."

A sigh wafted across the room, carrying with it a hint of jasmine. Eavin's head jerked up, and she searched frantically for the source. Instead she heard the sounds of shots outside, and perhaps the echo of a scream. In accord she and Jeremy raced for the door.

Even Hélène came stumbling down the stairs from her room, a frantic expression on her face as she saw people rushing through the hall. Eavin ran to the study, where Nicholas kept his guns, grabbing the pistol she had used earlier, leaving Jeremy to take the rifle. She sent Clemmie scurrying to find the overseer and to send Jim and several of the field hands to the front.

It was already too late by the time the household raced down the stairs to the darkened lawn. The black servants were there before them, and they watched with frightened eyes as a horse came galloping down the drive, its rider hanging crazily to the horse's neck.

"It's Malcolm!" The new overseer rode a distinctive Appaloosa. Eavin recognized it even in the dark. Dropping the pistol, she picked up her skirts and ran toward the wild-eyed horse, ignoring the shouts of warning behind her.

The rider was in enough control to bring the horse to a halt before it could ride her down. Slipping from the saddle, clutching his arm, the burly overseer jerked his head in the direction of the oaks. "That sneakin' Spaniard was back here with a carriage. It looks like he took Miss Gabriella with him. Let me get a couple of the boys from the stable and we'll ride after them."

"You're hurt! You can't go back out there like that. Let me see to your arm while the horses are saddled. Jeremy . . ." Eavin turned to find this friend already at her side, his usually genial expression twisted with anger.

"Let me see to this, Eavin," he said calmly, reaching for the wild-eyed Appaloosa. "A carriage can't travel fast on these roads. I'll have time to gather a few friends. It's better this way than sending slaves after them."

He wasn't giving her time to deny him. Malcolm readily relinquished the reins of his sturdy horse, and Jeremy was mounted and on his way before Eavin could find the arguments to stop him.

Perhaps he was right. Perhaps this was something a gentleman had to handle, and Jeremy was Nicholas's best friend. It was quite obvious that she had blundered badly.

Assisting the overseer into the house, Eavin called for hot water and bandages. Without a word, a pale Hélène stepped forward to take over the task.

It was the wee hours of the morning before a messenger returned saying everything was all right, that Gabriella was safe and with Madame Dupré in the city. Eavin and Hélène looked at each other through hollow eyes and rose together to find their beds.

Eavin didn't want to think what Jeremy had done to bring Gabriella back where she belonged. She would find out soon enough. The touch of Hélène's hand on her arm startled her, and she turned questioningly to the larger woman.

"I thought I was doing what was best for him. I was wrong," she said simply.

There was no reply Eavin could make. She understood far more than those words could ever say. With a nod she turned her weary feet to the guest house and her own bed.

She wasn't a Creole. She couldn't make Nicholas a proper wife. She was barren; she couldn't even bear him children. Hélène had seen that and had attempted to correct the situation in the only way she could. Had Eavin played the proper role of mistresses around the world and accepted Nicholas's marriage, Nicholas might still be here today, seeing to his wife as he ought, loving his mistress as he wished. Neither of them had known that Nicholas would react so strongly to their decisions. There was no fault to be placed anywhere. Eavin understood that with her mind. It would take her heart a little longer.

Jeremy came riding in after noon the next day. From the rumpled state of his attire, it was plain that he had been up all night and had not yet been home. His face was lined with weariness as he climbed the stairs to the gallery, and Eavin called for a hot drink to be brought in as she led him into the salon, where Hélène waited.

Jeremy made a slight bow and gratefully took the drink offered. The scent of the outdoors clung to him, filling the stuffy room with fresh air. Remembering the jasmine she had smelled the night before, Eavin knew Francine's spirit still haunted this house. For Francine's sake, she hoped Jeremy brought good news.

"How is she?" Eavin leaned forward in Francine's place, asking the question a cousin would have asked.

"She is fine now. Madame Dupré calmed her down. Raphael didn't hurt her. They meant to elope, but they agreed to let us accompany them back to town so there could be no question of harming Gabriella's reputation. Unless Malcolm wants to press charges, I think we can let the noise quiet down for a while."

"Nicholas wanted her to remain here. He feels the city is dangerous with the British so close," Eavin reminded him.

Jeremy frowned. "Then let Nicholas return and handle the matter. She is happy to be in town again. To be perfectly frank, I recommended a lawyer to her, and Madame Dupré has called on the priest. Gabriella informed me last night that Nicholas had promised she could have an annulment if she wanted one. I did nothing to dissuade her."

He waited for the repercussions from that announcement, and when both women simply sat there, stunned, he lifted his cup and drank deeply.

"Americans are very rash," Hélène murmured absently, picking at the needlework in her hands.

"It wasn't an American who ran away in the dead of night last night," Eavin pointed out with a hint of irony. She turned back to the weary man across from them. "You did the best thing, Jeremy, and we thank you. I'm not certain Nicholas deserves a friend like you, but I'm glad he has one. I think I better go into town now and talk to Madame Dupré."

"You will do no such thing!" The reaction was instant and spontaneous and, surprisingly, from both quarters.

Eavin looked from Jeremy to Hélène with bewilderment. "Why not? I am her daughter-in-law. We share an interest in doing what is best for Francine's cousin. Perhaps I can talk to Gabriella and make her see reason."

Jeremy left the floor open to the lady. Hélène gave him a gracious nod before turning a formidable scowl to Eavin.

"Gabriella is Isabel's problem. Jeannette is yours. Nicholas is mine. I see no reason to encourage a marriage that my son never wanted. If Isabel thinks Gabriella is better off in the hands of Reyes, then so be it. None of this has anything to do with Jeannette, so you have no need to bother with it. Isabel knows how to keep things quiet. Perhaps I should return to the city to help her manage. Father Antoine is a good friend of mine."

Those arguments seemed oddly irrelevant, but Eavin agreed to them because she wanted to believe them. It was thoroughly selfish of her. Gabriella didn't deserve a scoundrel like Raphael. Nicholas would be hideously wounded to discover his wife had left him for his enemy. But he couldn't be any more hurt than Eavin had been when he had brought a wife home unannounced. If he couldn't tell her a thing like that, she owed him nothing.

"Nicholas would worry less if he knew you were here," Eavin replied, avoiding the point. "I would worry less if you are here. I don't like being alone."

A look almost of relief crossed the other woman's face. "Very well, I suppose you are right. I promised Nicholas to look after Gabriella, but I can't very well be expected to run after the ungrateful child and leave you and Jeannette alone. What do you think, Mr. Howell?"

That the haughty Frenchwoman turned to him for advice left Jeremy momentarily stunned, but he responded with the graciousness of his nature. "I applaud your decision, *madame*. I'm certain we'll hear news if the British land. There will be time to go into the city and bring out both Gabriella and Madame Dupré if necessary. I think it would be better if Eavin and Jeannette were properly chaperoned by someone as respectable as yourself."

Eavin gave him a look of disgust at this pompous salute, but it served the purpose of making Hélène happy and taking away some of their guilt. When he rose to leave, she went with him.

"Do you think Belle will know how to reach Nicholas?" she asked quietly as they stood by the front door.

Jeremy looked startled as he gazed down into her innocent face. "What do you know of Belle?"

"I've met her and know who she is. Nicholas and I don't have a great many secrets from each other, Jeremy. Do you think she can help?"

A brief flicker of pain passed across Jeremy's expression before he schooled it into obedience again. "You're a fool to love him, Eavin. Nicholas has been damaged in too many ways to ever love you back."

"I know that. But love isn't something you bargain for, something you can take back and return if you don't like your choice. It happens, and you're stuck with it. Sort of like a plague, I guess." Eavin's smile was wry as she waited for Jeremy to answer her question.

Jeremy responded slowly, with a smile of his own. "A plague is a good description, I suppose. Nicholas should be the one afflicted, however. It would serve him right. But the answer to your question is no. I don't think even Belle's talents extend to Mobile. It's possible they're on the march by now. I sincerely hope so. This ghastly waiting can only mean the British are sending for more troops and supplies. We don't stand a chance against them as things stand now."

Eavin's expression sobered. "We don't stand a chance against them even if Jackson arrives. What fort there was has been burned for firewood these past years, and I've not heard word of anyone hurrying to reconstruct it. You'd think they almost want to be invaded."

"A wooden fort isn't going to stop cannon. They're merely hoping if they laugh and play, the threat will go away. You have to understand, Eavin, these people have been under the rule of three different nations over a period of twenty years. And despite whatever flag flies from the Cabildo, they go on doing what they've been doing for the last century and what they will do on into the next. Why do you think Claiborne had such a damned awful time prying the pirates out of their nest? They're an institution. He can't drive them out any more than he can ban slavery. They'll be back. And there's nothing the British or anyone else can do about it."

"Well, that's a relief." Eavin donned a bright smile. "I rather enjoyed Monsieur Lafitte. Tell him to stop by and say hello if you see him."

Jeremy grinned and kissed her cheek. "I'll do that. There's a band of the cutthroats making a nest in the swamp between here and my place. They're the ones who helped me find escorts for Gabriella last night."

He left to the sound of her laughter. It had been a long time since he'd heard that sound, and it still had the power to pull at his heart strings. Damn Nicholas, but it would serve him right if he set both Lafitte and Belle on his trail.

36

A tomahawk thudded into the tree trunk just a few feet above the ground, a few inches from their heads. Both men sprang from the thicket and slid down the embankment, rolling and catching bushes until they were almost into the river. Scrambling through the underbrush as arrows flew overhead, they dragged a pirogue from its hiding place and, shoving it into the water, climbed aboard and paddled furiously.

A volley of arrows erupted as they hit open water, but the current moved swiftly and they were soon out of range of everything but the angry war whoops behind them. Slapping water on his perspiring face, Michael ran his fingers through his hair, shoving the thick tangle out of his eyes as he scanned the banks while Nicholas forced the frail shell of a boat farther down the current.

"Join the militia, the man says!" Cursing under his breath, Michael checked the loading of the shotgun in his command, once certain they weren't being followed. "Fight the British! And all we've seen in months are a pack of lazy redskins and enough alligators to feed the navy."

"You'll see fighting soon enough." Guiding the boat more than paddling it, Nicholas kept to the shallow current. "The packet you're carrying will guarantee that."

Michael looked disgusted. "A glorified messenger boy, I am. I had visions of cannon in mind when I followed you out here."

"You don't know how to shoot one. I do. And the only person with cannon out here besides the British is Lafitte." Nicholas's aristocratic mouth curled in contempt at the remembrance of a certain conversation. "I can't believe even old Hickory is as prejudiced against pirates as

Claiborne. You Americans have a strange sense of honor."

"Will you keep your voice down?" Michael continued scanning the banks anxiously. "I've had enough near escapes to make me glad I'm the one going to the governor and not you. I don't ever want to see another swamp in my life."

Nicholas remained silent. Michael spoke the truth. They had risked their lives almost every minute of every day since they had left New Orleans. Once, the challenge would have thrilled him. Now it was growing old. Killing alligators and snakes, eluding Indians and quicksand, became a daily grind similar to the monotonous chores of sailing a ship. One did it to survive and got out of it as soon as possible.

Nicholas had thought it would be different once they reached Mobile, but it was little better than a frontier town and the women there held no appeal. He kept looking for an ebony cloud of hair, and when he found one, he waited for the flash of emerald eyes, the lilt of Irish laughter to ease his heart, but he had found none to compare to the woman he had left behind.

It should have been easy to replace one mistress with another. He had done it before. Women came easily to him. He had a fondness for women that they sensed. The ones in Mobile hadn't been any different. But he was.

Morosely, Nicholas pulled on the oars and watched the shallow river for snags. This last encounter had left him wondering if he would ever see Jeannette again. He tried not to think of the woman who would be holding her, but the man he was traveling with served as a constant reminder. Scowling, he tried to ignore Michael's mutterings.

"I've had my fill of these swamps. You can have your pirates. I want to see New Orleans again. Do you think Belle will see me if I call on her? Does she like flowers or should I bring her candy?"

"Leave Belle alone, you scoundrel," Nicholas growled. Night was coming fast and they were going to have to find a place to camp. Every bone in his body ached for rest, but he didn't want to stop. They were close now. Just a few miles more and they would be nearly home. He longed for just a sight of it. "She's not meant for the likes of you."

"And what is she meant for? Alligator bait? Or do you fancy sending off to France for a fresh marquis for her?"

This was an old argument. Michael had wormed every piece of information out of Nicholas that he would give on the topic of Belle. Nicholas wondered if he ought to tell him that Belle hadn't been a virgin since she was a child, that she had done things that Michael's proper Catholic upbringing would shudder to acknowledge, but those were secrets that weren't his to divulge. Belle was a survivor. She would tell Michael what she wanted.

"Belle chooses her own life, but she deserves better than some murdering Irishman who will pack up and go to Texas when things get a little too hot for him here. Just deliver your message to Claiborne and go back to the plantation and wait for me there. Jackson isn't that far behind us."

Michael helped secure the pirogue to a tree when Nicholas found a place to land. For a city boy, Michael was learning country ways quickly. This piece of bark had kept them out of more trouble than he cared to consider. He meant to hang onto it for as long as he was able.

"And my sister deserves better than a lying Frenchman who beds her and weds another. It's not a topic we'll be agreeing on anytime soon. Give me the hatchet. I'll find some wood."

Instead of handing him the pack, Nicholas sat where he was and stared at the man he had lived with practically every day these last months. "She can't have children, O'Flannery. Can't you get that through your thick Irish head? Eavin needs to marry someone with children of his own. I can't give her that."

Giving his partner a look of disgust, Michael bent over and grabbed the pack for himself. "And you'd take away her chances of finding it for herself. That's not love, Saint-Just, that's pig-headed selfishness. If she were mine, I'd give her what it took to make her happy, even if it killed me. I think your sister will be in better hands than mine is."

Michael removed the hatchet and walked off into the trees. Nicholas dragged himself up the bank and began putting together a hook and line to catch their supper. He didn't want to consider Michael's words, but they were there, just as the birds and the animals in the trees around them, unseen and unheard but present just the same.

Love wasn't an emotion Nicholas gave any priority to. He had never known it and didn't particularly believe in its existence. He craved Eavin's company, yes. She was intelligent and spirited, and he enjoyed the give and take of their conversation. She was passionate in bed. What man wouldn't crave her company? And Jeannette needed her. He couldn't send Eavin away and deprive the child of the only mother she had ever known.

But remembering the pale woman he had taken for wife, the one who would bear his children and sleep in his bed and be his companion for life, Nicholas felt the gaping chasm opening wider. What was the lack of children when compared to a life like that? His wife had the graceful airs and languid temperament suited to society, but they didn't suit him. Why in hell had he thought they would? Because he thought Francine would and that was what Francine was like? From this perspective, with an absence of months to distance himself, Nicholas could see that Francine would never have suited him as much as Eavin did. Francine had been the one lovely thing in his life, and he had placed her on a pedestal and worshiped her. He had never loved her. He couldn't even talk to her. At least with Eavin there was no lack of words.

It seemed a gross betrayal of all Nicholas had held dear to admit it, but Eavin was the woman he should have married all along. To hell with society and his mother and the wretched title that it had been drummed into his head to uphold. He had thumbed his nose often enough at them before. Why had he balked when it came to choosing a wife?

But it was too late now. He had married Gabriella, and unless she chose to call it off, there would be no backing out. She had nowhere to go, no one to go to, and Nicholas could not humiliate her by throwing her out. He had that much sense of honor. And while he had given up any thought of being a faithful husband, Eavin had made it plain that she wasn't going to play the part of adulteress for his sake.

He was going to have to let Eavin go. The thought hit Nicholas with the impact of a tomahawk to the head. It would have been easier if the Indians had killed him. He was going to have to let her free, let her marry another man. The idea shouldn't twist in his guts as it did. He couldn't have felt more pain if someone had stuck a knife in his middle and ripped it upward to remove his heart. Nicholas doubled over, bringing his forehead to rest on his knees as he fought the sickness welling up inside of him. He was going to lose her.

When Michael returned to the place where they had made camp, Nicholas was gone. Brush for a fire was gathered, their supply of provisions sat neatly on their bedrolls, a string of fish wriggled on the line in the water, but there was no sign of Nicholas. Or the pirogue.

Staring at the empty bank, Michael cursed, but he wasn't surprised. Nicholas had been a man in torment for months now, and the source of that torment wasn't far from the end of this stream. Glancing westward, Michael was thankful that he wasn't going to be there when Nicholas returned home.

She could be gone already. He had to prepare himself for that. Nicholas pulled at the oars until every muscle in his shoulders felt as if they would disintegrate.

At least his father's propensity for cruelty had been blatant, without the subtle finesse of his own. A blow could be seen coming and avoided. What Nicholas had done to Eavin had been much more devious. He had set her in her place and locked her there in view of everyone. *Mon dieu,* how could he have done that to the woman who had given him Jeannette, who had done nothing but offer herself and asked nothing in return? She had never spoken of love, that was true, but how could she? He would not have let her. He had taken everything she had to give and returned it with pretty lingerie and offers of houses. She should have killed him.

It was too late now to explain. Nicholas wasn't certain that he could if he tried. Women were commodities to be bought and sold, chosen with care, treated with respect perhaps, but it had never once occurred to him that Eavin would feel otherwise. Only Michael had begun to teach him something he would rather never have known. He wasn't certain what it was yet, but it hurt like the very devil. He had to cut it out and heave it away, exorcise it if he must, for it had no part in the life he was doomed to live.

He didn't even deserve Gabriella. He would probably kill her if left alone with her for any length of time. And he certainly didn't deserve Jeannette. That thought made Nicholas paddle harder. He would give Jeannette up to Eavin. Perhaps that would somehow assuage the wound he had inflicted. He would help them find a better life far from here.

Some of the pain lifted as he thought of Eavin's reaction to that news. She would be relieved. He would take the burden off her back. Nicholas knew the only reason she remained at all—if she remained at all—was because of Jeannette. She had far more consideration than he had ever shown her. She wouldn't take the child away from him, even when it meant ruin for herself. But he would set her free.

He didn't think it was possible that a sassy Irish maid could teach him what years of life and society had not, but he was beginning to suspect that Eavin knew more about love than he would ever know. If love meant this gut-wrenching pain at the thought of giving someone up, he was better off not knowing it.

But the memories of magical nights, soothing hands, lilting laughter, made a liar out of him. Without Eavin there, the plantation would become just a house again, not the haven Nicholas had found since she had arrived. He had thought it was the house that held him. He was not only a monster, but just as stupid as Belle had said.

When he came to the end of the stream and had to set out on foot, Nicholas wished for the horse he had left with Jackson's army. But he was close now, just miles from home. He tried to plan what he would say, but he couldn't. There wasn't enough time in the world to say everything that needed to be said, and he didn't have any time at all. He needed to get to Lafitte, warn him, guide him so he didn't turn on New Orleans in a fit of pique when Jackson marched in and refused his offer also. He only had time to get a few hours' sleep and let Eavin know that he would take care of her.

Not that she was likely to believe him or even listen to him, if she was there. But he knew she was. The closer he got to home, the more certain Nicholas was that Eavin was there. She was better than he was. She had promised to wait, and she would. That marvelous soft Irish heart of hers would watch over Jeannette and Gabriella just as he had asked. Damn, but he loved her. How could he not? She was everything that he had never had, that he had never believed existed, that he had never deserved.

Freed at last, that knowledge buoyed Nicholas the remainder of the way home. He loved her enough to do what was right for her. He wasn't completely heartless, after all. It wasn't going to be easy. He would have to send her somewhere where he couldn't follow, somewhere he could never find her, for it would be much too easy to go after her. Only honor kept him pinned to the plantation and Gabriella, and honor was a commodity easily sacrificed in the face of a life without Eavin. He could remain strong only if he knew he was doing what was best for her.

Exhausted, so weary he wasn't certain he could make it the distance down the lane to the house, Nicholas trudged past the spreading oaks and the hillock where he had made love to Eavin. He had wanted to build her a house there, overlooking the river and the land that he had carved out as his own. He hadn't realized that he would be building a cage for her, a setting where he could keep her while he let all the world admire what he possessed. A man wasn't supposed to enjoy showing off a woman with intelligence and passion, but he did. Only she wasn't his to flaunt.

Even his brain was too tired to think clearly. One flaunted a mistress and kept a wife behind closed doors. But Eavin wasn't meant to be a mistress any more than Gabriella was meant to be his wife. He'd straighten it out in the morning. Right now he needed sleep.

Nicholas reached the *garçonnière* before he reached the house. Throwing a look up at the darkened windows, he decided it behooved him to get a few hours' rest before disrupting the household. He glanced toward the attic windows of the house in the distance where Eavin and Jeannette were sleeping. All was dark there, too. He wouldn't let his selfish eagerness to see them disturb their slumber. Better to stop here for what remained of the night and come to them fresh in the morning.

Nicholas quietly let himself into the empty bachelors'

quarters. The place smelled of furniture polish and wax rather than neglect, but he was so accustomed to the stench of the bayou that he didn't register the difference. It only served to remind him of his own stench, and he went back outside to douse himself from the rain barrel. If he were going to sleep on sheets for the first time in weeks, he would do it in the relative comfort of cleanliness.

Stripped to his trousers, Nicholas strode into the downstairs parlor in bare feet, his hair soaked from the drenching of his bath. The cold water hadn't exactly invigorated him, but he felt almost human again. He would sprawl out in the comforts of a feather bed and rest until it was time for Eavin to go to breakfast. With luck he would be gone again before Gabriella rose.

That was a cruel thought. He would have to stay and politely inquire into his wife's health, then leave. He wouldn't let Gabriella bring out this streak of viciousness in him. But it would be so easy to do.

Sighing, Nicholas headed for the upstairs bed chambers. There were half a dozen to choose from, but instinct and the lingering scent of Eavin's perfume drew him to the one she had lived in those few days before he had left. As long as he was going to make his life a living hell, it might as well begin with sleeping on the pillows she had used not so many months before.

Nicholas knew his mistake the instant he entered the darkened chamber. He was not so weary that he didn't know someone was in the room. Perhaps he could be excused for not knowing who it was, but he never would have stepped forward and closed the door behind him had he suspected it was anyone else. He was drawn forward by a force he couldn't describe. The thought of Eavin lying peacefully in that bed just within inches of his fingers was beyond the ability of any mortal man to resist. And he was feeling very mortal right now.

Perhaps if he just took the chair beside the bed so he could be there when she woke. . . . But Eavin was awake before Nicholas could put words into action. Lying on her stomach, she turned her head to watch him as he came closer, and she made no attempt to escape when he sat down beside her.

Her hair tumbled in rich waves over her shoulders and

down her back. Nicholas gently reached to touch them. He realized she was wearing nothing when his fingers grazed the silken warmth of her skin. A shudder went through him, but still he would have done nothing had she not turned and reached for him. Her soft hand caressed his chest, drawing him forward, and Nicholas was beside her before he could stop himself, pouring all his longing into the kisses with which he showered her.

Succumbing to the dream, Eavin threw her arms around Nicholas's shoulders and crushed him to her breasts. In the morning she might wake aching with the emptiness as she had so many times before, but tonight she couldn't resist.

37

The dream groaned and pushed his tongue between her teeth and scooped her breasts into both his hands, and Eavin responded as if starved. The words he whispered in her ear were French and not words that Nicholas had ever said to her, but their meaning was clear, and her body responded joyously to their promise. It was only a dream. She didn't have to analyze a dream for lies.

His feverish kisses descended to engulf her breasts, and Eavin found herself grasping the sheets to keep from jerking upward under the sensations he induced. A feeling of panic momentarily swept over her as she realized her helplessness beneath these sensations, but the need was too strong to hold back. She reached to dig her fingers into his hair and allowed him to command her as he would.

Nicholas's kisses trailed lower, and Eavin cried out in pleasure and alarm as his hands captured and lifted her hips, holding her imprisoned as his tongue took his pleasure until she writhed with desire. Grabbing his hair more tightly, she jerked hard, pulling him away, pushing him back against the bed while she slid down his side to find the fastenings of his trousers.

She had never been so aggressive with the real Nicholas, but in her dreams she could do anything she desired. And she desired this. If she were never to know Nicholas's hard body again, she would fulfill all her dreams with imagination.

The dream hurriedly rendered assistance to her inexpert fumbling, and then her kisses were trailing naked flesh. She had never known dreams could smell and taste real, but she savored the experience, reveling in the maleness that Nicholas alone had taught her, thrilling to the tension she was arousing with her efforts. His moans and mur-

murs were music to her ears, and she knew a sense of
power she had never known when the real Nicholas had
held her.

Except this was the real Nicholas, she just refused to
admit it. The hands grasping her shoulders were hard and
callused against her skin as they jerked her upward. The
arms crushing her on top of him rippled with muscular
strength and not the stuff of dreams. And the mouth closing over hers was hot and moist and as demanding as the
needs of her lower body. Without giving herself time to
wonder or think, Eavin pulled away from his grasp and
positioned her hips over his.

Nicholas gave a gasp as he suddenly found himself inside her. He had never expected to achieve that haven
again, but his heart and soul rushed out to claim the moment. With fervent gratitude he turned her over and
buried himself deep.

Memories of plowing the rich land, releasing the odors
of sun-warmed earth, swept over Nicholas as Eavin's
body opened to his. He had visions of seed sending roots
deep into nurturing soil, and the vision filled him to
bursting with a desperate hunger he had never acknowledged. Nicholas threw back his head and surged forward,
burying himself ever deeper with each thrust until Eavin
had taken him as far as they could go, until there was
naught else to do but release his life into the furrow he
had plowed, and feel the heat of her welcome the seed of
his body.

Eavin's cries of joy were soon followed by sobs of another sort, and Nicholas gently pulled her into his arms
and held her while she cried. He didn't know by what
miracle he had been given these brief moments, but he
would cherish them to eternity, as he would cherish the
woman he held in his arms.

Overwhelmed as much by emotional exhaustion as
physical release, they fell asleep that way. When they
woke to the chill morning air stinging their skin, Nicholas
reached for the covers to keep the warmth they generated
around them, then proceeded to increase that heat by the
simple expedient of friction, skin against skin as he lowered his weight over Eavin and she wrapped her arms
around him.

Their lovemaking this time had a bittersweetness to it

that had not been there earlier. They were awake now, conscious of the wrong they were doing, unable to hold back once the breach had been made. The solace they found was marred by the knowledge of what lay on the other side of that door, but as long as the door remained closed, they could pretend nothing had changed.

Still, even as Nicholas's seed burned a path to her womb and her body convulsed with the joy of receiving it, Eavin knew this was the end, the farewell they had not been able to exchange before he left. She had cried her tears last night, and her face still felt swollen from the effects of it as Nicholas kissed the streaked paths of her cheeks. With the dawn she would have to be rational.

"I didn't mean for this to happen, *ma chérie*," Nicholas whispered against her ear, rolling over to ease his weight from hers but keeping her securely in his arms.

"I thought you were a dream." Eavin traced the unshaven growth on his jaw, judging it to be several days worth of beard, wondering at the oddity of the aristocratic Nicholas stooping to such depths.

He chuckled without humor. "I have been having dreams like that, too. They aren't quite the same, are they?"

"No, but I've never had them before, not even after—"

Nicholas hushed her with a kiss, then stroked her hair as he gazed down at her in the first rosy glow of dawn. "I know. I taught you what it was like to be a woman. I should be ashamed of myself, but I'm not. I think it may have been the best thing I've done in my life, but then, my life isn't exactly a noble one. I'm trying to change that, Eavin, but you're going to have to help me."

She stared up at him, at the wide, thoughtful brow, the sharp aquiline nose, the mouth a little too wide to be handsome, and wondered at the change she saw there. It was in the eyes perhaps, the little lines she hadn't seen before, the shadows lingering behind the golden glow, or the tautness behind a jaw that had already been too lean and was leaner still. She caressed the hollow of his cheek and tried to read the message his words couldn't convey.

"If I can't help myself, I'll not be helping you," she murmured.

Nicholas's lips curved at the hint of Irish lilt. "I could listen to you talk for the rest of my life and never tire of

it. You have a way with words and a voice that could
twist a man inside out if you wanted. Remember that, and
I daresay one of these days you can have everything you
want."

"I don't think words will buy me what I want," Eavin
said sadly, twisting a lock of his hair in her fingers. "You
had better go now. Annie will come."

"To hell with Annie. I'm not supposed to be here; I'm
supposed to be meeting Lafitte, but I had to see you first.
I wanted to tell you I know what a bastard I've been, and
I mean to make it up to you if you can wait just a little
while longer. Whatever happens, Jeannette is yours. I
know you'll do what is best for her. I can't keep holding
her over your head. If it hadn't been for you, I never
would have known her. You've given me more than I ever
deserved. I'll not repay you by keeping what isn't mine to
keep."

He dared say these things while his long, lean body
pressed her into the mattress, reminding her of all that
had gone between them, all that would end as soon as he
walked out that door. Eavin shook her head and turned
away from the urgency of Nicholas's expression. Perhaps
men were innately incapable of understanding what was
in a woman's heart. He was going to send her away; she
could hear it in his voice. He thought he would be doing
her a favor. Instead he was killing what was left of her.
She didn't dare tell him that, however, because she knew
she had to leave. But there was something he had to know
before he left.

"There's no measuring what we've been to each other,
Nicholas. We both got what we needed at the time; I understand that. I never expected more. We both have to go
on with our lives. I'm just sorry that I couldn't do a better
job of looking after Gabriella while you were gone. I
tried, but I suppose I didn't try hard enough. That was
wrong of me. I know you trusted me, but I really don't
deserve that trust. I don't make a very good saint."

Puzzled, Nicholas propped himself on his elbows over
Eavin and studied the pure porcelain of her face. He
couldn't believe the innocence in those emerald eyes was
capable of any wrongdoing, but they were filled now with
anguish and worry, and fear began to chisel its way into
his heart.

"Saints don't belong in my bed," he answered wryly. "I can't imagine you have done anything more or less than I would have done, up to and including murdering Gabriella. What is your imagined transgression?"

"It's not imagined," Eavin whispered, turning her head away so she didn't have to feel the piercing quality of his gaze. "She left you. She's talking about an annulment. She's in New Orleans now. And I did nothing to stop her."

Nicholas rolled over and stared at the ceiling, fighting the dizzying wave of relief at this news. He hadn't thought it of the weak-willed little child. He had hoped, but he had never believed. *Mon dieu,* but he must have terrified her worse than he had thought. He ought to be ashamed, but his heart was dancing with joy.

"It's not your job to stop her, Irish. It's mine. And I'm not certain that I want that job anymore. I've made some foolish mistakes in my lifetime, but Gabriella was probably the worst. I suppose I had better talk to her, though, if there's time. Jackson will be here in another day or two with his army, and I don't think the British will allow him much time to get settled in. She can't stay in the city now, however she feels about me."

"You don't understand." Eavin felt like shouting, but the words barely left her tongue in a whisper. "She went off with Raphael. He came back. Jeremy stopped him before he could ruin her, but she's still talking of marrying him. And no one is trying to stop her."

Nicholas closed his eyes and waited for the pain to take over, but it didn't come. He ought to at least feel betrayal, but he had betrayed Gabriella long before she had ever turned on him. Still, she was his wife and his responsibility until the law said differently. He couldn't let the foolish girl make the mistake of her life. The hope he had harbored just moments before faded with that knowledge. If he took away Raphael, they would be back where they started. Gabriella would have no one to turn to but himself.

"I'll take care of it, *ma petite.* As much as I wish she had stayed in Spain, I cannot wish a scoundrel like Raphael on her. Where is my mother? Did she return to New Orleans, too?"

With that heavy weight off her chest, Eavin could

breathe again. She didn't want to think about the implications of Nicholas's words. He had married Gabriella for reasons of his own, and those reasons had not changed. She was still going to have to leave, but not with the burden of guilt from Gabriella's departure.

"No, she is here. She gave Isabel permission to stay with Gabriella in the town house so she would be chaperoned, but she did not wish to condone her behavior beyond that. I think she is very worried about you and thought she might hear from you sooner if she stayed here."

That would be news to him. Nicholas grimaced at the ceiling, then turned and curled Eavin into his arms again. Rubbing her nose with his, he pressed a kiss to that delectable mouth of hers, then looked up to trace the redness his beard had chafed in her fair skin. "I suppose I must go in and reassure her. I would rather stay here, Eavin. I have spent months dreaming of being in this bed with you. How can I leave after just a few hours?"

His hand pleaded his case very well as it sought the soft purchase of her breast and aroused it to an aching peak with just a few strokes. Eavin met his amber gaze and held her breath at the smoking desire she found there. She couldn't stop him if she wanted to, and she very definitely didn't want to.

"Annie will be here. And Jeannette will wake." Her voice was already growing breathless as Nicholas pressed tantalizing kisses behind her ear. "Your mother . . ." She gasped as she felt him press the hardness of his arousal against her. "Gabriella . . ."

That was the one name that made Nicholas hesitate. He wasn't free to do what he wanted. He had to settle that matter before he could indulge in any other, but it was already too late to plead fidelity. What would one more black blot against his name matter?

He took her swiftly, before either of them could change their minds. One minute he was alone, and the next they were joined—and not just in body. Nicholas felt Eavin's life and love flowing through him, felt her joy and fear, and poured his own into her, shuddering with the relief of it. To never be alone again, to share what he was and wasn't with another who would accept him without complaint, that was a goal he had never hoped to achieve, had never known existed until this woman came along. And it was a burden also, one he would gladly carry, for he took her worries and fears into himself and felt them as his own.

Nicholas pressed a kiss to the single tear creeping from Eavin's eye. "I wish I could make promises, *ma chérie*. But I can't. I cannot ask anything of you. You are free to do as you wish, as you think best for yourself and for Jeannette. But I wish you would wait until I can come back before you make any decisions. This is your home; you belong here as much as I do. And there is no safer place to be right now. Michael will be in New Orleans shortly. He will know how to reach me if you should need anything. Stay."

Eavin heard the plea in his words and could scarcely credit it. She could not imagine Nicholas Saint-Just pleading with anyone. Her gaze rested on his face. Her heart felt the pounding of his as they lay with their bodies entwined. And she couldn't have denied him this any more than she could have denied him the other. Someday she would find the strength to say no. But now wasn't that time.

Gently she stroked his jaw, memorizing the lines as she answered, "I'll wait."

The promise he couldn't give her was in the words that she gave him. Nicholas could have wept for the joy of them. Crushing her in his arms one last time, he held her tightly against his chest, absorbing the love and gentleness and fierce determination that was this woman he wanted to call his own, knowing he might never be able to do so again.

"*Je t'aime.*" He whispered the words he had never thought to hear himself say. Then steeling himself for the coldness of separation, Nicholas threw back the covers and stepped out of bed.

Eavin clung to the warmth of the sheets where Nicholas had been just moments before, pulling them around her as she watched him dress in the golden light of the rising sun. He was the most magnificent man she would ever know, and probably the only man she would ever know. She watched his every movement greedily, storing it in her heart for that time when he would come no more. His words whispered and echoed through her mind, but they weren't quite real, not as real as the man drawing up his trousers and fastening his shirt, covering the body that had just been part of hers not minutes ago.

When he reached some semblance of respectability, he
bent and pressed a kiss to the crown of ebony hair spilling
over the covers, grateful that she had the sense to cover
the rest of her. Just the sight of her breasts would be sufficient to draw him back into her bed again.

"I will take Jeannette into the house with me and send
Annie with your tea. Stay here until I am gone. This is
where I want to remember you."

Nicholas smiled at the flush of red tinting Eavin's
cheeks at his tone, then refusing to think this might be the
last time he would see her like this, he walked out.

Eavin stared at the door long after he had gone. She was
crazed to think he meant anything by his words. Nicholas
had been charming women for years. But Nicholas wasn't
a man to make promises he couldn't keep or say words he
didn't mean. That thought terrified her, for if she translated
his French correctly, he had just told her he loved her. What
that could mean to both of them was disaster.

Lying back against the pillows, Eavin tried to remember
everything he had said, every nuance of his voice, every
shade of every movement, and she squeezed her eyes tight
in growing terror. He couldn't love her. He couldn't. He
was married. She could never bear his child. She was going to have to leave here sooner or later, or they would
break more commandments than they had done this morning. It would be much easier to leave if she thought Nicholas would be happier without her. She had to be
imagining things.

But when Annie appeared with her morning tea, she
knew she wasn't. The maid smiled knowingly at the single
gardenia blossom beside the cup. The man who knew how
to wield sword and gun and whip so well had never taken
the time to look at a flower before. Eavin touched it rev-
erently and looked up to the smiling maid.

"Belle will be proud of this day's work," Annie said
happily. "You drink up that tea and lie there nice and still
for a while, give it time to work, and see if everythin' don'
turn out fine."

And unable to do anything else while Nicholas was in
the house, Eavin did as told. The tea warmed her, and the
memory of Nicholas's hard body inside hers sent tingling
sensations through her middle that she would have cause
to remember for the rest of her life.

38

"The British are sailing into the lake! The fleet's going out to meet them." Michael slid down the earthen breastworks Jackson's militia had begun to build and landed in the trench where Nicholas was attempting to solve the constant problem of seeping ground water.

Nicholas glanced up to give him a scornful look. "Fleet! Five fishing boats and we call it a fleet. You'd better find an ax and start filling the bayou with the others, O'Flannery. Those boats don't stand a chance in hell. If your damned fool Americans had listened to Lafitte, they could have a navy out there now."

Nicholas's words trailed off into a string of French curses that had the Alabamians he was working with staring. One elbowed another as they stopped to gawk, but Nicholas caught them at it and issued a few curt orders in a language they could understand before climbing out of the trench and stalking toward the barricade of fallen trees blocking this entrance to the city.

Michael scrambled after him. "Jackson's listening. It's Claiborne who's holding out. He's the one who's going to have to live with pirates walking the streets after this is all over."

"After this is all over, he'll be lucky if anyone's walking the streets. It's time to get the women out of here. I doubt if Belle can be persuaded to leave, but try. Isabel and Gabriella can go on the *Enterprize* when it goes back upstream. Shreve said he thought he could dock easily enough at the levee."

Michael came to a halt, forcing Nicholas to stop and look at him with irritation. Belligerently, Michael placed his fists on his hips. "I'm not your whipping boy anymore, Saint-Just. I'll take care of Belle, but I'm not toting your damned wife back to the plantation to make my sister miserable. Let Raphael take care of her. He's naught better to do than sit at the coffee house and drink anyway."

Nicholas wiped a mud-smeared hand across his brow, adding more streaks to the dried ones already there. His golden hair rippled in the breeze off the water, but he wore no coat to cut the wind. Perspiration drenched the cotton of his shirt, and he shivered slightly as his body began to cool. Suddenly weary, he met the other man's furious gaze with a nod of understanding.

"I apologize, O'Flannery. I'm used to giving orders. I'll see to Isabel and Gabriella myself, if you can take care of Belle. Until I hear differently, Gabriella is still my wife. Eavin understands that better than you, I think."

Startled at this unexpected acquiescence from a man who usually exploded with fury when contradicted, Michael snapped his mouth shut and stared before daring to speak again. "I don't think you're feeling well. You'd better get back and get some sleep, or you won't be doing anybody any good. I'll see to the women. Your Creole buddies aren't of much use, and Jackson will be needin' you before this is over."

Nicholas managed a stiff smile. "You're beginning to sound like your sister. I'm fine. And after today I believe you'll find my 'Creole buddies,' as you call them, will be more than willing to lend a hand. The sight of the British Navy sitting in the lake with artillery aimed at them will turn rumor into fact fast enough."

Michael nodded dubiously. The gentlemen of New Orleans had looked down their aristocratic noses at General Jackson's crude militia since they had arrived. It didn't take half an ear to hear their scathing comments and to know they didn't think the rough frontiersmen were any better than the unruly keelboatmen who tore apart the riverfront on Saturday nights. But Jackson's pitifully small army was all that stood between New Orleans and the finest war machine in the world. A little crude meanness might be the only defense the city would have. It behooved the gentlemen to take that into consideration.

"Eavin will have my head if you come down sick. And then she'll be here to look after you, so you'd better keep that in mind when you're busy making a saint of yourself." Turning on his heel, Michael stalked away, leaving the bemused Frenchman to stare after him.

Belle was oddly agreeable when Michael approached her about joining the others at the plantation. She had taunted him for a week before taking him to her bed, and he wasn't prepared to let her go so easily, but she smiled and ran her slender fingers through his thick, dark curls, and he melted like butter.

"Don't worry," she murmured huskily. "I'll be back soon, when you're not so occupied. You must keep an eye on Nicholas for me. He is in grave danger, but he will not heed me."

"He lives for danger," Michael growled, pulling her into his arms and pressing her slenderness full-length against his stocky frame. "And you're not much better. You'll not be murtherin' poor Gabby while I'm gone, will you?"

She laughed softly against the curve of his throat and began unfastening his shirt. "In some ways you are much wiser than Nicholas, *mon chéri.* He lives by a code that no longer exists. But I think you do not. Will you love me one more time before I go?"

As intelligent as his sister, Michael knew her flattery hid an insult, but unperturbed, he scooped his will-'o-the-wisp lover into his arms and carried her to her bed. When it came right down to it, Belle needed an anchor to hold her to the ground, an anchor that he could provide. The time to live in another world would come after they had enjoyed this one. Smiling to himself, Michael meant to teach her that lesson.

"A steamboat! Thar's a steamboat a'comin'." The cry echoed up the gallery and through the halls, bringing dark and light faces alike to the windows.

Eavin stared out on the river with awe as the boat belched a stream of smoke and plodded along against the current without an oar or manpower. Daniel's letters had told her about an enterprising businessman who was providing supplies to New Orleans now that the British blockade and the dispersal of the pirates had successfully put an end to trade, but she had never actually seen the *Enterprize.* She stared in as much wonder as the slaves as the newfangled boat eased in toward the levee.

Toward the levee! It was landing here! Picking up her skirts, Eavin raced through the hallway and down the stairs, shouting orders to the gawking servants. Seemingly unruffled, Hélène drifted in her path, languidly waving a hand to indicate the placement of tea trays, nodding absently at an anxious question, and giving every appearance of boredom as the first steamboat ever to land at the levee maneuvered to the shore.

A carriage raced to greet the visitors while the kitchen fires were fueled to bake fresh rolls and boil water for tea and coffee. Eavin ordered fresh linen and water for the wash bowls, sent maids to scour the privies, and gardeners to cut magnolia leaves to fill the vases in the hall. It was nearly Christmas and it felt strange to decorate without the fresh scent of pine, but she was learning to compensate. Scooping Jeannette up from the floor, Eavin positioned herself at a window to observe the carriage as it arrived. Only Nicholas would commission a steamboat to stop here. Her heart couldn't help pounding with hope.

The first sight of their guests sent a sinking sensation to her middle, but Eavin fixed a smile on her face and joined Hélène in the hall to greet them. Isabel and Gabriella entered in clouds of perfume and rich pelisses, followed by a man introduced as the captain and a servant carrying stacks of gifts. The luggage was being loaded on a wagon that would follow, the captain assured Eavin as she led them into the *petite salle*.

Isabel and Gabriella were busy unleashing a torrent of French and Spanish on Hélène, and Eavin was left to entertain the American captain while Jeannette and the gifts were carried away to other rooms. Eavin wished she could concentrate on the agitated speech of the women, but she knew the rules of hospitality, and she applied them to learn as much as she could from the admiring man overwhelmed by the quantity of feminine graces surrounding him.

Discovering that Michael had been the one to book passage and that the man knew nothing more about Nicholas than that he was working with General Jackson, Eavin gave a sigh of relief when Hélène finally remembered her manners and turned to their guest. Excusing herself, she went to oversee the placement of luggage and the serving of refreshments.

The excited cries of the maids downstairs and the sound of strangely familiar laughter drew Eavin toward the stairs. Without considering what she did she started down to the servants' level, seeking the nagging familiarity of that husky voice, remembering it even as she came in sight of the speaker.

Belle. Nicholas's sister turned mocking eyes in Eavin's direction as she found the last step. The two women stared at each other until Belle's knowing gaze swept over Eavin and came back to meet her eyes with a look of triumph.

"So, you took my advice, *chérie*." Belle stood where she was, waiting for Eavin to come forward. The anxious black servants stepped away, suddenly nervous at this confrontation.

Eavin wasn't certain what she was talking about, but a slight flutter of knowledge stirred inside her and was quickly ignored. She nodded a greeting. "Why did you not come in with the others? Where is your luggage? I will have it carried up to a room for you."

Belle's laughter tinkled through the room, and a smile or two appeared on black faces waiting for the reply. Even Annie shook her head at her mistress's lack of understanding.

"You and your brother see with different eyes, *chérie*. I will not close them. Michael says he has rooms in the *garçonnière*. Perhaps I might use them while I am here." It wasn't a question but a statement, as if she had her choice of accommodations and preferred this one.

Eavin waded her way through the nuances and subtleties of Belle's words. Nicholas's sister had refined polite Creole reticence to a higher plane, requiring the listener to hear what wasn't being said. Her brow lifted slightly at the implications she heard.

"Of course, that is where I reside also. If Nicholas collects any more women, he will have to find another name for the *garçonnière*." She turned to the expectant servants. "Clemmie, see that Belle's trunks are carried to the room next to mine." She turned back to this unexpected guest. "The others are having coffee upstairs. I believe Nicholas would wish you to join them."

Belle laughed, but the mockery had left her eyes. "You are probably quite correct, but I do not always do what

Nicholas wishes. I will stay here, where I am wanted, and leave you to endure their disapproval."

For a fleeting moment Eavin wished she could stay down here, too. Once that was all she had hoped to be, a servant in this household that didn't need any more servants. Now she belonged neither here nor there, but for Jeannette's sake she would go above.

"That is your choice to make, but I don't think Nicholas's wishes are the only ones you flout. My brother has more pride than Nicholas when it comes to those he loves." Eavin noted she had scored a point when the other woman almost imperceptibly flinched.

"He will need it," Belle responded drily. Then glancing again at Eavin's midsection, she smiled wickedly, "And so will you."

Uneasy, Eavin only nodded and turned to give orders for lunch. She had enough on her mind without having to interpret Belle's innuendoes.

Upstairs, the news of the battle on Lake Borgne had their guests chattering in three languages to accommodate the steamboat captain. Eavin discerned it hadn't been much of a battle, but the brave American fleet had managed to postpone the British landing a while longer. Suddenly she was terribly glad that Nicholas had sent his ships away. He would have been on board if they had been here, and he wouldn't have fought to surrender. Knowing Nicholas's unleashed fury, she shuddered and mentally made the sign of the cross. For the first time the war suddenly seemed very real.

By the next week, the women were getting on each other's nerves, particularly when Gabriella rambled on about Raphael while Jeannette sat at her feet. With the child's dark eyes fixed solemnly on her, Gabriella still remained oblivious of the resemblance.

Eavin listened in disbelief as Gabriella blithely revealed that Nicholas had gone to see the priest and to sign the annulment papers. Didn't the girl have any idea how difficult that had been for a proud man? Yet there was not one word of praise for Nicholas's patience and understanding, only acclaim for the man who had made a mockery of her marriage. Perhaps the ignorance of youth could serve as excuse, but Eavin thought a thick skin the more likely culprit.

She fretted over the fact that the papers still had to go to the archbishop for approval. The American church hierarchy was engaged in open warfare with the Creole priests, and the archbishop chose to reside elsewhere than in the decadent domain of New Orleans. With the British blockade, it could take months for those papers to be received and returned, and they could be as easily rejected as approved. The annulment didn't seem as certain a thing as Gabriella would like it to be.

But at least Raphael had the sense to stay out of the way. Either that, or he preferred the Christmas celebrations in the city to the relative quiet of the countryside, Eavin thought cynically. Even with the British camping on their doorsteps, the inhabitants of New Orleans managed to dance until dawn. Eavin sincerely hoped Nicholas was among them, because the alternative was for him to be in the miserable army camps or the swamps with the pirates, and she didn't want to wish that on anybody at this time of the year.

Unfortunately, the British had grandiose dreams of spending Christmas in New Orleans themselves. Nicholas was with Jackson at noon when Gabriel Villeré arrived, his usually immaculate clothes torn and muddied from his escape through the swamps.

"They have landed! They are like ants swarming over the fields. They are flying their flag on my lawn!"

Jackson swore an oath Nicholas wished he had thought of, but soon the small command post erupted with people and orders, and there was no time to be wasted on curses.

To everyone's surprise, the motley army Jackson had pounded together out of inexperienced volunteers from Alabama, Mississippi, Tennessee, and Louisiana formed an organized show of strength as they marched through the Vieux Carré on their way to meet the British in the early hours of the evening. Crowds cheered from the banquettes and galleries, and women waved handkerchiefs at the army bravely singing their way through the streets, armed only with the rifles and squirrel guns they had brought with them.

The Kentucky volunteers had not yet arrived and the

pirates were still digging in their artillery, but the small band of men and boys confidently paraded out to meet the strongest enemy the world had ever produced. It was a brave show, but Nicholas knew it was just that. The British had the manpower and the weaponry to decimate them. Still, he walked with the others, his sword joined with those like his, side by side with fresh-faced farmers and merchants, Choctaws and free men of color, determined to fight for the American flag that had flown over this land for almost exactly ten years.

Under cover of darkness Lafitte's men were finally given their freedom to fight, and they sailed a small schooner toward the British encampment while Jackson's troops marched in from the right. Surprising the exhausted, frozen British with a sudden cannonade from land and water, Jackson's attack quickly became a wild melee that no one could win in the blackness of the bayous. Retreating as quickly as they arrived, the tiny American army began digging in on a strategic strip of solid ground between the Chalmette and Rodriguez plantations. The British, understandably, decided to wait for the rest of their army and postponed their Christmas plans for the city.

Nicholas breathed a sigh of relief when it became plain that the British would not attempt to advance farther this day. Time was on their side. The Kentucky troops could arrive at any minute. Now that Jackson and Claiborne had finally condescended to allow the pirates into their ranks, the cannon could be brought in from what remained of Barataria. Their troops were swelling with every day that passed, while the British troops would begin to lose numbers to the fevers and dysentery and other maladies that plagued the bayous where they were forced to make camp.

But even those differences were scarcely sufficient to close the enormous gap between the trained and experienced British troops and the rowdy, rebellious volunteers under Jackson.

As the days passed and ship after ship arrived to spill out still more redcoats and ammunition and stores, the city of New Orleans watched fearfully. Their only source of supply was the river now that the gulf had been cut off. British proclamations declaring the reasons why New Orleanians should rise up and join their cause against the intrusive Americans had coffee shops open until midnight. The city was rife with gossip as men argued and drew swords and tempers grew short.

As unofficial liaison between Jackson and the pirates, Nicholas could only curse the nature of mankind and continue preparations for war. He assigned Michael a different shift from his own so the Irishman's lilting accents wouldn't remind him so frequently of a similar voice at home. He stayed out of the city so he didn't have to be reminded of Raphael and his ilk lounging about the cafés asking why they should care whose flag flew overhead. The problem of Gabriella ached at the back of Nicholas's head, but he couldn't pursue it in the line of duty. He could only direct wagon loads of cannon through the bayous to the battlements that grew stronger with every passing day.

39

"*Regardez!* See there, the standard of the *canailles*?" Kerchief pulled tight to keep his hair from his eyes, the pirate aimed his cannon, set the fuse, and stood back as the powder exploded. A moment later, the British flag that had flown so proudly over the advancing troops disappeared in splinters of wood and silk. The pirate glanced triumphantly at the gentleman behind him.

Nicholas stared grimly over the battlefield. All around them artillery pounded, the pirates' amazing accuracy from land and water driving the British backward, away from the battlements. The day was turning into a triumph for the Americans, but he didn't feel triumphant. The British army was still camped on American soil, and there wasn't any way in hell that they could march forward to drive them off. The frustration of that knowledge compounded the other frustrations eating at his insides, and Nicholas clenched his teeth to keep the fury hidden. He needed to get home, to untangle his private life, to know that he was fighting for the future he craved, but he was trapped by duty and honor into standing in this mud hole behind a cotton bale, waiting to die.

The Christmas festivities had given them a brief respite from the escalating tension in the household, but with the gifts unwrapped and the parties over, the undercurrent of sniping and complaining began again.

To give Isabel and Hélène credit, their complaints were subtle and exceedingly polite, but Eavin was unable to deal with even the softest of voices. Her head ached and the ceaseless chatter left her feeling so tired she was certain she must be a hundred years old. Holding a scented handkerchief that Isabel had given her, Eavin made her excuses and crept out of the *petite salle* to find some peace.

In the hall, Hattie ran up to her to complain about one of the kitchen maids, and Annie came downstairs to say that Jeannette was fretful. Eavin closed her eyes and felt herself suddenly swaying helplessly. It was the most dismaying feeling, but she couldn't make her muscles move forward. Her head spun and she knew she was going to fall and she could do nothing to stop it.

When she came to, she was lying on the sofa in Nicholas's study, and Belle was berating a clamoring crowd of voices on the other side of the door she held against them. It took a minute for Eavin to realize where she was and that Belle had actually condescended to come upstairs, but the effort to discern that much brought back the dizziness and she closed her eyes again.

Slamming the bolt into place, Belle crossed the room and stood over her. Eavin knew she was there. She kept her eyes shut, but the image of Nicholas's sister seemed to be imprinted on her lids. She could see the challenge in Belle's eyes, the arrogant tilt of her head, and the triumph on her lips.

"You win," Eavin murmured senselessly.

"Did you have doubts?" Efficiently, Belle wrung a cloth in the basin of water she had ordered and placed it over her patient's brow. "Now you must take care of yourself. No more catering to the prima donnas. You will rest and they will take care of you, or I shall feed them all to the gators."

Eavin smiled at the certainty in Belle's usually languid tone. Opening her eyes, she took the cloth from Belle's hands and held it to her own head. "I don't think Nicholas would appreciate your feeding the animals."

Belle gave a very Gallic gesture to indicate her opinion of what Nicholas thought, then floated to the nearest chair and sat down. "You have what you wish," she announced arrogantly. "Now, what do you intend to do about it?"

Eavin slowly allowed her hand to drift downward and cover her abdomen. She had denied the possibility for weeks now. She still didn't believe it. She and Nicholas had spent months of summer in each other's arms without making a baby. It wasn't possible that one night could change all that. Not now, not when it was too late.

Belle gave her a look of disgust. "Even now you do not believe. You have been too much with Nicholas. But you will believe soon enough when your belly swells and grows round with his child. The whole world must scorn you when they find out, but you will have the child you craved. Before I return to the city, I must know what you mean to do about it."

Never wish for what you don't have or you just may get it. Those words flitted briefly through Eavin's mind as she waited for some sense of the child growing within her. Instead she smelled a waft of jasmine and imagined a ghostly laugh. Even Francine found her predicament amusing.

She was being overly superstitious. She would decide what to do when she was certain she was pregnant, and not before. Glaring determinedly at Belle, Eavin replied, "I will call her Isabel Hélène."

Belle broke out in chimes of laughter that carried outward and upward, filling the heavens and momentarily easing the fears of the people waiting outside the door.

"Something's wrong," Michael insisted, staring out at the drifts of gray fog clouding the street outside the window.

"Undoubtedly the stench of a Spaniard approaching," Nicholas replied idly, keeping his back to the loud party celebrating the coming of the new year. He hadn't seen Raphael in the crowd, but he kept hoping the bastard would try to sneak up on him so he could turn and punch him in the gut. Swords were no longer his weapon of choice.

"No, not here. At the plantation. I've got to go back." Frowning with as much puzzlement as determination, Michael turned to face the man who had once been his employer.

Nicholas raised a cynical eyebrow. "Belle sending you messages through the fog? Or does your cock just ache?"

Temper flared in eyes too similar to Eavin's to give him ease. Nicholas held up a placating hand just as the music came to a crashing halt and a voice somewhere in the front of the room yelled, "The British are advancing!"

Nicholas calmly turned to set aside his wineglass. When he turned back, Michael was gone.

Not until then had Nicholas felt fear. Now it was all around him, and it took all he could do to keep his feet moving toward the door and the other officers, instead of out the window and in the direction of the river. He had to believe that fighting the British was more important than running home.

But when someone came looking for Michael, Nicholas reported him sick and sent his prayers racing through the bayou after him.

"You cannot go back to New Orleans now!" Holding a candle over her head, Eavin stood in the doorway of the room next to hers and watched Belle wrapping the heavy cloak around herself.

"I must. There is grave danger, and Nicholas will not see it until it is too late. I stayed only to see that you understand and will take care of yourself. Now it is time to go."

"At least wait until daylight when someone can drive you in. There are too many strangers in the swamps these days. It isn't safe."

Belle gave her a look of scorn. "They'd best beware of me. You still do not understand all, do you? But there will be time. I gave Annie something to put in your tea to keep you and the babe strong. Drink it, or I will tell Nicholas and you will have no choices left."

Pulling the cloak closed, she waited impatiently for Eavin to stand aside. There seemed no other alternative, and Eavin stepped back, giving her room to leave. Belle's words had been a promise of a sort. She would not tell Nicholas of the babe unless necessary. That promise made the infant more real than anything else she could have done.

Without a word Eavin handed the gun she kept in her pocket to Belle. She looked at it, looked up at Eavin, then with a nod accepted the gift. A bond stronger than words was forged between them. Belle pocketed the weapon and swept down the stairs, leaving Eavin to stare into the nighttime loneliness with faltering hopes.

Belle drew her knife through the crude trap line, severing the rope that would have sent some poor unsuspecting wayfarer pitching forward into the grips of whatever fiend had set it. Snakes hid in the trees and beneath rotted logs, alligators mocked cypress knees, but only mankind was crude enough to set such easily seen traps. Belle preferred the animals.

Despite the crudeness of the trap, she shivered. She didn't like knowing that someone lurked in these hidden places she usually traversed alone. Her abilities didn't give her the strength necessary for a physical confrontation. She could only hope the trapper was elsewhere this night. But even as she thought this, she knew she wasn't alone.

The trees were her best resource. She blended between them, disappearing into their shadows, appearing moments later as a movement in their upper branches. What she saw below didn't surprise her. She had as many spies as did Nicholas's enemies, and the buck-toothed overseer was a favorite target for the people who reported his movements. That he would meet with Raphael even as the sounds of the first cannon fire echoed over the water should come as no surprise, either. Raphael had been dealing with the British for months now. It only meant that he thought his time had come.

Remembering the house full of unprotected women and the child growing in the womb of the woman Nicholas loved, Belle narrowed her eyes and touched the gun in her pocket. Nicholas had given her permission to protect his mistress. She would find it very satisfying to do so with a white man's weapon.

The pounding of cannon sounded like thunder as it shook the ground below. A night bird screamed in a flutter of feathers somewhere in the distance. Other sounds permeated the dark as Belle wrapped herself around the tree limb like a snake prepared to strike. No one who knew her in the city would recognize her now, and her high-pitched laughter sent the men below swirling in all directions as the sound of the gun cracked in the unnatural silence.

The wild cry of a wolf sent Eavin upright. Pulling the covers around her shoulders, she climbed from the bed to stare into the mist settling over the swamp. Thunder on the first day of the new year seemed vaguely ominous to her, but she would never get used to Louisiana weather.

No one else seemed to notice, but she couldn't throw off her sense of uneasiness. That hadn't been a wolf she heard, it was a woman's cry.

She sensed it, although she was certain anyone else would call her crazed. She couldn't remain where she was and wait, not knowing that Belle walked out there somewhere. Throwing off the blanket, Eavin began to dress.

When she arrived outside the kitchens, she found Malcolm and several of the field hands already there, weapons in their hands. There wasn't time to feel relief. Malcolm gave a brief nod of greeting and drawled his commands.

"Keep the women in the house until we get back. Them's cannon I hear. Don't reckon the redcoats will be here by morning, but start loading firearms."

So he hadn't heard the cry. Eavin hesitated, then nodded. She could have imagined it. But she would feel better with Malcolm out scouting the swamp. The other plantations would be rousing to the call, too. Whatever was happening, no one was going to sleep through it.

Eavin kept telling herself that as she sat in the window with a rifle in her lap, watching the dawn rise. Annie had come downstairs from the nursery and roused the maids. The scent of hot coffee was already drifting through the drafty rooms. But the rest of the household remained peacefully sleeping.

It was then that Eavin saw Michael riding madly down the lane between the oaks, a limp figure lying lifelessly in his arms. Pain twisted briefly in her middle, and Eavin halted in rising, placing a hand over the spot where her dreams grew. She concentrated on that one piece of magic God had given her, and the pain went away. She would be strong now. She had to be.

Eavin prayed with desperation as the rider appeared out of the fog. She didn't give her prayers any definite subject. To think of what she feared most would only bring misfortune. She could only pray mindlessly and hope God would understand. She needed Nicholas so much she could almost taste the need, but it was one that might never be answered again. She had to find a way to go on.

Crying orders to the housemaids, Eavin hurried down the back stairs to the stable yard, knowing instinctively that Michael would go there. They didn't belong in the gallery and the big house, any of them. Their place was in the kitchens and stables with the other servants. Michael would go where he most felt at home.

He was already handing Belle to one of the men when Eavin raced into the breaking dawn. His eyes were glassy with shock and grief as he slid from the horse and gently reached for the burden he had carried all this way. At Eavin's approach, he followed her through the silent yard to the *garçonnière*.

Michael hovered near the window as Eavin ordered hot water and bandages and began to pull at the dirt-encrusted remains of Belle's clothes. She was alive. She could feel her breathing. But Eavin could find no sign of consciousness as she threw the rags to the floor and began examining Belle's lifeless body for injury.

The broken leg was most noticeable. Eavin clenched her teeth and sent for the incompetent physician, who was never available when they most needed him. She couldn't set a leg. Her eyes were drawn to less obvious wounds, and she drew a deep breath at the placement of bruises and blood. She couldn't look up when Michael spoke.

"They raped her, didn't they? I could tell from what they did to her skirt."

There wasn't a note of emotion in her normally volatile brother's voice as he spoke. Eavin began to wash away the visible signs of violation. "Who, Michael? Who did it?"

"I shot one of them. A buck-toothed rogue with mean eyes. He already had one bullet in him. That's how I found her. I heard the shot. But it took me too long to get there."

A hint of self-condemnation tinted this last, but still not enough to be called emotion. Eavin sent a concerned look over her shoulder, but Michael was in one piece and Belle was not. She had to see to the physically wounded first.

"I've got to set this leg, Michael. I don't know how to do it."

Michael nodded and started for the stairs.

He returned shortly later with the old black priest Eavin remembered from her one Sunday at the slaves' church. Belle was modestly covered with a sheet by then, and he pushed it upward to reveal the crooked leg, touching it in places that made the lifeless body stir again. In a movement too swift for Eavin to follow, the priest twisted the leg and Belle screamed, a scream much resembling the one that had woken Eavin not too many hours earlier.

Silently the old man took the bandages and pieces of broomstick Michael handed him and began to wrap the leg. Once again Belle lapsed into silence.

By this time the household had been alerted to trouble, and Eavin heard women's voices in the yard outside. She ignored them, preferring to watch the man's capable hands as he set the leg and to linger beside her brother. Michael reached to hold her fingers, and she wrapped them around his, hoping to offer what little comfort could be given.

"I'm going to find whoever did this," he murmured.

There wasn't any reply Eavin could give, but the priest looked up and said, "Jenkins." When Eavin started at the familiar name of the overseer Nicholas had fired months ago, the old man nodded affirmation and returned to his work.

"That's the dead man," she whispered, "the bucktoothed man. Was there someone else?"

"I couldn't see him. He ran off when he heard me coming. Belle will know him. I'll wait for her to wake." Michael sounded quite sure of himself, as if all that needed to be done was for Belle to wake up and provide a name and the problem would be solved.

Eavin gave him an incredulous look, but she could see her brother was in a state of shock and not to be argued with. If that notion kept him from falling to pieces, she wouldn't argue with him.

"We'll have to send word to Nicholas. We can't keep it from him," she replied cautiously. The idea of hearing from Nicholas almost made things look brighter. She tried to keep the need from her voice.

That returned some of the proper proportion to the day. Michael looked up with the first dawning of realization and said to the room in general, "The British launched a surprise attack last night. They're fighting in New Orleans."

40

Michael didn't return. Nicholas didn't have time to consider the implications of this event once the British surprise attack was driven off. The arrival of swarms of rough-clad, malodorous Kentuckians kept him busy from dawn until midnight. The influx of fresh blood created excitement in the ranks, but Nicholas's fellow New Orleanians still looked upon the new arrivals warily. True, Jackson's rough recruits had held off the British for weeks, but who was to hold off the Kentuckians? Just their name had become synonymous with barroom brawls and reckless behavior. Nicholas harbored the secret notion that there was little difference between the hotheaded Creoles and the Kentuckians beneath their outward appearances, but he didn't voice the opinion aloud.

The news that his wife was seeking an annulment had gone the rounds of society, but Nicholas was too busy to feel the full effects of the gossip. Laughter that grew quiet when he entered a room was undoubtedly directed at him, but he was past caring. He had done the wrong thing for all the right reasons, and now he was paying for that mistake. Perhaps God found it amusing to shackle him to two women who preferred his worst enemy. It didn't matter anymore. Nothing mattered anymore. He was beginning to think the women back at the plantation would fare better without him. His death would resolve any number of problems. The anger within him was slowly dying as Nicholas realized beneath the hail of fire that his life had little meaning and less worth.

But in the few hours of sleep he managed each night, Nicholas still dreamed of a woman's arms and a child's laughter. These simple things kept him from throwing himself wildly into any affray that crossed his path. It would be too easy to cross swords with Raphael or dodge bullets with the pirates. The challenge was in staying alive to defeat the British and to return home to straighten out the mess he had made of his life.

Grimly he clung to that path, even when Raphael made it a point to speak of his courtship of Gabriella to everyone. Nicholas knew the scoundrel wanted to be called out, but he fully intended for the choice of weapons next time to be his own. There would be no more playing with rapiers. The next time Raphael would die. Nicholas could wait for that moment, for it almost certainly meant that he would have to leave New Orleans. And Eavin and Jeannette.

Nicholas knew that path would be best for everyone, but he was strangely reluctant to take it. The fact that Eavin hadn't packed her bags and left after his monstrous marriage told him far more than he wished to know. She was tied to this place more than he was. She needed the security of a home, of walls around her. She had told him often enough how much she loved the plantation, how she loved having a house where she had no one to take care of but friends and family. She didn't need to be returned to the brutal world where men thought of her as breasts and hips and nothing more. She had blossomed here, and there were men aplenty who respected her for her brains and charm. Nicholas couldn't ask her to go away with him.

So after he killed Raphael he would have to leave and Eavin would have to stay. He had done enough dishonorable things in his lifetime. Taking Eavin and Jeannette away from their rightful home wouldn't be one of them. And with Raphael dead there would be no reason for Gabriella to continue her pursuit of an annulment. He could not honorably ask Eavin to leave with him while he still had a wife.

Cursing, Nicholas shouted a surly command at a young soldier relaxing against a water barrel. With any luck at all, he would die a hero's death and disappear into oblivion beneath the feet of the invading British army along with all these other young boys.

When the morning of January 8 arrived, Nicholas was rather glad his wishes hadn't come true, but the carnage

that ensued drained his soul of any remaining anger he
may have harbored.

From his vantage point in the battlements, he watched
in horror as the British commanders ordered line after
line of courageous soldiers to march against the heavily
armed barricades standing between themselves and New
Orleans. Their greater numbers had to eventually send
Jackson's small army fleeing into the swamps—had the
Americans sense enough to recognize British strength.

Instead the rough recruits screamed triumphant Indian
war whoops as the pirate artillery raked through the sea
of redcoats, creating barricades of bodies for the steady
stream of British soldiers to climb over. The wild-eyed
Americans shouted and screamed encouragement as the
British continued to march, beyond the bounds of all
common sense. Like ants, the red-coated soldiers formed
their lines and plodded forward, secure in their officers'
commands that they would overcome.

When it became apparent even the pirates' artillery
wouldn't keep the swarms of British from eventually
crossing the battlements, Jackson ordered his men to do
what they did best—aim to kill and make every shot
count. The Kentuckians raised their borrowed muskets
and long rifles and leveled the first line of soldiers that
made it past the artillery. While they reloaded, the Ten-
nesseans did the same with the next line. Their accuracy
exceeded that of the pirates with their heavy cannon. The
carnage was tremendous—on the British side only.

By day's end, Nicholas wanted to scream at the arrogant British officers who thought life was so worthless
that they could send an entire army to their deaths over a
piece of worthless swamp. But by that time those officers
were dead and their men were scattered from the foot of
the battlements back to the sea. The Americans had less
than a hundred wounded, and only six had died.

It was a victory that sent the citizens of New Orleans
into a frenzy of celebration that welcomed even the rough
soldiers. Nicholas washed the gunpowder from his face
and allowed one of Jackson's aides-de-camp to treat the
wound in his shoulder as he listened to the riotous music
in the streets below. He had done his best to get himself
killed, but it wasn't enough. Now it was time to settle old
debts and go home.

Before Nicholas could seek out Raphael, he was ordered to report to the general's rooms. Grimacing, he pulled his coat over his bandaged arm, ignored the tie of his cravat, and limped to Jackson's headquarters. He had not yet had time to pull off his boot to see how much damage the fallen cannon had done to his foot.

"You know this man?" Jackson demanded as soon as Nicholas walked through the door. He gestured toward a slight man hanging between the captive holds of two lanky Kentuckians.

Nicholas concealed his shock at meeting Raphael's arrogant dark gaze. Assuming a languid pose, he reclined into the nearest chair and raised an idle eyebrow. "I do. Shall I make introductions?"

Jackson's craggy visage twisted into a scowl. "Cut that bullcrap, Saint-Just. I've had men following him for weeks after a report that he was spying for the British. We caught him trying to sneak out of the city just a while ago. He claims he was working for you and that he thought he was aiding our cause. Would you care to comment now?"

The smile forming on Nicholas's lips was a deadly one that drew some of the arrogance from Raphael's smirk. He didn't feel anger any longer. His soul had died and only coldness came to replace it. After the carnage of this day, Nicholas had no desire to ever lift another weapon, except against this one man. Raphael would have to die for what he had done to Francine and to prevent him from doing the same to Gabriella. Calmly, Nicholas reached for the cigars Jackson kept on his desk.

"I'd be happy to, General. Have someone bring up a bottle of brandy; it's a long, involved story. I was on my way to shoot him when you called. I'd be happy to see him hang instead."

Raphael hissed and began to speak in furious Spanish, but his guards jerked him backward and, at a signal from Jackson, led him from the room. The general raised his bushy eyebrows expectantly in Nicholas's direction.

Nicholas didn't feel any better later that night after he had emptied his soul to a man he would have at one time considered his inferior. He wished he could summon enough hatred for Raphael to lie and see him skewered as a spy, but he had no proof of those suspicions. Nicholas could only revile Raphael's character to the general and hope that was sufficient to hold him.

He couldn't help thinking of a proud old man and Raphael's younger brother. Francine was such a long time ago, and the fault didn't lie entirely with Raphael; Nicholas could see that now. A certain pair of accusing green eyes made many things clear. Eavin had not professed her love and then taken another lover, even after he had married and called her his mistress. Even now she was loyally waiting for his return while caring for those in his life who were important to him. She didn't believe the lies and untruths that circulated about him. She defended him against all odds. She did what no one else had done before—loved him without question.

Against common sense, in fact, Nicholas acknowledged wryly as he climbed the stairs to his room—with the same bravery and foolishness of the British soldiers slaughtered today. And for that loyalty he could not let her down now. She had a way of taking away the anger and filling him with hope. Perhaps it would be possible to end this thing with Raphael without death. If he could stay here, perhaps there was some way a fragment of his life could be rescued. Nicholas had a sudden need to believe in a future, and he swung the door open with a sense of hope.

That feeling was shattered the moment he met the gaze of the old black man sitting stiffly in the chair at the window.

"Are you sure, Belle?" Eavin stared out the window as if she could see through the nighttime. Instead, all she could see was the reflection of the woman lying pale against the sheets. The woman's black hair rocked restlessly back and forth against the pillow, supplying the only answer she would give.

Eavin swung around to face her. "You shouldn't have sent a messenger to Nicholas. He has enough on his mind. You should have let me report it to Clyde Brown. He could gather enough men to look for Raphael."

Belle sent a cynical look declaring Eavin's stupidity and closed her eyes.

Eavin wanted to curse and beat her fist against the

walls. Belle had said scarcely two words since she had recovered consciousness, and those words had been to an old black man who had promptly taken the first boat into New Orleans. She could strangle Belle were it not for the fact that the other woman was in such obvious pain already.

"Nicholas will have no choice but to call him out. He could be killed. And if he isn't, if he kills Raphael first, then he will be outlawed. Claiborne will not allow another infraction of the law. You are sending Nicholas to death or exile."

Her lips tightened into a straight line, Belle remained silent. Eavin could almost feel the helpless fury emanating from her. She knew what it felt like to be helpless and angry. There could be no more frustrating feeling in the world. Eavin clenched her fingers into fists and tried to speak calmly.

"If I tell Michael, he will go after Raphael, too. He doesn't know anything about swords. He will no doubt try to strangle Raphael with his bare hands. He could end up in jail or dead; either way, his past would come out. Should he live, it couldn't be here. I don't want to have to choose between Michael and Nicholas."

Belle opened her eyes and glared at her, defying Eavin to make that choice. Belle had been the one to make it; she was the one with the right to make it. Eavin grimaced and looked away.

"I won't be tellin' Michael. There's no purpose in it now. I'll be goin' into New Orleans myself tomorrow. Nicholas can't have found Raphael yet. There's time to stop him."

For the first time Belle looked at her with alarm and spoke. "You can't. You'll lose the baby."

Eavin felt a quiver of fear in her middle at Belle's words. She kept her hand from straying to that place where she felt the child beginning to grow. It wasn't noticeable yet, but it would be soon. Already her breasts were beginning to swell, and she could almost imagine her abdomen shaping into a curve. She kept waiting for the child's first movements, but it was too soon to tell. Yet the infant was very real to her.

She didn't want to lose this baby, but she didn't want to lose Nicholas, either. A cry of desperation escaped

Eavin's lips as she flung herself around to watch the darkness again.

"I will send Michael before I let you lose that child," Belle announced from the bed. "Nicholas can take care of himself. The child can't. I cannot promise there will ever be another one if this one is lost."

There was something in the anguished cry of these last words that brought Eavin around again. She stepped toward the bed, read the terrible pain in Belle's eyes, and knelt beside her to take her hand as the woman in the bed whispered her anguish.

"It's gone. I don't know what's happening. They took it away and I may never have it again. Please, don't lose this last piece of my magic."

The cry was hysterical and Eavin gathered the weeping woman into her arms and tried to hold her as the pain and fear finally poured out. Eavin didn't know what Belle was talking about, but she sensed it, and she mourned with her as Nicholas's sister cried herself into oblivion.

Whatever Belle's magic had been, it didn't exist anymore. Remembering her warning earlier of the danger that Nicholas was in, Eavin prayed frantically as she rocked Belle in her arms. She had no way of knowing if Nicholas was safe. The thunder that had rocked the skies all day yesterday had grown silent.

"You have behaved with dishonor, brought shame upon the name of Reyes, yet I cannot allow you to die a traitor's death."

The prisoner looked up with a glimmer of hope at the old man standing outside his cell. His father had aged immeasurably these last days, but he was a Reyes. He could accomplish miracles. Raphael had thought the evidence brought forward at his trial would have caused the old man to disown him, but he was the eldest son after all, and Alphonso was a weeping woman. He straightened his shoulders and ignored the rattle of chains as he stood to meet his father's gaze. "What would you have me do?"

Some time later the old man walked through the wide portals of the Cabildo and glanced upward to the square of heaven visible above the Place d'Armes. "God forgive me," he whispered in his native language, before straightening his shoulders in the same manner as his son earlier and turning his feet in the direction of the men waiting in the shadows.

A Reyes could not die a traitor. He would die honorably, as a man should.

Nicholas wasn't considering honor or safety. He was cursing himself for three sorts of a fool and parading through the Vieux Carré with murder in his heart. The fact that it was nearly midnight and the streets were full of drunken revelers didn't distract him in the least. He had one immediate goal in life, and that was to murder Raphael Reyes. Someone had to put an end to the fiend's existence, and if Jackson couldn't do it, Nicholas would do it for him. Honor required that he kill Belle's rapist.

He'd had two days to reflect on this decision while Jackson had kept him from the prisoner. Nicholas had gnashed his teeth with frustration as a hasty trial was called and witnesses were brought forward to seal Raphael's fate. He hadn't wanted to see Raphael hung by the cool justice of the law; he had wanted to see him suffering as Belle was suffering now. But he would have accepted that form of death. He would not accept Raphael's escape from justice.

This wasn't the furiously explosive anger that had ruled his life for so long. This was a different anger, a calculating one, a slow-burning fire in his gut that resolved to right old wrongs. Nicholas imagined even Eavin would approve of his decision now.

It would be better if he didn't think of Eavin. Her fits of anger were like brief summer storms, over and done with in minutes, leaving a cooling, healing rain behind. She didn't keep things inside and let them simmer into corrosion, nor did she lash out at everyone and everything in the way in her fury. She knew her target and struck it accurately, as she had struck him in so many ways. To think of her now would be to drain away this hatred that had kept him going.

But it wasn't even hatred that made him hurry down the street now. It was pain, a raw pain that Nicholas hadn't felt in years, that he had hidden and buried so long ago that he had no memory of it. The scent of coffee and *beignets* drifted from a nearby shop still lit and crowded with revelers at this hour. One of the men shouted an invitation to join them, but Nicholas was outside their sphere right now, living in a hell that prevented him from joining the world to which he belonged, a hell to which he had been consigned as a child. The pain had converted to violence long before he reached maturity. Its return diminished his ability to deal with the joyful everyday world around him.

The message had said that Raphael planned to escape at midnight. It was close to that now. There had been too little time to develop any plan of action. If it wasn't too late, he would warn the guards. But if Raphael was already free ... All he could do was hurry and hope he wasn't too late. For Belle, for Francine, for the life he couldn't have, Nicholas would fight, even if it meant his own death. He almost hoped for death. It would be the simplest alternative.

Before he could enter the unlit alley behind the barred exterior of stucco walls, a dark figure darted past him, followed by a second and a third. Without hesitation Nicholas ran after the first one, recognizing Raphael's slender form with ease. His injured foot pounded with pain, but he had no intention of losing the one goal he had in his life right now.

Nicholas shouted a command at two young soldiers staggering from a tavern. They grinned and joined in the chase, moving to cut off Raphael's escape from a different direction. In a street lined with buildings, there were few exits other than the alleys leading into private courtyards, and most of these were locked. Frantic, Raphael tried to dodge into the same crowded coffee house Nicholas had passed earlier, but a large form stepped from the doorway to block his path. Nicholas stared at Clyde Brown with incredulity, but didn't stop to exchange words as he followed Raphael's erratic path down the street.

It didn't seem possible, but some fool had left their carriage sitting in the middle of the narrow street. Raphael jumped into the driver's seat, only to jump down a minute later and rush toward a gated alley. Nicholas cursed as the alley door swung open and Raphael disappeared into the interior. He hoped Clyde was following and got the name of the cursed driver; there wasn't time to do it himself.

Pulling the gun he had carried with him, he recklessly pursued his own personal demon into the darkness.

The alley abruptly ended in a garden courtyard. A fountain splashed the noisome liquid that passed for water in New Orleans. Not a soul was in sight, but a black shadow swung around against the far wall as Nicholas ran into the light of the one swinging lantern.

A shot rang out and Nicholas felt the jolt, felt the searing flesh and the beginnings of a slow trickle of blood, but the pain he had carried with him disappeared as he lifted his arm and aimed.

The sound of his shot bounced off the garden walls, and the figure on the far end suddenly jerked, twisted, and crumpled to the ground. There was no satisfaction as the gun fell from Nicholas's numbed hand and he slowly started his own descent into hell.

Nicholas looked up to find the unsmiling visage of Raphael's father bending over him, but his last thought was of Eavin. She was going to be a rich woman now. He hoped the wealth would make her happier than it had made him.

41

Eavin stared at this bearer of bad tidings incredulously, her color fading until Michael thought she would hit the floor in another moment. Ignoring the other hysterical women in the room, he leapt to his sister's side and steered her toward the nearest chair. It was a measure of her shock that she didn't protest.

"It's not possible. That just wouldn't be fair," she murmured to herself as Michael pushed her into the chair.

"No one said life is fair, and he's not dead yet. Clyde just said he was injured."

The expression had been "mortally injured," but the finesse had escaped Michael in his concern for his sister. He turned to the lawman for reassurance, but Clyde merely shifted from one foot to the other.

"Well, man?" Michael demanded. "How bad is it? Raphael couldn't be that good a shot. Don't scare the ladies like this."

Clyde turned helplessly to the dapper young man who had entered behind him. Alphonso shook his head slowly, grief written across his features.

"It is not good, I fear. I understand the yard was small, and Nicholas is a large target. Even Raphael could not miss. And even crippled by the bullet, Nicholas managed to kill Raphael, my father reports. The physicians are amazed that he managed to do so. I cannot name the extent of my shame. I come only because Clyde asked it of me. I will go now and not darken your door again."

Eavin heard his pain and turned her eyes in Alphonso's direction. She still couldn't believe what they were telling her. Nicholas was dying, could already be dead at this moment. It just didn't seem possible. Nicholas was a life force of his own. He couldn't die, or her world would die with him.

"Please, take me with you. I must see him. Maybe it is not as serious as you think." She spoke faster as her own words gave her encouragement. Eavin started to rise, but Michael pushed her back down and she gave him a scathing look that he answered before she could speak.

"You're not going anywhere. Nicholas has a wife and mother to see to his care. You belong here with Jeannette and Belle."

Everyone turned to look at the hysterical Gabriella, who had fallen to the sofa with the news of Raphael's demise. Crying and screaming brokenly, she was beyond caring for anyone but herself. Hélène turned to meet Eavin's eyes.

"I will go," she murmured softly, rising from her place. "They have brought him to the house, I assume?" she asked of Alphonso, ignoring Clyde.

"Yes, but he knows no one, my father says," the Spaniard warned. "Already the fever has taken his senses."

"My God, don't tell Belle." Eavin clutched Michael's arm, forcing him to look down and see her fear. "She could have saved him. I know she could have. Perhaps there's some way . . ." She looked at him pleadingly.

"I will tell her it is one of the men. She hasn't forgotten how to use her herbs and potions. There may be something she can do." Michael looked up to Madame Saint-Just, who was preparing to leave the room, calmly ordering one of the maids to begin packing her bag. "I will go with you."

Hélène looked at him blankly, then nodded. She glanced over her shoulder at Gabriella. "We had best take her with us. Appearances are still important."

Isabel Dupré clenched and unclenched her fingers, then spoke hesitantly. "If you think I should, I will stay with Eavin and my granddaughter. I do not want to be in the way, but I think someone should stay here."

That this proud woman, who had nearly ignored her since she had arrived, now condescended to come to her aid left Eavin mildly astonished, but she had little room for any other emotion but fear. It mattered little to her where Isabel went. Her soul was already on its way to join Nicholas. Tears pooled in her eyes as she rose, still holding Michael's arm.

"Please, if you can, bring him back here. This is where

he wants to be. I know it, Michael. Belle and I can make him better. It will work. Tell me you'll try."

Hugging her to him, he kissed the top of her head. "I'll be doin' just that, colleen. Now lie down and rest. I'll tell Belle I'm taking the ladies back to town. You'll have to be brave until I get back."

Brave. Eavin felt like the entire foundation of her existence was crumbling to the ground. How could one be brave at such a time? But she had to be. Nicholas would be depending on her. That thought made her stronger, and Eavin closed her eyes and steadied herself before releasing Michael's arm. Then she turned and offered the vague shadow of a smile to her mother-in-law. "It would relieve my mind if you would stay, Isabel. Jeannette will need us."

As Eavin started for the door, she forced herself to stop before Clyde and Alphonso, touching Alphonso's arm in a natural gesture of reassurance. "I know you are not responsible for what has happened. Perhaps you will explain it to me later. I just don't think—"

Her voice broke and she hurried away, leaving the two men to stare after her with twin expressions of concern and sorrow.

Isabel hastily removed a sobbing Gabriella, leaving the men alone to stare at one another with varying degrees of suspicion and animosity.

"I'll be hearin' the full story now, gentlemen, before I leave. I'm after thinkin' it's a mite odd for a condemned prisoner to escape in the middle of the night."

It was Clyde who began to speak, and before he was done, Michael was punching his fist into the palm of his other hand and cursing vividly.

His body ached and he felt humiliation wash over him again. He shouldn't let his father do that to him. He shouldn't. He should stand up and kill the old man, wrap the stick around his neck. He was almost big enough to do it. He could. He could grab the stick and smash it against the old man's head, beat him into a bloody pulp. He was big now, not some terrified child. He had to do something. He had to stop him before he killed someone.

He groaned as pain lanced through him. His mother's voice whispered somewhere near his ear. His mother.

What in hell was she doing here? Those Barbary pirates were a scurrilous lot. She shouldn't be here. He had to get her out. Had she been captured? Of course not. His head hurt, and he couldn't think straight, couldn't remember. He'd taken this wound in battle, hadn't he? That blacka-moor with the knife between his teeth . . .

The familiar voice murmured again, a little closer now. A cooling cloth wet his head, and he was thrown back-ward in time again, back to the humiliated child. He struggled upward, wanting to get his hands around some-one's neck, feeling the violence building in him, waiting to get out.

"*Madame,* you cannot stay here. He is not well. Please wait until we call you." The voice was intrusive, not part of his dream, and Nicholas fought to locate it.

"He is my son and I will stay as long as I like. Now stand aside, sir."

Nicholas laughed. He was dreaming again. He was dreaming a new mother, one who would come to his de-fense. It was incredibly funny, and he laughed until he felt the tearing feeling in his chest, and then he coughed and grew silent again.

Hélène looked down at the pale figure of her son lying against the sheets. The color had drained from his weath-ered face, and his golden hair lay limp and lifeless against his brow. With his mouth relaxed in sleep, he looked years younger. She touched his cheek and he stirred and tears formed in her eyes. She had never allowed herself to care, but she couldn't hold back the tears. They trickled down her face as she applied the cooling cloth to his fe-vered forehead.

"Eavin." His eyes opened suddenly, but it was obvious Nicholas wasn't seeing her. A rakish hint of a smile formed along the corner of his lips. "Don't, *ma chérie,* or we'll both regret it."

His beautiful eyes closed, but the smile lingered on his lips. Hélène thought it was the first time she had ever re-ally seen him smile. Nicholas was very good at smiling without meaning it. Sometimes when he smiled, it cut her to the quick with the cruelty in it. That day when he had finally turned on his father and broken the cane over his head had been one of those days. He had looked up at her coolly over his father's fallen body, smiled that terrible smile, and bade her farewell. She hadn't thought she would ever see him again. He had been only fifteen, but he had become a man overnight, one with the same penchant for violence as his father.

But she couldn't help remembering the loving child, the golden head bent over fairy stories, the laughing eyes watching the dancers in the streets, the small boy who had wept when Labelle or her brother was beaten. That boy was still in there somewhere, she had seen it in his eyes when he played with Jeannette, as he had pulled Eavin into his arms when he thought his mother wasn't looking. She saw it in his smile now.

She hadn't been able to save the boy when he was young. Perhaps she could save him now, when he was strong enough to step out of the bonds of violence.

Clenching her jaw with uncharacteristic determination, she began speaking to the man sleeping feverishly beneath her fingers.

"That accursed Spaniard was here again, wasn't he?" Belle flung her pillow to the floor when it wouldn't move to suit her.

Eavin stayed out of striking range. Belle's irritability grew as her health returned. Confined to the bed by her broken leg, she could merely rant and rave to vent her frustration. It gave Eavin something to do besides worry about Nicholas. It had been over a week, and she had heard nothing.

"Alphonso is merely being neighborly. At least you cannot accuse him of courting Gabriella."

Belle had learned of Hélène's and Gabriella's departure, but no one had yet had the nerve to tell her of her brother's illness. She merely cursed the women for taking Michael away and fretted at the time it was taking him to return.

"Bah, the young rascal is not so foolish. He is courting you. When will you tell him you carry another man's babe in your belly?"

Eavin flushed at this bluntness. It helped no one to speak of the child. Everyone thought she was being sensible and respectable by staying here instead of rushing off to be at Nicholas's side, but all she was really doing was protecting his heritage. She couldn't tell anyone that, but Belle already knew and continued to throw the subject in her face.

"He will know soon enough. And he is undoubtedly foolish enough not to care. Alphonso is my friend, Belle. I need the few friends I have. Don't deny me my small pleasures."

Belle sent her a wooden look. "And what of Nicholas? What will you tell him when he returns? Has the man written nothing? They are saying the war is over, that we have won. Why does he not return?"

This was the hardest part, hiding the truth from clever Belle. She was starting to recover, she was speaking again, sitting up in bed and worrying about Michael, making some attempt to return to normal. The news that she had sent Nicholas into a death trap could set her back irreparably. But sooner or later, Belle would have to be told something.

"There are other complications." Eavin hesitated, then attempted a small lie. "I did not know how to tell you. Someone reported Raphael's activities to the authorities. He was sentenced to hang."

A dark light briefly illumined Belle's eyes, then shuttered quickly closed. "So? Why is Alphonso not holding his hand? What has that to do with Nicholas? I only wish I could be well again to watch the *canaille* die."

"It is too late. He's dead. I do not understand the complications. I believe Señor Reyes has become a trifle unhinged by having his son declared a traitor. He refuses to allow Alphonso to come to him. Men do not explain these things very well."

Belle's eyes narrowed with suspicion, but she said nothing. Her leg might be lame, but her mind was not. Michael's request for her fever potion had meant little at the time, but piece by piece she was acquiring bits of this puzzle. She watched as Eavin moved restlessly around the room, straightening draperies she had already straightened a dozen times, dusting shelves that were spotless, listening to noises that only she could hear. Eavin handled pregnancy well. There had been no bouts of morning sickness, only that one spell of dizziness, and no complaints of weariness. Belle doubted that anyone could tell if Eavin's figure was fuller. She hadn't seen a morsel of food pass Eavin's lips in days, and the circles beneath her eyes were beginning to assume a ghastly color. Belle was quite certain pregnancy played no part in that behavior.

Eavin turned and, seeing Belle's eyes closed, she thought her asleep and escaped from the room. It was all she could do to keep up a cheerful demeanor for a few minutes at a time. Her fears for Nicholas ate at her insides. She didn't have time to worry about herself, but someday she was going to have to. Her fingers strayed to her midsection. A child needed a father, even one who was not married to his mother. Please, Lord, let Nicholas come home.

Isabel watched her former daughter-in-law flit about the salon and ignored her feelings of uneasiness. Isabel was French by marriage, not by nature, and her upbringing balked at the insouciance with which Hélène accepted the fact that Nicholas would have his mistresses. Gabriella was her niece by birth, blood of her own blood. Eavin's presence was a constant threat to the marriage that would make Gabriella a wife or widow of wealth. With Raphael dead and Nicholas lingering on the edge of death, Gabriella would not be so foolish as to continue with her plans for annulment. Gabriella would take Francine's place, not this common Irish woman.

Still, Isabel held no grudge against Eavin other than that. Eavin had been Dominic's wife, she had taken care of Gabriella to the best of her ability, moved out of the house when Nicholas married. She was a good girl, if only a little misguided, and she deserved whatever chance could be provided for her. Isabel hadn't moved in the best of New Orleans society without learning a thing or two. She hid the letter that had arrived while Eavin was in the *garçonnière*. She would read it later and see if it suited her plans.

"Why don't you go up and see to Jeannette, *querida*? You will make yourself ill with this pacing about. Perhaps you should visit the Howells and get out of the house for a little while."

"I do not understand why I do not hear from them." Eavin walked the floor, wishing she could wring her hands and wail hysterically but too practical to fall into such dramatics. "Michael promised he would write. Do you think I should send someone to see what is happening?"

"I think your brother is like all men and forgets the passing of time. You must be content to know that all is well as long as there is no other message to the contrary. You really must begin making plans for your own life. The young Reyes boy will be a wealthy man some day, and he is much smitten with you if I am not mistaken. I speak from experience when I say that it is much better to be loved than to love."

Eavin stared out the glass panes at the desolate lane lined with moss-laden oaks. She heard what Isabel was politely telling her. Nicholas would remain married to Gabriella even if he lived. It would be dishonorable of him not to if Gabriella chose to cancel the annulment. At this moment Eavin didn't care. All she wanted to see was Nicholas riding up to the house, full of the health and vitality that she remembered so well. It would be time enough to consider the future then.

"I think I will go up to Jeannette. She likes to be read to, and Annie can't read." Eavin turned on silent heels and walked out.

Isabel watched sorrowfully as she left, then pulled the letter from its hiding place and tore it open, ignoring the fact that it was not addressed to her. Letters were frequently lost in these uncertain days.

42

Señor Reyes bowed low over Eavin's hand, straightened, and studied her face intently before handing her over to his son. Alphonso continued to hold her hand tightly as his father spoke.

"You have been good for my son. You have kept him from acting on impulse, prevented any further tragedies between our houses." He hesitated, then bowing his head with sorrow, murmured for her ears alone, "And you have taken my granddaughter into your arms and cared for her as one of your own. Do not think I have been blind to all that you have done."

Puzzled and not a little frightened at this unexpected visitation, Eavin tried to free her hand, but Alphonso would not let it go. This frightened her even more, and she turned to reassure herself that Isabel was still behind her. The sad look on her mother-in-law's face told her more than she wanted to know, and something in Eavin's insides began to crumble and fall.

"Jeannette is my own," she managed to reply. "I would not have it any other way."

"That is good. That will make things easier. I do not know of anything else that will make things easier. I wish I did not have to be the one to bear these tidings. Please do not hold the news against the messenger, my dear lady." The stiff Spanish-accented words held an undertone of grief.

Wildly, Eavin swung her gaze to Alphonso. His expression, too, was grave. She couldn't believe this, wouldn't believe it. Jerking her hand away, she confronted both men. "Please say what you have come to say and be done. I assure you I have no intention of shooting anyone."

"My father has just come from New Orleans, *querida*."

Alphonso held out his hand to her, pleading with her to take it. "Nicholas died last night. There was nothing anyone could do to save him."

The scream Eavin heard was her own, but it didn't seem part of her. It seemed to come from the wind rushing through the room, from the angry waft of jasmine circling and blowing away in the sudden breeze. Eavin didn't even realize she was falling until someone carried her to the sofa. She didn't recognize anything at all but the words that had snuffed out her existence. The tears pouring down her face were little more than the spring rain that darkened the day.

After that, it was as if she moved in a world isolated from the rest by some unseen window. Eavin could hear what the others were saying, see what they were doing, but they meant nothing to her. She didn't even try to reach out to touch them. She kept searching for Nicholas and not finding him. Surely she ought to be able to feel his spirit as she had felt Francine's. She ought to be able to feel his absence as she had felt the absence of the child she had miscarried. She sought Nicholas's room, held one of his cheroots to her nose to return his scent, buried her face in his pillow, but found evidence only of Gabriella's presence. There was nothing other than this dead numbness in the place where her life had been.

In the days that followed, Eavin heard the others discussing her. It seemed to be agreed that she should no longer be living at the plantation when Gabriella returned. Eavin heard Alphonso's proposal, but she didn't remember agreeing to it. Everyone just seemed to accept that she would, and she did nothing to disillusion them. It seemed too ludicrous even to consider.

Belle had to be told sometime, and there was none other to do it than herself. Eavin didn't know where Michael was, what he was doing. She had heard nothing from him other than a brief message sent back by the old black priest. That just said something about business in town and that he would arrive shortly. "Shortly" stretched into another week and the news couldn't be kept from Belle any longer than that. Word had already reached the servants, and the quarters were buzzing with gossip and uncertainty. With the master dead, there was no one to guide them. With no announcement made, they could not even express their grief.

Eavin left Isabel to make the announcement to the overseer and slaves, but she took on the task of telling Belle herself. It wasn't really necessary to say anything, she discovered when she paced the room searching for the words and Belle said them for her.

"Nicholas is dead, isn't he? I can't feel it, but I know it. I'm lame, not blind. Raphael didn't die by a hangman's noose, did he?"

Eavin burst into tears then, tears that had not broken through since she had heard the news. They poured from her heart, pieces of broken dreams, a watershed of misery. Until now she had never admitted how much Nicholas had become part of her heart and soul, and now it was too late. She cried for that, too, cried for what she had denied him, for what had never been and could never be now. And she cried for the fatherless child she carried within her.

It was when she reached that point that Belle's words reached her. Eavin looked up and stared at Nicholas's sister with incomprehension, wiping her eyes and trying to stop the quivering that made her feel as if she would never be in control of her life again.

"They say that your Spaniard has asked you to marry him. You must do it at once, give Nicholas's child a name and a home. He took in Jeannette, it is only fair that they take in his child. You must see that, don't you?" Belle demanded, forcing Eavin to meet her eyes.

"No, no, I don't see anything. I can't. This is Nicholas's home. This is where his child should be raised. I can't do it, Belle. I can't leave him. I must stay here."

"Fool!" Angrily, Belle pulled herself upright, ignoring the discomfort of the movement. "That witch will come back here and declare all this hers. She will soon find someone worse than Raphael to share it with her. She will treat you and the child like dirt, and so will all of society. You will have nothing, no power, no control, nothing! I have lost what is mine, but you cannot lose what is yours. You can be someone. You can make a difference. You must stand up and take it while you can. Promise me you will do this. Nicholas would want it of you."

To hear a voice of reason in her present state of confusion made it possible for Eavin to nod agreement. She wasn't even certain what it was she was agreeing to, but it seemed to make sense at the time. She believed the house would belong to Jeannette, but the house didn't seem to matter any longer. Nothing really mattered, but Belle was forcing her to realize there was more to this world than herself. Perhaps she was right. Perhaps she could make a difference. And Nicholas's child deserved a name besides bastard.

Isabel wept with relief when Eavin appeared to agree with her plans. Alphonso was overwhelmed and took her into his arms, only to set her down when Eavin stiffened and pulled away. He apologized, and she looked at him sadly, wondering what she was doing, but she touched his arm and remembered Isabel's words about it being better to be loved, and she hoped they came true.

After that, everything was done for her. The Howells swept down to take over the planning as if they were Eavin's family. With Mr. Howell in Washington on official business, they had no other affairs to conduct, and the quiet wedding that Eavin had envisioned began to turn into something only New Orleans could create.

She stayed out of the way of most of it, avoiding the sudden swarm of social visits. Isabel made it easy for her to escape, providing excuses so Eavin didn't have to listen to hypocritical condolences and congratulations in the same sentence. Eavin saw very little grief at Nicholas's death, and she despised his neighbors for not seeing what they had lost. As far as Eavin could tell, not one had even bothered to attend his funeral. She would have liked to hear of the people who had attended, but it was as if there were an unspoken agreement not to mention it to her. She suffered in silence, refusing to ask anything of anyone.

Eavin wished Michael would come home, but he was undoubtedly seeing to Nicholas's affairs in New Orleans. She had written for him to hurry back, but she couldn't bring herself to mention why. She just handed the letter to Isabel for posting and hoped Michael would hear the urgency. She wondered if she ought to write Daniel too, but the editor was strangely silent, and without Nicholas to bring home the scandalous news sheet, Eavin knew nothing of the outside world.

She assumed Hélène and Gabriella were politely staying in New Orleans until the wedding was over. Eavin would have preferred it if they had come forward and announced their plans and wishes, but that wasn't the way it was done in polite society. She hadn't even heard word from Nicholas's lawyer about Jeannette's guardianship. At times she feared Nicholas had changed his will and left the guardianship to his new wife. She feverishly wished the marriage was over and done with before then, so Alphonso and his father could fight for Jeannette for her. But those aberrations were few and far between. Mostly she dreaded the day that was getting closer with every passing minute.

Eavin didn't allow herself to think about it. She knew it had to be done. The child growing within her would begin to show shortly. She didn't have the nerve to speak of it to Alphonso. He knew she was a widow and no virgin. Perhaps he could be talked into imagining the child was his own. It would be better for everyone if that was so. She just couldn't picture doing the deed that would give Alphonso the right to think that way. Perhaps he would make the marriage act as simple as Nicholas had done. She could only hope for the best.

But when the day of her wedding arrived, Eavin woke to the morning sickness that she had not suffered until then. Heaving her insides into the chamberpot, she wept brokenly, unable to cope with the thought of what the next hours would bring. Eavin heard Belle yelling in the room next door, heard Annie come running, but she couldn't stop the churning of her insides or the sobs that left her breathless.

Isabel hurried over at the first mention of illness. Lying on the bed with a cool cloth over her head, momentarily calm, Eavin took one look at her mother-in-law and felt the bile rising and turned over and reached for the chamberpot again. The consternation forming around her had no effect on Eavin's soul.

Carriages were already arriving; Eavin could hear them from her window. The odors from the kitchen permeated the air. The scent of fresh breads and Creole spices drifted on the unnaturally warm breeze. Eavin's stomach heaved and tossed, and this time Annie reached for the chamberpot.

By noon the women had managed to get Eavin out of

bed and bathed, but she turned green every time they tried to get her into a gown. Annie went to fetch Jeannette, and Eavin calmed slightly at the sight of the child's laughing smile and tiny hands reaching for her. Holding Jeannette, Eavin forced herself to think of her future and the future of her unborn child. She had to go through with this. Alphonso would make an excellent father. He was kind and gentle and understanding. He was wealthy enough to keep the children in comfort. And if Nicholas's lands came into Eavin's guardianship, he was wise enough to help her manage them well. She was quite certain there wasn't a greedy bone in Alphonso's body. She was doing the right thing. Nicholas had showed her how it was done. He had married Gabriella because it was the right thing. Eavin could do the same.

Telling herself this over and over, Eavin allowed Isabel and Annie to lead her back to the house. They sneaked her up the back stairs and into her old room, the one Isabel had taken over. Hélène had been using the chamber Nicholas had converted for their use, and Eavin didn't even glance at the door now. She would remember Hélène in there and not those hot summer nights when she and Nicholas had lain between the sweaty sheets and become one with the other. That Nicholas was gone, but a part of him lived on inside her. She would do what Nicholas would want her to do.

Eavin had wanted to wear black, but the women wouldn't let her; Nicholas was no relation, after all. It was this inability to mourn him properly that brought home the point that she had only been his mistress, a relationship unrecognized by society even though it was closer than Nicholas had ever been to his wife. Eavin grieved anew at this discovery, but her grief allowed her to continue with the charade of dressing for her new life.

She had been married before. She knew all about the puppet performance that must go on. She hadn't loved Dominic, but she had entrusted her life into his hands with the hope that love would follow. She had tried to be happy that day, but she had actually been paralyzed by fear. This time she knew what to expect, and she could be calm about it. She was a mature woman, probably far more mature than her husband-to-be. She would go down and smile at the guests and give her vows, and Alphonso would take her home with him. She even knew what would happen when she got there, and what would happen after that.

For Eavin fully meant to take charge of her own life from here on out. She wasn't blindly handing herself into anyone's care ever again. Nicholas said he had included her in his will. There would be funds for her somewhere, and if they weren't enough, she had the little hoard that had grown in the years of Nicholas's care. With money in her pocket, she could afford to be independent. And she could continue writing and earning more. If Alphonso didn't like it, she could leave him. The child would have a name, and that was all that mattered at the moment. She wanted both children to have a father, but not at the risk of losing herself. Never again.

But the confidence Eavin had talked herself into dissolved when Isabel hurried in to announce that Alphonso and his father had arrived with Father Antoine. They were to be married by a priest, in the eyes of God, and Eavin's stomach turned inside out again and the small breakfast she had managed to get down spewed out.

Isabel was in near hysterics. Annie had Belle carried from the *garçonnière* up the back stairs to Eavin's bedside, but even Belle couldn't find a potion that would settle Eavin's seething insides. She sent the other women out of the room and leaning on a cane, slammed the door after him.

"What is wrong with you, girl?" Belle demanded when they were alone.

"Nothing. Nothing is wrong with me. It's just the babe." Gray-faced, Eavin stood up and steadied herself next to the vanity that Isabel had ordered installed. Unsteadily she wrung out a cloth in the basin and bathed her face.

"The babe, nothing. That child hasn't caused you one instant's grief since it was conceived. It's something else. You haven't buried Nicholas, have you?"

Holding the cloth to her head, Eavin slowly turned to meet Belle's eyes, playing the words in her mind. Belle was right. She hadn't buried Nicholas. She felt as if she were about to commit adultery. She stared into those knowing dark eyes and felt all her certainties begin to unravel. "I have to go to New Orleans," she answered.

Belle set her mouth, but her eyes turned thoughtful. "Maybe you're right. But how are you going to tell those people down there? If you go to New Orleans now, you could be throwing away any chance you have of giving that child a name."

"Will it be safe for me to travel? Really safe? I can't bear the thought of losing ..."

Belle narrowed her eyes and studied Eavin carefully. "I don't know. Once I could have told you. Once I could have told you when Nicholas's soul departed his body. Now I can't even feel his absence. I keep waiting for him to come home like I wait for your dog of a heartless brother. I don't know how people live like this, not ever knowing. I can't tell you."

Eavin sighed and set the cloth back in the bowl. "Welcome to the real world, Belle. Being human is a scary business."

Belle considered this a moment. Her beautiful oval face had regained some of its color, and her black hair was brushed to a liquid shine. Pulled back in a severe chignon, it still had the power to draw attention. She held herself with the same stately grace as before, even if it was slightly off balance from the awkwardness of the wrappings hidden beneath her skirt. Her eyes drifted to somewhere beyond this room as she spoke.

"Being beyond human is even scarier. You can't really touch someone, you can't feel his arms around you, hear his heart beat, for fear that he will get too close. Everyone must be kept at arm's length for the magic to work. And it had to work. So many people depended on it. And now there is no one for them to turn to. The power is in the hands of people with money and position. The power will be yours now. You must learn to wield it well."

Once Belle's words would have cast an enchantment of conviction. Now they merely reflected the loneliness of a woman cast outside society for too long. Eavin touched Belle's hand gently.

"Michael will come back. He's never been interested in just one woman before. He's ready to settle down now, and you have the power to hold him. It doesn't take magic to love."

Belle smiled wryly. "I am supposed to be comforting you. Do not look at me so. I have been raped before, many times. My body has not been my own for longer than I can remember. Michael will never understand that. He will only see me with pity. He will leave New Orleans shortly. I do not need my magic to know that. You had better decide what you will do before then."

Setting aside magic and superstition and a broken heart that kept dreaming the impossible, Eavin could see what had to be done. Without stopping to check her hair in the mirror or to adjust her gown, she gestured toward the door.

"Call Isabel. It's time I quit crying in my beer."

43

Eavin made it as far as the stairway leading down to the wide hall full of impatient guests. Her stomach began to roil as she saw the sea of upturned faces. She clasped the banister and forced her feet to take another step. A murmur went up from the crowd, and she saw the concern on Jeremy's face as she faltered. At his nod, his sister took the first step upward to meet her. Mrs. Howell's expression formed into a frown.

Eavin recognized her aristocratic neighbors from Carondelet. They were watching her with curiosity and growing concern as she hesitated, holding her hand to her stomach as it churned tighter. Even Mignon Dubois was pushing through the crowd, coming to stand beside Mrs. Howell and Jeremy's betrothed. Eavin felt as if the entire parish were staring at her, and her head began to spin dizzily.

Isabel rushed from the *grande salle* into the hall, followed by Alphonso and his father. She took one look at Eavin's green face and hurried to follow Lucinda up the stairs.

"Alphonso, carry her down before she falls! We cannot keep Father Antoine waiting any longer," Señor Reyes called from the doorway, encouraging Alphonso to move faster through the crowd.

Jeremy hastened to follow his sister while Mrs. Howell turned an outraged reply to the arrogant Spaniard. Eavin caught Jeremy's strong arm and found herself sitting on the stairs as Mrs. Howell's voice carried over the murmur of voices around her.

"It is obvious the girl is ill. You cannot force her to go through with this when she cannot even stand up." Huffily she ordered two of her neighbors to block the stairs while she ran up to sit beside Eavin.

Alphonso elbowed his way through the barricade, but
Eavin was surrounded and he could do no more than
hover solicitously as Isabel called from the bottom of the
stairs, voicing her concern.

It would almost be funny if she didn't feel so awful.
Señor Reyes was cursing in vivid Spanish while several
of their French neighbors were growing irritable and re-
plying in phrases that Eavin recognized from Nicholas's
vocabulary. Easily aroused tempers were escalating over
nothing, over less than nothing. Eavin thought if her
stomach wasn't already empty, she might enjoy spewing
its contents just to see the reaction that would follow. She
needed Nicholas here to appreciate this scene.

Jeremy and Alphonso growled at each other while Isabel urged them to carry her down. Mrs. Howell demanded
that they carry her back upstairs again. Belle appeared in
the upper hallway and was obviously making one of her
grand entrances, for Eavin could hear the crowd gasp
even though she didn't dare lift her head to look. She really did think she would begin to giggle hysterically soon
if someone didn't get her out of here. She didn't think she
was going to be able to stand by herself.

That was when Eavin understood what she was doing.
Despite all her brave, independent ideas, she was con-
signing herself into the hands of a man she didn't love
again. It hadn't worked the first time and it certainly
wasn't going to work this time. She couldn't sell herself
for a name. Feeling her stomach settle and her strength
begin to return as she realized she had other options, that
Nicholas had taught her not to fear and how to stand on
her own, Eavin raised her head to gaze over the crowd of
neighbors. They might be repelled by her decision, but it
was her decision to make. Even now she could feel their
sympathy surrounding her. She could arrange things on
her own. It wouldn't be so bad. She didn't need Alphonso
and his father to help her. Relieved at this discovery,
Eavin was free to pay closer attention to the happenings
around her.

There were shouts from outside just as Jeremy pushed
Alphonso's hand away as he reached to help Eavin up.
Alphonso's furious response was lost in the general con-
fusion as several of the guests below ran to the windows.
Screams from the general direction of the servants' quar-

ters brought more heads up and directed attention away
from Eavin.

Eavin's eyes widened as someone shouted "Soldiers!"
and a general stampede began toward the front door. She
ought to feel fear, but she only felt curiosity as people
pushed and shoved to get out of the two salons into the
hallway to see what was happening. Even Alphonso and
Jeremy straightened with looks of concern to follow the
action. Señor Reyes shook his fist and shouted something,
but his voice was lost in the clamor.

Some of the men had obviously found other ways onto
the gallery and were lining up outside, pulling swords and
pistols and whatever weapons that came to hand. Eavin
did begin to giggle then. It was her wedding and the British were coming. She couldn't think of a more suitable
guest roster.

She tried to hold the giggles, afraid to reveal her sudden lightheadedness as much as her earlier hysteria.
Alphonso sent her a worried look, but Eavin remained
seated, letting Mrs. Howell pat her hand as the men
tended to their unexpected guests. The sudden explosion
of voices reminded Eavin that she had heard the British
had lost and gone away. What soldiers were these, then?

She tried to rise, but the front door burst open before
she could, and she just sat there in amazement as strange
men began to push through the bystanders, sending the
women screaming into the salons and up the stairs toward
Eavin. Mignon collapsed in a heap beside her and hugged
her shoulders as a gap-toothed young man in leather jer-
kin and raccoon hat stared up at them, a wide grin beginning to fill his freckled face.

Convinced she was losing her mind, Eavin calmly
gazed back at the raged militiaman. "Why are you here?"
she asked reasonably while the others around her stared at
her with incredulity.

The militiaman grinned and shrugged. "Captain's orders to secure the place, ma'am. Don't question the captain's orders."

"I think I have a right to question the captain's orders.
This is my home. Where is he?" Eavin stood up and
looked around for some figure of authority. This was her
home. She could feel the knowledge seeping through her
with certainty. No one was going to drive her out or take

her away. This was the home Nicholas had chosen for her
and Jeannette. He would want his child raised here. She
would protect it with every means available, and her jaw
tightened with determination.

Behind her, Jeremy cursed as he and Alphonso shoved
downward toward the door and the intruders. Eavin
couldn't see anything or anyone to clarify the situation.
The men on the gallery had lowered their weapons in response to orders from someone outside, but they didn't
seem pleased about it. She set her teeth nervously as she
watched their hands rubbing hilts and handles as they
muttered and grumbled between themselves.

Ready to fight the devil himself for her home, Eavin
still wasn't prepared for what followed next. With the
priest wandering into the hall in his robes, a look of confusion on his face, Señor Reyes waving his cane and
shouting wildly, and Alphonso and Jeremy arguing vehemently with the grinning stranger and his squirrel gun,
the front door burst open again, this time with a phalanx
of trained soldiers—and Nicholas in the lead.

Eavin screamed, and the apparition looked up. His expression was grim and set, but his commands were quiet
as he sent his men to surround the room and restrain the
guests. Eavin shook off Mignon's hold and grabbed the
banister, staring in disbelief. Nicholas or his ghost didn't
take his gaze from her, but he continued giving commands, setting rough-looking men with weathered faces
and eyes like ice to disarming the guests, cornering
Alphonso and his father, imprisoning the priest.

Eavin drank in his appearance greedily, convincing herself this was real and not the onslaught of madness. This
strange Nicholas was pale, much paler than she had ever
seen him, which worried her. His golden hair was uncut
and straggled around his collar. He held his arm oddly, as
if it pained him to move it. When he stepped forward, it
was with a limp. But when Eavin saw the flashing golden
flakes of amber in his eyes, she knew he was alive, and
she stepped toward him as if in a trance, not daring to
feel the joy seeping through the cracks of her defenses.

"Father, we'll hold the services now, with all these
good people as witnesses." Gesturing to the astonished
priest, Nicholas reached the bottom stair and caught
Eavin's arm as she approached, dragging her down beside

him. Once he had her in hand, he scarcely gave her a second look, diverting all his attention to keeping the crowd in line.

It took considerable attention to do so. Alphonso shouted and tried to burst through the guard holding him pinned against the wall. Jeremy dodged his captor and seemed prepared to make his argument physical, but Nicholas stopped him with a glare. The women were the worst. Isabel talked breathlessly in French and Spanish, pulling his arm and pleading. Mrs. Howell and Lucinda were castigating Nicholas in strident tones, urging him to allow Eavin to lie down and recover herself. A rising tide of French and English began to flow through the hall, aided by the grinning, slow-taking, laconic strangers in their leathers and furs as they held out their long-barreled weapons in a barricade against the aristocratic crowd in silks and laces.

Nicholas purposefully ignored them all, drawing Eavin closer to his side, steering his way toward Father Antoine, his jaw set and his gaze fixed as he gave the command that kept the priest covered by a gun.

"Do not do this, Saint-Just!" Alphonso cried over the heads of his captor. "You are already married. Do not make a mockery of your vows."

Nicholas smiled grimly at the priest. "Tell them, Father. I want it to be perfectly understood that this marriage is legal."

Eavin swung her head to stare from Nicholas to the priest. Marriage?

Father Antoine nodded grimly and raised his hand to silence the noisy crowd. "The marriage with Gabriella Alvarez has been formally dissolved. She returns to Spain even as we speak." He returned his glare to Nicholas. "That does not justify what you do here today. You cannot hold all these people at gunpoint and force a marriage. Marriage is a sacrament. It will be denied if you do this."

The priest spoke in French, but Nicholas's reply was in a clear English that Eavin could understand without question.

"Deny me, Father, and I will carry her into the bedroom and have my men guard the door until her cries convince you otherwise. Now do you understand me?"

A collective gasp went up from the crowd, but the priest's lips twitched slightly as he turned his gaze to the stunned bride. "Are you willing to exchange this man for the other, *madame*?"

Eavin wasn't certain she was still breathing. She could feel the tear stains on her cheeks, but she couldn't remember crying. She looked up to meet Nicholas's golden gaze, reading the hunger in his eyes quite clearly. It wasn't anger that had brought him here but another kind of passion. Her lips turned up at the corners as she realized he was marrying her against all good sense. He didn't even know of the child. There were ten dozen questions yet to be answered, but she had the reply to the most important one of all.

"I will exchange logic and theory for love and hope, if that is what he asks," she managed to reply with some semblance of clarity.

"For my heart, *ma chérie,* for my life, my soul, for all that I am, if you will have me."

Nicholas's eyes darkened with the intensity of his reply, and Eavin was in his arms and resting against his chest before the words finished rumbling from inside him. She felt his hands around her back, and they were real. She could hear the beating of his heart beneath the bulk of his bandages, felt the tension drain out of him and become something else, and she knew he was alive and had come back to her. She needed to know nothing else.

The priest coughed delicately, but when the couple did nothing to acknowledge him while his audience waited expectantly, he began the words of the marriage ceremony. Women wept and a man cursed, but Eavin rested in Nicholas's arms, secure in his love as the words poured around them.

When it came time to repeat their vows, Eavin managed it in her hesitant French, then repeated them more strongly in an English heavily tinted with an Irish lilt. Laughter rippled lightly through the crowd as Nicholas did her one better and added Spanish for the benefit of the man who had nearly stolen her. The look Eavin gave him crackled with the chemistry between them, and the priest hid a grin and hurried to complete the ceremony that would seal their separate lives into one.

When the blessing was said that announced them man

and wife, Nicholas looked down on the small dark-haired creature in his embrace with growing astonishment. Running his hand through his unruly hair to brush it back from his face, he stared at her a moment longer before declaring with a tone that made no attempt to hide his surprise, "*Mon dieu,* I have actually captured the whirlwind!"

Laughter broke out behind them, and the cheers of the soldiers joined in as Eavin reached to bring Nicholas's head down to hers. What began as a simple kiss quickly flared into something else, and it was Michael's iron grip on Nicholas's arm that finally had to jerk them apart.

"You can molest my sister later. For now, I need to borrow your tactics and your priest."

Nicholas and Eavin looked up to find Michael keeping a precarious hold on a snarling, squirming Belle as she tried to elude his powerful grip on her waist. Her tightly controlled chignon had loosened in the struggle, and long strands of ebony trailed down her back and shoulders. Her elegant silk gown was twisted and hiked up to reveal a delicate, stocking-clad ankle and glimpses of a wooden brace. And her lovely, normally placid expression had erupted into a passionate fire that should have scorched her determined captor.

Keeping his arm around Eavin's waist, pulling her closer and giving her a quick look that asked the questions looming between them, Nicholas found the answer he sought now. Meeting Michael's eyes, Nicholas made a Gallic shrug and stepped aside.

"I'll not stop you if Belle won't."

Belle's shriek of rage was hastily quieted by the simple expedient of Michael placing his large hand over her mouth. He turned hesitantly to Eavin. "It means we'll be goin' to Texas after all, colleen. I'll not buy my wife or have my children named someone else's property because of some foolish law. You understand, don't you?"

Eavin glanced anxiously at Belle, who had suddenly grown still at this expression of Michael's intent. Meeting the sadness in the other woman's eyes, she nodded. "I understand. And perhaps you could take Annie and Jim with you. You are certain the Mexicans don't have laws about slaves?"

Belle relaxed and an understanding began to develop

between them. Working apart, their powers were not great, but working together, she and Eavin could accomplish a great deal. Belle's shoulders straightened and her hand went to her hair as the crowd pushed and murmured around them. Someone had discovered the punch bowl, and a mass exodus had already begun. Only the curious and the disapproving and those closest to them remained.

Michael looked puzzled at his sister's words, but the fact that Belle had grown quiet was not lost on him. He released his stranglehold and turned his attention to the priest.

Nicholas and Eavin didn't have time to learn how Michael would cajole the priest into the improper service. The outside world pressed in on them, forcing them to turn their attention away from each other, however briefly. One of the rough soldiers gave a shout as Alphonso shoved his way through his guards, a gun went clattering to the floor as one of Señor Reyes' bodyguards knocked it loose with his sword, and pandemonium threatened to break loose again before Nicholas could control it.

The sudden surge of violence swung the crowd's attention from the banqueting table, but instead of striking Nicholas down, Alphonso came to an abrupt halt before him. Nicholas made a dismissive gesture to the long-haired rifleman appearing at his side, and the man grinned and shrugged, leaning against a wall as he watched the scene with interest.

"You will understand that I knew nothing of this. I meant only to keep her from harm." Alphonso's declaration was made honestly but with pride.

Nicholas glanced over Alphonso's shoulder at the old man approaching with a slump in his shoulders and pain in his face. "I rather believe your father will explain. I hold no grudge against you. But perhaps it would be better if you followed Gabriella. I'm not certain I'll feel so generous another time."

Stiffly keeping his eyes from the woman he had been prepared to marry minutes before, Alphonso nodded and stepped aside to allow his father to approach.

Eavin didn't give Nicholas time to speak. Accusingly she glared at the elder Spaniard. "You told me he was dead, and I believed you. You let me grieve for nothing.

How did you think I would feel when Nicholas returned and I was married to your son? What did you hope to accomplish?"

Reyes straightened his shoulders and held his head up. "I hoped to make an honest woman of you. I hoped to give my son the love he craved as I denied it to my eldest. I wished to correct the mistakes of the past. My guilt is in thinking that I knew what was right without consulting you. I beg your forgiveness, *señora*."

There was more to be said. He wasn't the only guilty party. Eavin's gaze sought the woman who must have kept her letters and probably intercepted others. She clenched Nicholas's arm tighter as she realized Hélène had arrived and already cornered Isabel.

As if sensing they were being watched, the two women looked up. With a dismissive gesture Nicholas's mother left her antagonist alone. Catching the arm of Mrs. Howell as she approached the newlyweds, Hélène began making her way through the throng.

Seeing the direction of Eavin's gaze, Nicholas whispered, "She is the reason I am here today. I would see whatever differences are between you settled."

Eavin stared at him coolly. "There are no differences between us. We both love the same man." And with that pronouncement she left his side to hug her new mother-in-law.

The haughty Frenchwoman hugged her back with tears in her eyes. For Eavin's ears alone she whispered, "Isabel thought she did me a favor by inviting me to your wedding. She did not realize how right she was. Nicholas lived only to see you again. I have you to thank for returning my son to me."

Hélène had only to look up and see the tender smile on Nicholas's lips as he wrapped his arms around his wife's waist to know she had done the right thing. When Eavin leaned trustingly against him, giving herself to his hold and tilting her head to return his smile, Hélène nodded approvingly.

"Well, we shall have to teach you better French so you may write for our papers instead of that crude American rag," she announced primly before turning and walking away, leaving Nicholas and Eavin to stare open-mouthed after her.

As Eavin began to giggle helplessly, Nicholas scooped her up and shoved his way through the increasingly raucous crowd.

As his action was noticed, a ragged cheer rose among his troops. Someone fired a rifle into the ceiling, and a shower of plaster coated the guests in white. Another shout went up, this one in French and slightly risqué. Laughter rang out and a flute and a violin picked up the French anthem. Not to be outdone, the Spanish guests began to shout a wedding toast as they waved their cups of punch. The Kentuckians joined in, stamping their feet to the tune of the "Marseillaise" until the chandelier overhead started to swing and the floor groaned and shook with their energy. A woman screamed as a vase started sliding for the floor, but a soldier laughingly caught it and demanded a kiss in recompense. Her escort took offense and another circle of excitement formed.

In a separate corner, the priest watched with bemusement as two lines of black slaves began to form along the back steps and into the hallway, creating an avenue of retreat for the Irishman and the octoroon he had taken for a bride. Father Antoine's gaze met that of an old black man in priest's robes making the blessing over the young couple as they passed, and he repeated the motion, knowing the double blessing would be needed.

Caught up in and surrounded by the celebration, Nicholas serenely walked on, clutching his precious burden as he turned down the hallway to the newly decorated chambers he had meant for his wife.

He smiled as Eavin untangled his neckcloth and blew against his throat. His arm was going to cause him one hell of a lot of pain before long, but he was going to enjoy every minute of it.

44

Their progress came to a halt with the arrival of a man who set the soldiers to attention and the crowd into uproarious cheers. With a mild curse Nicholas returned Eavin to her feet. Keeping his arm firmly around her, he straightened to wait for the reprimand that was sure to come.

General Andrew Jackson sauntered down the path made for him through the crowd, his craggy face mildly amused as his gaze noted the disheveled bridegroom and his bemused bride. He came to a halt before Saint-Just, met the Frenchman's defiance imperturbably, and waited for his explanation.

"General, this is my wife, Eavin." Smoothly, Nicholas tucked Eavin at his side and turned the tables around, waiting for his superior officer to demand the explanations he wanted.

With a sage smile the general took Eavin's hand. "The lady responsible for dragging this sluggard from his bed, I assume. My gratitude to you, *madame*. I despaired of ever seeing him on his feet again."

Nicholas grimaced, as much with impatience as irritation at this delay. The bedroom door was only a few yards away. He had almost made it.

Knowing his impatience, the general grinned. "You're relieved of duty, Saint-Just. Stealing a squadron of soldiers and causing an insurrection are not the acts of a disciplined officer. Have you ever considered taking up politics?"

Laughter rose from those within hearing, and Nicholas gave a grudging smile. "I'll give it all due consideration, General, when I have nothing better on my mind."

Since Nicholas drew Eavin more tightly into his embrace with these words, more laughter followed at his implication. Before Jackson could reply, Jeremy had excitedly elbowed his way into their circle.

"That's an excellent idea, General! A Frenchman with American ideas! He would have instant support—"

Nicholas didn't take the time to hear the rest. With the general visibly distracted by the sudden clamor of excitement, he half shoved, half dragged Eavin into the side hall and pushed open his chamber door. Laughing, they both stumbled inward, slamming the door and throwing the bolt shut before falling into each other's arms.

"I can't wait another moment. It's been months, *ma chérie. Mon dieu,* how I have ached for you." Nicholas's kisses covered her hair and throat as his fingers rapidly found the fastenings of her gown.

"I thought you were a ghost. I thought you were dead." Emotion finally catching up with her, Eavin feverishly tore at the ties of Nicholas's shirt and cravat, needing to feel the heat of his flesh beneath her fingers to convince herself this was real.

"I could not write. My accursed arm ... But I did not dare come to you even if I could. I am sorry, my love, my life. I should never have shamed you as I did. I could not hold you if I was not free. I would not compound the wrongs. But I came as soon as I could, as soon as I heard ... *mon dieu!*" Nicholas clutched her tightly for a moment, stroking her hair as he sent an appeal to the heavens. "I was almost too late. I would have had to kill him."

"No, I would undoubtedly have thrown up on him and put an end to all pretension." Eavin hiccuped through her tears. "Don't dwell on it. Just love me, Nicholas. It's been so long ..."

Nicholas cupped her face in his palms and held her gaze. "I love you, Eavin O'Flannery Dupré. I did not think to ever hear myself say those words. I am not yet certain what they mean. I only know I could not face life without you. I will not let you regret what we have done this day."

"I will not give you time for regrets." Pulling his head down to hers, Eavin proceeded to show him what she meant.

They were in the bed before they could shed half their clothes. Determined to do this wedding night properly, Nicholas tugged Eavin's recalcitrant bodice until it fell away, then cursed when it revealed a chemise and a light corset. Using teeth as well as fingers to tear at the ties, and with Eavin's eager help, Nicholas slowly threw the garments to the floor. Stripped now of all but his breeches, he leaned over her, forcing himself to go slowly, to touch and relearn all those places he had loved over the past summer. As he ran his hand over a place he remembered as flat and hollow and found it slightly rounded, he lifted his gaze with hope and fear to hers.

"Eavin?"

The catch in his voice said what his words did not. This was what Eavin had been waiting for, the sharing that made what they had wrought real. Smiling through her tears, holding Nicholas's hand to her abdomen, Eavin finally admitted what she had feared to say aloud before. "This is the reason I could not come to you. I wanted to be by your side, but I dared not risk your son."

Incredulous, Nicholas spread his fingers over the slight rounding, trying to imagine his child growing there. As he realized the wish he had denied by marrying Eavin had come true after all, he whooped with joy and, grabbing Eavin, almost fell from the bed as he rolled across it.

As the cries from the bedroom resounded into the crowded hall where the guests reveled without their host or hostess, the French among them laughed knowingly and whispered about the speed of young love. The rough-clad soldiers elbowed one another and began to eye the delicate young women floating among them with more appreciation.

Standing beside Clyde Brown, Jeremy lifted his wine-glass in salute, and the lawman sadly did the same. Preparing to depart, Alphonso turned white at the sound emanating from the bedroom, but coming to bid him farewell, Hélène tapped his arm with her fan and shook her head. "I daresay Nicholas has just learned his wife carries his child. I'm certain you would have made as good a father as Nicholas is to Jeannette, but it is much better this way, n'est-ce pas?"

Looking startled, the young Spaniard agreed, but his gaze still wandered reluctantly in the direction of the bedroom. He would take his elder's advice for a change and

follow Gabriella, but he would always wonder what it
might have been like had things turned out differently.

And in a bedroom not too far away, where Nicholas's
whoops couldn't be heard but his joy was shared, a pale
oval face hovered above a grinning wide Irish one, and a
slender hand worked a different kind of magic on a man
who had never known love.

"You are a mad Irishman," she whispered as Michael
grabbed her hair and hips and halted her spell with an upward thrust that joined them physically and without a hint
of the supernatural.

"And I may never know what you are, Belle, but I
would keep you if you'll let me," he murmured huskily
against her ear as she lowered herself on him.

Almost purring as she heard what she wanted to hear,
Belle leaned over to kiss his ear. "I would some day visit
this place where you and your sister come from, *mon
chéri*. It cannot be the same as the rest of the world."

"Aye, it's the same. It's the leprechaun in us that keeps
you guessing." And with that, he turned her beneath him
and proved his reality better than her fantasy.

"Nicholas!" The name sighed between Eavin's lips as
their bodies rocked with the aftermath of their lovemaking. "Sometimes I love you so much that it hurts."

Nicholas lifted his weight with his good hand and
stroked her face with the other. He imagined her eyes
were the color of the wide Irish hills, and he smiled, a
gentle smile that appeared natural as it would not have a
year earlier. "Let me bear the hurt, *ma petite*. I have been
waiting a lifetime to hear those words."

Eavin caressed his stubbled jaw and drew him deeper
within her. "You will hear them every night and every
day from now on. You will grow tired of hearing them.
Someday you will say 'Bah, what nonsense!' and seek a
woman who does not talk so much. And I will have to
kill her."

Chuckling, Nicholas rolled over and drew her with
him, making the most of this opportunity to touch her all
over. "No, *ma chérie,* one *petite amie* is all I need, and
she is you. I think I know how to make you be quiet
when I need to."

Kissing her, he showed her how, until Eavin was laugh-

ing and struggling against his ardent attention. "Nicholas!
We cannot. Not again. We have guests. This is unconscio-
nable."

"No, this is New Orleans. They will not be surprised if
we do not come out for a week. I mean to keep you in
here and feed you well until you are plump and round and
everyone knows you belong to me in every possible way.
I want the whole world to know that you carry my child
for me. It makes me ..." He whispered a few French
phrases in her ear that had Eavin giggling again. "Just to
think about it," he finished, and nibbled on her ear.

"I have never seen you like this," she replied in wonder
when she was better able to speak. A lighthearted Nicholas was a man she could come to love even more thoroughly than the one she knew now.

"Give me time, and I will show you more." Nicholas
gathered her against his shoulder and stroked her breast,
admiring the weight of pregnancy and allowing some of
the joy to seep deep inside him, healing the wounds of
the past. "I cannot promise to be a saint, but I may have
to be a politician. The doctors say I may never use this
arm for a sword again. My fighting days are over. I married you under false pretenses."

Eavin laughed softly and smoothed the silken hairs on
his chest. "Oh, I wouldn't say that. It isn't your sword
arm that interests me. And saints aren't my style, either.
If you can settle for a wife who would rather write flam-
ing newspaper articles than gossip, I think I can manage
a husband who prefers politics to swords."

"Manage me, will you?" Nicholas quickly rolled over
and covered her with his long body to show her just how
unmanageable he was, and Eavin laughed and held him as
he did just precisely what she wanted, and they were both
the better for it.

In the other rooms, the guests ignored the sounds
from the master chamber as they discussed the spring
planting and the steamboat whistling loudly on the river as
it passed and the ball to be held in Jackson's honor on the
night after next. If one of the brave young soldiers took
this opportunity to slip out onto the gallery with the girl of
his choice, this minor indiscretion was smiled upon with

understanding. After all, was it not an American who had saved the city?

And was it not an American who had tamed the lion Saint-Just? Perhaps all would be well, after all. Glasses clinked, wine disappeared, and outside, dark faces stared at the candles gleaming in two bedrooms, and prayers were whispered to the rising moon, as the memory of jasmine slowly drifted up and away into the starlit heavens.